Cover Art by
Gilbert Arthur

Illustrations by
Gilbert Arthur

Shadows of the Heart is dedicated to everyone who supported me through the long days and late nights required to breathe life into it. Foremost among them is, of course, my beloved wife and biggest fan, Jessica. Without her, there wouldn't be a heart for me to write about. Our life set the cornerstone for my work.

Contents

Part One

Part Two

Part Three

Cast of Characters

Earth

Jillian Allen – the heroine of our story
Marisol Diaz - Jillian's best friend
Hector Thompson - Plague Man's reflection on Earth

Taerh

Hollis the Slender – the hero of our story
Asaege - Jillian's reflection
Aristoi - Hollis's closest friend and comrade / Songspear
Plague Man – Hollis's enemy / murderer of his friends

Gods and Goddesses

Olm – God of Justice, Creation. Twin Brother of Umma. Known as the Father of Justice, Lord of the Dawn
Umma – Goddess of Nature, Knowledge. Twin Sister of Olm. Known as the Mother of the Forest, Lady of Light
Sharroth – God of Shadow, Deception. Younger Brother of Olm and Umma. Known as the Master of Beasts, Father of Lies, Bringer of Shadows

Part One:

Hearts in Shadow

"The greatest enemy of knowledge is not ignorance, it is the illusion of knowledge."

-Daniel J. Boorstin

Chapter One
Fond Heart, Learned Mind

The woman closed her eyes and shook her head, determined to clear unbidden memories as if they were merely cobwebs amid childhood relics, too long untended. Despite the itch of fear that prickled at the nape of her neck, a small smile graced her lips as she remembered entire afternoons blurred by the scent of parchment and wood. *You are not here, tempting the fickle justice of the Binders, to reminisce on times long past their prime*, she scolded herself. Just the thought of the sworn protectors of the Great Library shocked her out of the warmth of remembrance. The Binders each took a vow to protect every scrap of paper stored within these walls with their lives should the situation demand it. They wouldn't take kindly to anyone stalking the stacks after the librarians had retired for the night, much less Asaege who had left the library under less than ideal circumstances.

With the hood of her lantern lowered, its feeble light barely eroded the darkness that surrounded Asaege, cloaking her in a hazy dimness rather than the velvet tapestry that pervaded the rest of the Great Library. To tell the truth, the woman had little need of its guidance. The fondest days of her life were spent beneath the mute witness of these stacks and the heavy volumes they contained. Aided by the meager light, her memory was able to lead her to the book she sought.

She placed the lantern on the marble floor and ran her fingers over the spines before her. Amid tomes dedicated to the ancient history of Granatyr was a thin book bound in worn calf skin. Time and use had long ago obfuscated the title on the spine, which was most likely the reason why it had remained undisturbed and misfiled for so long. Dialogues of the Chalice, while technically a historical work purely due to its age, was in all actuality a religious text.

When she found it misfiled years ago, Asaege decided to keep her discovery to herself. She told herself that unless she had the patronage of someone whose credentials could not be questioned, the find would be relegated to the long list of counterfeit versions; but she'd always known deep inside her heart that she selfishly wanted to keep it to herself. If none knew of her find, none could take it from her. No matter how the masters scolded her … no matter how many of her fellow students spurned her, jealous of the ease with which she navigated concepts that stymied them, she would always have this … her one perfect thing.

Lost in her own thoughts, Asaege suddenly felt the sensation of another's eyes upon her in the darkened confines of the library. She turned quickly, the words that had been insistently whispering in her mind like a petulant mantra all day coming to her lips in a blissful rush. It was almost as if the spell had a heart of its own and yearned with all of it to be free. The words were choked in her throat as the cold edge of steel pressed against its ivory flesh.

"Hush, Little Magpie," a low voice whispered, "it is a little late for research, yes?" The man's bulky form pressed against her, so the once cool confines of the stacks became at once close and warm. His free hand closed about her wrist loosely and raised it; The book tightly clutched in her hand was lit by the dim illumination of a moonbeam. "The night is infinitely better suited for skulking in the shadows," he said with an eyebrow raised, indicating the book with brown eyes so dark they appeared black in the dim light, "or perhaps taking things that do not belong to you."

The fear in her eyes momentarily was replaced by anger as she realized it wasn't a Binder that she faced. "How dare you? The Master Librarian sent me for this book … at the bidding of the Hand of Light himself." She stepped back a half a pace, her shoulders pressing against the bookshelf.

The man did not pursue, allowing his knife hand to drop to his side. He seemed to note that although her words were ones of indignation, her voice never raised beyond a tense whisper. A smile came to his lips, "Is that so?"

She bobbed her head quickly. "Yes. So, if you know what is best for you, I suggest that you find your way out of the library through whatever hole you crawled in. If you do so, I will forget all about this and not call for the Binders. They do not take intrusions on this, their self-anointed holy ground, lightly."

The man continued to smile at her, "So I have heard." He released her wrist and took a step back. With sarcasm tainting every word, he softly proclaimed, "Their devotion and purity of purpose have inspired me … I wish to turn from my unlawful ways." He looked up, as if to the heavens before continuing. "Perhaps Olm in his infinite mercy and wisdom will see fit to grant me forgiveness if I but admit to my sins and seek redemption." His eyes locked with hers as he whispered in a suddenly serious tone, "Call for them."

Asaege gulped once, her ruse obviously foiled, "They will slay you for your intrusions."

He shrugged softly, his grin broadening, "So they may … but your conscience would be clear. It was my choice … my responsibility." His tongue flicked out to lick his lips. "That is, unless you are here without their leave as well." She opened her mouth, preparing to double down, but he held up his hand to cut her off, "Save your protests, Magpie. My father always counselled never attempting to con a con artist or bullshit a bullshitter." He wiggled his eyebrows in her direction, "And I assure you I am in firmly in the ranks of both."

Her frown softened. "So it seems we are both using this night for its intended purpose."

"So it would seem."

Asaege pulled the book close to her, cradling it against her stomach. "Knife or no, there are a plethora of books to be found, this one is mine." Again, she brought the words reverberating in her mind to her lips, ready to release them should the man before her seek to press the issue. She needn't have been concerned.

He chuckled lightly. "I have neither the need nor the desire for your book. I seek something very specific, and I know for a fact that it is much more substantial." He winked before continuing, "No offense, of course."

Asaege forced a tight smile, bemused by the way she found the man's easy manner both comforting and irritating. In the dim light, she could make out his solid frame. While he could never be accused of being svelte, he was also not obese; solid was the best term, she decided. Her eyes kept returning to the long broad blade he held so casually in his right hand, almost as if it were an extension of his arm; but she forced herself to study the other, less obvious, things about him. Belted about his waist was an Uteli Wallin Fahr; looped over the hilt of the weapon hung a small, round buckler, within easy reach of either of the man's hands. Her appraising eyes continued to run over him.

An unruly van dyke reached the hollow of his throat, an easy smile nested within it like a cheerful bird. His cheeks and head were clean shaven and shone a bit, even in the dim light. The man was dressed in soft leathers dyed such a dark brown that they appeared black. The man continued, his smile remaining firmly on his lips, "As you have found that which you seek, would you mind aiding me in gaining my bearings? I believe I may have taken a wrong turn in Ancient Languages."

Her eyes snapped back to his again, the suddenness of the gesture causing him to flinch ever so slightly. She noticed his left hand tense but not quite clench. This was accompanied by a small almost imperceptible tic in his cheek. His right hand, the one with the knife, moved a split second later, catching the feeble light of the lantern. It wasn't a threatening gesture but one that tore her attention from his other hand. It was her turn to smile; while his blade was no doubt sharp, her mind was as honed on years of study as his knife was on whetstone. The way he'd gripped her wrist wasn't due to gentleness of character, but no doubt due to the fact that it was simply not capable of exerting any more pressure. His trick with the knife reflected light was meant to hide his deficit.

"How about it, Magpie? Help a fellow academic out?"

"To tell the truth, I have not the time to aid you with … "

In a flash of motion, the man closed the distance between them. Slipping around behind her, his right arm snaked around her throat and across her chest. Asaege began to speak the words of the spell as her training took over.

His left hand covered her mouth as his lips found her ear. He whispered, "Shh … we are no longer alone." Without releasing her mouth, he used his left hand to guide her eyes to an ever-brightening patch of bookcase. "I am going to let you go, snuff your lantern and follow me or scream and take your chances with whoever approaches." He pulled his hand from her mouth slowly as he returned his knife to its sheath. "I mean you no harm; I am not sure they will offer you the same assurances."

Asaege looked between his quickly disappearing back and the illuminated spot on the bookcase and made her choice, "Wait for me," she whispered as she snatched her lamp from the floor and pursed her lips. With a sudden exhalation, the lantern went dark. The two of them were barely able to cross into the next aisle before the three men turned the corner.

Chapter Two
Curious Soul, Adventurous Heart

"I will be only a moment and then you may return to whatever trivial task I have taken you from." The voice was soft but had a nasal quality to it that grated on Asaege's nerves. Although she couldn't see to whom it belonged, there was little doubt in her mind.

"The Binders live to serve, Lord Curate." The second voice was unfamiliar to her, but if it belonged to a Binder, that didn't bode well for Asaege or her companion.

"Of course you do." Curate Rethmus rarely made friends of those he deemed beneath him, which was mostly everyone, as he spoke for the current Hand of Light, Hierophant Graceous Trim. Despite the fact that he served the man who should have represented the authority and mercy of the Lord of Justice, Olm, Rethmus demonstrated none of the charity or righteousness that the Olmites professed. She could hear him shuffling through the books as he continued, "And the Hand appreciates your sacrifice this evening." While the words themselves seemed encouraging, his tone was flat and made him sound disinterested.

"It is no sacrifice to aid the church, Lord Curate."

Rethmus grunted non-committally as the sounds of his search became more frantic.

Her companion pulled on her cloak and gestured towards the far end of the aisle. She held up a finger and turned her attention back to Rethmus.

"No one has been admitted to these stacks, correct?"

"That is correct, Lord Curate, as you commanded. The Ancient History section has been closed to the public and the librarians have been notified that no book in these aisles is to be touched."

She could hear him groan as he sank to his knees, rummaging through the books on the lowest shelf. Asaege could see the light of his lantern filtering through the books as he brought it closer to the shelf to inspect the spines there. "Then tell me, Binder, why is the work that I … that the Hand requires not in its place?" A cold dread took up residence in her belly, beginning to radiate outward as a prickling sensation. Rethmus would never find what he sought; she clutched it tightly against her stomach. The swaying light stabilized as he set the lamp on the floor. "The Hand only entrusted this book to the Grand Library and its so-called guardians because we were assured that--" He paused mid-sentence.

"We continue to assure you that the library is a safe …"

"Silence, fool. There is a warm spot here … almost as if a …" She heard him pull himself to his feet. "Lock the library. Summon the other Binders. Have them confine the librarians to their cells. Notify me immediately of any that cannot be found."

"But, Curate, it is past midnight, and they are no doubt asleep."

Asaege could hear the sneer in his retort, "So I guess you should wake them. No one in the library will sleep until the book is found. None enter … none depart unless it is with my leave."

"The library is massive, that could take hours."

"Do you wish for me to tell the Hand that his needs are interfering with your slumber?"

"No, Curate."

She heard Rethmus shove the man. The Binder's weight shook the bookcase beside him; he didn't retaliate. "Then get moving. Send me two men immediately to aid with the search."

"As you will, Lord Curate." Asaege heard the man's footsteps disappearing into the distance.

Her eyes flashed back to her companion; he mouthed, "We need to go." She couldn't help but nod and allow him to lead her to the end of the aisle. For a man of nearly two hundred and fifty pounds, he moved like a shadow along the marble floors, eliciting no more than a soft patter on the stones. She could see his left hand flexing as he moved, as if he were trying to oil a hinge that had fallen into disuse. He made a right into the stacks containing works devoted to Kiel ecology and crouched down. "Am I to assume that the book Curate Fussypants searches for is the one in your hands?"

She pulled back suddenly, extricating her wrist from his grip. "And, if it is?"

He sighed softly, seemingly debating something and then answered her. "I guess we will deal with that if and when they catch us. At this point, even if it was not, they are not likely to believe us."

"Just being here after nightfall is punishable by …"

He held up his left hand, she saw that it did not open completely, "Let me be surprised. I have a feeling it is not a pat on the back and a stern 'attaboy'."

She simply shook her head. "If they have locked down the library, there is no way out."

He smiled softly. "There is a way in, which means there is always a way out." The sound of rushing feet reached their ears and they quickly flattened themselves against the shelves. A group of three men ran by their aisle without even a sidelong glance. Once the footsteps began to fade into the distance, he continued, "So we have already succeeded, all that remains is to get from here to there. Does that not make you feel better?" He smiled more brightly.

"Not particularly."

His smile dimmed. "Me neither." His eyes dipped to the book she still held, asking "What are the chances of you parting with that?"

"None."

"If they find it, they may have less enthusiasm in looking for us."

She felt her face set, as if in stone. "None."

Her companion frowned at her. "That important?"

"That important."

"I find that when gods are involved, they tend to get their way eventually."

"Churches are not gods," her voice was firm, leaving little room for argument. "This is not about what Olm wants; it is the will of one man."

The man shook his head and snorted softly, "Tell the million or so Olmites that." He slid his back along the bookcase until he stood at the edge of it, drawing his broad knife as he did so. "So, you are doing this for your god?" He brought the knife up, catching the reflection of what lay beyond his sight in its surface.

She slowly moved next to him. "To my knowledge, Olm has never done anything for me. The truth is the truth. A lot of things fall into a gray area between good and ill, right and wrong. There is one thing that is not open to interpretation: the way things work … for lack of a better term, the truth. I cannot allow anyone, even the Hand himself, to pervert that for their own goals."

Her companion slowly shook his head and said, "You remind me

7

of someone … someone I knew some time ago. He had a strong sense of right and wrong; but he allowed fear and the will of sovereign forces to intimidate him into silence." He sheathed his blade again. "The way is clear, at least for the moment."

Asaege nodded and began to move past him, but he seized her upper arm in his strong right hand.

"Tell me, Magpie, if by some miracle, we are able to escape this nightmare house of knowledge, what do you intend to do with the book?"

She shrugged. "I had not thought that far ahead when I set out this evening; but I suppose it would be a waste if I simply hid it away and allowed the lies of … what did you call them … sovereign forces to define its message." His grip didn't loosen as he waited patiently. "I will see that it finds its way into the right hands."

With that, he released her. "We need to move further into the library." He began to move towards the next stack when she grasped his arm.

"Why not make a rush for the exit before they have time to completely mobilize?"

"Sometimes, it is better to give ground in order to take it later. They, no doubt, will begin their efforts closest to the exits and it will be there that their search will be most vehement. As the night passes and they move further in, their eyes will be less clear and their enthusiasm less … well … enthusiastic."

"And they may be more spread out, allowing us to slip behind them." She watched his face, noting approval in his eyes. "They will be so focused on what is before them; they will not be looking back."

"Now you have it." He dashed across the aisle to the next stack and then turned to wave her on. She had already crossed half the distance to him. "Are you sure you have not done this before?"

She shook her head. "We are in Natural Sciences now. They will start their search in Historical Studies and spread out from there. The best place to hold up will be Mathematics; it is far enough from the Historical Archives and tucked into its own alcove that it should escape search for a while in the worst case, be ignored entirely in the best."

"Alcove? Does it have an exit?"

"That is the issue. The only entrance is a small bottleneck three stacks wide but the section itself is twelve by twelve. Enough room to hide but if we get caught there …," she let her voice trail off.

She could see him debating the options before closing his eyes. "How well do you know the library?"

Her answer was immediate, "Well."

"In your opinion, is Mathematics the best place to hide?"

She answered a bit more slowly, "Yes."

He opened his eyes. "Then I will place my trust in you, Magpie." He drew his knife again, extending it to her hilt first, "Put the book away so you have your hands free and tuck this into your belt. Even the best of hiding spots are sometimes discovered."

She opened the bag slung across her chest and slid the book into it before accepting the weapon. "Thank you."

"It is only a knife … and the night is not nearly over."

"Not for the knife …" she said before she turned and rushed in the other direction.

Chapter Three
Into the Heart of Danger

Asaege crouched with her back to a shelf devoted to theoretical geometry, watching the man before her. He sat arms akimbo and eyes closed, his breathing deep and regular. He'd been such since they decided on this spot; it offered a good view of the stacks at the front of the section but no direct line of sight from or to the main library. She wondered at how he could sleep so soundly when every moment offered the threat of capture or worse. By his side, sat the naked steel of his sword and round buckler.

She alternated between watching the entrance and the man. The light of the moon illuminated his face, smoothing the lines that his years had placed there. In sleep, she didn't see the hardened criminal she imagined him to be; here he was simply a man trying to make his way through the world. She silently scolded herself; he was here to steal from the library she'd called home for so many years. Just because he offered to help her escape the Binders didn't excuse his intended sin. Her eyes shifted back to the three stacks at the front of the section; when they returned to the man, he was regarding her, although his tempo of his breathing remained deep and regular. She averted her eyes quickly.

"You know the library so well and yet you are neither student nor teacher, Binder nor librarian." He spoke as if he were stating fact not confirming suspicion.

"How did you come to that conclusion?"

"Were you any of those, there would have been ample, not to mention safer, alternatives for retrieving your prize than skulking around the library in the dead of night."

She nodded. "What of you? Why are you here?"

He smiled easily. "I, my little magpie, am a thief. As such, I am here to pilfer and steal."

She sneered more than she'd intended, "Would not silver and gold be easier targets?"

Without thought, he responded, "Knowledge is more precious than any metal, more valuable than any stone." His response took her aback; he misinterpreted her expression. "Be wary of preconceptions; I am not the brute you seem to want me to be."

"I do not think you a brute, simply … "

"Simply a common criminal. If it puts your mind at ease, I am here to reclaim my own property. One cannot steal something that already belongs to you." She frowned at him before he continued, "The provenance before it came into my hands, however, is a bit more murky."

She laughed despite herself. "As is the case with a good amount of academic works. One cannot blame you, for sure."

He chuckled as well. "That is what I keep trying to convince folks; but alas for naught."

She wasn't sure if it was the heightened emotions of the situation or the absurdity of discussing provenience with a self-professed burglar; but Asaege began to giggle. This set off her companion, whose entire form began to quiver with silent laughter as he shook his head. The two took a moment to compose themselves before speaking again.

"I have shared my motivation for being here on this most unfortunate of evenings, Magpie. Care to share yours?"

She shook her head but began speaking against her best judgment. "I studied here for a long time … almost as long as I could remember. My family was neither wealthy nor powerful; but they are good people. They saw in me a hunger for knowledge and mourned the thought of it wasted as the wife of a fish monger; I have two sisters that can serve that role just fine."

Without realizing it, Asaege felt her mouth pull back into a grimace. "When I reached my eleventh year, they apprenticed me to the Great Library. At first I simply learned my letters and ran errands for the librarians; but I soon proved my worth as a talented researcher in my own right. Some of my happiest times were spent amid these books." She closed her eyes and became lost in the memories of days past. Realizing the conversation had dragged, she continued, "Soon I came to the attention of the headmaster of the Academy Athenaeum in the course of his research. He made no pretense that he wished for me to use my talents for the good of the Academy and arranged for my apprenticeship to be transferred from the general library to him. I trained as a teacher as well as fulfilling the role of his personal research assistant. If I had remained, I have no doubt that I would at this very moment be instructing the next generation of noblemen and clerics."

The man seemed lost in her story as he prompted, "Why did you not stay?"

"Knowledge should not be the exclusive right of the wealthy and powerful. I spent my free time teaching those who could not afford to walk the halls of the academy. This was not viewed kindly, I was told. How could the academy maintain itself when the commodity it charged dearly for was given to every street urchin and shopkeeper? How could men who made their livings writing letters and contracts feed their families when their customers could now write for themselves? How could the clergy deliver the word of Olm to their flocks when those same sheep could read for themselves? He claimed that knowledge was a commodity; but what he really meant was that it was a yoke, a method to deny the lower classes the tool of their own improvement." She shook her head, "I could not be a part of that ... I could not let knowledge be used as a weapon against the defenseless."

He gestured towards her satchel. "And so you do to this day, hmm?"

She shrugged, coloring slightly. She hadn't meant to share so much; but once she opened the gates, she couldn't stem the tide. Asaege couldn't put her finger on it; but there was something about this man that forced her to lower her guard without realizing it.

"Why that book? And why after so long?"

"I have said too much."

"And yet not enough so I may understand the connection. The church seeks that book, or at least the Hand of Light does. That much is clear. It is important enough to them that they risk alienating both the Great library and the Binders that serve it. The Hand would definitely qualify as a sovereign force. What is in that book that he is so afraid of?"

She opened her mouth to rebuke his roundabout attempts to squeeze more information out of her when she heard voices. Both of their heads turned towards the stacks at the same time, their conversation falling into silence.

"Stay here," a deep voice boomed, "Augathra, Feldur and I will search Mathematics and then we can tell His Royal Bossiness that it was clear."

"Yes, Sir," a pair of voices intoned.

Asaege's companion held up five fingers and he slowly and silently rose to his feet before retrieving his sword and buckler.

Again, the unseen voice thundered. "If there is someone in there, we will flush them out to you. Be ready."

A pair of voices responded in a crisp, "Yes, Sir."

Asaege drew her borrowed dagger and nodded in a direction away from the bottleneck. Her companion followed quickly.

They heard rather than saw the three men search the stacks. As much as they'd wished the search would be half-hearted, it was quite the opposite. The men expertly cut off the section and searched it systematically. Each time the pair sought to break free of their grid, they barely avoided being spotted. As the net closed nearer and nearer about them, Asaege's companion leaned in towards her.

"Are all the aisles the same width?"

She nodded. "All except the ones at the back, they were built first and butt up against the interior wall. There is enough room for a man to stand; but not enough for two to pass."

He sighed softly and then smirked, "Then there is where I will make my stand. Once all three enter the stacks at the back, move towards the front. Their backup should enter soon after. That is your chance to run."

"You cannot ask me to leave you to face five men alone."

He growled, "I am not asking … I am telling you that is what is going to happen."

Asaege frowned. "Do not tell me what to do." She tapped her temple with an extended finger. "I have weapons at my disposal that have neither hilt nor edge."

He raised an eyebrow. "Such as what?"

"I learned more during my apprenticeship than history and geography. The Academy Athenaeum is also home to some of the finest thaumaturges in Granatyr."

He chuckled softly and bit his bottom lip, "Now you tell me. I suppose it serves me right for not asking."

"The dweomers I was able to master are not powerful but used properly, they can be of aid. The Binders may guard a library but do not mistake them for librarians. They are trained soldiers to a man."

He struggled with his pride for a moment but to his credit, he won. "Fine. Stay behind me and do what you can. Nothing that burns or flashes. Agreed?"

Asaege nodded quickly, "Agreed."

They made their way to the back of the Mathematics Section as quietly as they could manage. The man put his bag down and began to stretch. She watched him with a raised eyebrow.

14

"Do not judge. Proper stretching wins more combats than you can imagine."

"Mm hmm," she agreed although the look on her face raised doubt.

"Well it does … "

The first Binder came into sight, lifting his lantern to spread its light to the back of the aisle.

"Good evening, milord," Asaege's companion purred, "I was wondering if you could direct me towards a good recipe for meat pies? I have a serious craving."

"Over here!" the man yelled and launched himself at the thief.

"Mistake," her companion intoned as he took the charge against his buckler, sliding his sword along its smooth surface and between the Binder's ribs. A soft gurgle accompanied a surge of blood from the man's lips before he fell to the marble. His comrades were right behind.

"Lay down your weapon and I promise you will only lose a hand tonight." The speaker belonged to the voice they had heard leading the search. "You have Binder blood on your hands but this does not have to end in your death."

Asaege brought to mind an incantation and allowed it to flow from her memory to her lips in a rush. Although the words of the spell filled her ears, she could hear beneath it others. "Now you make me feel bad. Unfortunately, I will have to decline. You see I only have the one good hand and I am afraid I am going to have to insist on keeping it."

Another sound filled her ears. It began softly, the barest hint of rustling. "Then you shall arrive in the afterlife with both of your hands intact, Deadman." The rustling began to multiply, as if it were coming from everywhere at once. The third Binder arrived, his sword already drawn but he couldn't press the advantage with his comrade in his way. He turned as the thought of flanking the two intruders occurred to him only to be met by a buzzing cloud.

The cloud engulfed his face in an instant, the stinging insects crawling into his ears and nose. Before he could think about it, he opened his mouth to scream and they swarmed into the open orifice. Dropping his sword, he began to claw at his face in panic. The leader turned at the sound; immediately thinking better of it. Unfortunately for him, immediately was a split second too late. The thief's buckler batted the man's sword aside and his own blade laid his throat open. He slumped to the floor without a further sound.

Watching the frantic struggles of the flailing third Binder, Asaege's companion turned to her. "Not powerful? Was that what you had planned for me?"

She held up her forefinger and thumb a small distance apart as her only reply.

*****

The pair easily avoided the last two Binders as they rushed to check on their comrades. Once in the library proper, they carefully made their way towards the librarian's entrance. It was smaller and known only to those who navigated the building often. Asaege hoped that fact would mean it was also less well guarded. In the end, her hope was true. There were only three men between them and freedom. One of which was the Lord Curate himself.

"Do you have another trick in that beautiful brain of yours?" her comrade asked.

She nodded. "Not as dramatic; but it may serve the purpose."

"Olm help us," he whispered and crouched, moving from shadow to shadow towards the closest of the men. He gathered himself for a moment before lunging into the light. The point of his sword took the man in the side, slipping between his ribs. The Binder slumped to the floor, blood loss taking first his consciousness and then his life in short order. The awkward fall wedged her companion's blade between two ribs, prying it from his grasp. To his credit, he drew a thin Slazean knife from a sheath strapped to his leg but now faced two armed men with nothing more than a dagger.

Asaege brought to mind another dweomer and allowed it to move from memory to lips with ease. She saw the Lord Curate glance in her direction, allowing the remaining Binder to move forward to engage her out matched companion. Words also began falling from Rethmus's lips as he pulled upon his own arcane resources. A cold feeling of dread washed over her body as she recognized the words. He was channeling fire.

The spell on her lips was designed to fatigue the body and slow the mind; but it wouldn't be enough to prevent the Lord Curate's own spell from burning her alive, not to mention the priceless books on the shelves behind her. In that moment, as time slowed to a crawl, her only thought was which outcome she found more distressing: the loss of her life or the destruction of the knowledge contained in those books. As his spell began to take effect, Asaege felt her skin tingle and smoke. She closed her eyes and threw everything she had into what was to be her final act on Taerh. If she could weaken her companion's enemy, it would give him a fighting chance against Rethmus. She felt the words lodge in her throat as her fear robbed her of her wits for a moment. That instant was all that was required to foul the ritual. The spell she'd spent so many nights repeating until she knew it as well as her own name flew from her memory like so much dust from an unused shelf.

As she felt air in her lungs began to burn her from within, Asaege

16

saw something catch the building light of the flames that crackled across Curate Rethmus's fingers. Beyond the range of the lanterns, some small object glinted in the flickering illumination, making the shadows of the stacks quiver as if they breathed. Her vision wavered, the heat mercifully threatening to steal her senses before the flames devoured her body. As everything around her grew dark, the undulating shadows coalesced around that of the Curate. His voice was choked off as suddenly as if a hand had closed around his throat. His shadow and that of her companion's opponent seemed no more than a patch of writhing darkness although their bodies seem untouched.

The library fell into silence as the last word echoed amid the stacks and she cracked open an eye. The Lord Curate stood with his arms out stretched and his mouth hanging open, the words of his own dweomer suspended upon his tongue. The Binder also stood frozen mid lunge, Asaege's companion looking dumbfounded between her and the frozen man. All he could manage was, "Serve the purpose?"

She shook her head and shrugged, "Not my spell."

He tilted his head. "Pardon?"

"It was not my spell … I do not know what happened."

He nodded quickly. "Fair enough … let us not question the machinations of the unknowable." He carefully stepped around the Binder and towards the door.

"Should we not finish them?" she asked, not sure of whether she truly wanted to.

He shook his head as he pushed open the door. "I have enough blood on my hands for tonight. The Binder was simply fulfilling his pledge and as for the Curate, I am sure his night is not going to get any better."

They stepped outside into quickly approaching dawn; Asaege took a lungful of clean night air. A voice in the back of her mind marveled at the taste of it. It seemed to hold so much … so much of everything. Not like … She shook her head to clear it.

"Will you tell me now what that book contains that made it worth both of our lives?"

A smile came to her lips as she looked at him again, this time in the quickly lightening sky. His deep brown eyes looked into hers, mirroring her smile. "It occurs to me that through everything we have shared, I do not even know your name."

He laughed. "Fair trade. My name for the significance of the book."

Her eyes darted back to the building they had just left and then to him, with that same self-satisfied smile on his face, "Agreed …"

He extended his hand, taking hers gently, "I am called Hollis, Magpie," as he brought it to his lips. Her heart rose in her chest as her fingers closed around his …

Chapter Four
Shadows of True Knowledge

She'd lied to him, of course. The thief would have known that even without the gifts bestowed upon him by the Well of Worlds. Rather than eroding Hollis' respect of the woman, it confirmed it. Had Asaege surrendered her interest in the leather-bound prize for which she risked both of their lives, it would have made her unworthy of keeping it … at least in the thief's estimation.

Hollis had kept his own side of their bargain; but his identity wouldn't have remained a secret for long anyway. There was not a surplus of bald, bearded thieves pushing eighteen stone in the city of Oizan. Were she to have inquired strenuously enough, she would have come across the name Hollis the Slender eventually. Unfortunately, the two men he'd allowed to live during their daring escape would have no more difficulty identifying him.

He cursed beneath his breath; before the situation with the Well … before he'd 'met' Stephen, he would never have made that mistake. Immediately, the word turned sour on his mind's tongue. It was a choice he wouldn't have made six months prior; but in his heart, Hollis didn't feel that it was truly a mistake. Along with the other gifts that the fabled Well had bestowed upon the thief, it also tied his soul inexorably to that of his reflection. What was left behind was neither completely Stephen nor himself. Rather their personalities, their very identities merged together into something altogether new. He could recall the memories of his reflection as clearly as his own; but both seemed equally natural and familiar.

"Frowning at your plaques will not change them, Slender One." Hollis's eyes rose slowly from where they had been staring unseeing at the stained oak table before him. Upon its surface lay six elongated octagons stacked atop one another in a tight fan. The back of each was adorned with a beautifully rendered painting of a tree, lanterns hanging from its branches. Leaned against its wide trunk were a sword and a plow. "You may have all night to wait on them to do so; but others of us have places to be … people to see … money to win."

The thief's eyes continued to rise, meeting the gaze of the voice's owner. Elias wore a confident smirk painted across his too lean face. The man broke eye contact to take in the players sitting to his right and left before darting back to his own cards held before him. The sailor was too eager … too nervous. A few hands prior, he'd bested Hollis's trio of plows with his own run of swords. During that hand, he'd sought eye contact rather than avoiding it. His motions had been slow and deliberate, not the inpatient, rodent like gestures he now exhibited.

Hollis casually reached out with his right hand to push the fan of cards before him into a neat pile as he regarded the other two men at the table. Before the incident in the Well, the thief had always been confident in his abilities; but the fabled site had gifted him with a surety that hung about his heart like a thick winter cloak. It had also granted him what he had termed to himself as 'the understanding'.

'The understanding' was just as it sounded; the thief could instinctively recognize how things worked. It was a boon in his line of work, as locks and mechanical traps that would have posed issues for him beforehand simply no longer did. Hollis also tended to pick up on things that most people would miss. He could tell you how many nails fastened a man's sole to his boot and if he put his mind to it, where to apply pressure to best peel one from the other. This extended to people as well. For example, he could tell that the man to his left was debating surrendering his plaques by the way he flicked them against his bottom lip.

The same instincts told Hollis that the talkative sailor across from him held little more valuable in his fist than a low-ranking pair … perhaps as much as three of the same card across suits. The thief's run of lanterns had nothing to fear from any hand at the table. He casually picked up his cards and began shifting their order front to back in a smooth, methodical way; it was a tell he had been cultivating since sitting down hours before. Each time his cards were weak, he had used it as an opportunity to display this behavior in preparation for this very moment.

Elias spoke up again, "The bet is three nobles to you, Hollis." The man's brash insistence had softened, as he attempted to coax the thief into matching his wager.

Hollis tilted his cards in his hand, fanning them as he did so. He took a purposeful deep breath and let it escape his lips in a slow drawn out sigh. The thief pushed three silver coins from the pile to his left into the center of the table. He resisted his urge to increase the bet; it never paid to be too eager, as Elias would soon demonstrate to the room. To his left, the man continued to fidget with his cards as his eyes moved between the haphazard pile of coins in the center and the neatly stacked but dwindling one before him.

Hollis felt a pang of sympathy for the man, a farmer only in the city of Oizan to sell his harvest. The money stacked in front of him was all that would come between his family and a hard winter. Cursing himself for a sentimental fool, the thief retracted his hand and pushed another four nobles into the center. Just as Hollis knew he would, the already spooked farmer placed his cards down in front of him and slid them towards the center. Without a word, the man rose, gathered the coins before him and walked towards the Virgin Mermaid's massive double doors.

The thief's eyes shifted back to the man across from him. Elias studied his cards with what he no doubt believed was a passive expression. Hollis could see the corner of the sailor's mouth quiver as he weighed his options. In the other man's contemplation, resided the distinct possibility that the thief's time cultivating his ruse was going to be wasted. Quickly, Hollis changed tactics; he could feel his lips curl into a sly smirk as he parroted the man's words back to him, "Money to win?"

That final push was all that was required; Elias shoved his remaining coins into the center of the table. It was a gold imperial's worth of silver, give or take a few. "It is a good thing that you have a little weight to fall back on, Slender One, because you may not be able to afford to eat for a while."

The thief's smirk blossomed into an amused smile, "Is that so?" He gathered a handful of nobles and dropped them atop the substantial pile already between them. "There is a saying where I grew up, wharf rat," Hollis winked at the sailor, "would you care to hear it?" He didn't respond; but Hollis could see realization begin to filter into the greedy man's face. As he again shifted his cards in his hand, he continued, "You rarely have issues leading a horse to water; but the trick is convincing him to drink." The thief stopped shuffling his cards and slowly began laying each on the table face up. Knave of Lanterns. Squire of Lanterns. Knight of Lanterns. "Tonight, my friend, you were indeed thirsty." Princess of Lanterns. "So very …" Queen of Lanterns. "… very …" King of Lanterns. "… thirsty."

As the thief revealed his cards, he watched the color drain from Elias's face. Once the king was laid on the table, however, a rushing wave of crimson spread from his cheeks like a still pond disturbed by a thrown stone. The sailor slammed his hands on the wooden surface and rose to his feet in a sudden, violent movement. "In the name of Olm's sacred hall!" Hollis settled back in his chair, his right hand resting on the hilt of the dwarven steel dagger secured at the small of his back. "I will not be cheated!" The 'Mermaid's common room fell into a tense silence as all eyes turned to the pair.

The man on Hollis's right slowly rose from his chair and backed away from the table, his empty hands held before him in a calming gesture. The thief simply raised an eyebrow, "I assure you that you still have not been … I suppose I have no need to see your cards to infer that they cannot best my Court of Lanterns?"

The sailor's face had taken on the shade of an autumn sunset. He reached into the pile of coins in the center of the table to retrieve his losses. "I will rot in Sharroth's cage before I let you cheat me out of wages, fairly earned."

Hollis leaned forward as he smoothly drew the thick bladed dagger from its sheath. "That is between you and the cage's current occupant, Elias; but if you do not put my winnings down, rest assured you will have a few less fingers with which to hold them." Although his smile never wavered, the thief's voice had taken on a tone sharp as the blade he held. The man let the coins drop to the table and reached for the curved Oenigh dagger tucked into his belt.

The occupants of the closest tables leapt from their chairs, not wishing to be embroiled in a conflict that wasn't their own. Elias sneered at him, "How dare you draw steel on me? Have you no idea of who I am?"

Hollis rose slowly and pulled the sheathed Uteli Wallin Fahr from where it hung on the back of his chair. "Well, kindly enlighten me."

"Elias Fairborn of the Witches' Murder. My crew and I have killed more men, women and children than clear pox. So many, as a matter of fact, that the Liege Governor himself granted us a commission so that we would turn our sights on Mantry rather than his own kingdom."

The thief shrugged. "I had no idea … but at the risk of overstating the obvious, your crew is not here." Placing his dwarven dagger atop his winnings, he pulled the sword smoothly from its leather home.

"They are but a shout away."

Hollis nodded slowly, placing the sword's sheath and belt beside his dagger. "That may pose an issue …," Elias's lips pulled back, revealing a ragged toothed smile, "… for me. You, of course, will be quite beyond their not so timely aid when they arrive."

Elias' eyes shifted from the thief's own to the Uteli long sword and then dropped to the right. "I have no need of them to finish one such as you. This knife has drunk the blood of more men than I can count." The pace of his words began to hasten as he continued, "I will allow you to buy your life with the paltry coins on the table there. Walk away now and you will have a tale for your grandchildren. Tell them of how you cheated death this night."

The thief moistened his lips with the tip of his tongue as he grunted non-committedly, "Mmhmm." Apparently the same tells Elias flaunted at the card table extended beyond it. It was clear that the man knew he was over matched and sought to extricate himself from the situation. The issue was that pride and self-preservation were often at odds.

The sailor began to pace frantically. "All of these people will bear witness to the fact that you were offered a reprieve."

Hollis chuckled. "Which I am sure they will do with pleasure." He moved around the table, his weapon held at waist height, the point angled upward towards Elias's throat. "Just as they will, no doubt, attest to the fact that I did not heed your offer."

The sailor cackled suddenly, the laugh clearly nervous and forced. "You cannot even face me on equal terms. That alone shows your cowardice. I will give you one final chance to save yourself."

Again, the thief shrugged as he laid his left hand upon the weapon's hilt as well. "You are the one who brought a knife to a sword fight. However, allow me to extend to you the same courtesy you offered me. Put your weapon away, apologize to these fine folk for disturbing their evening and leave the 'Mermaid."

The man's eyes darted nervously; it was obvious to Hollis that he knew he was in an impossible situation. Elias valued his reputation as highly as his life and he was being forced to sacrifice one to preserve the other. The sound of the door opening behind him brought a look of relief to the sailor's face. The men who entered the Virgin Mermaid weren't who either of them expected.

The bearded man wearing the ivory and gold chalice of Olm was flanked by two city watchmen in their dark gray cloaks. Two men with steel drawn in the center of the bar room floor certainly didn't escape their notice. If the newcomers' purpose was in doubt, the leader's words removed it all, "Hollis, called the Slender, you are wanted for questioning in connection to an incident earlier this evening in the Great Library. Put down your weapon and come with us."

Cursing to himself, the thief stepped back a few paces so as to keep the three men and Elias in his sight. "Are the Binders so short-handed that they are outsourcing now?" The look of confusion on the faces of those gathered reminded him that he'd used an English word, as 'outsourcing' had no Trade Tongue equivalent.

The bearded man spoke again, "No doubt the Binders have a few questions for you as well; but Hand would like to speak to you about the death of the Lord Curate this evening."

Figuring it would make no difference in the moment, Hollis declined to inform the men that he had, indeed, left Rethmus alive. The thief stepped back again, placing the table between himself and the trio.

Allowing his eyes to quickly scan the room, the thief saw that while many eyes were on him and the forces of the law, such that it was, an equal amount were glued to the table before him. It held eight gold imperials worth of coins, give or take a silver noble. With a quick motion, Hollis snatched his sheath from where he'd laid it on the tabletop. As he did so, he dragged it through the pile of coins, making sure they left the surface and arced into the crowd. Those gathered dove to recover the glinting precipitation and effectively blocked the men's path. Quickly mourning the loss of income for the evening, Hollis snatched his dagger from the table before putting his head down and running towards the kitchen and freedom.

Chapter Five
Heart of the City

She'd lied to him, of course, but something told her he'd expected her deception. Asaege lay in the bed that dominated the corner of her small room above the weaver's shop. The weaver, Lange, and his wife had lost their own daughter to the crimson lung a few years before; they had rented her the room after she'd been cast out of the library. The couple cared little about the reason for her exile from academia, as did most in the Ash.

A small section of the area commonly referred to as the Common Quarter, the Ash was only slightly poorer than the rest of its neighbors. In the end, everyone who lived north of the Forest Gate were seen as little better than beasts of burden in the eyes of the nobles and merchants of the Oizan.

Between a so called 'transit tax' levied on people traveling through the Quarter's only gate and the fact that the majority of its population worked as unskilled labor, there was little hope of their improving the situation they were born into. Their station was kept in place with a law prohibiting laborers from joining a guild or even forming one of their own. Without a guild of their own, they were denied representation on Oizan's city council. Owing to the poverty of their customers, Common Quarter craftsman and merchant couldn't afford to pay guild dues, thus they were often in the same straits as their laborer neighbors.

The people were more concerned with putting food on their table and clothes on their backs than what they could find beyond the walls of their grime coated prison or in the pages of a book. As a matter of fact, only a very small minority of the men and women who made their homes in the northern district could read. Asaege had offered to teach the skill to Lange and his wife, Tawn, to make up the difference between the value of the small room and the paltry amount she could afford to give them, but they'd always refused with one excuse or another.

Asaege clutched the book for which she had risked so much to her chest, breathing in the rich scent of old paper and candle wax that clung to it. She ran her thumb over the spine, long since worn smooth of writing by the passage of time. The truth was that her deception was less about wanting to keep her plans for the book a secret and more due to not having a real plan to begin with. As her driving desire to possess the work faded, it was replaced by an intellectual aimlessness.

In its empty expanse, surrounded by the miasma of better times brought on by the comforting smell, she fell into the abyss of a numbing slumber. Upon her lips was the name of the mysterious man who still haunted her thoughts. "Hollis."

Chapter Six
Legacy of Apathy

"Hollis," Jillian murmured as her eyes fluttered open. Looking around her darkened bedroom, she let a dejected sigh pass her lips. She could still smell the ghost of the book's scent … see the memory of his face in her mind's eye. The dream seemed so real; in some respects more real than her one bedroom apartment. Her heart still beat quickly in her chest as she brought her hand to her cheek.

After rubbing at her eyes, Jillian turned to gaze at the digital clock that stood sentry on her bed side table. It flashed 12:00 in a lazy tempo; the electricity must have gone out at some point during the night.

By the red pulsing light, she searched for her cell phone and thumbed at the button on the side. It was a little after six a.m.; she had to be up for work in less than an hour. Using her elbow to push herself into a sitting position, she tried in vain to hold on to the euphoria of the dream. The crush of reality blotted out the spark of it, but not the details. When she closed her eyes, she could still see Hollis's face against the darkened lids … the way his self-assured smile nested within his ragged goatee … the look of mischief that bordered on insanity in his deep brown eyes.

Jillian shook her head to clear it of foolish thoughts. Only a child would be enamored by a dream. She slowly rose to her feet, reaching for the bathrobe that lay thrown over the chair that she called 'clothing purgatory'. The articles consigned there were not fresh from the laundry but still too much so to be cast into the hamper. As she pulled the cotton garment around her, she padded into the living room and flopped on to the faded futon that served as a couch. Fumbling for a moment under the avalanche of pillows that covered the surface, she found the television remote and clicked it on.

The woman stared at the images moving across the screen, listening to the buzz of voices that emerged from it for almost ten minutes before she realized she neither comprehended nor remembered anything they'd said. Her mind still wandered the paths of her dream. "Come on, Jillian," she whispered harshly to herself. "Enough is enough. It's time to return to the real world." Jillian climbed to her feet and headed for the shower.

After emerging from the revitalizing embrace of the warm water, she felt much more herself. She walked into the apartment's small galley kitchen and opened the refrigerator. Liberating a yogurt from its depths and pulling a spoon from the drawer, she returned to her quickly brightening bedroom to choose an outfit for the day.

The container and spoon held in one hand, she pulled out a pink sleeveless blouse and a pair of black pants, hangers and all, from the closet with the other and tossed them onto the bed. Despite being September, the weather had been mild all week and there was no reason to assume today would be different. The principal kept the school uncomfortably warm, so if she didn't wish to be so as well, it paid to wear a lighter fabric.

Jillian dressed quickly, looking longingly at her unmade bed as she fastened the blouse's last button. In addition to the normal school day, there was a staff meeting scheduled for four p.m., after which she still needed to grade papers and prepare for the next day's class. Her apartment was only ten minutes from the school at which she worked; but it was unlikely that she would be seeing it again much before ten that evening. Taking a deep breath and exhaling it in a deep sigh, the woman mourned the death of her weekend. It had, as it always did, passed too quickly.

A musky, vaguely skunk-like scent caught her attention as she walked around the bed towards the door. She scolded herself for not cleaning up last night and turned around to gather up the clear plastic bag and glass pipe that lie on her bedside table beside her still blinking clock. Her vivid dreams made much more sense now; her friend Cyrill had bought from a new guy. It was a strain that neither of them had been familiar with and must have been stronger than she'd anticipated.

*****

The day had passed quickly and for the most part, pleasantly. She was able to concentrate on the portion of her job that continued to thrill her, even after five years and three school districts. Some would say that teaching elementary school was only glorified babysitting; but Jillian wouldn't trade a moment with her kids for a year spent with even the most gifted grad students. Despite the continually shrinking duration of childhood, there was something about teaching a young mind, one not weighed down by the burdens of the world around them.

Having no children of her own, the woman held each and every child that passed through her classroom door close to her heart. Far from being lenient and permissive, Jillian elicited from her students not only their love, but their respect as well. It was always with a heart heavy with equal measures of pride and sadness that she watched each class move on to the fifth grade. If she could only be allowed to teach … to show her students the wonders of knowledge and the satisfaction of success earned not given, every day would be more rewarding than the last.

Life, she lamented, was rarely so kind, however. It may have been memories altered by nostalgia, but she swore that when she was in school it was more about learning than testing … more about helping a student become a better version of themselves than protecting oneself. The majority of her co-workers were so concerned with keeping a low profile and not making waves that they couldn't put themselves out in a place where they could make a difference in their students' lives.

She recalled the moment she realized that not everyone put the children under their care before their own interests. She'd formed an after-school group of students who felt they needed extra review or simply a place in which they could focus on their studies in relative peace. At first, she offered it to her own students; but slowly over a few weeks, children from other classes and even other grade levels had filtered in a few at a time. Jillian hadn't minded; she'd even found that the older children took to helping the younger ones. In doing so, they reinforced their own understanding of the material.

She asked for nothing to compensate her for her time and effort, but the satisfaction that each of the children who shared those hours with her left a little better than they had entered. That is where the trouble began.

A trio of her fellow teachers was haunting her doorway one rainy Wednesday morning as she arrived. They had asked to speak to her for a moment; not waiting for her to reply, they stepped into her classroom … her only sanctuary within those walls. She remembered fighting down the surge of anger at their violation. The women quickly explained to her that by offering extra help to those children, it weakened the position of other teachers in the school. The look of contempt on their faces when they lamented that they, too, may be asked to do the same shocked her to her core. If the derision of her co-workers hadn't dissuaded her from continu-

29

ing, the letter she received a few days later from the union certainly did. It was on that day that the ideal she held for teaching died.

Jillian shook her head as if with that physical act, she could also shake her thoughts free of the dark path they were walking. Her cloudy mood faded quickly; she couldn't quite put her finger on it, but something had buoyed her spirits throughout the day. The closest thing she could liken it to was wonder, no matter how misplaced that feeling seemed to her. She felt as if she saw everything around her with fresh eyes, as if she were experiencing it for the first time.

A knock on her open door broke her free from her reverie; Marisol stood in the doorway, a soft smile upon her lips. "As much as we both may like to 'forget it'", the young teacher made quotes in the air with her fingers, "I don't think missing a staff meeting will win us any points."

Jillian smiled at her friend, the only person she could truly call such in the building. "I am so far behind at this point, I'm not sure that a few more either way will make much of a difference." She laughed briefly, but stood from her desk all the same. She'd liked the young Puerto Rican woman the moment she met her. Jillian wasn't sure if it was that her dark skin and accent marked her as different and thus a kindred soul or Marisol's easy but confident demeanor, but the two had bonded quickly. Among the storm of disapproving glares and whispered condemnations, they represented a united front, small though it may be.

"Come on, don't you want to be there when Janice finally frowns deeply enough to make the corners of her mouth touch?"

Collecting the binder containing her lesson plans and her purse, Jillian walked towards her friend. "Well, as an academic, I should at least be there on the off chance that it does occur."

"It would be the only responsible thing to do."

She laughed softly. "We cannot have anyone thinking we're not responsible, after all." Arm in arm, the pair made their way to the school library. The feeling of jamais vu clung to the edges of Jillian's consciousness; but the delightful high brought on by its renewed sense of newness washed any concern from her mind.

*****

The other teachers were seated in groups according to their grade level as the two women opened the door to the library. All eyes in the room seized upon them momentarily, but most immediately dropped back to whatever they'd been doing previously. At the front of the group stood Reginald Peterson, vice principal of Rolling Meadows Elementary School. Peterson shuffled papers absently as he surveyed the room, his lips moving slightly as if he were counting. Marisol and Jillian sat with the other two fourth grade teachers. At the head of their table sat Janice

Roberts, a perpetual frown pasted on her face like a suit of armor.

Jillian smiled and nodded in greeting to her co-workers just as Mr. Peterson decided he was satisfied by whatever had occupied him by announcing, "Alright folks. I know we have limited time, so let's make the best use of it." He passed a blank sheet of paper to the nearest teacher. "Let's all sign in while we get started."

Jillian consciously prevented herself from rolling her eyes. Each teacher in the room had at least a bachelor's degree, most had completed their masters, but they were still required to sign in during every meeting as if they were suspected of trying to ditch seventh period biology. In the grand scheme of things, it was only a minor inconvenience, but it spoke to the larger issue of trust and respect within the school.

"As you are aware, if you read my email from last week, today we will be discussing some staffing changes."

Several concerned gasps peppered the room, mostly from newer teachers who hadn't yet secured tenure. The more experienced teachers simply stared at the vice principal with barely contained boredom.

"Due to an unexpected resignation, we will be forced to reorganize our child study team." Jillian frowned deeply. "Not to worry, folks, I am assured that the remaining members are ready, willing and able to pick up any slack this causes."

I am sure they assured you of that, Jillian thought, *they didn't want to lose their jobs as well*. Her thoughts went to Thomas Krieger, one of her own students. Thomas was a sweet boy, kind and generous as the day is long. He struggled in class, however, having issues with his reading and staying in his seat during long lessons. Jillian had contacted Mrs. Krieger a few times to discuss Thomas's in-class issues as well as his chronic missing homework. When the woman deigned to respond, it was to inform her that it was the school's job to teach her son, not her own.

"In order to assist with this process, each teacher will need to help the study team evaluate cases on which they need to focus."

Jillian started to raise her hand, only to be stopped by a sharp pain in her shin. Across the table, Janice's eyes were hard steel as she mouthed the words, "We talked about this."

They had spoken about Thomas briefly, but Janice's sarcastic solution consisted of moving the boy's seat. In the end, her strongly worded advice came down to 'If the mother isn't making a big deal about it, now is not the time to do so either.' It made Jillian sick to her stomach. Tucking her legs deeply under her chair, she raised her hand again.

"Miss Allen?"

Ignoring Janice's angry sneer, Jillian spoke. "I have a student, Thomas Krieger, that I believe would benefit from the team."

Mr. Peterson raised an eyebrow. "Is that so? I believe that may be more appropriate for your grade level meeting. We have other more pressing business to attend to." Without pausing to allow Jillian to respond, he shifted his eyes down to his notes and continued, "As you all know, back to school paperwork was due last week. We still haven't received it from everyone. Please remember that all sections should be completed and alphabetized by last name or it will be returned to you for resubmission."

A collective groan arose in the room, but the vice principal continued as if he hadn't heard it. "With that paperwork, should be included the name and contact information for your class parent." He paused momentarily to look up and sweep his gaze across the gathered teachers before his eyes shot back down to his notes. It was no doubt a technique he'd picked up from an overpriced public speaking course or self-help book. "If you haven't done so already, you should be in contact with them. It is your responsibility to have something planned for the Fall Festival during the week of parent / teacher conferences."

Peterson looked down at the notes scattered on the podium before him, the corners of his mouth drawn into a tight frown. A soft murmur rose to fill the silence. After a moment of searching, he cleared his throat insistently before saying, "Ladies and gentlemen, we still have a fair amount to discuss. If I could have your attention, we could continue." The room settled into low hum; although it wasn't the silence he obviously was looking for, he continued. Holding up a stack of papers, Peterson announced, "This is the list of books listed as concerning by the PTA —" The muttering rose, but he spoke over it, "— and the board of education agreed that in situations such as this, it's better to be safe than sorry. Please take one and pass the rest along."

He bent forward to drop the pile on the nearest table, in front of Mrs. Rossi. The graying fifth grade teacher peeled off the top sheet and handed the rest to the man next to her. Her jaw tensed as her eyes moved over the substantial list. Mrs. Rossi's head snapped around to glare coldly at the vice principal.

Peterson cut her off by speaking over any objection she may have had, "I know at face value, it may seem excessive but it's what we have before us. There is no use fighting both the PTA and the board."

When the stack made its way to Jillian, she took one and passed the pile to Marisol. Her eyes skimmed the list: Harriet the Spy, James and the Giant Peach, Bridge to Terabithia, A Wrinkle in Time. The list went on, but she felt her eyes skimming over the words without really comprehending. *A Light in the Attic by Shel Silverstein? For encouraging poor behavior? This is insanity!* The last entry on the list was simply an author's name: Judy Blume. Before she could stifle herself, Jillian said, "You have got to be kidding me."

A tense silence hung in the air for a split second, every eye in the room on Jillian. Marisol's voice broke the stillness. "A Wrinkle in Time is banned for," she made air quotes, "'occult themes'?"

With that, the dam broke as a rush of voices rose to fill the room.

Mr. Peterson held up his hands, "They have not been banned, only labeled as concerning."

"What does that mean?" The voice came from the back of the room where the eighth grade teachers sat around a small cafe-style table.

"Well," he began, shuffling though his notes again, "Any of these books could be assigned, read or discussed but prior to being made part of a lesson plan, approval would need to be given by the board. The administration is in agreement that to avoid that sort of unpleasantness, it is best that we steer away from anything on the list."

"How is that any different than banning it outright?" To Jillian's surprise, the voice was Janice's.

"Because it is," Peterson stammered, "Any of them could be taught with the proper approvals; we just would prefer that they be avoided."

"So they're not banned, we simply can't read, teach or discuss them without prior approval from not one but two different committees."

"Exactly." The vice principal had taken on an ashen pallor with the exception of two scarlet splotches high on his cheeks. "If any of you would like to discuss this further, feel free to make an appointment with my secretary and we in the administration would be happy to discuss the matter with each of you individually."

Jillian rolled her eyes. *Divide and conquer*, she thought.

The raised voices quieted as the sound of pen scratching paper replaced them. Almost every teacher made quick notes to remind themselves to follow up. Mr. Peterson took advantage of the stillness to continue. "But be aware that with contract negotiations coming up, there may be a delay in scheduling." It was a subtle threat that didn't go unnoticed, based on the narrowed eyes and tight lips of the teachers present. "Now, if we could return to the agenda, we still have a fair amount to cover."

The remainder of the meeting was a tepid blur of expected duties and only vaguely polite reminders that had more to do with bureaucracy than education. As it became clear that the meeting was winding down, Jillian closed her portfolio and tucked it into her bag. As soon as the first of her co-workers stood, she leapt to her feet and quickly approached the vice principal.

Looking at her in shock, he managed, "Can I help you, Miss Allen?"

"I wanted to circle back around to Thomas Krieger." The blank

33

look on his face indicated that he wasn't making the connection. Jillian continued, "He has some issues with attention, and I believe it is affecting his reading skills as well as his other class work."

"Have you spoken to the parents?" His tone became accusatory.

"I have emailed the mother several times, but she doesn't seem interested in a conference."

Peterson shrugged. "Then it most likely isn't that big of a deal. Have you tried moving his seat?"

*****

By the time Jillian returned to her one-bedroom garden apartment, she could feel the fatigue of the day settle upon her shoulders like a physical thing. The woman hung her bag and purse over the wooden chair that stood beside the entrance and made sure to both lock and chain the door.

Below her feet, her neighbor's yappy dog began its nightly serenade. Once she was home for a bit, the dog would quiet but every time her apartment door was opened, whether it was to leave or return, Jillian was greeted by a high-pitched chorus of displeasure. Muttering beneath her breath, she quickly moved into the large common area that served her as both living and dining room.

Despite the gnawing sensation in her belly, she collapsed on the futon rather than grabbing something from the refrigerator. Laying her head back on the eclectic wall of pillows behind her, she closed her eyes and tried to imagine the stress of the day flowing from her with each measured breath. For the most part it worked; but the tightness in her shoulders and back, physical manifestations of the tension she'd carried home with her, stubbornly resisted the exercise.

After a few moments in the dim, still confines of her apartment, she felt like she could at least muster the energy to rise and find a snack to quiet the nagging rumble in her stomach. Moving aside the Tupperware bowl of sliced vegetables that she promised herself she would choose over other less healthy alternatives, she pulled a plate of homemade meringue cookies free. "Sweets over veggies ... great call, Jill," she scolded herself. She, however, didn't feel contrite enough to forgo the sugar and its egg white delivery system.

She placed the plate of cookies on the low cocktail table that stood between the futon and the television before walking to her bedroom. Again, she felt a rush of discovery as she turned on her bedside lamp.

Nothing in the small room had changed; but part of her felt that she was seeing it for the first time. Shaking away the sensation, Jillian opened the drawer of her nightstand and pulled free the small plastic bag and glass pipe. Despite the weariness that hung upon her, she didn't feel that she could shake the tension enough to not sleep fitfully. Shutting off the

34

light, she walked out to where cookies and a delightful buzz awaited her.

Chapter Seven
Downfall of a Kind Heart

The blanket of dream fell from Asaege's shoulders as her eyes flickered open. The dream was in itself unremarkable; she'd walked the paths of her childhood, arm in arm with her sisters as she enjoyed a simpler time. What haunted the woman, instead, were recollections of dreams she couldn't remember. They were only glimpses, but each was so clear, as if they were memories rather than fantasies. She could remember standing in a brightly lit room, surrounded by tiny desks and chairs, although she'd never taught a group larger than a half dozen while at the library, there were easily four times that number of desks in their neat little rows. The other strange thing about these recollections was that it all seemed to be washed out, like too little paint spread over too much canvas.

That same faded quality clung to each false memory; she could clearly recall the sweet, airy treats combined with the deep, rich taste of the pipe weed. Asaege generally avoided smoking a pipe, as the scent tended to cling to her hair and clothes; but the weed from her memories had a pleasant, almost intoxicating aroma. Even that seemed to have a deluded quality to it.

Taking a deep breath, the woman sat up in her small bed as she reached towards the ceiling in a long, lounging stretch. Even as the dregs of her childhood dream faded into nothingness, the memories persisted as clear as if they were her own. Although they lingered, Asaege tried to force the strange sensation from her mind and rose, turning the lazy stretch into a full body one. Her eyes were clamped tight against the aches from the previous evening, but she relished every one. They were physical proof that the previous night hadn't been a flight of her imagination.

Another, infinitely more important reminder lay half concealed by the flaccid pillow upon her recently vacated bed. The sight of book's worn leather spine filled her heart with pride as it peaked out from beneath the linen depths. With the pride, returned the previous night's aimlessness with regard to her next course of action. She was proud to have liberated the work from the hands of those who would use the words contained within to press their own agenda; but other than the hollow victory of denying the Hand access to the physical book itself, she was unsure what triumph she'd actually achieved.

Through the miasma of doubt, one thing shined through as the dawning sun cuts through the early morning fog. She had to do something with it worthy of the words found within. Just as a candle's purpose is to shine forth and drive the hungry fingers of darkness before its luminous touch, knowledge yearned to be free. Just as the night fled before the light, so ignorance must surrender to understanding. An idea struck her as she pulled the book out of its linen and feather prison. The Dialogues of the Chalice, although towering in significance, was in reality rather diminutive in page count. She could most likely copy it in its entirety within less than a day.

Her buoyed spirits quickly sank as she remembered how adamantly Lange and his wife fought her attempts to teach them to read the Trade Tongue. Providing even the brief work in written form to a largely illiterate population would do no more for them than explaining the formulae and rituals of her arcane studies. There had to be another way.

Asaege thought about perhaps taking the book to one of the scholars who hadn't completely shunned her after the library had finished its character assassination. Even if they believed her story of the work's liberation, they, as devoted academics, would insist on seeing the original. All it would take would be one of them thinking to leverage her identity in order to secure the Binders' favor and Asaege would lose both the book and her freedom. The same situation could arise if she sought to bring it to any clergy of Olm within the Ash District, with the Hand of Light's good graces replacing the Binders.

Her mind became trapped in the ensnaring tangle of doubt and paranoia, each thought pulling her further and further into their grasp as if the feelings were quicksand in her own mind. It wasn't until the third knock that the insistent rapping forced itself into her perception. After placing the Dialogues under the pillow once more, Asaege padded to the door.

Despite its five decades, Tawn's face still held a measure of the beauty she possessed in her youth. As a matter of fact, to Asaege's eyes, the small wrinkles that pooled near the corners of her eyes and lips were no less than a sculptor's loving chisel marks upon marble. Each moment, whether they were filled with joy or grief, could be seen upon the canvas of her rounded face. In this moment, her normally serene countenance was stained with a worry that darkened her blue eyes. The concern that hung around her almost seemed a tangible thing in the small dim stairway.

Asaege reached out to take the woman's hand. "Tawn, is everything alright?" The woman's worry was infectious; Asaege's heart pounded in her chest as her already frantic mind raced to conclusions as to its source.

"Let me come inside, dear." Her eyes darted down the stairs and then flashed up to meet Asaege's.

She retreated further into her room, leading the woman by her already captured hand. "Of course. Is Lange ill? In trouble?" Asaege's mind swirled with the possibilities.

Closing the door behind her, Tawn squeezed the younger woman's hand. "He is well, Asaege. We both are just fine."

"That brings me great relief; yet you still carry a burden."

Tawn nodded slowly, her eyes shifting down and closing as a sigh left her body like a stilled sail. "Normally, I would not concern myself with your comings and goings, sweetness." Her eyes opened and met the woman's again. "Lange and I think of you as family ... more than family ... "

"I know, Tawn; have no fear of that. Please tell me what weighs so heavily upon you."

"A man came by this morning ... a man from the library." Concern for Tawn was replaced with dread in an icy hot flash that radiated from her heart; it took all Asaege's self-control to remain silent, hoping the woman before her would continue. "He asked if we knew where you were."

"What did you tell him?" the woman asked more quickly ... more forcefully than she'd intended.

Sadness fought with concern in Tawn's eyes, but it didn't filter into her voice, "Nothing, of course." She placed her free hand atop Asaege's, "We would never betray your trust like that ... not many in the Ash would. In the minds of those who dwell here, they are too clean ... too fancy to be trusted." Concern returned full force. "However, there are some who would see themselves in a better position and would use the favor of outsiders as a path to it."

"You do not think …"

She shook her head, "If the man knew anything he would have demanded rather than inquiring. He has suspicions for sure; but that is all they are. Silver does have a way to turn suspicion into knowledge, though."

Asaege nodded numbly. "The Great Library does not have a lack of the first two when it comes to procuring the last."

The woman's eyes filled with an intensity that Asaege rarely saw in them. "He said that something was stolen." Tawn lowered her voice to a whisper, "He said that men were killed."

The younger woman felt as if a great weight had settled upon her shoulders. She opened her mouth to deny her friend's accusations; but found that she couldn't give voice to the lie. Asaege simply shook her head quickly and averted her gaze.

Tawn reached up and cradled the woman's face. "My dear, if what he said is true, I am sure the Binders will not stop at merely asking a few questions."

Asaege found her voice, "That they will not." She looked up to see the sadness that colored Tawn's features. "I will go if that is what you would like."

The woman shook her head slowly, considering it for longer than Asaege would have liked before pulling her into an embrace. "Nonsense, dearest. I am sure whatever happened, you had your reasons. Lange and I know you for the woman you are. No fancy Binder's questions are going to change that."

Chapter Eight
Walker Among Shadows

By the time the rosy tint of daybreak had begun to drive the inky dimness from the city's alleys, Hollis had emerged from the tunnel that connected an unassuming book bindery to a similarly nondescript wine shop on the outskirts of the Oak District. It'd taken him almost an hour to shake his determined pursuers within the Dock Quarter before he could enter a fish monger's with neither a sign nor a name to place upon it. In reality, the anemic income that the small shop earned was a minuscule portion of its immense worth.

Its true value lain in its location against the wall that separated Dock Quarter from Merchant Quarter and the Grand Market that was located within it. A cleverly disguised tunnel ran from beneath the unremarkable building into an equally easily overlooked one on the opposite side of the wall that ostensibly held the stall of a notably dim barrister named Duvale. Again, the stall's lack of regular traffic was preferred as both it and the fish mongers served primarily as a method of egress between districts without the need of traveling through the gates that separated them.

Dominating the northern and eastern portions of the Merchant's Quarter, the Craftsman's District contained the homes and shops of a wide variety of craftsmen and tradesmen that did business within the city itself. The remainder of the Merchant's Quarter was taken up by the Grand Market. If the Craftsman's District was the lifeblood of Oizan's economy, the Grand Market was its heart. If one was to be in need of their heart's desire, chances were it could be found within the frenetic depths of the sprawling bazaar that sat at the center of the great city.

A smile came to Hollis's lips as his thoughts turned to simpler, some would say better, times. The majority of his ill spent childhood was spent within the pressing crowds of the 'Market. The sheer amount of humanity made cutting a purse or pocketing a trinket while passing a stall so simple as to almost be thoughtless. In addition, the proximity of a passerby's fingers to their coin made them easy marks for beggars with ailments both real and expertly feigned.

This night, however, he'd rushed through the virtually empty area. Once the sun fled the sky, so too did customers and merchants alike. Few walked among the empty stalls this late, so the city guard rarely included the Grand Market in their nightly patrols. Hollis decided not to rely upon his luck this particular night, as it seemed to be wearing thinner as the evening progressed. Exiting the Grand Market's northeastern edge, he'd hurried north into the area known as the Knot. The Knot was a tightly packed concentration of homes, shops, and warehouses of the less affluent tradesmen in the Merchant's Quarter.

Hollis had known these uneven cobblestone streets as he knew his own childhood memories. In the center of the huddled buildings lay the entrance to the headquarters of what some would say was the most powerful of the guilds in Oizan: the Thieves Guild. While not wielding the obvious, public power of the masons or goldsmiths, the thieves exerted the scalpels of blackmail, extortion and bribery to remain in nearly every conversation that occurred within the halls of power.

Under normal circumstances, the subterranean halls of the guild house would have been the thief's destination, as his membership in good standing earned him a measure of protection from a common run in with the law. His compound issues with the Binders and the Hand of Light himself, however, posed a special circumstance that he surmised would put him beyond the guild's ability to safeguard him. Furthermore, Hollis feared that even if it were within the council of masters' capability, the good will purchased with his head may prove too sweet a prize to pass upon.

As such, the thief had given the guild hall a wide berth as he continued north towards the wall that separated the Merchant's quarter from the Oak District in the Common Quarter. Despite having lost the physical pursuit of the men that chased him, Hollis still felt as if a noose closed around his throat. His avoidance of the River Gate between the Dock and Merchant Quarters certainly bought him some amount of time as the forces of the law continued searching the southern quarter of the city;

however, his passage wouldn't have gone unnoticed.

If his luck held for a little longer, the guild would remain unaware of his movement until word of the search reached their ears. Once his 'brothers' were made aware of his crimes and the advantage that could be squeezed from them, the logbooks of each pass through would be reviewed and his path quickly ascertained. There truly was little honor among those who traded in the shadows.

It had taken all his resolve to remain calm and jovial as he made his mark in the log kept in the basement of the wine shop. To his Well gifted perceptions, his presence prompted no more than a passing interest in either of the apprentices that manned the tunnel. No doubt it had been a long and uneventful evening that was soon to come to an end. Hollis had flirted with the idea of offering to return the logbook to the guild house for them, thus freeing them to return to their homes or austere cells provided by the guild within the underground complex should they lack the former. The risk of awakening suspicion, however, wasn't worth the trouble.

If the only logbook that had come up missing was for this pass through, it would indicate his course as sure as drawing a map. When he had finished the horizontal flourish of the H that graced the space besides his name, he favored the younger of the two with a wink and bid them both a good day.

*****

The thief took the most direct route he could through the Oak District, his game of cat and mouse becoming a foot race instead. Already the logbook was on its way to the guild house and no doubt into the waiting hands of the registrar. This man, charged with the maintenance and dissemination of each meticulously kept record of the guild and its members, on a normal night would give each a cursory review and file it among its brethren. This wouldn't be a normal night. Hollis had no doubt that the guild's massive network of informants would have brought word of his pursuit and the events that precipitated it to the ears of those who would very eagerly desire details of his movements. Although there was only a hand full of pass throughs within the city, it would take time to locate the ones that the thief had used. It was this time that Hollis raced against.

When he reached Birch Street, he slowed his pace and tried to match it to that of those around him. He'd learned early in his career that often times walking was a surer method of escape than running. What one sacrificed in speed was more than repaid in camouflage. One man running was easy to follow; one man walking among a crowd is less so. This knowledge didn't quiet the itch between his shoulder blades, however, as he strolled across the street far from the sheltering cover of the recently vacated alley. Hollis was surprised by the amount of relief that flowed through his body when he passed out of the morning sun into the claustrophobic depths of the slums.

No map of the city labeled the area as such; it had been given the more optimistic title of Ash District. It was meant to fit with the other neighborhoods of the Common Quarter: Maple, Oak and Elm; but as it became the bin into which was deposited the population that even the Common Quarter didn't wish to think about, much less see, its name became more appropriate. It was certainly the slum that many characterized it, but it was normally known simply as the Ash.

Cast away like their namesake, those who called the Ash home were often so far down on their luck as to have never had any at all. Most worked as day laborers or servants to their fellow citizens, although there were quite a few shops and craftsmen who lived there as well, hoping to someday do well enough to leave it behind forever. Unfortunately, almost all who dwelled within the Ash lived and died on its filth lined alleys. Any wage earned outside the Common Quarter was almost offset by the cost of passing through the Forest Gate, the only point of egress into the city proper.

In the wine softened moments between anger and sleep, Hollis's father had eluded to better times for himself and his wife; although the thief had never known any world outside of the Ash before the argument that drove him to the streets. That fight and his subsequent flight from the one room hovel that he and his father had shared represented the first faltering steps into Hollis's new life. Found and raised by the guild, cut throats and scoundrels were more a father to him than his biological one had ever been.

For years, Hollis had refused to step foot into the Ash for fear that the knife that had ended that final argument with his father hadn't ended the man himself. Over the years, as he grew in both size and skill, the thief found the district an ally as dependable as his brethren within the guild … sometimes more so. The Ash was a fickle and deadly place, offering betrayal and blood more often than hope and joy; but one could depend on the nature of the place and its people as surely as the sun rising in the morning. It was that dependability that he sought now.

His first stop was a squat, two story building flanked by three story tenements. Although it was one of the more affluent businesses in the Ash, it needed no indication to differentiate it from its neighbors. It was both shop and home to Bearon the Broker. If one was in need of quick coin in exchange for an object of dubious providence or quick access to something of questionable use, Bearon was the man to see. Despite fulfilling an essential role within the district, his access to large amounts (at least to Ash standards) of coin and the unwillingness of the guard to involve themselves in anything within the borders of the Ash, Bearon was the target, from time to time, of theft or outright robbery.

Years before, Hollis had struck a deal with the fence; the thief would look out for his interests as well as allow it to be known that he had a vested interest in keeping Bearon in business and unmolested. In exchange, the fence kept safe for Hollis a cache of weapons, documents and coin. It was one of many the thief had secreted around the city; but one of only two within the confines of the Ash, so it was suddenly much more important.

Although he still carried a fortune by Ash standards, it only amounted to seven silver nobles and a few copper commons. The majority of the money the thief had brought with him into the common room of the Virgin Mermaid paid for the diversion that allowed him to slip the grasp of the guard the previous evening. Everything else he owned hopefully still remained locked in his room above the same inn. If he was to make sense of what occurred in the library after he and the strange woman had left, a handful of silver wasn't going to carry him very far.

Chapter Nine
Shadow of Suspicion

When the thief emerged from the small attic of Bearon's shop, he felt a small measure of his worries had lifted from his shoulders. His concerns still remained but a few hours of sleep and a change of clothes combined with the comforting weight of coin pressed against his hip buoyed his spirits a bit.

The sound of multiple voices in the shop below told Hollis that his host had customers. The tone of the fence's voice reached his ears before the actual words became clear. Notes of tension floated beneath the dulcet tones of feigned casual conversation. Hollis paused at the top of the stairs and crouched just out of sight of the main shop.

" … are partners; but sadly I have not seen him in weeks. With his newly discovered wealth, he apparently has found more desirable places to spend his time."

"Is that so?" The second voice was a rumbling baritone, its timbre indicating that its owner was accustomed to deference. A tense silence hung in the air as Bearon's guest waited for the fence to supply more information and potentially allow him to provide enough metaphorical rope to hang himself … and Hollis with him.

Bearon was far too familiar with the machinations of those who sought to interrupt his business to fall into that particular trap. He remained silent and no doubt continued to blankly stare at the man. Hollis had been on the receiving end of that particular gaze more times that he could count … or cared to.

The voice continued, "What if I told you that I had it on good authority that your partner passed into the Common Quarter just this morning?"

Bearon's answer was as smooth and fluid as lamp oil. "I would say that you are more well informed than I am. I would honestly expect no less of one under the employ of the Great Library. Information is the currency they trade in, is it not?"

"It is. And if I have it on the same authority that he was seen passing into the Ash?"

The fence allowed a beat and a half to pass before answering, allowing him to no doubt feign surprise. "I would say that authority may not be as good as you believe. No one comes here unless their options are severely limited." Another pause. "You never did say why the Binders search for the minority partner in a humble mercantile shop far off the beaten path."

"Not so humble, as we both are well aware; but you are correct, I did not." Again, a question hung in the air unasked and unanswered. "Suffice it to say that I believe his options may be becoming more limited by the day."

"Is that so?" Bearon repeated the Binder's words of a moment previous and let the silence linger as he had done. The gambit was no more effective when reversed. Hollis began to feel some small measure of respect for this man; with it came a small measure of dread. "Why would he come here, the one place within the Ash that someone such as yourself would be sure to search for him? That would be foolish, do you not think?"

"I would certainly agree with that. Tell me, Bearon, have you ever lost something? I do not refer to something of great value but instead something common … something that you use every day?"

"I would say everyone has at one time or another."

"I know, speaking for myself, that drives me insane. I mean big things … special things, they are in some ways easier to find. They tend to be either shiny or distinctive in some way. It is this significance that makes them easier to find. They stand out in some way from their surroundings. It is the familiar things that often prove themselves frustrating to locate. Your eye is accustomed to them, so it tends to pass over them more readily. Very often that which you seek … once you finally locate it, ends up being right under your nose … in plain sight." He paused again, but it was evident that Bearon wasn't going to fall for that particular gambit any more readily than he had previously. Hollis could feel the man's frustration; but none of it filtered into his voice. "You are well aware of both the reach and generosity of the Great Library. Understand that if you realize that after consideration, your partner was actually closer at hand than you had thought, the Binders are as forgiving as they are appreciative."

Despite Hollis's history with the fence, his hand tightened on the bone pommel of his sword. Within the Ash, loyalty was a commodity like any other. A twinge of doubt fluttered in the thief's heart like a restless moth. He and Bearon had been partners for more than a decade; in that time neither had found a reason to sever that relationship. Hollis hoped that the Binder below hadn't brought with him an excuse for the fence to do just that.

When the man replied, his tone put the thief's doubts to rest. "I understand more than most give me credit for, milord," the word oozed from his lips like day old pudding, left to go rancid upon the table. "I say again, I have not seen Hollis in almost a month's time." Another silence reigned in the shop below but this one held an edge sharp enough to slice.

The Binder broke first. "I will take my leave then. Please remember my words: the Binders forgiveness has its limits, and it is far more limited than their memory."

"I shall endeavor to do so."

"See that you do." The Binder's hard soled boots clicked their way to the shop's front door. It closed with a solid thump. The interior of the shop was like a tomb until Bearon's voice broke the stillness.

"He is gone, my friend. You may cease your skulking. We have some things to discuss."

*****

Hollis half leaned, half sat on the corner of Bearon's desk in the back room of the fence's shop. "He was alive when I left him. Angry and frozen like a mouse in a snowdrift but definitely alive."

The fence leaned back in his chair, his fingers steepled before him as he listened to Hollis recap the events of the prior evening. Once the thief fell into silence, Bearon laid his palms on the desk and leaned forward. "What about the book that brought you to the library in the first place?"

"I never found it. As I said, things became complicated."

"The girl?"

Hollis shrugged. "We went our separate ways." He left the leather-bound volume she'd stolen out of his recap of the previous night's activities.

"The Binders would not have come this far from their beloved library did it not involve one of their precious books." The fence studied

Hollis across his desk. "Are you sure you did not miss anything? No one would blame you; it was a heightened situation."

He could feel Bearon's gaze and allowed a small smile to come to his lips. "Is that not what the Binder said?"

Bearon simply shrugged.

The Hollis of a year ago would have confided in his partner, he owed the woman nothing. Situations like this were where Stephen's influence starkly stood out in the thief's personality. Bearon had the opportunity to betray him and hadn't; that fact gave Hollis confidence. He didn't feel that the fence would show the same loyalty to her. The thief wouldn't expose her to the Binders' justice in the name of his own comfort. Besides, the book held some importance. The curate came specifically looking for it and there was a good chance that it was what had gotten the man killed. Hollis wouldn't mourn him but he felt he had to do what he could to prevent the mysterious woman from sharing his fate.

"We escaped with our lives and nothing else." The lie came easily to his lips.

"Mm hmm." Bearon obviously didn't believe him but seemed to let the matter drop. "As much as I enjoy your company, Hollis, you cannot stay here for long. The Binder may not have pieced together how much I know, but he has figured out that I know something."

The thief nodded. "I understand."

"It is not safe."

Hollis noted that the fence didn't expand on for whom it was dangerous. He didn't press the man. He simply repeated, "I understand."

Bearon reached under his desk and laid a small, iron bound strongbox on its surface, "Do you need a few nobles to carry you over the rough patches?"

Hollis shook his head. He could have used the money, but he needed something far more valuable. In his mind's eye, he could see his fleeting partner in crime.

Although her linen blouse and breeches were free of stains, they had held a subtle scent of stagnant air and gathered humanity. It had been the smell of places too infrequently visited by fresh air. Although Oizan was heavily populated, it was fairly open as far as cities were concerned. There was one place in the city where that scent hung like a wet sheet: right here in the Ash. For it to permeate into one's clothes, someone would need to dwell there for an extended period.

The thief brought to mind everything he could remember about the woman. An Ash-rat so far afield as the Great Library was an oddity, but what drew his attention and curiosity in equal measure were her fingers. Between her first and second finger, he could see oval calluses, stained

50

bluish-black. Those weren't the calluses of a laborer or even a craftsman; you only earned them by writing, hour after hour and day after day. She had the hands of a scholar. More and more, the woman continued to intrigue the thief.

"I have been away from the Ash for a while but I heard that August the Scribe succumbed to the clear pox this past spring. Has anyone taken his place?"

The fence frowned. "Do you need a letter written? A contract read?"

It was Hollis's turn to shrug noncommittally.

Bearon studied him again before slowly responding, "Trelis the tinker rents space to a woman named Asaege."

The thief waited patiently for him to continue.

"She lives above the Lange the Weaver's shop."

Hollis nodded once and turned on his heel. Over his shoulder he grumbled, "Thank you for your hospitality … and your discretion, Bearon. Friends are hard to find."

The fence called to him, "We are not friends, Hollis. But we are partners. There is no profit in interfering in your business."

Turning in the door jam, the thief regarded Bearon. "As long as it stays that way." He could feel the ice in his eyes as their gazes met. Bearon looked away first. By the time he looked to the door again, Hollis was gone.

Chapter Ten
Lightened Heart

When Asaege stepped into the street, she felt as if a dozen sets of eyes were suddenly upon her. She forced herself to realize it was entirely in her imagination, as was the impression that the conversations around her became hushed as she emerged. The woman closed her eyes and shook her head in an effort to sweep the cobwebs of doubt from her mind.

When she opened them again, her perception of the street had returned to a rosier one. Asaege felt her spirits buoy a bit as she took a deep lung full of crisp autumn air. This simple act, performed countless times before, brought with it a feeling of wonder that surprised the woman.

As she walked through the district that had become her home, she saw it for the community that it truly was, beneath the grime that clouded the perceptions of many outside the Ash. Beneath thread-worn awnings people gathered to greet the day and catch up with their neighbors. Many of them had a warm smile or a friendly wave for those that passed. Outsiders often received a cold, almost hostile reception as most were all too familiar with the prejudice that those living in the Common Quarter in general, and the Ash in particular, drew when they passed beyond the Forest Gate. The issue didn't arise often; few chose to enter the Ash of their own free will.

One commonly held belief of the Ash by those outside of it hap-

pened to be true. During the day, the community found there was no different than anyone would find in the towns that dotted the Kings Road, in affability if not affluence. Once the sun went down, however, most of the Ash's hardworking population shuttered themselves in their humble homes. The district's streets then belonged to those whose business could only be done in the dark: the feckless, the lawless and the desperate.

People, once fallen on hard times, become willing to do anything to survive. Often, when someone is born into the Ash, that fall is short indeed. With such a concentration of poverty, most residents are forced to look outside the Common Quarter for whatever low paying work they can find. What small amount of silver that those jobs bring is further degraded by the tolls charged to even pass through the Forest Gate and into the city proper. While most outsiders attributed the nocturnal activities in the Ash to a perceived barbarism of those who dwelt in poverty, it was in truth a self-fulfilling prophecy. The combination of poverty and lack of proper policing leads to a bastion for those who operate outside the law. The Common Quarter had just one import: criminals.

She made her way down the narrow street, surprisingly crowded for the late morning hour. As she did, her eyes searched the crowd for anything out of place. Her gaze only found her fellow residents hurrying about their business. The sense of tranquility clung to her mind like fresh honey; however, through its muslin cloak, flashes of unease filtered through as the events of the previous evening settled themselves within her. Asaege wondered for what must have been the tenth time why she felt the need to venture out into the streets, knowing full well that the Binders searched the Ash for her. She'd come to rely on the loyalty and honor of the people that shared her fate in Oizan's forgotten district.

Even as the thought formed in her mind, she eliminated it out of hand. Her new circumstances were out of the ordinary. While many resented and hated those who didn't need to dwell within the twisted streets of the Ash, there were always a few of that weren't above using her safety as a means to break free themselves. It would only take one. The thought was a chilling one, causing her to look around suspiciously once more. The main street was intersected at frequent but irregular intervals by alleys that at times made the Ash seem more of a rats' nest than a proper district of Oizan.

From her perspective, each of these alleys seemed to dissolve into shadow only a handful of feet from the bright sunshine that beat down upon the street itself. Her mind created silhouettes within those shadows, just out of her sight, assailants who lurked there, waiting to lunge forth and pull her into the depths of the alley. She shuddered once more and pulled her wool cloak tighter about her shoulders. Her destination lay only a few blocks from the candle shop but it stretched into a journey of almost endless distance as her mind continued to play tricks upon her.

By the time she reached the place where Trelis the tinker had set up her shop, Asaege realized she was walking with such speed that it bordered on a run. The shop was no more than an alcove between two claptrap buildings covered by a threadbare canopy, but it served its proprietor well enough. Trelis was a sturdy woman, seemingly all angles and sharp edges from her razor like cheek bones to her long, knife-like fingers. She'd practiced her trade in the Ash for as long as most of its residents could remember; she was as much of a part of the district as any building of wood or daub.

Trelis's perpetually firm set mouth blossomed into a rare smile when she saw Asaege. "Good morning to you. This late in the day, I feared you had forgotten our arrangement."

"Late? It is no more than a few hours past dawn, Trel."

"Indeed it is." The tinker nodded as if Asaege's words proved her point.

Chuckling as she shook her head. "Judging by the rush of customers, I do not believe that I have kept anyone waiting."

"… except myself."

"Except you." Asaege pulled her satchel from her shoulder and set it down beside the grim tinker. "Did you have business for me?"

"No."

"Then why …" Asaege let her question fade into the morning air as she realized the futility of arguing with the woman. Instead she abruptly changed the subject, "How has business been this morning?"

"Slow. Old Hehn came by with a broken awl, but other than that, no one has brought any business."

Asaege let out a soft breath, once again feeling foolish for her paranoia. She reached into her satchel and pulled free a worn blanket, laying it upon the earthen floor of the tinker's shop. Once seated on the blanket, the woman retrieved a wooden case from the bag and carefully opened it. Inside were the tools of her trade: a small ink pot, a brass tipped pen and a small knife. The set could feed her for a week should she choose to sell it, but if she took that step, Asaege felt she would forever give up who she had been. She wasn't sure she was ready to do that.

Looking at the silk lined box brought back memories of her time spent in the University District. It had always seemed sunny there, the golden light streaming in through floor to ceiling windows, opened to allow the smell of lavender carried on the breeze from the Garden District. Despite the years that separated Asaege from that time, she could almost hear the voices of students like the sound of a babbling brook over smooth river stone. She felt the pain of loss squeeze her heart like a greedy claw; of all of the wonders of her time in the library, the most intoxicating was the joy of teaching the children. Their unending questions frustrated some, but to Asaege, they were as the singing of nightingales. Too quickly, curiosity became apathy, and the weight of everyday life replaced the desire to learn for its own sake. Through the children, she was able to hold on to the warmth of spring even as her own season approached autumn.

The sound of a clearing throat broke her out of her reverie. Looking up, Asaege saw a woman burdened by years that hadn't yet passed waiting patiently. She smiled up at the woman, "Good Morning, Ruth."

Ruth's face split into a gap-toothed smile, "Good Morning, Asaege. My son sent another letter from the Blades." The woman extended the creased parchment toward her. "I worry so about him. The Points are such savages, and he is such a kind hearted boy."

Recoiling slightly at the derogatory term for the elves that inhabited the continent known as the Blades, Asaege reached up and took the letter from Ruth and patted the blanket beside her. "Well, Ruth, let us see what news young Rhoth has for us this morning."

*****

Asaege had been forced to return to the candle shop via a longer, less direct route. Just as she prepared to step from Trelis's alcove, Asaege had spotted the tell-tale white cloak and bulky armor of a Binder as the man spoke to a pair of day laborers under the cool sun of the autumn afternoon. Ducking back inside, she forced herself between two boards that formed the back of the stall and walked with all possible speed in the opposite direction.

By the time Asaege stepped into her small room, candle in hand, the sun was disappearing behind the Ash's ragged crone's smile of a skyline. By the flickering light, she was able to locate the rust spotted lantern that served as her primary nighttime light source. Lifting the hood, she touched the candle's flame to the lantern's wick, and it blossomed to life. As its light pushed back the shadows of the room, Asaege's heart leapt into her throat. She wasn't alone.

Hollis sat on her small bed, his arm draped casually over his doubled up left knee. In his right hand, he held the Dialogues. A sly smile was painted on his lips. "Well, Magpie, it certainly took you long enough to come home to roost."

Her hand still clutched to her chest, Asaege stepped toward him as the anger rose within her. "What have you done with the—"

The thief frowned. "The weaver and his wife? I have done nothing to them. As a matter of fact, you no doubt will cause them more conster-

57

nation with your raised voice than I have in the time I have spent here." His smile broadened into a grin that bordered on arrogance. "I am very good at what I do, Asaege."

She stared at him for a moment before speaking again, "What do you want?" Her eyes snapped to the book he held.

Hollis lifted it for a moment. "This? I have no need of it —"

She quickly interrupted him, "Then give it back."

Nonplussed, he continued, "What I do need, however, is an understanding of the importance others place in it … why you would risk the wrath of the Binders and City Guard for it … why it was worth the Curate's life."

Shock struck Asaege like a hammer to her chest. "The Curate is —"

"Dead," Hollis finished for her. "For some reason, everyone seems to believe that we … or more accurately, I am responsible."

"You killed plenty of men last night."

The thief agreed, "That I did; but each of them sought to do the same to me."

"As did the Curate."

"Yes, but there is a difference between a soldier and the Hand of Light's second in command."

Rage rose in Asaege. "Are you saying that one man's life is worth more than another's purely because of his position?"

Hollis held up his hands, "It is not my opinion; it is simply true."

She frowned deeply and made a noise, half growl and half grunt, deep in her chest.

"I never said I liked it. As someone whose life is on the lower end of any exchange in that regard, sometimes you just have to work with 'the way things are'."

"Sometimes 'the way things are' is unfair."

"Fairness has nothing to do with it."

"It should."

Hollis nodded slowly. "That is certainly not in dispute."

Silence fell between the two, but Asaege could feel the thief's gaze upon her, as if he were looking through her. In order to break the tension, she asked, "May I have my book?"

He extended it to her. "Absolutely." When she reached for it, he pulled it back just out of range. "Humor me, though. The Curate's death falls squarely on my shoulders … a death quite possibly caused by the loss of this very tome. I deserve to know what makes the book worth it, at least." With a flick of his wrist, he tossed the Dialogues to her. "Do you not agree?"

Guilt settled on Asaege's shoulders like a heavy snow, cold and heavy. "I suppose you do."

Chapter Eleven
Shadows Converge

Hollis leaned back against the wall, watching the woman before him. The Well had gifted him with powers of observation that he was still coming to grips with, but he needed none of them to tell that she'd been truly surprised by the news of the Curate's death. Her wide eyes and sharply indrawn breath told that tale all by themselves.

He could tell the ramifications of their previous night's activities were still settling upon her by the way she fidgeted nervously with the mismatched buttons on the front of her linen blouse as she gathered her thoughts. When she began, Asaege's words trembled for a moment before she found her voice.

"It is known as the Dialogues of the Chalice, one of the pillars of the modern Olmite church." The thief nodded, letting Asaege find her way through the explanation. "It documents a series of conversations between a previous Hand of Light and Olm himself. As such, it is the only record of what passed between God and Man. "

"I could see where that would make it important in a dogmatic way. If it was so important, then why is it not housed in the Ivory Cathedral?"

"That is an excellent question. When I found it years ago, I had assumed it was misfiled. Each time I checked, the book had not moved. When the library and I parted ways, it was where I found it last night. For a few years, the Hand of Light has been using excerpts from the Dialogues more and more in his sermons. At first they were innocuous, tying the good harvest to a prophesied time of plenty or noting that the fall of the Walker was foretold within another passage."

Hollis chuckled softly at the last, remembering the hand he played in Walker's downfall.

"Recently, however, he has begun hinting that the Dialogues have more to tell us … more immediate and impactful things. Within the final pages of the book, it is said that Olm spoke about a person that would purify his church, root out those who shadowed the people of Taerh from his merciful light. I have read these very passages many times and from a certain viewpoint you can interpret them as such."

"But if the book remained lost in the library, how could the Hand quote from it, much less make such grand predictions?"

"I wondered that myself, which is why I returned last night to see if the Dialogues had been discovered. My fear is that the Hand seeks to paint himself as this destined figure."

"It would not be the first time something like that has happened."

Asaege nodded slowly. "The crusade on the Blades is not as popular as it once was and there is a more and more vocal minority who claims that making war against the elves is not the Lord of Justice's true will. I have witnessed, as you have as well, the venom some people hold towards the elves. This venom was injected into them by the church itself. It certainly does not aid the church's reputation that more and more tales of its abuses on the Blades as well as the streets of our very city are coming to light."

Hollis began following her train of thought. "But if the Hand was a figure of destiny, ordained not only by the church but by the very words of Olm himself —"

Asaege interrupted, "All thought of resistance would disappear."

"Or be crushed suddenly and brutally by those who sought to fulfill the word of their god."

She seized her bottom lip between her teeth before continuing, "I could not in good conscience allow my discovery to be so warped."

"So, when you found it, you sought to remove it from his reach."

"Correct. Take the arrow from his quiver, so to speak." Asaege squared her shoulders in an expression of pride.

"But the Curate must have known it was there as well." The thief frowned deeply as he allowed the repercussions to settle upon his mind. "If he allowed it to remain there, he assuredly believed it was best that it remained lost."

"But why keep it from the Hand?"

"That is precisely what I am struggling with. The Curate serves the Hand in all things. It is his only purpose." Just as in the 'Mermaid's common room, Well-given understanding filtered into his thoughts. With it came a now familiar sense of calm. Hollis began to see connections that had eluded him until that point. He remembered a decades old meeting with the Hand. Silvermoon and he had gone before Olm's chosen to beg for his aid with their comrade, Haedren. On that day, the Hand had seemed small and frail. When Haedren challenged him, the man had reacted with trepidation rather than the strength of his position. "Unless the Hand's sermons come not from the Lord of the Dawn, but instead from the minds of men."

"Even so, why would the Curate keep the work the Hand has been quoting from him?"

"Insurance." Hollis realized he'd used the English word as there was no translation for it in Trade Tongue.

As he searched for an equivalent concept, he saw Asaege nod in understanding. "The power behind the throne must continue to provide value or they become replaceable."

Taken aback, the thief stumbled for a split second. He was sure he'd used the English word but Asaege hadn't missed a beat. "Exact … exactly. By feeding him the book in edible chunks, the Curate maintained his place and did not suffer any unfortunate accidents."

"Except that he did."

"Except that he did," Hollis agreed as he absently rubbed at his goatee. He watched the woman before him with new interest. Her lips were drawn tight with concentration, but her shoulders held a tentative tension that seemed to go beyond the danger they both faced. "Could we be looking at a mafia-style internal struggle?" He purposely used the English word 'mafia' and watched her reaction.

Without hesitation, she replied, "That would indicate a much larger problem. Two are a plot, any more is a conspiracy." Even as she spoke, Asaege's eyes floated side to side as if she were suffering from vertigo.

When she stumbled, Hollis's hand reached out to seize her forearm and stabilize her. Firmly but gently, he guided her to sit on the bed beside him. She opened her mouth to make some apology, but he dismissed it with a shake of his head. "Whether the Hand was looking to remove the middleman or someone else is looking to move up, for the moment, is not important. This has landed squarely on our shoulders. In addition, you … we have something for which they clearly are willing to kill."

The trembling began in her fingers, but Asaege clenched her fists to hide it. "How can you be so calm?"

Hollis shook his head and chuckled, "First, it may surprise you, but this is not the first time that someone has wanted me dead. Second, what makes you think that I am calm?" Releasing her arm, he stood and began pacing the room. "Inside, I am positively in a panic, but it never pays to let that particular demon behind the wheel." This time, he used the Trade Tongue word wheel but the English turn of phrase.

Asaege paled slightly and wavered on the bed. Two steps brought Hollis to her side, taking hold of her shoulder. Each time he referenced something from Stephen's world, the woman reacted as if her feet were being swept out from under her. He could recall the first few times he experienced the confusion that reflection carried with it, but he didn't remember anything this extreme. He also never fought the act very hard; Hollis and Stephen had recognized their kinship almost from the beginning. There was little doubt in his mind that before him sat another 'traveler', for lack of a better word.

The thief squeezed her shoulder softly and stepped back, "We have to focus on one thing at a time." He nodded in the direction of the book that lay on the thin blanket. "We have the book. That may put us in danger, but it also gives us currency."

Asaege's disorientation seemed to pass quickly. "What will it buy us? I have less intent to give it to them now than I did last night."

"Are you firm on that?"

"As a mountain."

Hollis shrugged. "It was worth a try." He turned to pace the room again. Over his shoulder he said, "If the book itself will not purchase us anything, perhaps what is contained within will."

As he turned back, Asaege was on her feet as well. "The Hand uses the words of Olm to motivate, but inspiration is not solely the purview of the church."

The thief smiled. "Indeed it is not, although they do have a platform from which to spread it, that gives them a decided advantage."

Her shoulders slumped a bit, "True. No matter how strongly you shout, the Hand's voice will always be louder."

He sighed. "No one in their right mind would set themselves in opposition to the Olmites, they wield too much power."

Asaege laughed nervously. "You mean besides us?"

The thief joined her briefly. "Yes, but we have nothing to lose."

She stopped suddenly, seizing Hollis by the wrist. "We have nothing to lose. That is the key, Hollis."

He raised an eyebrow. "Having nothing to lose? Then the entire Ash is a key."

Asaege squeezed his wrist tightly before releasing it. She ran to the window and threw open the shutters. "Exactly! What do you see out there?"

The thief looked out over her shoulder, grumbling softly, "Poverty and filth in equal measures."

She glared at him out of the corner of her eye for a moment before continuing. "Why does religion have power?"

"Beyond the coin that fills their coffers? Beyond the powerful friends that their favors buy?"

"Where does that coin come from? What do the Olmites trade for those favors?"

Hollis shook his head slowly. "I feel like you are trying to get somewhere."

She rapped him on the chest with the back of her hand, "Influence … influence with a massive amount of worshipers, most of them so poor that the idea of a better place waiting for them is all they have to hope for."

Realization dawned upon the thief. "What if those same worshipers found out they had been lied to?"

"These people have given all they have, some more than that, to the church and those they support."

Hollis stepped back and regarded her again. "If you think folks have an issue with your possession of the book, it pales in comparison with the fury you will bring down on you for shining light upon their lies. What do you have against the Olm?"

"Olm? Nothing. Those that use his words to take advantage of good, hard-working people? That is another story."

He collapsed onto Asaege's bed and folded his hands behind his head. "Motivations aside, do you have a practical way to get any of this done? Not to mention how to keep it from coming back to roost on our certain graves?"

She shook her head. "I have not gotten there yet."

"You understand that this could have far reaching repercussions?"

A nervous, self-conscious smile came to Asaege's lips. "I am beginning to come to that realization."

"We can still return the book." Smile turned to angry sneer. "Apparently your feelings on that matter remain resolute. I am not sure how long I can keep ahead of Binders and templars, not to mention the City Guard and my own guild. At least your name has not been associated with the theft as of yet."

Asaege studied the floor, biting her lower lip again.

"Am I wrong?"

"A Binder was here this morning. Tawn sent him away."

"That will not last for long. I have a feeling the same Binder paid a business associate of mine a similar visit. Can you trust the weaver's wife?"

She nodded quickly. "Of course. Can you trust your associate?"

A graveyard chuckle rolled from the thief's chest. "Of course not. It is the Ash. I can depend on the fact that, up to this point, I am worth more to him as an ally than not. That is likely to change if the search goes on for too long."

*****

Hollis slipped into the back of Bearon's shop as quietly as he could manage. The bell meant to warn the fence of intruders dangled impotently wrapped in a small piece of cloth the thief kept with him for just such a purpose. As he closed the door gently behind him, his ears picked up the soft tones of voices. Hollis drew a thick bladed dagger and crept forward towards the curtain that separated front room from back. He sank into a crouch as the voices became clear.

"— loyalty is an admirable quality, Bearon," the voice was soft but had an edge to it that was sharp enough to cut flesh. "The boy is your partner; you may even be under the mistaken belief that he is your friend. I have known him since before he sprouted his first man beard. I assure you that he has no friends. He is a killer, born and bred." The voice remained low and friendly, but that only added to the threat held within it.

"But I have already told you —" It was Bearon's voice. Despite how much he fought to keep his tone even, the thief could hear the trembling in it.

"Do you want to guess how I know he is a killer?" The voice paused, clearly waiting for an answer. When none was provided, it continued, "Because I made him everything he is. He is a killer because I taught him to be one."

"But —"

Suddenly, the voice rose in volume, "Do not!" As quickly as it rose, the tone softened again. "Do not lie to my face. Believe me, I appreciate your position. Please understand mine." Hollis heard the sound of steel on leather as the voice's owner drew a blade. He could picture it clearly in his mind; it was a thin, Slazean stiletto, designed to slip between rib or armor in order to find the softer vitals beneath.

Hollis drew the curtain back and stepped through the doorway. "You came in search of me, Seran, here I am. The fence has no part in this."

The man standing between Hollis and Bearon was as short and slender as the deadly weapon clutched in his left hand. His thick hair had been dyed a deep crimson and was pulled back into a hasty pile at the back of his head. With the grace of water over stone, the figure stepped back to regard the thief without losing sight of Bearon. The hue of his hair making his olive Slazean complexion and pale blue eyes all the more

66

obvious, Hollis could hardly mistake his mentor for anyone else. The slight widening of his eyes was the only indication of Seran's surprise before his face split into a smile, "Perhaps you are correct, my boy." He gestured toward Bearon with the tip of his dagger and then the door. "Find your way out, fence. We will be sure to lock up when we are done."

Nodding quickly, Bearon turned and fled through the front door, letting it slam behind him.

Seran turned back to the thief. "You certainly did not make it easy to follow you, boy."

"I have not been a boy for a long time, old man." Hollis concentrated on keeping his breathing slow and steady, in through his nose and out through barely parted lips. Despite his natural inclination to clutch the dagger tightly in his fist, he forced himself to hold it firmly but with a light touch.

His mentor nodded lightly. "So you have not. Then tell me: why I am still picking up after you?"

"I did not kill Rethmus."

Seran snorted once. "I do not care." He turned his back on Hollis, casually examining the various goods scattered on the counter. "What I do care about is that you did not clean up after yourself. It was very sloppy to leave witnesses." He picked up a pair of roughly cut emeralds and turned to face the thief, "No witness, …" He paused, looking to his student expectantly.

"— no crime", Hollis finished. "Olm knows that you repeated it often enough that it is etched upon my brain."

"And yet both seem to remain." He began to roll the gems around each other in the palm of his hand.

Despite himself, Hollis felt like he was ten again under the withering glare of his teacher. "There were other concerns."

Seran shook his head, "None more pressing than escaping clean."

The thief repeated, this time more adamantly, "There were other concerns. I have it under control."

His mentor raised a pierced eyebrow. "Is it? The guild hunts you as surely as do the Binders and City Guard … not to mention every damned Olmite who values their soul. If that is under control, perhaps it is time for you to teach me a few things."

Hollis frowned. "The entire guild?"

Seran's smile reminded one of a well-fed cat in the best of times, so despite the fact that he wore one as he responded, the thief was cautious. "We have history … you are my blood as sure as if I had fathered you myself."

A nervous smile came to Hollis's lips. "I did not hear you say no."

"No. Of course not." His voice dropped low and dangerous, "Were I to have wanted you dead or captured, you would be so."

Although his mentor's face maintained an air of casualness, Hollis noticed that his jaw remained tight despite his smile. Combined with the slight drawing of his eyebrows, the thief suspected that Seran was hiding something and whatever it was, at least on some level, saddened the man. The gifts bestowed on him by the Well continued to fascinate the thief even as what they revealed made him uneasy.

Hollis rolled his eyes and drawled, "That will no doubt bring me a great deal of comfort in the nights to come."

Seran laughed softly as he slipped the emeralds into the pouch at his waist. "Are we going to discuss the woman?"

The thief swallowed suddenly, looking at his feet to hide his surprise. "She was in the wrong place at the wrong time," he replied more quickly than he would have liked.

"I could say the same thing about you. Why were you there in the first place?"

"I was looking for a book."

"In a library? That much is obvious. Please tell me you are not still chasing after ghosts and legends."

Hollis avoided the question. "The Well is more than ghosts and legends. Nonetheless, the book belongs to me … bought and paid for."

Seran shook his head sadly. "You have been in our rarefied profession long enough to understand that ownership is relative."

Hollis opened his mouth to respond as the front door was kicked in.

*****

As the door slammed open, the two men turned as one. The first through the door was Noth, an Uteli expatriate that had served his apprenticeship under Hollis. With a flick of his wrist, the thief sent his dwarven steel dagger spinning through the air. Noth threw himself to the ground but wasn't quick enough to completely avoid the thrown weapon. Instead of sinking into his chest, as the thief had intended, the razor sharp blade drew a deep furrow along his bare bicep. Before his dagger clattered to the floor, Hollis drew his Wallin Fahr.

Out of the corner of his eye, the thief saw Seran move forward in a low, stalking motion as he pulled the calf length cape from his shoulders. Holding it by the thick, raised collar, he allowed it to drape over the back of his right hand. Before Noth could find his feet, Seran was upon him. From his semi-prone position, Noth swung his thick, chopping sword at his opponent. The Slazean interposed the cloak between himself and the weapon, stealing most of its momentum in its voluminous depths. With a swift snap of his wrist, Seran tangled the blade within the cloak and

68

pulled it off to the side. Taken off guard, Noth allowed his arm to go with it. Before he could regret his inaction, Seran dropped to one knee and drove his stiletto into his armpit. Once. Twice. Three times. A choking exhalation was the last sound from Noth's lips as steel punctured his lung and he began choking on his own blood.

Hollis moved past Seran and his dying foe to engage the pair rushing through the door. He recognized neither of them but from the grim expressions painted on their faces, they seemed familiar with him. A short side-to-side swing of his Uteli blade slowed their advance, trapping them in the doorway. Foregoing the buckler at his belt, the thief placed his left hand below his right on the hilt of the sword. As long as the pair remained in the doorway, Hollis maintained the upper hand. He could take full advantage of his weapon's length while his opponents seemed to only get in each other's way. The larger of the two gathered himself and surged forward. The thief brought the Wallin Fahr around with a quick rotation of his wrist, opening a long, shallow gash across his linen clad chest. A short return swing drove his foe back into the doorway beside his comrade.

Soft, catlike steps were Hollis's only warning as his mentor came up beside him. Despite their history, the thief's gaze shifted quickly to the side, estimating Seran's intentions. His ice blue eyes were narrowed and focused on the two men in the doorway; a brief rush of relief flashed through Hollis as he turned his attention back to the pair before him. The larger of his opponents' pained grimace turned into a tight sneer. In a low voice, Seran snarled, "Let them in." Conditioned by his years under his mentor's tutelage, Hollis responded without thought and took three short steps back and to his right as Seran mirrored his action.

Baited by their retreat, the pair charged through the door. Obviously holding a grudge, the larger of the two pressed Hollis while his comrade advanced on Seran. The thief heard the smaller man mutter something to the Slazean before he was forced to devote his complete attention to the assailant before him. Wielding the same machete-like sword as his companions, the large man swung the weapon in short chopping motions. Hollis was able to parry them easily but the ferocity of the man's attacks left him little room to turn defense into offense. His opponent's long loping strides kept the thief from back pedaling fast enough to regain the reach advantage of his longer weapon. As his foe's relentless press became more frantic, Hollis swiftly changed tactics.

As his opponent gathered himself for another advance, Hollis lunged forward rather than retreating. Releasing the sword's hilt with his left hand, he grasped the weapon halfway up its blade and brought it around in a short arc. The ivory and steel pommel met jaw with a dull crack. The strike stunned the man for a brief second as he was rocked back on his heels.

That instant was all the thief required. He stepped back, returning his left hand to the hilt of his sword and bringing it down in a diagonal slash, opening his opponent from throat to hip.

As the man sank to his knees, Hollis swung the blade left to right across his throat. The move had been instinctual, as natural to him as putting one foot before the other. Deep in his heart, however, Hollis felt a stab of sorrow. *Had I let the book go ... had I not been in the library that night*, he thought, *This man might be enjoying the earthy taste of cheap ale or the warm touch of someone tender.*

Over his decades of life, he had taken more lives than he could, or even cared to, remember; he recalled the number and faces of all that fell before his blade since the Well. Sixteen. Hollis had a sinking feeling that he would be forced to add to it significantly in the coming nights.

Hollis's eyes flashed to where his mentor circled with the remaining assailant, his cloak swaying to and fro like the tail of an agitated cat. Hollis ate up the distance between himself and the two men with five quick strides. Seran's opponent must have heard him coming because he turned to face the charging thief. The man sneered at him, bringing his sword around to meet Hollis's rush.

A genuine look of shock crossed his features as Seran smoothly stepped up behind him and looped his forearm under his chin and across his throat. Pulling his head to the side, Seran drove his stiletto into his exposed throat twice in rapid succession.

The dying man struggled to speak before collapsing in the Slazean's arms. Seran let his body drop unceremoniously to the wooden plank floor. Hollis couldn't miss the look of betrayal on the man's face as he passed into death.

Chapter Twelve
Tradition's Legacy

The autumn sun warmed Jillian's sleeping face, pulling her slowly from the vivid dream. She could almost smell the smoke clogged air of the Ash in her tiny garden apartment. Compared to the oil painting of a dream, the confines of her bedroom seemed to be rendered in watercolor. Even the crimson display of her alarm clock seemed less vibrant as it declared 7:11am.

Swinging her legs around to dangle from the edge, Jillian stretched and allowed a languid yawn to roll through her. Normally, her dreams slipped from her recollection like smoke slips through grasping fingers but even as she washed her face, she could recall them as certainly as her own memories.

She absently picked a black and white blouse and matching skirt from her closet when her heart began to quicken. With a sudden, too hard jerk, she turned off the light and rushed from the closet. Its confines reminded her too much of ... what? Images flooded her consciousness.

Darkened library stacks filled her mind's eye as she ... Asaege rushed through them. Jillian recognized the Great Library from her dreams of two nights prior. Despite her pursuers, she remembered a feeling of exhilaration rather than fear. Beside her was the roguish figure of Hollis, an unexpected but welcome companion on that night. Last night's dream crashed upon her like a lightning cloven oak. *I am not sure how long I can keep ahead of Binders and templars, not to mention the City Guard and my own guild.* His voice had been so calm but the thief's eyes danced side to side with barely contained panic.

Jillian felt Asaege's fear as if it were her own life in danger. She could feel her heart pounding in her chest, standing safely in her own home. Hollis ... the library ... everything was nothing more than a product of her overactive imagination. Then why did it all seem so real? Why did the events seem just as pressing to her wakened mind as anything during her school day? She shook her head in an attempt to shake the images from it. Stubbornly, they clung to her recollection as surely as any of her 'real' memories.

A sharp chirp from the phone left by her bedside snapped Jillian from her reverie. In quick succession, the device chirped again. Rolling her eyes, she crossed the floor and picked up the offending object. The screen showed that Marisol had sent two text messages within a few seconds. As Jillian traced a simple pattern on the screen, the lock screen dissolved into her application crowded wallpaper. She absently opened her friend's text messages and read them quickly.

Hey girl! Rise and shine for another day in paradise. The second message was a winking emoji with its tongue out. Jillian laughed despite herself. Marisol always seemed to bring the right amount of silliness and camaraderie to their friendship. Amid the often unfriendly faces that filled the teachers' lounge, Marisol was a rare spot of sunshine. With quick sweeping strokes of her thumbs, she wrote a response and stabbed send. *We all know how well that turned out for Adam and Eve. See you soon.*

Tossing the phone onto her unmade bed, Jillian shuffled into the bathroom and turned on the shower. Not checking the temperature before stepping in, she found it acceptably warm, just as it was every morning. The water was neither pleasant nor unpleasant, it simply was ... for as long as she could remember. Combined with the uncomfortable sense of thinness that surrounded her, the mediocrity pulled at her spirit like a thick spring mud. Impulsively, she reached out and twisted the hot water knob clockwise. The deluge of heat rolled over her body in a wave of breathtaking warmth. It was exhilarating ... until it wasn't.

The warmth turned blistering quickly. Jillian reached out desperately and turned the hot water off, turning the scalding spray into a bone chilling one. Another quick twist stopped the cold water as well, leaving her wet and shivering in the early morning light. Chuckling lightly to herself, she drew the curtain and reached for a towel. *Perhaps smaller steps, Jill*, she thought. Even though her experiment in altering her morning routine had't gone as she imagined, it still left her with a feeling of accomplishment. Quickly drying herself, Jillian rushed into her bedroom to dress, not wanting to be late for work.

*****

"Finish up those journal entries, kids," Mrs. Schmidt prompted, "There's only thirty seconds left in this section." She'd taken a weekend course in Atlantic City earlier in the year, so the school had billed her as a 'literacy specialist' but there was something about her that made Jillian uncomfortable.

Perhaps it was the way the pitch of her voice lifted when she pronounced the word 'kids', turning it into something patronizing. Perhaps it was the breathless way she sighed when Jillian had asked for clarification on the new procedure. Whatever it was, she came across about as genuine as cheap theatrical scenery.

Jillian watched the woman's bored expression out of the corner of her eye as she studied the children. Each of them scribbled furiously in the spiral notebooks provided for the lesson. Their jaws were set in a hard look of concentration, the stress of the timed exercise stamped across their furrowed brows. She always asked for her students' best effort when in her class but the five pages in the abbreviated time frame of five minutes seemed to be a recipe for failure.

"And … time," Mrs. Schmidt announced. "Pencils down, please." Timothy Harris squinted down at his notebook and quickly made a few more flourishes, perhaps completing his thought. "I said, pencils down." Her tone was sharp and direct. Abrupt as a slap, it held the sound of flesh on flesh.

Timothy dropped his pencil in shock, and it bounced from the desk to roll beneath the radiator. The boy rose to retrieve it, only to be greeted by another terse barrage. "Stay in your seat, Mr. Harris. The lesson is not over." Although the words were spoken rather than shouted, each held a razor's edge.

Jillian stepped between them, breaking the teacher's line of sight. With her back turned to Mrs. Schmidt, she spoke gently, "He's just getting his pencil. Go ahead, Timothy, and then sit back down."

When Jillian turned, Mrs. Schmidt had seized her with a withering glare. Furrowing her brows and pursing her lips, Jillian allowed the annoyance that had plagued her all period to boil to the surface. Were it a physical thing, her expression would have set the other teacher ablaze. Despite her tenure and experience, Mrs. Schmidt averted her eyes first. Jillian stepped back to lean against her desk, wordlessly surrendering the class to her co-worker once more.

Mrs. Schmidt cleared her throat, turning her eyes to the class again. "In the next section we're going to share what we've written with our classmates." Jillian saw every eye in the class drop to their desks as one.

73

Her colleague didn't seem to notice. "Do we have any volunteers?" Not a single hand twitched. Without missing a beat, she flatly stated, "You don't want me to choose." Her eyes were fixed firmly on Timothy's averted face.

In an attempt to break her concrete focus, Jillian spoke, "I think we all are interested in the educational purpose of sharing such a personal thing as a journal, Mrs. Schmidt. Can you please tell us more about this section?"

Through clenched teeth, the woman hissed, "Of course, Miss Allen." After a deep sigh, Mrs. Schmidt turned to the class. "The theme of this journal entry was something that changed your life. In sharing it, we'll see that each of us is not all that different than our classmates. Friendships are often found in the things we have in common."

And ammunition for teasing is often found in the differences, Jillian thought, *If you had told them that they needed to share, perhaps certain topics would have been avoided*. Looking around the room, her eyes settled on a hand full of children whose home lives weren't the best. Jennifer's father was a highly functional alcoholic, but an alcoholic, nonetheless.

Brent's older brother had enlisted in the military after high school and recently came home from overseas missing his left leg below the knee.

Timothy's parents were in the midst of a contentious divorce, one of their major disagreements centered around how to handle the boy's educational struggles.

"Let's begin sharing, shall we?" Again, Mrs. Schmidt found Timothy's down-turned head. "How about Mr. Harris? Timothy, please share your journal with us." Her voice turned to gravel as she said, "Read it aloud to the class."

The boy's head snapped up, his eyes darting to and fro in panic. He shook his head in a series of jerky motions.

Mrs. Schmidt stalked between the row of desks like a shark that has sensed blood. "Oh come now," she chided, "We're all friends here. Tell your classmates what has changed your life, Mr. Harris."

"I don't wanna." The words emerged from Timothy's lips in a barely audible squeak. His eyes sought out Jillian's, a pleading request obvious within their depths.

She stood quickly and covered the distance in a half dozen rushed steps, "Mrs. Schmidt, perhaps we can pick someone else?"

Her co-worker either didn't hear her words or simply ignored them. She snatched the notebook from under the boy's clenched fists and flipped it open. A tight smile spread across her lips for a moment before she turned to the rest of the class. "The assignment was five pages but Timothy seemed to think that didn't apply to him. He decided to do three pages."

Jillian's gut began to clench with disgust.

"Perhaps young Mr. Harris made up the difference by writing a really good journal." Mrs. Schmidt dropped the notebook carelessly onto Timothy's desk. "Don't keep your classmates waiting, Timothy."

Slowly he began to read, "I have a dog. His name is Leon." The snickers began quietly. Jillian turned a dark glare on the class, and they softened but didn't stop completely. Timothy's voice dropped to a whisper, "Leon is brown and white with black on his ears. Leon is my friend." He looked up to see several of his classmates laughing.

"That's enough. Does anyone else have something to share?" As she made her way to the front of the room, Jillian saw Timothy recede into himself, pulling his arms into his midsection in an attempt to make himself smaller. When Mrs. Schmidt turned, there were still no hands raised. "Still no one? Perhaps I can choose another —"

"It's almost time for PE class, boys and girls. Please line up in the hall and I will be out to escort you to the gym in a moment." Jillian tried to keep the fury that boiled within her from her voice. She was only partially successful. Mrs. Schmidt turned to regard her, her jaw set. Jillian held a finger, her lips pursed in anger. Her colleague remained quiet until the last child had closed the door behind them.

"What was that all about?" Mrs. Schmidt didn't try to conceal her frustration.

"I was about to ask you the same thing. Didn't you see the fear in that boy's face?"

She shrugged. "Sometimes stepping outside our comfort zone can be frightening."

"He's nine," Jillian stated in as calm of a voice as she could manage. "Timothy's comfort zone is all that keeps him from falling apart."

Mrs. Schmidt shook her head slowly, "The lesson requires sharing with the class. I find that public humiliation helps with that every time."

"Not in my class, it doesn't." Jillian crossed her arms across her stomach in an effort to quell her growing desire to slap her co-worker. "The only thing that your method accomplished was to drive him further into his shell."

"I don't see it that way, Jillian."

'Ms. Allen," she corrected, "And you don't need to. I read the lesson plan and am sure I can teach it with no further assistance from you."

"I've set aside another period for this." Obstinacy stained the woman's tone.

"Then I suppose you have some free time on your hands." Jillian turned her back and walked to the door. She stopped before opening it, her hand loosely gripping the knob. "I'm going to take my students to PE. I don't expect to see you when I return."

*****

Marisol was waiting for Jillian at her car as she exited the building. Her friends broad smile wiped away the last vestiges of Jillian's bad day from her mind. Returning Marisol's smile, she said, "Happy Friday Eve."

"Is it Thursday? I didn't realize." Without missing a beat, Marisol followed with, "That's a lie. This week's seemed to drag on for a month."

Flashes of the days that had passed in her dreams the previous evening barraged Jillian as she murmured, "You have no idea."

Wrapping her arm around Jillian's shoulders, Marisol chirped, "It's almost over though. Then it's two glorious days of sleeping in and freedom from 'the old guard', right?" Quickly raising her other arm, she waved to a trio of teachers leaving the school, stern expressions stamped on their faces like minted coins.

Jillian rested the side of her head on the crown of her friend's. "I can't wait." She felt Marisol tense briefly before untangling herself from their hug.

"Speaking of the weekend, Jill, what are you doing tomorrow night?"

She shrugged her shoulders and rolled her eyes, "I haven't thought that far ahead. Nothing, I suppose."

"Great. Are you free for dinner?"

Jillian perked up. "Absolutely! That could be just what I need."

Marisol nodded, a glimmer of mischief glinting in her deep brown eye, "How about Lobster Johnnie's at seven?"

A sense of foreboding settled across her shoulders like a wool blanket. "That's fine." Jillian squinted at her friend, "What are you up to, Mari?"

A sly smile crept onto Marisol's lips. "Nothing." Her half joyous, half guilty expression told a different story. Jillian simply seized her with a stern glare. Her friend broke quickly. "There's this guy at church."

"Mm hmm."

"He'd be perfect for you."

"Mari!"

"Or if not, at least you'll get out of that damned apartment."

"After the last time —"

"— that wasn't my fault. How was I supposed to know he —"

"— stop right there! I spent months trying to forget how he —"

"— I know, right?"

76

The lightning exchange was both invigorating and exhausting in equal measures. In times like this, Jillian felt that the two shared at least part of a single brain. "I don't need a blind date right now."

"When does anyone ever think, 'Do you know what I need? A good blind date'?"

"Never."

"But millions of people do it every week. They can't all be wrong."

Jillian frowned and mumbled, "You severely overestimate human-kind as a whole."

"It's one dinner. What could be the harm?" Marisol avoided her friend's eye as she repeated, "It's one dinner." Jillian sighed deeply, which Marisol took it as a sign of acceptance. "His name is Charles."

"One dinner," Jillian stated.

"One dinner," Marisol agreed, "but you're going to regret saying that. I think he is a good one."

"That's what you said before."

"Yeah, but I was just getting my radar synced. This one's the guy." Marisol flashed her pearly smile. "Trust me."

"Why is it that when people say that, it seems to have the opposite effect?"

"Because you are a cynical woman, too old before her time?"

Jillian shook her head briefly and then reached into her purse to find her keys.

"Love you," Marisol chirped.

In a begrudging tone that she didn't feel, she responded, "Love you, too."

78

Chapter Thirteen
Shadows of an Idea

Despite his mentor's assurances, Hollis couldn't shake the trepidation that pulled at the back of his mind after his reunion with him. Seran had slain two of the guild's hired swords without hesitation, but the second man's strange behavior bothered the thief. As his list of allies continued to dwindle, alienating any of them might very well spell the difference between life and death.

Yet the final expression of betrayal on the dying man's face haunted him enough to not return to Bearon's shop. The loft above an abandoned stable served him well enough as a makeshift bolt hole but he couldn't rely on it forever. Navigating through the maze of alleys, his feet brought him to the candlemaker's shop. In the hazy dimness that seemed to define the evening within the Ash, he could see the candlelight filtering from between the closed shutters of the second-floor room of his new-found ally.

Despite the stiffness in his left hand, the thief's fingers were able to find purchase on the walls of the rough daub structure. Supporting his weight on his toes and the fingertips of his right hand, he made quick work of the latch holding the shutters closed. As they swung open, Hollis slid inside.

Asaege was beginning to stir, years spent in the Ash having no doubt robbed her of the ability to sleep deeply. The candle's flickering illumination highlighted her sleepy expression nestled in her sleep tangled chestnut tresses. Even when woken from the depths of dream, the woman was still striking. The hard years spent in Oizan's slum had replaced the porcelain smoothness of youth with the shallow lines of experience, but these did nothing to detract from her beauty. Even in the midst of the confusion brought on by waking suddenly, her face was set in a look of quiet determination.

Hollis brought his finger to his lips, "Magpie, it is only me." It was only then that he saw the glint of candlelight from the steel of the dagger she clutched in her right fist. The thief held his hands up before him, empty palms facing out as he waited for her to recognize him. When she allowed the knife to drop to the thin mattress beside her, he let his hands fall to his sides. "Do you know how to use that?"

Asaege frowned and muttered, "I had *you* worried."

"That you did. Was it under the pillow?"

She shook her head. "Between the mattress and bed frame." Impressed, Hollis nodded lightly. "But you did not come all the way here to discuss the finer points of hiding weapons, I assume."

The thief chuckled briefly. "That I did not. I paid a visit to my associate after I left you last night."

Asaege's forehead furrowed into at tight line of worry. "Has he had a change of heart?"

Hollis shook his head. "Not yet but I do not believe it will be too long until someone changes it for him."

"What makes you say that?"

"When I arrived one of my guild mates was already there. I got the impression that if Bearon was not prepared to change his mind, cold steel was going to be the last thing to cross it. Fortunately for me, that particular brother did not bear me ill will."

"Why does the thieves guild care about a stolen book? Or even the curate's death for that matter?"

The thief shook his head sadly. "They care about neither. What they do take very personally is how my part in both reflects upon them."

"I assume that would be badly?"

"I think it is safe to say that my tenure with the guild is at its end."

Asaege's eyes narrowed. "For what it is worth, I am sorry."

"It is worth plenty, but that does not change the fact that when at odds with the guild, the Ash does not provide the armor that it would against the Binders or City Guard. A great deal of my brothers are as at home within its borders as I am."

"Can your guild mate help us?"

"Can he? I believe that Seran can do anything he puts his mind to, even if he has to burn the city down around his ears. The true question is 'will he?' Much like Bearon, I do not believe Seran feels that my death is in his best interest. Unlike my associate, however, Seran is less easily swayed by the desires of others, whether or not they are expressed at the tip of a dagger." Hollis sighed, "The problem is that should his interests change, his blade at our throats may very well be our only warning."

"How well do you know him?"

"Seran might as well have raised me. A great deal of what I was able to accomplish within the guild is thanks to him." The thief shook his head sadly, "That being said, I am not sure Seran lets anyone truly know him. He brings a new meaning to 'keeping your cards close to the vest'."

Again, Hollis's Well-given insight witnessed the woman's gaze turn to glass for a split second. Before he could reach out to grasp her arm in an effort to stabilize her, the look passed. Asaege's voice shook momentarily as she said, "So, we are back to where we started." As she continued, the flutter faded, "Does no one you know feel loyalty towards you?"

Despite the direness of their shared situation, he couldn't suppress a chuckle. "It does not appear so, does it?" A sharp pain stabbed into his heart as a parade of faces echoed through his mind: Silvermoon, Rhyzzo, Jeff, Mike, Ren. The final face hung in his recollection like an accusing Dickensian spirit. It bore such a close resemblance to Ren that the two might have been brothers. The truth was that they were much closer than that. Just as Stephen was before their merging within the Well of Worlds, Alan was Ren's reflection on Earth. Or was it the other way around? Hollis could never decide which world was the real one, if there truly was such a thing.

Very much as Hollis had taken Ren under his wing, Stephen had supported Alan through his own tragic younger years. Despite their almost ten year difference in age, Alan had been Stephen's best friend until his death. A death which the mingled being that was Hollis never could quite absolve himself of blame. As his reflection, when Alan died so too did Ren follow him into the cold clutches of the grave, but it was his inability to prevent his friend's passing that started the ball rolling. While it was true that without that triggering event, Hollis and Stephen would never have fallen under the magic of the Well and been tied together forever. Stephen, and by extension Hollis, would have traded every gift the magic portal had bestowed upon him for just another hour with Alan.

The weight of Asaege's increasingly more impatient stare brought the thief out of his guilty recollections. He repeated, "It does not appear so." His mind went to the last person that he could truly call a friend, Aristoi the Songspear. The two parted ways almost a year before, the Kieli traveling south to bring her decades of wandering to a well-earned end and Hollis in search of Maggie.

He hoped his friend had found more peace at the end of her journey than he had. The letter he'd sent to Aristoi a month or two prior had gone unanswered, but that wasn't unexpected. If he had need of her, the Songspear would come. Hollis had no intention of calling, however; too many had suffered for knowing him. He wouldn't condemn the last of his friends to the same fate.

"So, it appears that it is you and it is me."

"Tawn —"

"— should remain as far from this as you can keep her. No one involved in this situation will treat her kindly."

Hollis saw the woman draw a sharp breath as the realization settled upon her. "Have I already placed her in peril? Does my continued presence place her and her husband in more?"

The thief shrugged his shoulders lightly. "Most likely, but if you were to flee, it would only confirm any suspicions any party already holds."

Asaege sat upon the bed in a half-collapse, "Is there nothing I can do to safeguard those I love?"

Again, a knife of guilt pierced Hollis's heart. He gritted his teeth through the pain. "That is not what I said." Taking a deep breath to center himself, he continued, "It is my name on the lips of those searching for both murderer and book. As far as we know, you were not seen … if you were, you certainly were not identified."

She stood from the bed in a sudden motion and demanded, "How do you know that?"

Standing firm against the woman's advance, the thief stated flatly, "Because if you were, you would already be dead." Asaege paled a shade. "Please take no offense but with such high stakes, no one involved would hesitate to kill an ash-rat to get what they want … even one as principled as yourself."

"And you will be safe?"

He laughed briefly before shaking his head. "Far from it, Magpie. Anyone coming for me, however, will show more caution; my reputation buys me at least that."

"How long will that last?"

"Based on my experience with my guild-mates this evening, I fear I may have spent that particular currency. I can simply hope that when they do not return, it manages to fill my coffers a bit."

"But eventually —"

"— the guild will decide that their potential losses are overshadowed by the cost of inaction … or one of the other involved parties will decide that for them. I am a human like any other. I bleed. I die. The odds are not in my favor."

"There is nothing we can do?"

"If that were true, I would not be here. I may be a lot of things, but a martyr is not one of them."

"But you said that they would not stop until you were dead."

Hollis nodded. "Either that or they find the book."

Asaege's eyes shifted to the vaguely rectangular lump beneath her thin pillow. "I will not give it to them."

"So you have said. That refusal has a price, though."

"Your life?"

"Let us hope it does not come to that."

"Then, what is the price?"

"We are going to have to make it more expensive to chase the book than the church cares to pay."

Asaege frowned. "I do not see that happening. The Hand's power depends on the prophecies that lie within its pages. Unless …"

"Unless what?"

The corner of the woman's lips turned up in a sly smirk. Hollis liked the look of it on her. "If we cannot make the chase beyond their willingness to spend, perhaps we can make the words they seek worth less. The concept of value is simply what you would pay for something, correct? "

The thief tilted his head, intrigued. "Correct."

"What is the value of something freely given?"

Hollis smiled broadly. "Precisely nothing."

"We have the Dialogues. What if we give the words found within to anyone who would listen?"

"We touched on this last night. The problem is that no matter how loudly you shouted, the Hand's voice is always louder."

Asaege's smirk turned into a broad smile, "What if they were not shouted at all? What if the voice that carried them came from the very soul of the listener?"

The thief raised an eyebrow but didn't speak.

"What if we could give each person the words of Olm … free of messenger … and let them decide for themselves their meaning?"

"How many ash-rats can actually read?"

"Virtually none."

"And you do not see that as barrier to your plan?"

"People can be taught if they want to learn. When someone has nothing, they cling on to the promise of a better life. If that promise comes at the cost of learning to read, I have no doubt that they will pay it."

"Even if you could make enough copies, they would be confiscated

83

as quickly as you could pass them out."

Asaege walked to the open shutters and pointed across the narrow alley. Etched on its surface was a sloppy oval bisected by a crooked line, no doubt the territory marker for one of the minor gangs that haunted the Ash. "What if they could not be?"

*****

Asaege's hand moved across the daub wall with broad strokes of her brush. In its wake, the words passed from Olm to his chosen hand were left in foot high letters: *Each of my children are warmed by a measure of the flame used to mold Taerh itself. The rich and poor are as one in the eyes of the creator.*

She stepped back with a weary smile, wiping the sweat beading on her forehead with the back of her hand. To her left, her partner in crime crouched, lantern in one hand and a broad bladed dagger in the other. His attention was on the far end of the alley, concern etched deep lines in his forehead.

He spoke in a rasping whisper without turning to face her. "Are you almost through, Magpie?"

"I have just finished, Hollis." She took the opportunity to study the thief while his attention was elsewhere. A week's growth of hair stubbled his previously bald head and cheeks. It softened his appearance, like a well-worn cloak. Asaege thought she could catch a glimpse of the man below the hard surface the thief maintained. He turned to examine her handiwork, smiling briefly before turning back to the mouth of the alley. Even in that smile was a tension that reminded her what was truly at stake.

"The paint will hold up to the elements?"

Asaege joined him, settling into a crouch beside the thief. "It would take more than a day and a wire brush to scrub it from the wall and even then, it should leave behind a shadow. It is more stain than paint; it sinks into daub, wood and stone alike. I would not be surprised if it outlives both of us."

Hollis licked his lips. "We can be assured of that fact if we do not get moving soon. I can feel something gathering itself. Less and less folks have been by over the last hour." He nodded into the street, "It is empty … very unusual for this time of night. The Rusty Plough is two blocks from here."

"Why did you not say anything?"

He shrugged. "Would it have helped you write any faster?"

She shook her head. "Not likely." He nodded, squinting into the shadows that flanked the dimly lit street. Asaege began to rise, but the thief's hand clamped onto her forearm like a vise, pulling her back down beside him.

"Do you see the alley between the weaver's shop and that of Adale the seamstress?"

"Yes."

"Wait for a moment. Watch the shadows on the right side, at thigh height."

Asaege narrowed her eyes and stared into the darkness. After a moment there was a quick flash, a reflection of light off of something metal from within the alley. "Some —" In her excitement she raised her voice. Immediately realizing her mistake, she let it drop into a whisper, "Someone is over there."

Hollis nodded, "His name is Tormand. He wears a cloak pin that his woman gave him. He believes it is his good luck charm. There are at least two others hidden further back. I saw them enter together ten or fifteen minutes ago."

"Again, I ask why you did not mention anything?"

"Again, I ask would it have made things easier? A passage half scrawled is worthless to us."

"But now we are trapped."

The thief's voice was flat and still like glass as he said, "Perhaps. But so are they."

"How do you come to that conclusion?"

"Their masters want me dead. They have cleared the street to make that as much of a certainty as possible."

"How does wanting you dead trap them?"

"There is the possibility that they have seen you. That information cannot find its way to the ears of anyone else." Hollis set the lantern down on the dirt crusted cobblestones. "It has to die with them tonight."

Despite herself, the casual way that the thief spoke the words caused a chill to run through Asaege. In the library, those who lost their lives had been actively trying to kill him. The thief now spoke of murder, planned and premeditated. Part of her, however, felt a rush of gratitude that he cared enough for her safety to kill for it.

"Do you have the sword I gave you?"

She gripped the sharkskin wrapped hilt of the Uteli short sword. "Right here."

"Draw it and move further back into the alley. Do you still remember the spells you used in the library?"

"'Remember' is an over simplification but yes, I do."

"The bugs. Can you focus them on one person or do they attack everything in the area?"

"It is called Io's Infestation." He regarded her out of the corner of his eye. "They will concentrate on one person, but insects are unreliable allies. I have no guarantee that they will not wander."

"It will have to do. There are three of them. None can walk out of this alley. That means that I must be between them and its mouth."

Asaege felt her stomach drop with realization. "You have to let them by you."

She could see the concern on Hollis's face. "They must get past me. Stay as far back as you can and set your bugs on the closest. Be prepared as there is a good chance that he will charge you to end the spell."

"The spell cannot be stopped once it is cast."

"I doubt he knows that."

Asaege swallowed hard. "Alright."

"Keep your blade between you and him and hope that he is armed with knife rather than sword. The greater reach of your Talis Fahr should keep you out of his range long enough for your magic to do its work."

"And if it does not?"

"Keep your slashes short and do not let your blade come off line. If he gets inside your guard, it will be he who has the advantage. Give ground if he chooses to take it. As long as your spell is in effect, time is more your ally than his."

Asaege felt her heart flutter in her chest; the tremor danced its way into her hand. She clutched the hilt of her borrowed sword tighter to fend off the shuttering. "Are you not frightened?"

Without hesitation, Hollis replied, "I am scared to death."

Shocked, Asaege said, "You are?"

The thief nodded, "Every time. No matter what anyone tells you, the only person without fear is a dead one."

Swallowing hard again, she managed, "How do you know they will come?"

"Because I have something they do not."

"What is that?"

"Patience."

Chapter Fourteen
Shadows of Things to Come

True to his prediction, Tormand and his two companions grew impatient quickly. Hollis saw them leave the sheltering shadows of their alley at a run.

The thief rose from his crouch, taking a few steps back as he drew his own Uteli weapon. The Wallin Fahr came free of its sheath with a soft whoosh of steel on leather, the dwarven steel blade glinting softly in the dim light. When the last of them crossed into the alley, Hollis sprung forward.

Tormand was in the lead, wielding a wickedly curved dagger in each hand. He tensed as he prepared to meet the thief's rush.

He was disappointed when Hollis dodged by him, offering only a token slash for his efforts. The thief's eyes were securely set on the furthest of his guild brothers. The second of the thugs was so surprised by Hollis's movements that he didn't offer even token resistance to his rush by him. The final guild-member was able to duck under the thief's high, horizontal cut and move further into the depths of the alley. The cut was, of course, a feint; Hollis stood between the three assailants and freedom.

As the thief pivoted and brought his sword into a low guard position, he felt rather than heard the words of Asaege's spell crashing onto his soul like waves upon a stony beach. The words were lost to his memory as soon as they reached his ears, almost as if his mind refused to understand them. The sound of the words hung in the air for a second longer than they should have, like honey dripping from a comb. Just as in the dim confines of the stacks, a rustling sound rose to replace them. It was soft at first but began to build exponentially upon itself.

The two thugs closest to Hollis advanced upon him, but the narrow confines of the alley didn't allow them to stand shoulder to shoulder and retain enough mobility to fight effectively. Their bodies partially blocked his view of Tormand but the thief could see the cloud of thick, black flies that surrounded him in a miasma.

Asaege was lost to his sight completely. Tormand let out a shrill cry as his arms windmilled about him in a vain attempt to swat away the stinging swarm; the ineffectual motion only seemed to agitate the insects as their buzzing grew louder. His scream was cut short, replaced by a choking cough as the flies, no doubt, found their way into his mouth.

Taking a short, fortifying breath, Hollis focused his attention on the two assailants before him just as the rearmost one released a short, bladed throwing knife. Allowing his body to rotate as he dropped his right shoulder, the thief bladed his body and bent his knees. The knife passed his head with only six inches to spare. Despite the life and death circumstances they faced, the thief was able to reach out and grasp the calm cloak granted by the waters of the Well of Worlds. As it settled upon his shoulders, his perceptions sharpened, and time seemed to slow around him.

The closer of the two thugs gathered himself for a charge, dropping his knife hand as he began to lurch forward. The thief used the coiled strength of his bent legs to spring forward, sword leading the way. His guild-brother's face had time to register shock before dwarven steel pierced both lung and heart. He collapsed to the grime covered alley as a rush of crimson vapor exploded from his lips.

Hollis completed his lunge, releasing his left hand from the hilt of the Talis Fahr as he moved past the dying man. The thugs own weight pulled the blade from his body. His companion's eyes floated right and left as the thief saw the realization of his dire predicament fall upon him like an avalanche. "For what it is worth, brother," Hollis began. He brought the tip of his sword back on line at mid chest height, slightly away from his body to maximize his reach advantage. "I will mourn your passing."

His opponent sank into a crouch and tried to make a rush for the mouth of the alley and freedom. The thief swept his blade in a short, chopping arc, opening a deep gash along his bicep. "Wrong place."

He reversed direction in time to avoid Hollis's return stroke but came no closer to escape. Not giving the man a chance to recover, the thief pressed his advantage. He feinted with a short thrust, driving the thug back into the prone body of his wheezing comrade. Instinctively, the man looked down at his partner.

Hollis brought his sword down in a swift left to right diagonal slash, biting deeply into the thug's body between neck and shoulder. Drawing his blade free, the thief widened the wound and reversed his stroke. An angry red mouth opened across his chest and the thief's opponent collapsed across the body of his comrade. "Wrong time."

The air was filled with the thunder of insect wings as Hollis drove his blade into each of the dying men a final time before stepping over their bodies. His eyes searched the shadows of the alley for Asaege and Tormand. As he'd counseled, she'd retreated and allowed her spell to do its work. Tormand swung more at the stinging cloud surrounding him than at Asaege. She held the Uteli short sword in front of her like a knife fighter, keeping the man at range. The man's tentative gait told the thief that her longer weapon had stung as surely as the products of her spell when he didn't respect that range.

As he closed on the pair, Hollis could see through the undulating black cloud the savaged flesh on Tormand's face and neck, the product of thousands of tiny insect bites. He winced at the thought of the agony that the man had endured. Until that moment, the thief had never truly understood the reality of a death by a thousand cuts. When he came within a hand full of steps, the roar of the insects rose to an almost unbearable volume. A few of the fat flies separated themselves from the cloud and floated towards Hollis.

Asaege called to him, "Stay back!" She thrust out with her sword quickly, sinking the tip into Tormand's thigh, eliciting a choking gasp from the man. "A swarm of this size will not remain if presented with a fresh victim!"

The thief took a step back and the insects lazily returned to the miasma surrounding Tormand. Raising his voice to be heard above the drone, Hollis shouted, "We cannot tarry! We need to be gone before curiosity overcomes whatever threat my brothers used to clear the street!" Tormand turned in a jerking motion as he heard his voice.

"They will disperse when the magic loses its hold over them!"

"How long will that take?"

Asaege simply shrugged.

"If we leave him here, all of this is for nothing!" Tormand groaned loudly, trying to force words through swollen lips and tongue. If he could speak, no doubt he would assure the thief that he had nothing to fear from his guild-brother. Despite Tormand's plans for him, the bittersweet sting of pity filled Hollis's heart. He voiced the words that rang in his heavy conscience. "We cannot take that chance!" He was not sure whether his words were for Asaege or Tormand. Regardless of their intended audience, the truth of the words remained.

Hollis watched as Asaege marshaled her courage. He assumed that as the caster of the spell, the insects wouldn't turn on her as she was much closer to Tormand than the thief had been when the fat biting flies had begun to focus on him. He was sure that the knowledge didn't make the act of stepping into the cloud any easier. Although he couldn't hear the sound of steel in flesh above the roar of the swarm, its effect was clear when Tormand collapsed to the cobblestones, taking the miasma of insects with him. Asaege was revealed as the greasy black curtain fell from around her, her jaw rigid and set. The flies settled on the motionless body of Tormand like a rippling black carpet and the thunder of their wings quieted to a persistent buzzing.

Looking into her tight face, the thief could almost feel the turmoil that raged inside Asaege. She clenched her left fist at her side, her right filled with the instrument of her first kill. Hollis remembered the feeling well, the wearying mixture of elation and regret dragged at the limbs like a week of sleepless nights. He refrained from telling her that she did well, knowing before the words left his lips that they would sound condescending.

He settled for, "He was dead when he made the choice to come after us. Everything that came after that was just the path to that end."

The part of him that had been Stephen wanted to wrap his arms around her and assure her that it would be alright. No one had done any such thing for him when he had, reflected in Hollis's mind, killed his first opponent. Hollis wouldn't lie to Asaege as he didn't lie to Stephen that night.

There was no guarantee that anything would be alright ever again.

Chapter Fifteen
With a Heavy Heart

The silence that had been the pair's companion on their return to Asaege's room above the candlemaker's shop clung to them as she searched for a way to break it. Asaege was aware of the way she absently rubbed at her right palm with her left thumb, but couldn't seem to stop the vaguely comforting gesture. *He was there to murder me ... murder us. If I had not killed him, he would have succeeded.*

Her thoughts made sense when spoken from a logical frame of mind, but they brought her no more comfort on their hundredth uttering than they had on the first. So, she continued to rub at her palm.

Hollis sat on Asaege's bed, watching her pace through hooded lids as she scrubbed at her hand. She waited for him to speak … to say something, but he simply sat there, still as a statue. *Comfort me*, she thought, *Yell at me, lecture me but say something!* Her eyes flashed up to meet his as if, by force of will, she could force her thoughts into his mind. In the depths of his deep brown eyes, she found neither condemnation nor the cold apathy she would have expected from the career criminal she assumed him to be. Instead, there was a softness that pulled at her heart like the unrelenting force of quicksand.

Within those eyes she found a sad sympathy. She was prepared for anger or impatience, instead that gaze stripped away any walls she had erected to protect herself from them. "I am sorry," she whispered.

With a small shake of his head, the thief said, "You have nothing to be sorry for. You did not bring Tormand or the other two into that alley."

"Did I not? It was the book that brought them there. The book that I stole. The book that I foolishly seek to keep from them."

He stood in a smooth motion and gently gripped her by her upper arms. "They came there of their own free will. They were sent by a guild that is more concerned with their own power than loyalty to their brothers … also of their own free will. If it were not the book, eventually it would be something else. People who crave power often do such to the exclusion of all else."

"But —"

"— but nothing. I would cast my lot with someone who stands for something every time over those who represent nothing but their own greed."

"They want you dead."

"Yes. They would not be the first and certainly will not be the last. I have made more than my fair share of enemies over three decades; it is a side effect of the life I have chosen for myself. A friend once told me that, no matter how unpleasant, we all have the responsibility to stand against those of evil intentions. Sometimes it comes at great cost; that cost is not always personal."

"I had no right to ask this of you."

"Whether or not we have the right, the responsibility remains." Slowly, he released her arms and took a step back, "But that is not what is really eating you, is it? That is not what caused you to rub at your palm hard enough to push clear through your hand."

"That man …"

"Tormand."

"Tormand. I have … had never …"

He laid his hand on her shoulder, "I know. If I could, I would have taken that from you. To take a life is a serious thing, it weighs upon the soul. If each time, a part of you does not perish with them, then you are already dead … in spirit if not in body."

"I know he was a bad man."

Hollis nodded slightly, not correcting her.

"He would have killed either of us."

Again, Hollis nodded, this time more vigorously.

Asaege rubbed her palm again with more enthusiasm. "I saw the fear in his eyes, as if he were a child alone in the dark."

The thief seized her left wrist. "There is no spot to rub away, Magpie."

A rush of images crashed upon Asaege's mind like a raging waterfall. She saw a crowded theater and a dimly lit stage. The actors upon it spoke words she only half understood. *Out damned spot! Out, I say!* an actress spoke vehemently as she scrubbed at her hands. Asaege's head swam as her heart tried to beat its way out of her chest. Despite herself, she muttered, "Out damned spot."

Hollis smiled softly and responded, "Yet who would have thought the old man to have had so much blood in him." He slipped his arm around her waist and guided her to sit on the bed.

Wavering slightly, she seized him in an accusing glare, "How do you know that?"

"It may not have been my favorite, but the Scottish Play was one of the building blocks for the burgeoning sense of honor of my younger self. Well, not me exactly …" Hollis sank to one knee, "A more important question is how did you know it?"

"It came to me in a …," Asaege searched for the proper word. She decided on, "Vision."

Nonplussed, the thief retorted, "Memory is more appropriate."

"I have never been in that theater. If it is a memory, it is clearly not mine."

"It is and it is not."

Asaege closed her eyes and tried to focus on her now clear memory of the theater. She could almost feel the stifling closeness of the air against her skin and smell the scent of bodies pressed too long together. As she did, her head swam as her attention turned to fighting to retain consciousness. Again, Hollis's strong hands slowed her fall as she listed to the side and collapsed onto her side. Asaege's throat tingled, and she felt as if her head was filled with soap suds as she fought the closing darkness. Through the panicked confusion, a soft voice clove.

"Magpie, listen to me." Like the crack of a whip, the whispered words cut though the swirl of images and emotions she didn't recognize. "Breathe deeply … in … and out … again … in … and out. That is it. Try to relax. The harder you try to cling to the memories, the harder they will fight to escape you. Let them go for now. Feel the bed beneath you, the blanket on your skin. Focus on your breathing. In … and out … in … and out."

Asaege lost track of how long she lay on her side breathing before the vertigo passed. Slowly her eyes flickered open to find Hollis sitting tailor style on the floor, his hand resting lightly on her back. "What is happening to me?"

"It is complicated," Hollis began. She focused on his words, but memories not quite her own still haunted the edges of her thoughts. "It is called reflection." He frowned in frustration, as if he grasped at something just beyond his reach. "At least that is the best term that I had found for it."

"Reflection of what?"

"Another world? Another place, for sure." A small smile crept to the thief's lips despite the seriousness of the conversation. "Truth be told, I had very limited experience with it before …"

Asaege locked eyes with him, "Before what?"

Hollis dismissed her question with a shake of his head. "It does not matter. You are seeing memories of someone in this other place."

"How?"

He chuckled, looking abashed. "I have no idea. I mean I have some understanding of the mechanics of it but the majority of it has eluded me."

Asaege couldn't help but smile at his confession. "You are a great help."

Hollis shrugged. "It is better than nothing."

"Tell me what you know."

"From what I understand, each of us on Taerh has a like soul or reflection in the other place, with neither aware of the other until a certain herb is consumed on that side. I am not sure if there is a similar plant on Taerh. I have only seen it work the one direction. Your reflection sleeps there and awakes her within your mind."

Asaege gasped. "They subsume you?"

The thief seized his bottom lip between his teeth for a moment before answering. "That is where it becomes complicated. Sometimes they can only bear witness to what you see and do."

"And other times?"

"Yes, they can force your consciousness to recede for short periods of time. It is my understanding that two reflections' interactions vary depending on the pair. Your reflection should be as your twin, but it does not always seem to be so."

"So, these memories …"

"Belong to your reflection."

Asaege closed her eyes again, "How do I get rid of them?" As the alien recollections brushed her consciousness, she tried to focus on pushing them further away. Rather than having the intended effect, they became more distinctive and caused her head to swim again.

Hollis felt her tense and rubbed her back gently. "To my knowledge, you cannot. At least I have never heard of anyone being able to."

"How many times have you seen this?"

"Seen? Besides myself?"

Her eyes still closed, Asaege nodded.

"Three."

Asaege's eyes snapped open. "Three?"

"I told you that the majority of it has eluded me."

"The ones you have seen, perhaps they know more?"

"I imagine getting satisfaction from them would be quite difficult."

She felt her brows draw together in a scowl. "And why is that?"

The thief turned away from her accusing glare. "Well … two are dead. The third and I have … um … history."

"What sort of history?"

"He came within a whore's conscience of killing me once. I returned the favor less than a year ago. Even if I had not, he is a positively unsavory individual."

"Do you know any other kind?"

Hollis quietly chuckled. "A few, but not many. I have read about others reflecting."

She perked up. "Have you looked for them?"

"They are all dead as well."

Asaege's shoulders slumped. "And the books?"

The thief winked slyly at her. "That is where there may be some good news. I am fairly sure I know where to find them."

"Wonderful. Are they in the Great Library?"

Hollis's tongue flicked out to wet his lips. "Not quite."

Chapter Sixteen
Legacy in Reflection

Jillian woke with a start, Hollis's words echoing in her ears as if they still hung in the air. *They are in a flower shop on Earth, between a wine seller and a restaurant. The sign reads: Florist and Holistic Medicine.* She didn't need remember the address; she knew the shop that he described. She'd taken her friend, Cyril, there many times to buy weed from his connection. Jillian had stayed in the car each time but was very familiar with the parking lot and surrounding businesses.

She tried to remember the owner's name. *Harold? Henry? I know it started with an H.* Jillian lay back against sleep warmed sheets, once again baffled by the vividness of the dream. She could still see the swollen wreckage of Tormand's face; the copper-sharp stink of his blood still stuck in her nostrils as if he were standing before her now.

The recollection caused her to tremble slightly. Dream or not, the guilt of the man's fate pulled at her soul. She felt as if that face, those memories would stay with her until the day of her own death.

Jillian rubbed her eyes with the backs of her hands, partially to scrub the sleep from them but mostly in a vain attempt to purge the sight from her mind's eye. The former was notably more successful than the latter.

She swung her legs over the edge of the bed as she sat up. A quick glimpse around the dim depths of her room showed Jillian that she'd spent far too much time focused on things other than basic housekeeping. Clothing purgatory had expanded beyond the white brocade chair under the room's only window and now occupied the top of the wicker trunk that held her extra linens. On her bedside table, a green glass pipe lay beside a half empty plastic bag that held the last of her most recent purchase.

After tucking the bag into the table's drawer, Jillian scooped up the pipe and walked towards the kitchen. As she chipped away the tar from the rim of the bowl, Jillian's mind returned to the flower shop. Could Hollis's description of the location of his journals be nothing more than her mind's way of rationalizing the purchase of more weed? Jillian had split the price of the eighth ounce of *Dreamtime Dank* with Cyrill the previous weekend and she'd only smoked it a few times. The remainder would last her at least another week. Then why was she so focused on getting more?

Jillian set the pipe down on the wad of paper towels set aside for the purpose and stared out the kitchen window. Was it the weed that had her so keen on visiting the flower shop or was it … something else? The more she tried to dismiss the possibility that it was the dreams that were pushing her to investigate the florist more carefully, the more she believed it. Before she realized it, she had her phone in her hands and was dialing Cyrill's number.

"Hey, Cyrill. It's not too early, is it?"

Her friend's sleep hoarse voice responded in the affirmative.

"Then I'll make it quick. Could we drop by that flower shop for more *Dreamtime*?"

Cyril responded with a clipped, "Sure."

Trying to force a cheerful tone to her voice, Jillian said, "Great. I'll meet you there at five?"

*****

The mildly crisp autumn breeze did its best to offset the stifling air that sat in Jillian's classroom like a squatting toad. Without the open windows and door, even her own motivation would begin to wane. She couldn't help but smile softly as she watched the faces of her students, the collective potential shining forth from their eyes brought a sense of humble appreciation to her heart. Each of them was capable of so many things … things of which they could not comprehend in the midst of the lesson on verb tenses.

"If today I catch a fish, how would I tell people about it tomorrow?" A few hands shot up immediately. "Come on, guys, you know all about irregular verbs," she gently chided, "If you were at the ballpark last weekend and snagged a foul ball, what verb would you use to tell your friends about your catch?" In twos and threes, hands were raised until almost all were in the air. "Reuben?"

The shy boy smiled broadly. "Caught," he declared in a confident voice.

"Very good. Rita, if you knew you wanted to catch a fish tomorrow, what would you tell people?"

The girls chin length red hair bobbed as Jillian could almost see the answer pop into her head. "I will catch a fish!"

"Awesome." Jillian gave the class a thumbs up. "Irregular verbs aren't so hard, are they?"

The class shook their heads, a few even adding, "No, Miss Allen," in an only half enthusiastic droning.

"What about a harder one? Who's up for a challenge?" Only a few hands didn't remain in the air. Jillian smiled, "How about 'am'?" She watched the wheels turn in the children's heads. "I am a teacher now. What would I say about something I did ten years ago? Aaron?"

The slim, brown-haired boy chewed his bottom lip for a moment before chirping, "Was? I was a student?"

"Very nice, Aaron. Claire, what could I say about something I want to do in the future?"

She furrowed her brow for a moment. Jillian could see her body tense as the silence stretched.

"You got this, Claire," she prompted gently.

"Will be?"

"Excellent. I will be a teacher for many years to come." Jillian softly clapped her hands, "See, they're not so scary. Verbs have nothing on you guys."

A soft murmur of excited voices rolled through the room as her students felt their success. She let it persist for a moment before continuing, they deserved the feeling of achievement. "I want you each to finish pages eight and nine in your language workbook tonight." A chorus of groans replaced the sounds of success. "It's exactly what we just covered," Jillian smiled at her students, "You've all got this."

Through the open door came the sound of a raised voice, "How many times have I told the two of you that when I am talking, you are not?" The voice belonged to Janice Roberts. "Now you're quiet? Both of you know I already have a meeting scheduled with each of your parents for next week and neither of you have the sense to modify your behavior before then?" Jillian could hear her anger building with the volume of her voice. "I'm going to have to call your parents again tonight, is that what you want?" A pair of soft voices responded, only to be cut off by Janice, "Now is the time to speak up, boys."

In unison, the boys responded, "No, Mrs. Roberts."

"Well, that is exactly what is going to happen." Janice's voice echoed through the tiled hallway. Jillian walked towards her open door. "Let me tell you what else is going to happen. Both of you will stay in during recess for an entire week." As Jillian closed the door, the pleasant cross breeze ceased but the stream of angry words was only dulled. "Furthermore, each of you will write me a one page apology paper due Monday morning."

As she turned back to her own class, Jillian couldn't decide which was more stifling: the now motionless air or the weight of the system in which she labored.

*****

Marisol was in the teacher's lounge when Jillian entered. Her friend's presence offered a balm to the struggles of the day. "Hey, Mari," she chimed.

Marisol's face brightened, "Good afternoon, Miss Allen."

Jillian rolled her eyes. "Settle down, Miss Diaz." They both laughed as she sat beside her friend.

"Rough one?"

Jillian responded, "Didn't start out that way but …" she let her words trail off.

Marisol finished for her, "Janice's afternoon performance?"

She nodded. "It sucks that I am right across the hall from her. The breeze was so nice until I had to close my door."

One of the third grade teachers, Mary Ellen Garrett, chimed in from across the room, "I know. I am all the way down the hall, and I have to close my door when she gets loud."

Jillian turned to face her and asked, "Has it always been this bad?"

Mary Ellen shrugged. "For as long as I can remember. Janice is … passionate."

Marisol murmured, "That is one word for it, I guess."

"She used to just yell at them in class. That was better."

Jillian frowned. "For whom?"

Mary Ellen stammered, "It was less noise in the hall. Besides, it's not like the kids can't hear her from the hallway."

"Doesn't make it right." Rage simmered in Jillian's gut.

Mary Ellen dismissed her words with a casual wave of her hand. "She's been here forever."

Marisol interjected, "So has Mrs. Lee, and you don't see her screaming at her kids in the hall."

Mary Ellen nodded, "I would say something but —"

The lounge door creaked open and Janice Roberts swept through it

100

in a rush of cashmere and frustration. "I swear these kids are going to be the death of me," she said to no one in particular.

Mary Ellen's face transformed into a broad grin, "I know, right? They have no gratitude for what we go through for them." She rose from her chair, staring daggers at Jillian and Marisol from the corner of her eye. "The parents could stand to teach their brats something ... manners, respect ... something."

Jillian rose as well, reaching down to cradle Marisol's shoulders in a one armed hug. Without another word, she walked past the two women and through the open door.

*****

Cyrill was already outside the flower shop when Jillian pulled into the parking lot. She had met the dusky skinned man in college, but the combination of a desk job and his passion for home-cooked Greek food had filled out his cheeks and waist since then. He leaned against the side of his leased Kia, studying something intently on his phone.

As Jillian turned off her own car and opened the door, he tucked the device into the pocket of his thin windbreaker and walked towards her.

"Did I wake you this morning?"

Cyrill chuckled. "Not really, I was fighting it for a while. I had an eight o'clock meeting but was putting off getting up for as long as I could."

Jillian narrowed her eyes, "Must be nice working from home."

"It has its moments. I mean, you can't beat the commute."

The two laughed momentarily and then a tense stillness hung in the air. Jillian broke the silence. "So, should we go in?"

He raised an eyebrow. "You want to come with?"

"I figured it would be OK. You don't always want to be my go between, do you?"

"Good point." Cyrill crossed the small parking lot and pulled the frosted glass door open. She stepped in behind him. A heavy air hung in the interior of the shop, despite the crisp evening outside. Combined with the motley collection of wooden tables, packed with greenery, it made the front room seem positively claustrophobic.

One wooden table was devoted to a plant that Jillian didn't recognize. It seemed like some sort of ground cover, low and thick. Its deep green leaves were small and heart-shaped with dark purple veins running through them. An ancient cash register stood atop a tall counter flanked by two squat, glass vases filled with fresh flowers.

"Hector!" Cyril called.

Hector, that was his name. I knew it started with an H, Jillian thought.

A figure emerged through a curtained doorway, carrying a pair of cellophane wrapped bouquets. Thin to the point of emaciation, the man's jeans hung precariously from his hips. The pants' threadbare cuffs pooled around a pair of thick soled shoes. A beard that matched his cuffs dotted the light brown skin that spoke of Latin American ancestry. A broad smile bloomed on the young man's face, "Cyrill, what's up?"

Cyrill took a step forward and clasped the man's shoulder, "Not much, bro. That last stuff was awesome; I hoped you still had some left."

Hector's smile dimmed a bit as his eyes moved past Cyrill and settled on Jillian. "I sure do, my man. But first, who's this? 'You decide to finally swipe right?"

The tips of Cyrill's ears reddened as he sputtered, "N…no … this is Jillian. We're college buddies."

Hector set the flowers on the counter as he slipped free from Cyrill's grasp, "College? Long time ago, ese."

Jillian corrected, "Not that long."

Hector squinted at her for a moment, his gaze moving up and down over her form before responding, "So it isn't." He wiped his right hand on his jeans before extending it to her, "Hector."

She accepted the handshake and repeated her name, "Jillian."

"Charmed, as they say. I figured Cyrill was sharing with someone. A light weight like him couldn't go through an eighth in a week."

Jillian nodded, continuing to study the man before her. When he looked at her there was something behind his eyes that made her slightly queasy. It was more than his unsubtle leering.

"It's good stuff. Did you enjoy it?"

Again, she nodded. There was a coldness beneath his casual, stoner façade.

"Some people say it gives them real strange dreams. 'You have any of those?" In contrast to the casual tone of his voice, Hector's gaze suddenly became more intense.

Suddenly uncomfortable, Jillian simply shrugged. "Strange is relative." She found it peculiar and more than coincidental that he was pressing her on her dreams, considering that those dreams had brought her here in the first place.

"Right." Hector drew out the word, almost turning it into a question. When Jillian didn't respond, he simply turned back to Cyrill. "How much do you want, big man? If you're splitting it, I would say at least a half. Not that I don't like visitors."

Cyrill looked to Jillian, who nodded quickly. "Yes, a half will be great, Hector."

"Right," Hector purred again. "Come in the back and I'll set you up." He pulled the curtain to the side and stepped into the back room.

Cyrill followed behind him, holding the curtain for Jillian. If it was possible, the room was more cluttered than the storefront. Packed with thickly cushioned chairs and wooden tables of disparate sizes and styles, it reminded her of an antique shop. The smell of weed clung to the humid air like a physical thing. It wasn't unpleasant but simply a little over-powering. Jillian stepped past her friend into the dim room. Only lit by a pair of tabletop lamps, pools of shadow crouched under furniture and in corners.

"Have a seat," Hector suggested. "I'll take a few to get the stuff together." He absently gestured to a cluster of Queen Anne wingback chairs surrounding a low wooden table. The surface of the table was cluttered with rolling papers and pipes of various shapes and sizes. Stacked beside one of the chairs were a half dozen leather bound books. Like a gulp of cold water, a sense of dread settled in Jillian's gut. Hollis's words from her dream rang in her ears, *There would be five or six of them, bound in brown leather and only a touch longer than your hand from wrist to fingertip. There in nothing fancy about them, but they do stand out, if only in their plainness.*

The weight of another coincidence settled upon her.

Hector and Cyrill stared down at a metal food cart containing a scale and a small pile of stems and buds. "Where do you get *Dreamtime*?" Cyrill asked.

"That's a trade secret, my man," Hector responded. "If everyone knew, why would they need me?"

"I guess that's fair," Cyrill agreed.

Jillian settled into the chair beside which the stack of journals rested and while their attention was focused elsewhere, she scooped one up. Flipping it open, she began to scan the page.

*****

Although I only slept for a little over eight hours here, that time translated to almost four days in Taerh. I continue to wonder why time seems so fluid between there and here. I have turned to the writings of Dirac and Hilbert to understand this concept of relative time in both places. I have learned more about theoretical mathematics in the past few months than I had ever done in six years of college, or ever wanted to. The frustration I feel when trying to understand the phenomenon is nothing compared to that I feel when reflected.

Silvermoon continues to search for Haedren after their last encounter at the Crown of the First King. The Walker insists that he searches for what she refers to as the 'Well of Worlds'.

I'm put off by the contrast between Beatrice and her reflection, although I cannot help but see the wisdom of her words regarding the herald. The longer we cooperate with The Walker, the more her erratic nature becomes apparent. Sometimes, I believe she is not necessarily of two minds, but two separate people.

I fear the consequences of bringing my worries to Samantha, as each time I do, she becomes visibly upset. Her heart condition prevents her from using adder Root, and her inability to reflect weighs heavily upon her.

*****

Through the swirl of her confused thoughts, Jillian heard Hector say, "One seventy." She closed the journal quickly and folded her hands over it and her lap.

Cyrill let out an astonished grunt. "One seventy? The eighth was only thirty last week."

Hector snorted. "It's popular stuff, you said so yourself. It's simple economics: supply and demand."

"I have one fifty with me."

"Then you will walk out with the same amount and nothing else." Hector's voice dropped to a dangerous growl. "One seventy."

Jillian stood up. Hector's dangerous tone caused an inexplicable dread to wrap its frigid fingers around her spine. "Cyrill, I have some cash in my purse. I'll go grab it."

Hector nodded in her direction, "See, Cyrill old boy, you should bring her more often. She knows better than to haggle with her dealer."

She quickly walked through the curtain with the journal clutched against her midriff, calling over her shoulder, "Be right back."

"Take your time, darling," Hector called in a more amicable voice.

With her heart beating in her ears, Jillian threw open the flower shop's door and stepped out into the autumn air. Like removing a hood from around her head, she could breathe more easily. She was unsure if her breathlessness was more due to the close air of the shop, or the book clasped in a death grip against her stomach. Rushing to her car, she fumbled to unlock the door and slid into the driver's seat. She felt the accusatory eyes of the journal on her, despite the fact that it didn't possess them. *There is still time. I could just return the book and say I mistakenly took it with me when I came out for the money.*

Shaking her head, Jillian knew what the right thing to do was but slipped the book into her purse all the same. Too many coincidences were providence. She pulled a pair of tens from her wallet and stepped from the car. No matter the cost, she would get to the bottom of at least one mystery today.

104

Chapter Seventeen
Traveler's Legacy

The journal was still on Jillian's passenger seat as she pulled into the restaurant's parking lot. The owner of Lobster Johnnie's must have had high hopes for franchising his brilliant idea for hamburger-seafood fusion but despite a loyal local following, the fact that there was only one location spoke volumes.

Primarily popular with the high school and college crowd, the red and black Greek Revival building's silhouette reminded her of a discount Parthenon, all neon and square column. Although it was a Friday night, the early hour made finding a parking spot less troublesome.

Jillian stepped out of her car and took a deep, fortifying breath. The light blue blouse and pencil skirt she'd worn to school served her well enough as blind date wear; her only compromise was to swap out her flats for a shiny pair of black patent leather Mary Jane pumps. The shoes only added a couple of inches to her 5'7 height but always seemed to boost her confidence. After all, this wasn't her first blind date.

Clusters of teens milled around near the restaurant's double glass doors, but leaning against one of the faded ivory columns was a man who stood out by at least a decade. His attention was fixed on the scrolling screen of his phone, an unfiltered cigarette hanging from loose lips. Occasionally, he would tense his mouth and the tip would glow red and snap up horizontal as he took a deep drag.

Twin streams of smoke would roll from his nostrils as he continued to browse whatever held his attention on the cell phone. He didn't seem to notice Jillian's presence until she softly called his name.

"Um … Charles?"

His eyes rose from the screen quickly, a smile coming to his lips. It caused the cigarette to dance briefly. "You must be Jill."

"I prefer Jillian," she corrected.

He shrugged dismissively, "You can call me Chuck. All my friends do."

I bet they do, Jillian thought but pasted a smile on her own face. "Okay, Chuck, do you want to go in?"

Again, he shrugged but pushed off of the column and gestured towards the doors. "Absolutely. I am starving." He took one final deep draw from his cigarette and then flicked it still lit into the parking lot. Chuck pulled the door open and stepped through, allowing his trailing heel to drag behind him to keep it from swinging closed on Jillian. "I love this place," he said as he approached the hostess's station.

Jillian caught the door and stared at his back in frustration. *It's going to be one of those nights.* "I've been here a few times when I was in college." She focused on maintaining an upbeat tone in her voice. "Do they still have the King Crab Patty?"

He nodded absently as he spoke to the girl behind the podium, "Table for two. By the window." He looked back to Jillian before quickly adding, "Please."

The hostess rolled her eyes and pulled two menus from a box besides the podium. "This way, folks."

They followed her to a small two person table near the back of the dining room, where she laid the menus on its surface and commented, "Lester will be your server. Have a nice night," before turning to walk away without waiting for a reply.

Chuck pulled out the chair facing the door and sat down. "They added Seafood Cheddar Biscuits last month. They're sort of like cheesy shrimp toast, you'll love them."

Jillian pulled out her own chair and sat down as well. "Sounds delicious. I love shrimp toast; it's always a treat."

"I'll get us an order." He raised his hand and beckoned a passing waiter with two fingers. "Hey, dude. Can you grab us an order of biscuits?"

The young man's eyes faltered a moment as Jillian could see him debating whether to mention that he wasn't the couple's waiter. In the end, he simply nodded and rushed towards the kitchen.

Chuck turned back to Jillian. "Marisol tells me you're a teacher too." Jillian nodded. "What's that like?"

"I love the kids but sometimes it can be a bit—"

"— I played lacrosse in high school. State champs three years in a row." Chuck's rugged good looks and close cropped, dirty blonde hair were offset by the smug smile that marred his expression, an expression that sat upon a face at least a decade past the accomplishments that he was about to regale her with.

Jillian felt an awkward smile come to her lips, "Sweet." Making a conscious effort to move beyond the casual way he'd interrupted her, she prompted, "What school?"

"Pope Innocent. Class of twenty eleven." She waited for him to return the courtesy, but she was disappointed. "I played defender, our line called ourselves the Legion of Stone."

"Because you were so good?"

"Damned right." Their server approached the table, biscuits in hand, interrupting what no doubt would have been a less than fascinating recap of Chuck's high school lacrosse career.

"Welcome to Lobster Johnnie's. My name is Lester and I'll be your server tonight. Can I start you off with some drinks?"

Before Jillian could respond, her date chuckled, "I don't know, Lester, can you?" He turned conspiratorially to her and said, "Kids today, hmm?" Chuck put his hand on Lester's forearm and gave him a condescending smile. "Les, the word 'can' indicates whether or not you are capable of a thing. I'll give you the benefit of the doubt that you are more than capable of taking our drink order. What you meant to say is 'May I start you with some drinks'."

Jillian saw the server's cheeks begin to color.

"Do you want to try again, big man?"

Clearing her throat, she spoke up, "Water is fine for me, thank you."

Chuck glanced at her from the corner of his eye but then added, "I'll have whatever light beer you have on tap."

Lester nodded and quickly turned from the table.

"Was that really necessary?"

Chuck shrugged. "I was just having some fun … busting his balls a bit. It's a guy thing."

Jillian just responded with, "Mm hmm." *Definitely going to be one of those nights.*

*****

It wasn't the worst date Jillian had ever been on but that had more to do with the plethora of unpleasant dates she'd experienced over the last few years than Chuck's company. As they left the restaurant, he pushed his way through the door first and favored her with the same heel drag

107

and hold to prevent it from slamming closed on her. Before Jillian had walked through herself, he had a cigarette pursed in his lips as he lit it with a mirrored chrome lighter. Exhaling a plume of gray-blue smoke, he turned to her. "Whatcha want to do now?"

Jillian looked over her shoulder towards the parking lot. "It's been a long day at the end of a long week. I think I'll head home."

Chuck's eyes brightened. "Alright, where're you parked?"

She pointed to her black subcompact. "Right over there, but I think I'm going to call it a night, Chuck."

A mixture of frustration and resentment hung in his eyes. "If you say so. I'll walk you to your car … if you want."

Despite herself, Jillian said, "That'd be nice."

As they reached her car, she used the key fob to unlock it. "Thank you for a nice evening," Jillian started as she turned to face him. Chuck was right behind her, causing her to have to brace her hand against his chest to prevent from colliding with the man.

"Yeah," he said, "Good night." She felt his hand at her waist as he pulled her closer.

Jillian stiffened her arm to maintain the small distance that remained between them. "Good night."

His face tightened into an angry scowl and turned on his heel. "Take care," he muttered over his shoulder and walked back towards the restaurant.

A thought flashed through Jillian's mind of its own accord, *Hollis risks his life and kills three men in order to keep Asaege's identity secret, but this guy can't even hold open a freakin' door.*

*****

Greeted by her typical yapping welcome, Jillian tossed her bag on the pillow filled futon that served her as a couch, content to forget about work for the weekend. In truth, she would likely surrender to the responsibilities of teaching that simply didn't fit within the school week tomorrow. For tonight, though, she had every intention of remaining firm in her pursuit of a work free couple of days. The apartment was dim, only illuminated by the flickering lamps that lit the central courtyard of her garden apartment building. Her feet knew the way down the hall of their own accord; she didn't bother to turn on any lights enroute to her bedroom.

As she stepped into the cluttered room, its cozy confines closed around her. The combination of the darkness and stillness seemed to draw the stress of the week from her like a sponge. Jillian took a deep breath and slowly exhaled through parted lips, releasing the last bit of tension as she collapsed on the unmade bed. She wasn't sure how long she laid there

108

like a spent balloon before she fumbled for the bedside lamp. A quick twist of her fingers and the room was thrown into a warm glow.

Reaching into her front pocket, Jillian pulled free the small plastic bag containing her share of the weed she and Cyrill had bought from Hector. Holding it up before her eyes, she noticed that while the buds seemed plump and fresh if not slightly small, there was still a fair amount of shake pooled among them. Both the buds and the detritus were a dark shade of green that she recognized from earlier in the week when Cyrill had brought over the first batch. Shaking the bag slightly, Jillian marveled at the way the light highlighted an almost purple tint to the leaves at the bottom.

Still studying the bag, she fumbled a bit and pulled open her bedside drawer. Her pipe and lighter were still sitting where she had left them. Wiggling herself into a sitting position, Jillian carefully opened the bag and took out a fair-sized bud and a pinch of shake, packing them both into the bowl. With a flick of her thumb, the flame leapt to life. Touching it to the bowl, she inhaled smoothly igniting the contents.

Jillian took two quick puffs before tamping the bowl with the end of her lighter. The smoke held in her lungs, she pulled her purse closer to where she was sitting. The weight of the journal felt like an anchor within the bag's confines. As she exhaled, Jillian pulled the small leather-bound book free and examined it carefully. Its cover was unremarkable and free of any symbol or writing. She flipped the journal open to a random page. The handwriting was neat and without flourish although it had a flow that Jillian's eye found pleasing.

As she scanned the page, her heart rose in her throat. There on the page, was Hollis's name.

*****

February 7, 2010

When I came to my senses in Taerh, Silvermoon was seated in an open window, overlooking a trio of fields in mid-harvest. A hard packed dirt road my reflection recognized as the Kings Road was visible on the edge of them. As I have come to expect, the forester's memories came rushing back with my first few breaths of the other world's air. After our confrontation with Haedren on the road, Walker accompanied me, Mika and the injured Ret to the town of Pinebrook where a priest of Olm was able to tend to the Northman's wounds.

After three days, Ret was finally on his feet once more, contrary to the frustrated cleric's advice. Although the gangrenous otherworldly bites were well on their way to healing, they remained raw and angry. Only by refusing to continue on were Silvermoon and Mika able to convince the Rangor to rest, although I do not believe that his promises would last more than a few more days. Mika sat across from Silvermoon, in mid conversation.

"... do not understand why the Herald left if Haedren and the broach were such a concern."

My mind reeled as I desperately tried to find a frame of reference. It came slowly as I tried to buy more time. "Neither do I."

My tone must not have been as convincing as I had intended. Mika studied me from the corner of her eye before continuing slowly. "Do not misunderstand, I would much rather be the ones to deal with the priest; he is one of ours, after all. I simply feel that the Walker is not telling us the entire tale."

I nodded slowly, "Mages seldom do. I do get the impression that she has no harmful intentions towards us, however."

Mika shrugged. "If you say so, 'Moon."

Even now, I shudder to think about the events on the King's Road the last time I was reflected. The venom in our friend's voice combined with the seemingly effortless way he dispatched the three of us still haunts me, even when I am safely within my own mind on Earth. What chills me to the core, however, is the dispassionate casualness in which he chose to end the lives of the men and woman who had traveled with him ... fought beside him for nearly fifteen years. "I have to believe Haedren is still in there but the man on that road bore no resemblance to our comrade. If ... when we catch up to him, we will have a difficult choice set before us."

Mika muttered, "Not so difficult should he turn his magic on us again."

I felt Silvermoon's horror at the woman's words. "He is our friend."

"... who tried to end all of our lives as one would step on an ant, Alexei." Mika's use of Silvermoon's first name told of her fear more accurately than any other words ever could. "Benefit of the doubt afforded him the opportunity to kill me once. I do not plan to give him another chance."

There was a tone of finality in her voice that gave me pause. Mika could not be more different than the Beatrice I know. My head spun as I sought to come to terms with this version of my lifelong friend. All I could manage was, "Let us hope it does not come to that."

She nodded once before rising in a sudden, almost violent motion. "I am going to take a walk ... check on Ret."

I let her go with a short wave. Although I don't know Haedren on this side, I am having issues coming to grips with sentencing him to death, given Silvermoon's memories of the man. Do I risk sharing what I have experienced with Beatrice and the others in an attempt to moderate the actions of their reflections? Do I have the right to control the actions

110

of Mika and Ret by subsuming their will with that of others? These questions weighed on me for the next two days as we waited for Ret to recover enough to travel and they continue to weigh on me as I write this. The crux of the matter is how much moral latitude does one possess in the name of 'doing the right thing'?

Although I only slept for a little over eight hours here, that time translated to almost four days in Taerh. I continue to wonder why time seems so fluid between there and here. I have turned to the writings of Dirac and Hilbert to understand this concept of relative time in both places. I have learned more about theoretical mathematics in the past few months than I had ever done in six years of college, or ever wanted to. The frustration I feel when trying to understand the phenomenon is nothing compared to that I feel when reflected.

Silvermoon continues to search for Haedren after their last encounter at the Crown of the First King. The Walker insists that he searches for what she refers to as the 'Well of Worlds'.

I'm put off by the contrast between Beatrice and her reflection, although I cannot help but see the wisdom of her words regarding the herald. The longer we cooperate with The Walker, the more her erratic nature becomes apparent. Sometimes, I believe she is not necessarily of two minds, but two separate people.

I fear the consequences of bringing my worries to Samantha, as each time I do, she becomes visibly upset. Her heart condition prevents her from using adder Root, and her inability to reflect weighs heavily upon her.

February 8, 2010

Marcus and Hollis had caught up with us in the time that I slept on this side, bearing mixed news. Their research within the Great Library turned up a treatise on the nature of possessed objects, referred therein as 'monstrae'. These objects are often imbued with a measure of their owners anima.

When used by a thaumaturge, it allowed them to draw upon that essence to fuel the taxing process of true magic. Although Marcus claims it is an arduous process to create one, it makes the owner quite a bit more dangerous than they would be without it. What makes this particular bit of trivia of concern to our current circumstances is what happens when a monstrae passes from the hands of its creator.

Coming into possession of another thaumaturge's monstrae gives the new owner not only a measure of the creator's power but also access to a portion of their knowledge as well. This would seem to provide a convenient way to circumvent the years of sacrifice and study in order *to secure insight into magic, which was the language of creation itself. Although seemingly quick and easy, it comes with an extremely puissant drawback. The anima within the object is not simply power and knowledge, but a measure of the creator themselves.*

Just as the new owner has access to the deepest secrets of the creator, so too is the depths of the new owner's soul open to the essence trapped inside. A plethora of cautionary tales spread across a score of works discovered by Hollis and Marcus tell of monstrae thieves literally possessed by the object they intended to harness for their own purposes.

When last we faced Haedren, he had in his possession a brooch of dark steel and bright silver. That same brooch was in the possession of the fallen Hand of Lies, Theamon, when the five us slew him months before. Marcus believes the brooch may be a monstrae containing a portion of the dark mage's soul and it is this that has caused Haedren's dramatic personality change. Silvermoon's memories, normally as clear as a mountain stream to me, were clouded when it came to the subject of Theamon. It almost seems as if my reflection is fighting to keep the knowledge from me. Any recollections prior to the battle on the road that I witnessed myself is fractured and disjointed.

I fear that Silvermoon and his five companions, self-dubbed the Band of Six, had a part in the former Hand of Lies' ascension to the power he wielded on that terror filled night. It's this shame that causes him to struggle to keep the truth a secret. Even Hollis's perpetual sunny demeanor becomes overcast when Theamon is mentioned, even in passing. Of all of my friends' reflections, it is Hollis that most pulls at my heart's strings. Silvermoon's love for the boy mirrors so closely mine for Stephen that I can scarcely bear the thought of him putting himself in danger. But put himself in peril he does, often and with seeming joyful abandon.

Knowing that the death of one's reflection here inevitably leads to one's own death in our world, I can't help fearing for the boy. Perhaps I should spend some of that fear on myself because Hollis may well have gotten a measure of his penchant for risky behavior from Silvermoon himself. Taerh continues to prove to be a paradox. Never have I felt so alive and so frightened for that life in the same breath.

*****

That final statement echoed in Jillian's mind as the weight of her eyelids finally overcame her will to remain awake and she drifted off to sleep. Beneath the languid feelings that pulled at her, Jillian's mind reveled in the journal entries that bore out the words of her dream-time co-conspirator.

Chapter Eighteen
With an Open Heart

Asaege woke as waves of dizziness crashed against her as the tide pounds the shore. She struggled into a sitting position, fighting the vertigo that washed over her. Her memories roiled like boiling water with recollections not her own bubbling to the surface as clearly as those of her days in the Great Library.

Her mind sprung to life with images of places she'd never visited and people she'd never known, yet each held a familiarity that she couldn't explain. In the center of this maelstrom was the face of an herbalist and a stolen journal. This must have been the journal of which Hollis spoke. A world apart from her, it remained forever out of reach … at least out of hers.

It is securely in the grip of my… what was the term Hollis had used? My reflection. Asaege focused on the image, but the light-headedness threatened to overwhelm her. Bracing her hand against the wall beside her humble bed, she tried to fight through the feeling and bring the memories to the surface. *Jillian. Her name is Jillian.* The vertigo redoubled as Asaege felt as if she were falling away from her own body. Instinctively, she reached out, releasing the wall beside her. Asaege fell to the hard wood floor in a heap.

With the dizziness came a flood of memories and sensations belonging to Jillian. She saw a brightly lit building full of teachers and students; it was a miasma of smiling eyes and disapproving frowns. The taste of light, sugary treats and thick, dank smoke filled her senses. She could picture the faces of friends and acquaintances, lovers and enemies; Asaege knew none of them. The blur of Jillian's life was an ever-expanding tapestry of memories. Asaege rode upon the crest of the wave of recollections as driftwood upon the ocean.

Her own consciousness fought against the deluge as if she were drowning. Asaege struggled against the wash of alien recollections that sought to overpower her personality. Fear gripped her heart as the tenuous grasp she held on herself began to slip away. As suddenly as it'd appeared, the vertigo faded and with it the foreign memories. Curled upon the floor, Asaege lay still, herself once more.

She focused on simply breathing.

In and out. In and out.

Asaege had no idea how long she had lain there, eyes clenched tightly shut and breathing slowly. Carefully, she opened her eyes and experimentally tried to sit up. The dizziness was gone as if it had never been. All she felt was the soreness in her shoulder where she'd landed after falling out of bed. Bracing her hands against the floor, she slowly climbed to her feet. The mid-morning sun seeped through cracks in the shutters, throwing the room into dappled relief. The academic in her was tempted to try to recall Jillian's memories again but fear seized her.

I almost lost myself the last time, she thought, *I am not sure I am prepared to give it another attempt so soon.*

The choice was taken from her hands when there came a light rapping upon the door to her humble room. "One moment," Asaege called as she gingerly climbed to her feet. When the expected vertigo didn't return, she brushed the dust from her dressing gown and opened the door.

Tawn stood on the other side, her hands clasped before her. The thumb of her right roughly massaged the space between the thumb and forefinger of her left. "Asaege," she tentatively began, "There are some people here to see you."

Asaege silently mouthed, "Binders?" She poked her head through the door and risked a glance down the stairs. No one but her landlord and friend was within sight.

Shaking her head, Tawn continued, "It is Risa, the weaver's wife, as well as Dunst and Yarl from down the block." Asaege recalled that the brothers had managed to scratch out a meager living as unskilled laborers in the Dock District.

"Did they say what they wanted?"

Her surprise evident on her face, Tawn whispered, "They are all here to learn to read."

114

*****

As Asaege climbed the stairs, she felt as if her heart floated ahead of her. So lost was she in the joy of teaching, a cherished although lapsed visitor, that she almost missed the now familiar figure in her small room. Hollis had once again made himself comfortable on Asaege's bed, his hands tucked behind his head. His right eye opened slightly, revealing only a slit of his deep brown iris. Mostly containing her gasp of surprise, Asaege growled, "I am afraid that this is becoming too much of a habit, Hollis."

The thief slowly closed his eye and smiled softly. "It would be less so were you here when I came calling."

"I would be here if you let me know when you were planning on stopping by."

Hollis pulled his arms from behind him and stretched unhurriedly before pushing himself upright into a sitting position, "Seems like an impasse to me."

"Not as much as you seem to believe," Asaege muttered. Without waiting for a response, she continued, "Is there something I may do for you, Hollis?" She found that the annoyance in her tone didn't have a match in her heart. She wasn't sure if it was from the high of teaching again ... or something else.

"Can not one friend visit another?" He nodded at the small table to her right. "Besides, I came bearing gifts ..."

Asaege absently shifted her eyes to see what he'd brought. She nearly choked when she saw what lay so casually on the rough wooden surface. The tome was wrapped in stained leather so dark it almost appeared black. Although it bore indication of neither title nor author, the meticulously inscribed platinum buckle left little doubt as to what was contained within its pages. Written in a kind of shorthand used by those initiated in the ways of magic, the inscription read simply: *Property of Marcus the Green. Trespass at your own peril.*

"Is that what I think it is?" Asaege knew the answer but uncharacteristically found herself at a loss for words.

Hollis nodded. "It belonged to ..." He paused, his eyes going blank for a moment, before continuing. "It belonged to an old friend who no longer has need of it."

She eyed the book suspiciously. "Is it locked? Will it —"

"Blow your hand off?" Hollis finished, crossing the room in a few quick steps. "Most likely. Marcus was quite possessive of his things and went to frankly disturbing lengths to safeguard them. I would be surprised if you escaped with just a bloody stump, actually."

Asaege tried to contain her excitement but felt it straining to escape

115

her chest in a bubbling laugh. In a low, childlike voice, she whispered, "Can you open it?"

Hollis nodded quickly and muttered a pair of words that hung in the air like the echo of a great pipe organ. There was power in those words, power that Asaege recognized.

That recognition tempered her excitement slightly. "I studied some magic designed to safeguard during my time in the library, but I have never been able to actually feel the discharge of protective magic before."

"As I mentioned, Marcus was fairly serious when it came to his possessions." Hollis casually shrugged before continuing, "I think it had something to do with his childhood."

Asaege's curiosity about the book and its owner warred within her, but the book won out very quickly. "Is it safe to open?" Her hand already hovered over the leather cover.

"It should be. The same words lock it again."

She didn't wait for him to finish before pulling the worn leather strap free of the buckle. "I thought you said you were not initiated," Asaege said as she opened the long unused grimoire.

"I am not. The words themselves hold no more power than the spell laid upon the book gives them. As such, they do not fly from the mind in the same way that other thaumaturgical syllables do."

"You must have been a good friend indeed for him to share them with you."

"He did not exactly give them to me." Asaege glanced up quickly to see the now familiar glint in the thief's eye. "As I said, Marcus was not much for sharing." She broke eye contact and returned to examining the book, despite her interest in Hollis's story. "Although cryptic, like I said, the words were not shrouded in any real way. I simply listened each time he opened the book and eventually was able to master his pass phrase."

On the vellum pages before Asaege were formulae for spells beyond anything she'd ever seen before. Each one was written in a precise hand, using the same shorthand notation as the buckle's inscription. Flipping to a random page, she found a mystical incantation and its accompanying instructions. According to the notes, it was designed to soften a section of earth, causing it to become as mud beneath your feet.

Written across the top of the page was 'Trologue's Transmutation'. The spell itself seemed brief to the point of being concise although the instructions were anything but. They seemed to go on for three pages, offering changes to emphasis and intonation depending on the material to be transformed or depth affected.

Asaege lifted her eyes to meet Hollis's. "This is worth a fortune." It was a statement, but her question was obvious.

He purred, "Perhaps," not giving her the satisfaction of answering it.

"I do not wish to look too closely at a boon's nature but …" she let her words trail off.

"Look a gift horse in the mouth?" Hollis spoke the familiar phrase in English before repeating it in Trade Tongue. It came out as 'Feel the gums of a free horse' and felt wrong in his ear.

Asaege regarded him briefly through crinkled eyes before returning her attention to the book.

"You certainly have more use for it than I do, and I do not normally move in circles that would be interested in such an item."

Feeling silly arguing the point, she continued to indulge her curiosity. "Anyone in the Great Library would have given you a prince's ransom for this book, perhaps even traded it for the book you sought there."

Asaege heard his teeth clicking closed, his voice forced between them. "The book is mine, bought and paid for. I am not in the habit of paying a second time for something that I already own." So extreme was his reaction that it tore her attention from the pages, but when she looked up, Hollis's easy grin was again painted on his lips. "I thought it made a better gift for you but if I was mistaken …"

When he casually reached for the book, she gathered it in her arms. "I never said that!"

Hollis let his hand drop to his side, nodding shallowly. "That is what I thought." His eyes shifted away from hers, "I will admit to having ulterior motives, though."

Wryly, she responded, "Witness my lack of surprise."

Hollis squinted at her, "We have not known each other for nearly long enough for you to be this jaded."

"The evidence would seem to say otherwise." Despite her mocking tone, Asaege's heart fluttered in her chest, something she wasn't all together sure had to do with the thief's gift.

Watching him through hooded eyes, she admired (not for the first time) his easy smile. Although beyond the thin walls of her tiny room, pursuers on both sides of the law sought his blood for crimes not his own, the man before her could grin as easily as a child at play. In the depths of his mahogany eyes, beyond the mischievous sparkle, was something that Asaege could only describe as steadiness. More than confidence and stopping a hair's breadth short of arrogance, Hollis's calm stare spoke of a path through their current troubles, even if it wasn't apparent to those around him.

A warmth rose in her cheeks, tucking her head further into the book clutched in her arms, she awkwardly changed the subject. "You mentioned some sort of ulterior motive?"

"If we are going to continue to 'tag'," Hollis used the English word, "buildings with quotes from your book, we are going to have to have more to rely on than luck and positive thoughts."

A wave of lightheadedness swept through Asaege; the foreign word hit her ear like a bee sting, yet she understood its meaning. She shook her head softly to clear the fog. "You believe the book may contain that very thing?"

"I do. Marcus was the most talented thaumaturge I have known this side of the Walker ..." Hollis paused for a moment too long. She watched the corner of his mouth twitch as he spoke the Herald's name. He closed his eyes and continued, "I think the contents of that book give us a much better chance of coming and going in safety."

"I can try. I was barely initiated before I left the library and from what I can tell, there are some pretty advanced concepts in here." She continued to clutch the valued tome against her chest, her fingertips white against the leather binding.

Hollis reached out, hooking his finger under her chin and tilted her gaze up to meet his. "I have faith in you, Asaege." The words sank into her heart like rain on parched sand. "Do what you can; anything you can learn is more than we have now."

Again, the thief's soft brown eyes bored into hers. In their depths, Asaege found no trace of trepidation; she found it infectious. She pulled away from his finger, the heat of his flesh on hers leaving a phantom sensation even when removed. Turning her back on him, Asaege stalked towards the small table in the corner and laid the book down.

As she pulled the cover back, she spoke over her shoulder. "I do not have any students coming by until tomorrow, so I can get started right now."

She imagined his raised eyebrow as his voice dropped to a growl, "Students?"

Asaege nodded "Yes. A handful of locals who want to learn to read."

Suspicion crawled into Hollis's voice. "Do you not find that a tad bit convenient?"

She continued to focus on the book in front of her. "Word of messages written on alley walls throughout the Ash has spread." Asaege could almost feel the thief's glare against her back. "It has ignited a desire to read them for themselves."

"And they came to you?"

"It is common knowledge that I used to teach at the Academy Athenaeum."

"Common or not, it puts you squarely in the sights of any motivated to make sure those in the darkness of ignorance stay there … not to mention any who are able to make a leap of logic from a troublesome teacher to the message's true author."

"That would have to be a hell of leap."

"The sun shines on even a dog's ass some days."

Asaege turned on him, "What would you have me do, Hollis? Turn them away? Tell them, 'I am sorry, I have the skills to help you better yourself, but I choose to let you drown in squalor because I am afraid of a mutt getting a tan'?"

Hollis nodded, "I am not sure I would use those words but that is absolutely what I would have you do."

"Did we not intend to make people think? Is that not what we wanted when we started this endeavor?"

Hollis sighed deeply. "In theory, it seemed a more sound principle than it does in the harsh light of reality. I was far more comfortable when it was someone else doing the teaching."

"So, you are comfortable putting some faceless stranger in danger than ourselves?"

"Damned right, I am. We are already taking plenty of risks."

Without thinking, Asaege snapped, "You are selfish."

Hollis recoiled a moment. "How do you figure that?"

"For the good of the many, the few must make sacrifices. Does the fact that they are faceless make it easier to abandon them? Just because you do not know them does not make them any less worthy of help." For the first time since meeting the thief, Asaege saw anger filling his eyes like a fast moving, summer storm.

Through gritted teeth, Hollis hissed, "I did not know you, did I?"

His words did what the fury in his eyes could not. "I am sorry. I should never have said that. You aided me when you had no reason to do so and I will always be grateful for that."

He remained silent, his slow, deep breathing causing his nostrils to flare rhythmically.

Asaege placed her hand on his forearm and repeated, "I am sorry."

With a shallow nod, Hollis spoke, "A great deal of people have a great deal to say about me. Not a lot of it is complementary, but the one thing that cannot be said is that I have not known sacrifice."

"I know. I spoke too hastily."

"You did."

Asaege managed a guilty smile. "But you only have yourself to blame."

He frowned. "Is that so?"

"Yes. You are putting yourself in a tremendous amount of danger for someone you barely know. How can I not be willing to do the same?"

Hollis smirked, opening his mouth to respond, no doubt something wry and sarcastic, but paused as her words truly struck him.

Encouraged by his silence, Asaege continued, "It is a case of 'learn by example' gone wrong. I have never been a 'do as I say, not as I do' kind of person and I am willing to bet that you are not either."

"Do you realize the risk?"

"I do … and I will be the one taking it. If we are truly partners in this, then we need to be partners in risk and reward."

He muttered, "I suppose."

"You trust me to go through that," she nodded towards the book on the table "You trust me to go out night after night with you to commit Olm's words to brick and mortar. So, which is it? Am I charity … a poor wretch on which you have taken pity, or are we partners?"

Hollis nodded. "Partners."

She smiled softly. "I knew you would see it my way."

His smirk blossomed into a 'cat who ate the canary' smile. "And seeing as we are partners, perhaps you can do something to help me …"

*****

"I am not sure about this," Asaege protested. She sat tailor style on her small bed, Hollis kneeling in front of her. He held her left hand in both of his.

"Relax, Magpie. I know it is uncomfortable at first, but I assure you it is as natural as breathing. Close your eyes."

She did as requested, but almost immediately opened her right eye a slit.

"Both eyes, please," his voice was a soft rumble, barely above a whisper. "Let your mind relax and drift. The key to trying to reflect lies in not trying at all. The more you force it, the harder it is to do."

Asaege's curiosity got the best of her. She blurted out, "How did you learn?"

Without a trace of irritation in his voice, Hollis simply responded, "I had help." He squeezed her hand gently. "Now, please just let your mind wander … let it go where it wants."

"I am trying," she muttered.

"Stop. I understand that it is hard but let everything go. Be in this moment, right here … right now. There is nothing outside this room … outside of the two of us." He gently squeezed her hand. "Our hands and my voice."

Asaege took a deep breath and let the tension she hadn't realized she'd been carrying escape her body with her exhale. She felt the warmth of Hollis's skin on her own; the sensation of it caused a delicious chill to spread up her forearm and caused the fine hairs found there to stand on end. As he spoke, the subtle force of his breath caressed her throat where it met collarbone.

"Listen to the tone of my voice but let the words wash over you like the waves on a beach."

His dulcet voice made her feel as if she were wrapped in a lamb-soft blanket and caused her head to spin. At first, she fought for control, as would a swimmer rolled in the undertow. Hollis's thumb rubbed the back of her hand in slow, gentle circles; his voice continued to drone in an increasingly arcane tapestry of placating sounds.

As she gave herself to the comforting vertigo that spun around her, she felt as if something inside her snapped. As the maelstrom of sensation swept her away, the last image in her mind was that of another woman … one she'd never met, but recognized as if they shared the same womb.

Chapter Nineteen
An Unexpected Legacy

Jillian opened her eyes in a room she didn't recognize, her hand clenched between those of a man she'd never met. She snatched it away as she recoiled from him. Her back struck the wall behind the narrow bed on which she sat. "Who are you? Where am I?" The two questions exploded from her in rapid succession. Even the sound of her voice seemed strange to her ears. She recognized it, of course, but it seemed richer somehow. The words themselves had a crispness to them, seeming formal and unfamiliar at the same time.

Her mind reeled with the unfamiliarity of her surroundings, but beneath the panic a steady stream of words not her own repeated themselves with the insistent agony of a favorite song, seldom heard but encompassing in its desire to be vocalized.

Like a hidden itch begging to be scratched, the alien phrases surged to the forefront of her thoughts. Acknowledging them seemed to cause them to redouble their efforts to break free, almost as if the words had a mind of their own and demanded release. It took a moment to realize that the man before her was also speaking.

He spoke gently, his tone sure and even as he repeated himself, "You are safe." Once Jillian's eyes focused on his, the man continued, "But reflection can be disorienting. Please just focus on breathing."

She understood his meaning, despite the fact that his words themselves struck her as a rush of odd sounds. She felt a sensation like the pricking of needles at the back of her eyes as her head began to swim, but she was able to push the alien thoughts to the back of her mind for the time being and focus on the man before her.

He spoke again, his voice low, "Take a few easy, deep breaths."

The stranger's voice … his face pulled at her mind like a forgotten memory, just beyond her reach. Each time she thought it within her grasp it slipped through her fingers like smoke. She felt a tightening in her chest as her heart beat a staccato rhythm in her ears. Jillian clawed at the simple, homespun dress she wore as she gasped for air that wouldn't seem to come.

Again, the stranger was there. "Listen to my voice. If you do not calm down, you are going to pass out and neither of us wants that." He reached out to take her right hand between his again. "Breathe with me. In … and out … in … and out."

She closed her eyes tightly and despite her fright, tried to focus on his voice.

"In … and out … in … and out."

Gripping his hand as if it were the only real thing in the world, she did as he bid and shortly, the wicked claws around her chest loosened. As her breathing slowed, she opened her eyes once more. Before her was the same familiar - not familiar face. While not conventionally handsome, the soft curves of his cheeks and fine lines at the corners of his eyes certainly didn't make him unappealing. His bald head was coated in a fine sheen of sweat; it glistened in the afternoon light that filtered through the window behind him. A wry smile hung on his full lips, nestled in a bushy mass of salt and pepper facial hair.

"That is it," his smile deepened. "Do you feel a bit better?"

Jillian nodded absently. "I do not understand." Her brow wrinkled, the words hitting her ears wrong. She repeated the statement in English; the words felt strange on her tongue. "I don't understand."

The man before her responded in the same language, flawlessly switching to it. "I know. I'll do my best to help you put the pieces together."

His kind brown eyes held an understanding that threatened to overwhelm her. Like water from a broken dam, realization crashed over her. She recognized the man before her, but not from her waking hours. The dreams. "Hollis," she blurted before she could stop herself.

He simply bobbed his head.

"But you're just a figment of my imagination."

Hollis shook his head slowly. "Not exactly." He squeezed her hand gently as he spoke, "I thought that as well … at least at first."

"At first?"

"Not so long ago, I was in your place, except the only person willing to help me was doing so ..." he paused for a moment, the corners of his mouth turning down in a tight frown. "Let's just say they had their own reasons for aiding me and my well-being wasn't among them."

Beneath the smooth tone of his voice, Jillian could hear the hollow echo of pain. As quickly as it came, the cloud that covered his features passed and his frown disappeared like fog in the morning sun. "I'll do my best to make sure you don't have that problem."

"Thank you?" Jillian's voice was tentative but the steady look in his eyes and confident smirk steadied her nerves. "Is this a dream or not?"

Hollis chuckled softly before responding, "It is and it isn't." He released her hand and vigorously rubbed at his cheeks. "It's been too long since I've spoken English. It's almost as if it requires a different set of muscles."

She dismissed his complaint with a quick shake of her head, trying to bring him back to the point at hand. "It is and it isn't?"

"In your world, you are indeed sleeping but it's that slumber that gives your consciousness the ability to cross over to Taerh." He spread his hands out, palms up to indicate the world in which they occupied. "Normally, it requires a nudge though. Did you drink tea before you fell asleep?"

Jillian shook her head. "Caffeine keeps me up."

"This would be a special tea, made from a plant called Adder Root." He held up his right hand. "Deep green leaves the size of your pinky nail with purple veins."

A feeling of dread washed over Jillian, as if ice water rather than blood flowed through her. In a small voice, Jillian whispered, "I think I've seen a plant like that."

"Where?" Hollis's words snapped like a whip, the man suddenly seeming too anxious.

She narrowed her eyes suspiciously, "I'm sure you wouldn't know it."

His voice dropped to a rumbling growl, "Try me."

"Marcheur Florist and Holistic Medicine on —"

"Spring Street next to the Castor and Pollux Diner?" Hollis chuckled, although it wasn't a jovial sound, "I'm acquainted with it."

A rush of questions fought within Jillian's mind, demanding to be asked. She settled for, "How?"

Ignoring her question, he pressed forward with one of his own, "What of the old woman who owns the shop?" Despite the calm aura Hollis tried to maintain, Jillian could feel his panic as if it were a heat radiating from him. His eyes shifted back and forth, studying something that he alone could see.

She frowned deeply. "I don't know about any woman. The flower shop is owned by a man. I think his name is Hector-Something."

Hollis closed his eyes for a moment and exhaled as if he'd been holding his breath for a lifetime. "That's still pretty bad news but it's miles better than the alternative."

It was Jillian's turn to reach out and seize his hand between both of her own. "Stop." His mouth slowly closed as his eyes shifted to their intertwined hands. "I'm missing something ... several somethings from the sound of it. Start from the beginning."

*****

Hollis's story would have been completely unbelievable was Jillian not currently in the middle of her own equally improbable one. "I'm fairly sure that the Plague Man has the brooch now. It's too dangerous to be allowed to fall into anyone's hands, much less ones as deranged as his."

Jillian placed her hand on his shoulder, "It's not your fault."

"Whether or not I can be held accountable, I am responsible. A chance to put an end to it in that cave was right there and I missed it."

Her head swam for a moment as her stomach lurched with vertigo. Jillian was forced to squeeze his shoulder tightly to avoid pitching forward. A rush of memories that she only half recognized threatened to overcome her. Images of a hurried retreat through a forest of dark wood bookcases assaulted her. She felt her heart pounding in her chest as within a split second, she relived the terror of Asaege and Hollis's first meeting in the Great Library. *He came to the library looking for a book.* A thought not her own forced itself into her mind. *His book must have something to do with the brooch.* Jillian felt as if she were falling as her eyes rolled back into her head.

Hollis's arm wrapped around her, giving her something real to seize onto and find her center again. She could have sworn she felt a flash of anger as the light-headed feeling faded. "Take a few deep breaths."

"I remember a library," she began as she slowly opened her eyes. "You were looking for a book."

"That's correct. It was stolen from me a month or so ago in Ghath. I had thought it simply an unfortunate coincidence but if Hector has a steady supply of adder root, it's almost assured that he and his own reflection are in contact."

"Is that bad?"

"It's not good."

"Why do I remember your book so clearly? I had a dream a few nights ago —" A wave of impatience rolled through her again.

126

Hollis filled the silence with an explanation, "Your reflection's name is Asaege. She and I ran into some issues a week or so ago in the Great Library. That same trouble prevented me from retrieving my property and then I got ..." He seemed to search for a word but settled on, "Side-tracked."

"Do you mean that Asaege is in," Jillian tapped her temple, "here?"

Hollis nodded. "That she is, and I have a feeling that she's not all that pleased."

Remembering the white-hot anger, she lowered her voice to a tense whisper, "She's pissed."

He laughed out loud. It was a deep, ringing sound that broke the tension that filled the room.

"It's not funny."

Hollis's laugh settled into a soft chuckle, "The two of you are going to have to learn to get along or neither of you is going to get anything done."

"And how do you propose that we do that? How did you and Stephen make peace?"

He shrugged. "I —" He quickly corrected himself, "We just did. Despite our differences, we were at our foundations, very much the same."

"Not helpful."

Hollis spread his hands helplessly. "Try to focus on your similarities rather than your differences. What drives you?"

"I am a teacher ..."

"That's something; Asaege is as well ... despite how vehemently I object."

Jillian closed her eyes and pictured herself in her classroom. She could smell the sweet-sour scent of dry erase markers and freshly printed worksheets. The remembered scents brought a smile to her lips; despite the frustrations of administration and co-workers, she felt the freedom that came at the front of her classroom. The faces of her students turned towards her in rapt attention caused the stress of the day to fall from her shoulders like a woolen blanket and allowed her soul to fly.

A sense of calm settled on her like the feather light touch of the season's first snow. Her mind still wrestled with the implications of Hollis's words, but those worries seemed wrapped in cotton gauze, the troubles of another day. In place of the simmering annoyance that had haunted the edges of her perception since awakening in Taerh, she only felt a fortifying presence in the back of her mind. Layered with her own memories of crisp autumn days in her own classroom, there were images of places she never visited. Unfamiliar faces watched her, lit by candlelight and curiosity. Although she recognized neither surrounding nor student, they seemed familiar.

These must be Asaege's memories, she thought, *although worlds separated us, it's amazing how similar our experiences are*. Jillian found the experience intoxicating, delving further into her reflection's memories. With no more effort than it would've taken her to remember her ATM password, she brought to mind Asaege's happiest days, spent among the towering shelves of the Great Library. Once she'd completed her duties for the day, her time was her own. Very often, she'd lost entire afternoons wandering the seemingly endless stacks. *So much knowledge in one place, free for any mind inquiring enough to seek it out*.

Jillian's stomach twisted, shattering the cloak of calm that had lain across her heart. Unbidden, another memory came to the fore; dirty-faced teens staring longingly at the massive oak doors of the library. Two armor clad men stood guard before them, their faces twisted into sneers of disgust. The remembrance shattered like fine crystal, making way for another. A half dozen soot-stained faces huddled around a single candle, listening as Asaege read from a purloined tome. As this memory gave way to yet another, a feeling of dread not her own began to gnaw at Jillian's gut.

Dark cherry wood and gilded ivory dominated the headmaster's office. It would have been beautiful if not for the deep frown of the red-faced man standing across the massive desk from Asaege. His words, hissed through clenched teeth, were as clear as the day they were spoken, "If we simply give away knowledge, it becomes worthless." Jillian felt Asaege's despair as he continued, "You have stolen from academy and library alike and given to those undeserving of its gifts." His final words rang like a churchyard bell, "You are banished from these halls."

Jillian felt the anger rising in her again, but this time directed elsewhere. She wasn't certain that some of her own wasn't mixed within the emotion. No matter the source, the fury shattered the last of the tranquility, leaving Jillian confused. She slowly opened her eyes to find Hollis watching her patiently.

"The first time is often the most difficult." He again spoke Trade Tongue, its clipped proper tones hitting her ears awkwardly after their time speaking English.

She was slow to respond, forming words carefully in what should have been an unfamiliar language, "I do not understand. I do not know this language and yet, I can speak it."

"Do not focus too much on it. Someone once told me that the best way to deal with the complications of reflection is to try not to try, if that makes sense."

Despite herself, Jillian laughed softly. "That is ridiculous."

128

"Is it? At some point you learned to ride a …" He paused, searching for a word and ended up settling for the English term, "… bike."

She nodded.

Returning to Trade Tongue, Hollis continued. "It is very much like that. If you focus too much on the process of it, it becomes more difficult to do. But if you let your body remember how to ride, everything just sort of works. Skills from this side are very much like that, except it was not you who learned them but your reflection."

"So, anything that Asaege can do …" Jillian allowed her question to hang in the air.

"Theoretically, you can as well," Hollis finished. "But," he added, "For now, I would focus on building a relationship. If you are anything like her, I fear there is a good deal of stubbornness to overcome."

She frowned at him, feeling indignation for them both. "I can feel us building common ground already."

He flashed her a smile. "You do not need to thank me."

"I was not going to."

Hollis shrugged, "In the meantime, can we get back to how you ended up here in the first place?"

"You are the expert."

He chuckled. "I am familiar with the phenomenon; what I am more curious about is the specifics. You said that you did not drink the adder root tea and I am sure that if you had eaten it, there would be no doubt in your mind that you had done so." Hollis grimaced, indicating a not so pleasant first-hand experience.

Jillian shifted her eyes downward, inexplicably feeling self-conscious. "I must have smoked it."

A short-lived expression of confusion crossed Hollis's face. "Oh?" It quickly blossomed into understanding. "Oh! I suppose that is one way to get around the taste."

"Adder root has a taste?"

"I suppose not when put into a marijuana cigarette," the last two words were spoken in English.

Jillian couldn't contain the bubbling giggle that rushed from her lips. "A what?"

Hollis repeated sheepishly, "A marijuana cigarette."

She snickered, "No one has called it that since the days of Reefer Madness in the thirties."

He snapped, "That is illegal," obviously before completely thinking it through.

"Are we seriously going to discuss legality, Hollis the Slender?" Jillian smiled, trying to soften her words. "At least I paid for it."

129

Hollis opened his mouth to retort, but seemed to think better of it. Furling his brows, he conceded, "You make a reasonable point." He dismissed whatever train of thought boiled behind his eyes with a quick shake of his head. "I feel that it is not much of a leap to assume that Hector is using the florist shop as a front to sell …" He searched for an appropriate term.

"Pot," Jillian supplied.

"Pot," Hollis repeated, "Pot that he is lacing with adder root for some reason."

"Why? What good does it do him?"

He thought for a moment before responding. "That is the sixty-four thousand noble question," paraphrasing the English saying into Trade Tongue. "I can only think of one reason someone would want folks you do not care for reflecting." Hollis's expression darkened as if a cloud covered the sun that was his usual jovial demeanor. "And it does not bode well for anyone he is selling the adder root spiked product to."

Jillian frowned. "I am missing something."

"The only thing that can activate a Well is the blood of another reflection."

She felt as if a lump had formed in her throat, the ramifications of his words settling upon her. Mouth suddenly dry, it took a pair of swallows for her to form the words, "He wants to kill me?"

He bit his bottom lip softly, allowing a moment of silence to hang in the air between them. To Jillian, it seemed to stretch into eternity. When Hollis finally spoke, he'd found his soft comforting tone once more. "I do not think he is targeting you specifically. I imagine he is casting a fairly wide net; any caught within it will suffice for his purposes."

Neither his tone nor his words helped mitigate her panic. "Is he capable of carrying through with it?"

"Without a doubt. He was extremely dangerous before learning to reflect; I do not imagine that it dulled his edge any."

Suddenly breathless, Jillian rasped, "What do I do?"

Hollis sighed. "The good news is that, most likely, you are one of many he has seeded with the adder root. There is no reason to believe you are in any immediate danger."

"Most likely? No reason to believe? I am not hearing anything that is filling me with an abundance of confidence."

"Plague Man, Hector's reflection, is based in Slaze, which is at least a half week's ride from Oizan. There is a good chance he is not even in the area."

"'Good chance' still does not sound certain."

"I will admit that, from a certain perspective, it seems grim." Jillian simply watched him with furrowed brow. "Do you know him well on the other side?"

She shook her head, "I only met him once. It was an introduction by a friend."

"Well, there you go. It sounds like you are not even on his radar," the last word was spoken in English, as there was no equivalent in Trade Tongue. "His target is most likely someone else, someone he already had his eye on."

"There is 'most likely' again."

"Sometimes 'most likely' is the best you can expect."

"Who is this 'someone else'?"

"Does it matter?" Despite his attempt to keep his face impassive, Jillian saw Hollis's brow wrinkle with concern.

"It kind of does. There is someone out there marked for death by a murderer. What if it is my friend? We have to stop him."

Hollis rolled his eyes. "We? I hope you are referring to yourself and Asaege."

Jillian smiled meekly, "I am sure we cannot do it alone."

Cursing beneath his breath, he muttered, "The two of you are more alike than either of you would like to realize. Courtesy of Stephen, I have been known to have an altruistic streak; you both more than give him a run for his money."

"I did not hear you say no."

Hollis exhaled sharply. "No, you did not." Her smile broadened, causing him to raise a finger. "But I am not going to do it alone. It will require work on both sides. I can try to locate the Plague Man and if …" Hollis dropped his voice, "… if I can find out where he is, perhaps I can convince one of the dwindling number of folk who are not actively looking to betray me to keep an eye on him until I can attend to it personally."

The consequences of Hollis's words settled on Jillian's mind like a heavy cloak. "Do you mean kill him?"

He slowly nodded. "I do not see another way to stop whatever he has planned."

She felt her heart rise into her throat. "I have never been responsible for someone's death."

Hollis laid his hand on her shoulder, "And you will not be responsible for his either. Plague Man has taken far too much from me; his death or mine was inevitable since The Stone City."

Jillian wanted to believe him, so closing her eyes, she decided to do so. Changing the subject, she spoke, "You mentioned something you needed from me."

Studying her, Hollis took a moment to respond. "If we can prevent

Hector from reflecting … from causing others to do so, it will buy us some time to sort things out. You know what the adder root looks like, correct?" She nodded. "All you need to do is deprive him of it. I do not much care what you do. Steal it, Kill it. Burn down his store. Dealer's choice." He met her eyes with an intense glare. "Whatever you need to do in order to make sure he cannot use the plant or sell it to anyone else, get it done."

"That is it?"

Hollis thought for a moment, a self-assured smirk returning to his lips. "While you are there, he has possession of some journals that belong to me. Save enough adder root so we can continue to talk. I need to know what is in those journals."

Chapter Twenty
Legacy of a Dream

The sun filtered into Jillian's room through half open blinds, coloring her vision a soft crimson behind closed lids. She tried in vain to cling to the adder root fueled dream but the harder she struggled to sink back into its numbing embrace the further from her grasp it drifted. While the dream state faded like so much smoke in the breeze, the memories of it were as clear in her mind as if they were her own. Opening her eyes slowly, she felt a tinge of disappointment at the sight of her small, cluttered bedroom.

Beside her on the bed was the journal she'd been reading before slumber had taken her the night before. It lay, half open, on the rose-colored duvet, a leather tumor against the backdrop of soft linen. Jillian reached out for it, but stopped, her fingers hovering scant inches from the weathered spine. She was an educated woman, free of the fancies that she'd indulged in during her childhood. Yet, this book evoked in her a trepidation that she couldn't easily explain.

It was simply a book, a leather-bound collection of paper and ink. Its nature wasn't what made it so frightening to the woman; rather what the writing held within represented. Its pages reinforced the delusions that Jillian desperately wanted to dismiss as a handful of vivid dreams. *But is that truly what I want?* Just as it had before she drifted off to sleep, the last line she read echoed in her mind: *Never have I felt so alive and so frightened for that life in the same breath.*

When she dreamt, Jillian felt something she'd somehow lost in her waking life: freedom of purpose. Even when her dreams consigned her to the role of an observer, she could taste the sweet flavor of liberty … the liberty to make the world a better place, free of the crushing weight of expectations and bureaucracy. Asaege sought to change her small section of Taerh in spite of how 'things were done'. She'd struggled through disappointment and disaster, yet her motivation never wavered. There was inspiration in that.

Closing her eyes, Jillian focused on her breathing. She could almost hear Hollis's voice in her ear. *Breathe with me. In … and out … in … and out.* She imagined his hands in hers … the sensation of his skin on hers. *In … and out.* A sense of calm fell over her, softening the edges of her unease. Beneath it, she could feel a sense of wonder not quite her own. *Asaege?* she thought. Of course, there was no answer. That's not to say that there wasn't a reaction. Memories crashed upon Jillian's recollection like the white-capped rapids of a swollen river.

Peeking through squinted eyes, she remembered Hollis's stubbled cheeks and concerned frown. She could almost feel his callused fingertips against her palms. Faster and faster, memories flooded her senses: Reading by candlelight, the pages between her fingers darkened by age. Running through the maze-like streets of the Craftsman's District with her childhood friends beside her, their laughter echoing from the daub and brick buildings. The agony-rush of releasing a spell from her mind, like scratching a previously unreachable itch. As if a dam had broken, recollections not her own began to sweep away Jillian's sense of self.

Panicked, she snapped her eyes open; the treasured calm and unwanted memories evaporated as if they'd never been.

Jillian's heart beat a furious staccato rhythm in her chest, forcing her to half sit, half collapse onto the bed. Her eyes settled on the journal once again. Her sudden weight dimpled the mattress, causing the book to slide towards her until it rested against her thigh. "Either all of this is real or I'm going insane," she mused to no one, "Either way, I suppose there is no going back now."

With trembling fingers, Jillian picked up the journal and opened it tentatively.

*****

March 13, 2010

I woke this morning with a heavy feeling in the pit of my stomach. Despite never having met Haedren, Silvermoon's anguish at his fate clings to my heart like rotten honey, thick and cloying. While I slept on

134

this side, the Band of Six was able to catch a scent of their comrade's trail, although none of us liked what we found. It was near twilight when Silvermoon and company crossed over the bridge that marked the boundary of the town of Traeth.

Although the failing sun hid from our eyes the evidence of Haedren's passage, the stink of blood and death hanging in the air filled in the blanks more than adequately.

As a crossroad town, Traeth employed a professional militia rather than relying on citizen-soldiers as most rural settlements did.

Neither their training nor experience seemed to save them from their eventual fate. The first bodies were grouped tightly, seeming to indicate that some of their number had turned on each other. I could not help but recall the ease with which Haedren was able to turn the Walker's pet wolves against her. I shuddered to think of these people pitted against one another: brother with brother and friend with friend. How do you fight someone whose weapons are the very people who rise up against him?

Those who seemed to have resisted Haedren's influence sprawled in the street, their bodies more gangrenous wound than unmarked flesh. I heard Ret's sudden intake of breath before the big man could get his emotions under control. Before him lay examples of his own fate had the Walker not intervened. It must have indeed been an uncomfortable dose of reality, even for a hardened Rangor warrior.

The King's road passed through Traeth before forking. One road continued east through the mountains, the other turned south towards Utel. A sudden gnawing grew in the pit of my stomach as the revelation that despite the obvious message that ~~our~~ their comrade had left, the chance of following him fell to a coin flip. As it turned out, I needn't have worried; in the town center, Haedren waited for us.

He was seated impassively on his horse, waiting for our arrival. Arrayed in front of him was a half dozen townsfolk, their eyes wide and jaws slack. As Haedren lifted his head to regard our group, all of his thralls turned their attention to us as well, in perfect unison. Even after the veritable abattoir we had just ridden through, that is what chilled my soul to the core. As one, the townsfolk took a step forward, interposing themselves between our group and their master.

Haedren spoke in a soft voice that seemed to echo through the deafening silence that hung in the air. "I had thought that I made myself clear, Forester." The hair on the back of my neck stood on end, although I could not immediately put my finger on why. "If you continue to chase me, I will take whatever measures required to end your pursuit." Leaning forward in his saddle, Haedren locked eyes with me; within them, I could

135

see no sign of Silvermoon's friend. "Is this truly the hill you wish to die on, Forester? How many more lives do you intend to spend in the name of pride?"

A wave of dizziness crashed over me, bringing with it unfamiliar images. They were Silvermoon's memories, forced upon me by my reflection. Haedren referred to Silvermoon in many ways, none of them were 'Forester'. That backhanded term of endearment was the chosen eccentricity of Theamon.

Haedren smiled softly, obviously identifying the look of recognition in my eyes. "There it is" Sitting back, he shrugged. "I will be honest. I find myself disappointed that it took you this long to make the connection."

Not able to help myself, I quipped, "I am not feeling quite myself."

Haedren's voice grew cold, "So I am becoming aware. I underestimated you once before to my own detriment —"

"If you can call your death simply a detriment," I interrupted.

True to the possessing entity's nature, anger crossed Haedren's face but it passed like a summer storm, leaving it placid once more. "The proof seems to be clearly in evidence before you. My former form may no longer draw breath but I still live."

"For now." Something about his turn of a phrase bothers me now but, in the moment, it was lost in the storm of emotions.

Haedren made the slightest of gestures with the fingers of his left hand and the townsfolk began walking forward one plodding step at a time. "You are a formidable foe, Forester, I will give you that. Perhaps given time and the proper allies, you could carry through on your implied threat." He reached out and beckoned with his right hand, as one would rudely summon a waiter. From between two buildings another score of townspeople emerged in lockstep. "Fortunately for me, I doubt that you will have another opportunity."

The sound of boots on dirt emerged from the darkness behind us, no doubt heralding the arrival of more thralls. I heard Marcus muttering beneath his breath and felt the power of his words deep in my chest. He shouted the last of them, although it fled my mind as soon as it reached my ears. A whip crack of thunder rent the night as everything was cast into blinding daylight for a split second. A spider web of violet-blue lighting swept the town square like a neon broom. In the center of it all, a pulsing cloud as black as a killer's heart surrounded Haedren, shrugging off the effects of Marcus's spell.

"Impressive. Were I you, however, I would save it for them." From every side, towns-folk thralls closed in on us. Ret and Mika dropped from their horses, each slapping their mount on the flank to send it

136

running into the ever-closing circle of zombie-like citizens. Hollis's own horse spun in slow circles as the boy tried to control it. "I believe this is farewell, Forester." The sky returned to the dimness of twilight, with it the protective shadows that had surrounded Haedren receded as well. "Perhaps you will surprise me, though." With a dismissive backhanded wave of his hand, he turned his horse and began to ride deeper into the night. "Who can tell?"

As much as I wanted to give chase, our dire straits demanded my full attention. Hollis unceremoniously tumbled from his horse as a trio of thralls laid hands on it. He tucked his shoulder and rolled to his feet, seemingly no worse for wear. Marcus stood between Mika and Ret, his lips moving quickly as he prepared another spell. Too close for Silvermoon's bow to be of use, I drew the Uteli sword tied to the saddle and turned my mount.

*****

Jillian was so engrossed in the journal that she nearly jumped from her bed as the chirping alarm on her phone broke the stillness of her room. Silencing the device, she softly cursed herself. She'd only meant to spend a few moments to convince herself that the words found within the book were no more worthy of fear than any others but had spent too much time to accomplish the opposite effect. Jillian was no less convinced that her dreams were visions of another world than when she woke. Furthermore, now she was running late.

Rushing into her closet, Jillian pulled a green and black floral pencil skirt and ivory blouse free from their hangers. Tossing them on the bed, she stormed into the apartment's only bathroom to evaluate if she could forgo the shower that her schedule would no longer allow. Often when someone first wakes, they claim to not recognize the disheveled image staring at them from the depths of their mirror. This is normally a considered exaggeration to illustrate the absurdity of the situation.

In that moment, any trace of exaggeration was absent.

Jillian felt a sense of vertigo as she stared at a reflection that she truly didn't recognize. Reaching behind herself, she lifted her chestnut hair from the back of her neck and pulled it into a messy bun, squinting into the mirror. Slowly her familiarity with the image before her returned as she recognized the curve of her throat and slope of her nose … the shape of her lips and sweep of her cheekbones. Like an early morning mist, her confusion receded and revealed her sense of self. It didn't take with it the pangs of panic that echoed through her stomach.

"What's happening to me?" she asked her empty apartment, praying that silence would be her only answer. Forcing a tight smile to her lips, she repeated, "You're not going insane. You're not going insane." Hard-

137

ening her glare she stressed each word, "You. Are. Not. Going. Insane." Unsure of the actual impact her self-affirmations had on the growing unease in her gut, Jillian released her grip on her unruly hair and began to muscle it into a more proper bun.

An artificially joyful tone chimed from the bedroom as she was pushing the last hairpin through the tightly packed mass of hair. Rotating slightly from side to side, Jillian examined her work. *Not my best work*, she thought, *but it'll have to do.* Unbuttoning the over-sized men's shirt that served as her favorite sleepwear, she tossed it in the general vicinity of an already overflowing laundry basket and fled the bathroom.

Marisol's 'good morning' text no doubt awaited her in the next room; beyond that certainly lurked a day filled with disapproving stares and bureaucracy.

*****

Jillian hadn't realized how tightly she'd been clutching the stylus until the lunch bell rang. With her awareness, a burning ache blossomed across the back of her hand. Gritting her teeth against the pain, she rubbed at the building cramp with her thumb. As the bell's siren call faded into silence, Jillian looked up to find twenty-four expectant faces stared at her. Suddenly self-conscious, she smiled at them, "Who's tired of social studies and ready for lunch?" Two dozen small hands launched into the air. Chuckling softly, Jillian shook her head. "Alright, then. Mrs. Lister had lunchroom duty today. Put your books away and join her class in the hallway." The sound of scraping chairs and excited voices rose like thunder. "Carefully, please," she cautioned, "No one wants to spend recess in the nurse's office."

With as much restraint as can be expected of a group of pre-teens, Jillian's class filed into the hall. Mrs. Lister poked her head through the door and flashed a quick smile before turning her attention to herding the veritable mob of children toward the lunchroom. Once her students were safely in the hands of her co-worker, Jillian slumped into her chair. It audibly creaked beneath her sudden weight but despite its age and penchant for dramatic noises, it was a comforting constant in her maelstrom of a day.

Pinching the bridge of her nose between the fingers of her pain-free hand, Jillian closed her eyes and sought the peace of a moment's respite. Serenity wasn't to be found, however. Memories not quite her own waited to greet her as her lids flickered closed. As if he was in the room with her, Jillian saw Tormand's face contorted with pain and fear as Asaege's summoned insect cloud literally ate him alive. Despite her lack of breakfast, Jillian's stomach rebelled.

Sitting bolt upright, she tried to suppress the wave of retching that

138

rolled over her.

Mixed with the sense of revulsion was a crippling feeling of guilt. Although in that moment Jillian was simply a spectator, her heart ached as if it were her words that called forth the stinging cloud of agony … her hand that drove a yard of steel into the suffering man's gut in the name of protecting her own life. Although it did nothing to sooth the nausea, a strange sense of calm settled over Jillian's heart. The sound of blood pounding in her ears dimmed to a quiet rush.

Just as it had in the dream, this sensation of unity with her reflection dulled the edges of both her revulsion and Asaege's projected guilt. Perhaps Hollis's words were more accurate than Jillian had first believed. Tentatively, she opened her eyes with the hope that the simple act would not disturb the delicate tranquility. As they fluttered open, they did so to a world both strange and familiar. Her classroom was the same as it'd been since being decorated for the first day of school, but she also viewed it with a sense of wonder normally reserved for children.

The crepe paper streamers and multi-colored wall decals evoked in her an excitement that could only seem to come from one source. Asaege's barely repressed personality strained at the confines of Jillian's will, her sense of amazement palpable through their connection. The feeling only intensified as her eyes roamed over the quietly buzzing fluorescent lights and softly glowing smart board. Jillian felt a sensation very much like carbonated bubbles behind her eyes as her consciousness began to fade. Taking a slow, deep breath she forced Asaege from her mind. The calm evaporated instantly, leaving Jillian reeling and exhausted. It was only then that she noticed the figure standing in the classroom's doorway.

"Jillie?" Arms akimbo, Marisol stood there with furrowed brows.

Letting her head slump against the chair's high back, Jillian forced a smile to her lips. "Hey, Marisol."

"Where were you? Because you certainly were not here."

Feeling her vigor return slowly, she stood carefully. "I'm not sure what you mean."

Squinting in confusion, Marisol studied her friend through hooded lids before responding. "Alright," she said slowly in obvious disbelief. "We were supposed to grab lunch today. You know, seeing as neither of us has lunch duty."

Jillian exhaled sharply, the last vestiges of fatigue leaving her with the breath. "Of course, it must've slipped my mind."

"It seems like it may have had some competition for resources." Jillian just stared at her. "I called your name three times, but you were in your own world."

If you had any idea of how right you are, Jillian thought. "I've just got a lot going on is all."

Marisol weaved between the tiny desks that filled the room to close the distance between herself and Jillian before whispering, "Are you okay? Because you know how people talk around here." She pressed her thumb and forefinger together and subtly touched her lips to remove any doubt as to the origin of her concern.

More sharply than she'd intended, Jillian hissed, "You know I don't smoke before or during school."

Her friend's apology was plain in her soft eyes. "I know. These hens are just looking for something to cluck about and it's not like you have gone out of your way to make friends."

"You're my friend —"

"— and a damned good one, which is why I worry."

Jillian repeated, "I've just got a lot going on."

Marisol's skepticism was evident in her rolling eyes, but she seemed to let it pass for the moment. "Let's grab some lunch while the lunchroom still has those big chocolate chip cookies."

Jillian smiled and gestured for her to lead the way. As she followed Marisol from the room, she desperately wished she could confide in her but couldn't bear the thought of her friend believing that she'd lost her mind.

Interlude: Hector
Poison to the Root

The open window swept the cloud of exhaled smoke from the car, causing it to swirl in the crisp autumn air. Hector brought the stub of a cigarette to his lips absently as he watched Jillian follow her co-worker from the room. He drew deeply, causing its tip to glow crimson-orange momentarily before fading to salt and pepper ash once more. The thumb and ring finger of his free hand tapped an uneven rhythm on the Toyota's steering wheel as he continued to stare into the now empty classroom.

"There is obviously more to you than first impressions suggest, Miss Allen," he purred releasing a stream of smoke from his pursed lips. "Perhaps if I'd had a teacher like you during my formative years …" Hector let his words drift into silence as he took another drag. He shifted his eyes to the car's threadbare passenger seat where a pair of leather-bound journals lay beside a half empty sleeve of generic snickerdoodles. "But on the other hand, the fact that you came to my place of business and walked out with something that clearly didn't belong to you hints at your duplicitous nature."

Hector couldn't decide whether he was more annoyed or intrigued by the woman. In the back of his mind, a dark thought festered. She made his life complicated, and complications rarely lead to success. His reflection valued simplicity in all things and whatever her reason for taking the journal, there was little chance of it being simple. Options for excising this particular obstacle from their path began to filter unbidden into Hector's thoughts, bringing a sly smile to his face.

He was becoming more intrigued by the second; anything that so frustrated the normally unflappable Plague Man was worth consideration.

So lost in both his thoughts and those of his reflection, Hector didn't notice the crossing guard until her frame filled his side mirror. "You can't park here,"

He lifted his eyes slowly, bringing the last bit of his cigarette to his lips. "It's a free country."

"This is a school," she snapped, scowling at his cigarette, "A tobacco-free zone." Studying him with disdain, she prompted, "Do you have a child here?"

Hector drew a lung full of smoke before responding. "Me? Not that I know of." He flicked the smoldering butt past the crossing guard with a snap of his wrist.

"Then you have to leave."

He exhaled, causing a steady plume of smoke to roll over the woman's day glow vest and flannel shirt. "No problem, ma'am," he muttered not trying to keep the contempt from his voice. "Thank you for your service."

The crossing guard shouted something that Hector couldn't make out as he pulled away, reaching into her vest for what he assumed to be a notepad. Even if her eyeglass prescription was up to date, the mud that he'd smeared on his license plate would make any attempt at reading it futile.

Chapter Twenty-One
Shadows of Memory

Hollis couldn't help but smile at the striking similarities between Asaege and her reflection, despite their self-professed differences. As Jillian's presence faded from her, Asaege's face tightened into a stiff frown. "I am not accustomed to being a passenger in my own body."

"I admit it can be disconcerting," Hollis replied, trying to keep his tone sympathetic. "I can assure you that your reflection did not find the experience all together pleasurable either."

Furrowing her brows and snorting softly, she snapped, "Good."

"I will tell you the same thing I told her." His fingers brushed her skin lightly before he rested his hand on her wrist. The sensation sent not unpleasant shivers up his own arm. "The two of you are going to have to learn to co-exist."

Asaege didn't look convinced.

"It is more than convenience that drives my advice, Magpie. The reflection of a very bad man has her squarely in his sights …" He allowed his words to fade, watching her eyes for recognition. When her frown deepened, he continued, "What happens to her, happens to you, Asaege. If Plague Man's reflection kills Jillian, you go with her."

A wicked knife of sorrow drove itself into his gut at the thought. He covered it by forcing a smirk to his lips, a defensive trick that had worked for him throughout his life. "Who then would complete your crusade to teach the world to read?"

"She is so —"

"Stubborn? Self-righteous? Frustrating? Yes, I am aware. She reminds me of someone I have recently become acquainted with."

"I am not —" A slow smile blossomed on her face. "Alright, you may have a point."

Hollis squeezed her wrist softly. "None of those things are bad. Principled is often characterized by folks as all three when it does not fit their narrative. You are two sides of the same coin, although neither of you have realized it yet."

He felt Asaege relax, the tip of her tongue flicking out to wet her lips. "The loss of control is maddening."

"Understandable. Both of you are fighters, and that is bound to lead to conflicts, but if you can get on the same page," he used the English expression without thought, "You will find yourselves unstoppable. There comes a point, when you are in sync, that everything around you slows to a crawl and a sense of contentment settles upon you. It is in those moments, when two worlds converge, that you will be capable of incredible things."

Asaege raised an eyebrow.

"Take my word for it," he assured her, "It is indescribable."

She sighed, resignation replacing obstinateness. "I can try."

"I have a few things to do before tonight; they should take me no longer than a few hours." Hollis reluctantly released her wrist, immediately missing the heat of her skin against his palm. Turning on his heel and walking towards the window, he spoke over his shoulder "I should be back before dark."

*****

Hollis watched the Forest Gate from the safety of a nearby alley, hidden in shadows despite the early afternoon sun. The only passage between the Merchant Quarter and the Common Quarter (and thus the Ash) was manned by four members of the city guard; it was twice the normal compliment of guardians.

Under normal circumstances, the guards would scarcely glance at the steady stream of traffic that flowed past them. They would ensure that each person passing through the gate deposited the required toll in the bulky lockbox but paid not closer attention than was strictly necessary. On this day, each one studied the line carefully, pulling citizens free of it at what seemed like random intervals.

Not so random, Hollis thought, *Anyone going hooded or even marginally matching my description seems to be warranting further interest.* He closed his eyes for a moment, finding the calm center that he'd tried to describe to Asaege. It came easily, another gift of the Well. Hollis and his reflection, Stephen, were not simply two sides of the coin; since activating the Well of Worlds, they were the spiritual equivalent of a Möbius strip. There was no longer a pre-Well Hollis nor Stephen, there was a new personality that combined the best (and worst) of both.

It wasn't that particular gift of the Well that Hollis was interested in at the moment, however. Just as he had in the Virgin Mermaid, Hollis studied the soldiers guarding the gate from within the shelter of tranquility. The 'Understanding' blossomed in his brain, casting the situation into perfect clarity. As two of the guards pulled a portly merchant out of line, whispering tersely but forcefully to him, the other two stood a half dozen steps away, watching the press of humanity passing by them from both directions. Their eyes were hard and focused, squinting in intense concentration. There would be no way for him to sneak by them given their level of attentiveness. Another solution would need to present itself.

Hollis turned his attention to the men and women around him. They seemed no more aware of his presence than the gate guards, even though they passed within a few arms' reach of where he leaned against the alley's wall.

He focused on a passing couple; young lovers he guessed by the way they huddled together in the afternoon chill. They whispered softly to one another, but he could see their lips. Like a razor, the thief honed his awareness on them; the ambient sounds around him seemed to hush. Hollis was unsure if he actually heard what passed between them or if the 'Understanding' simply translated what he read from their lips so quickly that it seemed like it. In either case, their conversation was as obvious to him as if he stood between them.

"— very different things. How can we take his word for it over that of the Hand?" The young man seemed distressed.

The woman frowned deeply. "What has the Hand's words ever done for us? His message always seems to come down to 'Shut up and do as you are told. Your reward will be found in Olm's Hall; do not look for it in this life."

"The Hand speaks for the Lord of the Dawn." The man's response was instant but by the way his eyes danced, his words were not backed with the confidence he wanted them to be.

"What if he does not?" Her boyfriend recoiled, pzutting distance between their heads. Before he could respond, she continued. "The Prophet brings us Olm's words … from the god's own lips."

"But the Hand —"

"— lives within the Ivory Cathedral. Draped in silk and gold, he tells us that Olm's plan for us is sacrifice. Where is his sacrifice? Where is his —"

The couple passed the alley's mouth, concealing any further conversation from Hollis's eyes. *The Prophet? What have you gotten yourself into, Hollis?* A trio of laborers passed the guard post, walking towards him. Their furtive glances back at the soldiers spoke of conspiracy. Hollis furrowed his brows and focused the 'Understanding' on the conversation that passed between them, suddenly more interested in it than what should have been the more immediate problem.

"— scares the Lord Mayor and his goons. The truth always frightens those in power." The smallest of the three frowned deeply.

His companions nodded in agreement, one of them speaking quickly, turning his head from where he'd been watching the guards behind them. "How many nights has Lord Mayor Stranfort had to decide between filling his children's bellies or his own?"

"None," the small man snapped through gritted teeth. "He has plenty and to spare. Enough that he can shower the Ivory Cathedral in enough coin to keep 'Olm's Chosen' in the luxury they have come to expect … nay demand."

The here-forth silent member of the trio muttered, "Just two nights ago, the Prophet wrote of just this situation on the wall of the old stables." His face contracted in concentration before he continued, "If a leader does force service for a purpose contrary to the good of his people, throw them down. Faith can forge chains more unbreakable than steel." For a moment, the man looked sheepish. "Or something along those lines."

"You cannot read, Plath." The accusation came from the smallest of the group.

"Garreth read it to me. He learned some letters when he was apprenticed to the silversmith off Peddler's Way."

"The one that dismissed Garreth after spilling acid on his hand?"

Plath nodded. "The same."

"I suppose there was no shortage of boys to accept apprenticeship in his stead. Meanwhile, Garreth is forced to beg for iron drabs from passers-by with his one good hand."

The trio passed beyond Hollis's line of sight, but he felt he'd heard enough. *The Ash is tinderbox of frustration and resentment; Asaege's damned book is just the spark that will cause it to blossom forth into a raging inferno.* Not for the first time, the thief wondered why he'd involved himself. Their nocturnal vandalism brought him no closer to his lost tome or, more importantly, clearing his name of the curate's murder. *A year ago, I preyed upon these people as surely as those they so despise. Why should I care for their fates now?* Hollis knew the answer before the question had completely formed in his mind. When the Well had worked its magic, he and Stephen had become one and what remained could no more abide injustice to those who didn't bring it upon themselves as he could do so with regard to himself.

Simmering beneath the assuaging sanctuary, Hollis could feel a building anger. He took a gentle, deep breath and compelled the heat that burned in his heart to cool before it robbed him of his cloak of tranquility. He was so lost within this internal struggle that he almost missed the solution that he'd so dearly hoped for.

Pushing their way through the press of humanity passing through the gate, a squad of armored templars approached the guard post. Each of their clean-shaven faces were set in a grimace, a mixture of annoyance and contempt. The crowd parted before them like dirt before the plow, but it wasn't the citizens' reactions to the newcomers that interested Hollis. The guardsmen themselves stood a little taller, their ferret quick motions betraying trepidation. All four approached the soldiers, their postures exclaiming deference and platitudes. With their eyes on the approaching group, none were spared to watch the flow of people through the gate in the opposite direction ... the direction in which Hollis needed to travel.

*****

Once he'd passed through the gate, Hollis easily disappeared into the crowded streets of the Merchant's Quarter. There he was simply just another face in the crowd. It was only a few minutes until he stood before his intended destination: the Gilded Courtesan. Places such as this went by many names: house of ill repute, brothel, bordello; the Gilded Courtesan was both none of these things and all of them. Within its walls, one could pay to spend time in the bed of a willing partner, but it wasn't a common whorehouse. If sex for money was all you sought, there were plenty of other places that offered more reasonable prices. The Courtesan dealt in sympathy and companionship rather than physical release.

Pulling his hood closer around his face, Hollis mounted the three stone steps and slipped inside the straw-colored door. It took a quick moment for his eyes to adjust to the dimness of the building. Before he could see the lavish interior, he could smell it. Perfume and sandalwood warred with one another to caress his senses. After the crisp autumn day, the Courtesan was positively stifling; it wrapped the thief in its aromatic embrace as he grew accustomed to the soft illumination of the room. He resisted the temptation to shrug his cloak from his shoulders, valuing anonymity over comfort.

Hollis had known the proprietor, Torae, since their shared childhood in the Ash. Neither the woman's appearance nor manner betrayed her humble origins. Torae's hair had been dirty blonde in her youth but the

147

halo of short jet-black locks that hung around her rounded face showed no sign of it. A deep purple dress of crushed velvet clung to all the right places as she approached him, flanked by two muscular, shirtless men. Hollis pulled his hood back slightly and winked at his old friend; she dismissed her companions with a slight motion of her fingertips.

"Lord Marcae," she exclaimed more enthusiastically than was necessary. "How delightful to see you again." Any eyes that had turned the way of the cloaked newcomer returned to their business. It never paid to be too curious when it came to the aristocracy. Torae took Hollis by the arm. "This way, milord. I have arranged for your favored room."

Hollis allowed himself to be led up the grand staircase to the second floor, placing his hand over hers. "Milord? I could get used to that," he whispered softly.

"Do not become too accustomed to it." Torae's voice held a sharpness; he knew that tone well.

"One would think you were unhappy to see an old friend."

"What was your first clue?"

"Then why the 'Lord Marcae' business?"

"Would you rather I announce to all present that the fugitive murderer of the Hand's curate stood among them? Word spreads faster than clear pox between these walls."

"I cannot say that I would." The pair reached a pair of oak doors at the end of the hall. Pulling a key from her bodice, Torae unlocked them and gestured Hollis inside.

Once the doors closed, she spun on him. "What were you thinking, coming here?"

Hollis shrugged. "You said it yourself, a sheer avalanche of information passed through the Courtesan. I am simply in need of a handful."

"And if you were recognized?"

A sly smile rose to his lips. "It would do nothing but help the place's reputation."

Torae scowled at him, "And my own?"

"You could not be blamed for the predilections of a wanted fugitive."

"Are you so certain that none who pursue you would dig deeply enough into your history … or mine, for that matter, to make a connection?"

He hadn't planned that far ahead; the thought caused a chill to crawl up his spine. "That was a long time ago, Torae."

"The church has a very long memory."

Hollis dismissed her objections with a backward wave of his hand, "You are nothing if not resourceful. I am sure you could turn the situation to your advantage. I am sure the coin that is your knowledge of their quarry would spend like any other." He could tell that his words had stung her; she recoiled as if struck.

"If you think that I would trade in that particular currency, you do not know me as well as I had thought."

As he reached out for her arm, Torae studied his hand but allowed him to lay it on her sleeve. "I am sorry, Tor, I know you would never betray me but —"

"— But what?"

"The past few days have brought some stark truths to my attention."

She turned towards the dark oak cabinet that dominated the chamber's far wall. "Stark or not, the truth is that no amount of money," she turned to regard him with a disapproving glare, "or careless words can wash away the paths we have shared. Cradle to grave —"

"— Ash is always Ash," he finished for her.

Opening the cabinet, Torae revealed a selection of glass bottles containing liquor of varied colors. She gestured to them absently. "I am fairly certain that you did not take time from your no doubt daring escape from justice, or injustice as the case may be, to reminisce about times passed."

"You are as perceptive as you are beautiful, my dear."

She regarded him out of the corner of her eye. "Indeed. Why are you here, Hollis?"

Chuckling softly, he said, "Since you mentioned it, there is perhaps something that you can help me with."

"Witness my lack of amazement," Torae drawled sardonically.

Hollis ignored it and continued, "I have heard unsettling rumors about an old friend. I do not particularly care for surprises and would rather know when to expect him."

"What makes me think that you use the term friend loosely? Does this 'old friend' have a name?"

"The Plague Man."

Torae licked her lips in a nervous gesture, swallowing twice before she found words again, "You do not choose your enemies carefully, do you?"

"With no more care than I do my friends." Her head snapped around to regard him. He amended, "Present company excluded, of course."

"Of course."

"Can you help?"

"I can ask around. He is not exactly inconspicuous; if he is in the city, someone will have seen him." She seemed to purposely avoid using Plague Man's name.

Hollis's face broke into a boyish smile. "Great, I shall amuse myself

149

here." Kicking off his boots, the thief collapsed onto the four-poster bed's overstuffed mattress. "Is the kitchen still open? Even fake aristocracy has to eat."

Torae murmured, "I can perhaps find you something." As he cradled his head on cupped palms, her voice took on a scolding tone, "As long as you do not leave this room. We were fortunate that none looked too closely, Lord Marcae; I certainly do not want to press our luck."

"I will be right here."

As she stepped into the hall, closing the doors behind her, Torae grumbled beneath her breath, "Until something shiny catches your eye. Olm save me from those closest to my heart."

Chapter Twenty-Two
Shadows of the Smoldering Flame

Hollis had meant to keep his promise but shouted words bleeding through the chamber's thick walls peaked his often unhealthy curiosity. *It could not hurt to just have a tiny look-see*, he thought as he pushed himself up from the bed. As he approached the door, the voices grew clearer.

"— was not a request!"

The response was in a more rational tone and reasonable volume, obfuscating its details from the thief's ears. No matter how reasonable, however, it didn't seem to soothe the fire within the owner of the boisterous voice.

"I ask for simple things, apprentice. The fact that you cannot seem to accomplish them is no doubt the reason why others eclipse you in both stature and standing!"

Hollis opened the door a crack and focused his attention on the voices in the hallway.

"I am sure that I do not need to remind you, Master Dhole, that I was elevated to the rank of journeyman several years ago."

Hollis knew the voice immediately. It belonged to a former rival of his known only as Toni. While Hollis's path within the guild became smooth after his ascension to the rank of journeyman, Toni's seemed to progress in fits and starts. Despite sustained absences, he'd attained the rank of lesser master, where Toni never passed that of senior journeyman.

"You will always be my apprentice!" Dhole's voice lowered to a dangerous rumble, "Much to my near constant embarrassment."

Twenty years before, Toni and Hollis had been two shining prospects among a crop of mediocre apprentices. Many were the nights that Hollis wished harm upon his rival; almost as often was he tempted to take a more active part in bringing it to pass. In the end, Alexei Silvermoon arrived in his life, spiriting him away from the oppressive world of thieves guild politics. When he returned, Toni seemed to have lost the faith of the masters. Hollis had never inquired further; now part of him wished he had.

Sinking to one knee, Hollis peeked through the partially opened door. Master Edrich Dhole stood, naked to the waist, in an open doorway. His face was blotched with abnormally shaped scarlet patches; these carried down to his flabby chest and stomach, making him appear like a shabbily sown flesh quilt. Before him in the hall stood a pair of figures. The closest was a boy not yet old enough to coax more than a spotty copse of fuzz on his cheeks. His eyes seemed to search for somewhere to look that was neither the master before him nor the person to his left. Staring directly at the enraged man was a lithe figure dressed in deep purple leather and silk.

When they were apprentices, there had been a great deal of gossip about whether Toni was a girl or boy; the years had done nothing to solve that particular mystery. The epicanthic fold at their eyes betrayed a southern island heritage but it seemed as if Toni had hardly aged in the decades since their apprenticeship. Besides where lithe muscle had replaced the gawkiness of youth, they matched Hollis's memories.

"But Master Dhole, I am concerned that the—"

Like the sound of stone on stone, Dhole's words crashed out of him, "Your concerns are none of mine!" His hooded eyes swept between the two thieves before him. "Just do as you are told," Dhole grumbled before turning and closing the door behind him.

"Why do you have to challenge him like that?" The young boy spun on Toni, venom dripping from his words.

They squinted and turned to regard their accuser with a casualness that bordered on disrespect. When Toni spoke, all doubt was removed. "Were I you, Felst, I would be more concerned about my own words." Their tone was cold and hard as steel, "Dhole is on the other side of the door." Toni leaned in, laying their hand on the boy's shoulder. Pressing a thumb against his throat, they hissed, "While I stand in front of you."

"My apologies, Toni," Felst croaked, trying to pull away from their long-fingered grasp.

"Words are a privilege, chose them carefully else someone may revoke it." Despite the obvious danger of having members of the guild so close, Hollis couldn't help but feel impressed. This was the Toni he remembered from childhood: confident, calculating and capable. That they hadn't been advanced beyond journeyman was a loss to the guild as a whole. Toni released the boy and turned on their heel, "I have something to attend to, I shall return before Dhole concludes whatever degradations he has on his mind."

"But," Felst began to argue. When Toni turned to regard him over their shoulder, he thought better of whatever his objection was going to be and simply said, "Have fun."

Toni smirked and chuckled once before disappearing down the stairs.

*****

The room's lock was never meant to keep out a determined party but Hollis took his time in opening it all the same. Felst wouldn't regain his wits for some time and he would need quite a bit longer to free himself from the silk bonds that Hollis had found far too easily, in a bedside table. The thief felt it far more important to enter Dhole's chamber unnoticed than quickly. The master's moans made quiet entry easier than Hollis had any right to expect. What he saw as he slipped inside would haunt his dreams for weeks to come.

Dhole lay bound face down across the room's large bed, clamps of various sizes and shapes attached to wads of fat across his back. The room was filled by a low moaning not unlike a contented heifer. His companion stood above him with another clamp clutched in her small fist, her back to the door … and Hollis. The deep carpet and his years of practice made sneaking up behind her simplicity itself. He wrapped his right arm around her stomach, his left hand covering her mouth. As she exhaled in surprise, Hollis applied pressure to her diaphragm to prevent her drawing further breath.

Lifting her from the floor, he retreated towards the door before setting her again on her feet. "I am going to let you loose. Do not scream." Despite his hushed tones, Hollis gave each of the last three words an almost physical punch. He waited for her to nod her head against his restraining hand before slowly releasing her and taking a half step back. She spun on him, gulping air like a drowning victim. Hollis winced, expecting her to reject his advice but the courtesan seemed content to simply breathe deeply as she watched him as a canary does a tomcat.

Not wanting to press his luck or waste any further time, Hollis reached into the pouch at his waist and pulled forth two gold imperials between his first two fingers. Wordlessly, he let his gaze linger on the

153

shiny coins before darting to the door. The woman understood his meaning immediately and took the bribe before slipping through the door on silent feet. He couldn't help chuckling under his breath, *The capacity of the human soul for self-interest never seems to disappoint.*

"Enough anticipation, girl," Dhole snapped, "I am not paying you to stand and gawk."

Hollis strolled casually towards where the rotund man lay strapped to the bed, slowly drawing the Dwarven steel dagger from its sheath at his waist.

"Do you hear me, whore?"

The thief entwined his fingers in the guild master's hair, drawing his head from the soft confines of the stacked pillows and slid the cold blade between duvet and throat. "I can hear you just fine, Dhole, but were I you, I would choose my words more carefully from this point forward."

Dhole reacted as if a red-hot coal had been placed on his bare skin; Hollis was forced to remove his knife to prevent the guild master from mistakenly slicing his own throat. "You have no idea who you are threatening," he growled, straining against the thief's grip. "You are a dead man!"

Hollis tightened his grasp and forced the guild master's eyes to meet his own. A cruel smile spread across his face as Dhole's body went slack upon recognizing the thief. "Now that it is perfectly clear that both of us understand the situation in which we find ourselves, perhaps we can make more constructive use of the time that remains to us."

"How did you get in here? Felst! Toni!" Dhole tried to pull his hair free of Hollis's grasp, his eyes desperately looking towards the closed door.

"Scream all you like. Your companions are otherwise engaged and as for concerned passers-by … well someone of your unique predilections can hardly expect anyone to come running due to a little yelling." Hollis saw realization dawn in his prisoner's eyes and felt him relax beneath his hand. "That is better, Master Dhole. Our well documented differences aside, I always knew you to be a pragmatist at heart."

"What do you want, Hollis?" Dhole had obviously meant his words to be a demand but he didn't seem to have the spirit to commit to them.

"I had thought we could have a conversation about loyalty, guild master." Hollis tightened his grasp of the man's hair, "You betrayed me, Edrich Dhole. Along with the more practical skills of the trade, do you know what was drilled into me during the seemingly endless nights of apprenticeship?" He paused, waiting for an answer. When he didn't receive one, the thief pushed the guild master's face into the plush surface of the bed, smothering him within its confines. When Dhole began to flail,

Hollis lifted his head and whispered, "A conversation has to be a give and take for it to truly be considered a conversation. Do you know what all apprentices are taught from their first night?"

Through clenched teeth, Dhole hissed, "Brotherhood."

The thief's voice took on a tone of sarcastic joy, "That is correct. No matter who you were before you entered the guild, we are all brothers and sisters. None care for you but the guild. You can depend on none except the guild and it, in turn, will depend on you. Money. Power. Love. All of these things pale in the face of the steadfast bulwark that is the iron clad social contract that is the Brotherhood of the Night."

Dhole remained silent, his entire body tense beneath Hollis's hand.

"Does that sound familiar, Guild Master Dhole?"

"They are my words."

Again, sarcastic joy emerged from Hollis's lips, "That they are." His tone cooled to icy steel, "Tell me, Edrich, where did things go wrong? How did you fall from your lofty goals to the depths of ordering one of your own killed?"

"You said it yourself, Hollis, I am a pragmatist. You are hunted by both church and city alike, not to mention the Binders. The guild operates due to the unwillingness of those more powerful than us to act against it."

"Whose fault is that, Guild Master? Under your predecessor's leadership, the thieves guild was a power unto itself … a veritable shadow governor."

"The cost of one brother's life is a price I am happy to pay in order to continue operation."

Hollis felt a heat rise in his chest and was forced to take a deep breath to prevent it from overcoming him. Dhole took the silence as a sign that his words had found a home in the thief's heart.

"Are you so selfish as to pull the rest of the brotherhood down with you in a bid to escape the maelstrom of your own crimes?"

The thief laid his blade across Dhole's throat again. "Keep that word out of your mouth." His words were quiet but far from soft. "Anything you knew about brotherhood was forgotten the day you traded the fates of those under your protection for a few pieces of silver and the favor of politicians."

"Do you plan to punish me for what you perceive as my sins, Hollis? Play judge and executioner? You will lay claim to the role of martyr as well, if that is the case."

"I am no longer a murderer, Dhole, no matter what your valued friends may think. That time is passed. I remain a killer, perhaps, but not a murderer. I was not responsible for the curate's death, and I will not be responsible for yours." He felt the man relax beneath him. "Not this

155

night, at least. Whether my hands remain clean of your blood, however, is entirely in yours."

"How so?"

"The guild stops hunting me. Tonight."

"I cannot give that order. I have made assurances."

Rage rose in Hollis once more; Dhole seemed to be doing his utmost to test the thief's new leaf. "If they continue to chase me, I will be forced to defend myself. Six guild-mates have already paid for your assurances with their lives." He clenched his fist in the man's hair hard enough to elicit a grunt of pain, "If I have to dip my hands in the blood of my brothers and sisters again, yours will be the next to pass through my fingers." Hollis felt a deep gulp radiate through Dhole's body. "I see now that letting you live if you refuse to see reason is pointless." Although muffled by the thick walls, he heard raised voices in the hallway. Quickly, Hollis leaned down to whisper in the guild master's ear. "Am I wasting my time?"

Emphatically, Dhole shook his head. "No. I will call off the hunt … make some excuse to the council. You have my word."

Dragging his head up to meet his gaze, Hollis removed the knife from Dhole's throat. "I am not sure how much that is worth, but I do not suppose that I have much of a choice." Quickly, the thief rose from the bed and rushed towards the door. Stopping before he reached it, he said over his shoulder, "Do not force us to have this conversation again. I assure you that you will not like how that one will end."

Hollis threw open the door to find an unbound Felst leading two men down the hallway towards him. *Perhaps the boy has a future as a thief after all.*

Chapter Twenty-Three
Shadows of Shared Truth

"Good evening, gentlemen," Hollis chirped with a mirth that he didn't feel, "Let us not allow hasty conclusions lead us to ill-advised actions." He stepped into the hall, keeping his knife low and at his side. His Uteli longsword remained sheathed on his hip; the corridor was too crowded for it to be of much use. If it came to it, tight quarters combat was much more suited to knife work anyway.

Through the open door, Dhole roared, "Kill him!"

Pasting a smirk on his lips, Hollis's eyes moved between the three men before him. "Dhole always did have an inappropriate sense of humor. Always joking at the most inopportune times."

"Twenty gold imperials to the man who brings me the traitor's head!"

Hollis let his shoulders slump. "I do not want to fight you, brothers." It was obvious that the trio heard his words, but it was Dhole's promise that still echoed in their ears. Felst hung back and his two brawnier companions moved forward, short, stabbing swords held before them. Hollis brought his knife up in front of him, it's thick point between himself and his two closest attackers. Sharpening his tone to a razor's edge, he said, "If you test me, boys, you will breathe your last in this hallway. That is a promise." When his last attempt to defuse the situation failed, Hollis did what he had to … he turned on his heel and ran.

His opponents' shock was evident in the fact that he was able to reach the room at the end of the hall and slam the door shut before their cries of surprise reached his ears. He twisted the key in the lock and then snapped it off with a sharp kick with his booted foot. Their fists rapped furiously on the door as he pushed the oak liquor cabinet onto its side to create a makeshift barricade. The crash of broken glass drowned out the pounding for a second. *Torae is going to be so pissed*, Hollis thought as he scanned the room for another way out.

The only egress that presented itself was the tall window that over-looked the Silver Courtesan's central courtyard. Before he could think better of it, Hollis dashed across the room and threw open the leaded glass shutters. Sheathing his knife, he stepped onto the window's wide sill, a cold flash of panic pulsed through him in a wave.

Before the events at the Well of Worlds, Hollis and Stephen had been two separate people, each with their own lives and personalities. The magic of the Well coalesced them into a single mind, for good or ill. Somewhere along the way, Hollis's reflection had developed a rather serious case of acrophobia. It was Stephen's residual fear of heights that reared its ugly head as he stood perched on the edge of a two story plunge. Closing his eyes, Hollis tried to calm his mind. As a youth, the city born thief had made leaps far more dangerous than this, all that was required was to remember the feeling: the cold razor sensation of adrena-line in his veins, the thrilling feeling of weightlessness as for the barest of moments he floated free of the world that had birthed him. His trepidation didn't flee completely but it dulled like a candle's light through silk.

The pounding at the door ceased, replaced by a manic scratching. The fallen cabinet blocked the keyhole inside the room, so there was little chance of his pursuers pushing the broken key through on that side. Hollis hoped they wasted the time to try, however. Before he could think about it any further, he stepped off the windowsill and into the crisp autumn air. After a brief but exquisite second of weightlessness, the thief plunged towards the garden below him. A thick arbor broke his fall, sav-ing him from serious injury. He lay cradled within the embrace of bark and leaf for a moment before a white-hot pain erupted in his arm. A rigid branch, sharp from recent trimming had impaled his left forearm, causing the limb to feel like it had dissolved into a crimson mist of agony.

Above his head, he could still hear Dhole's shouts and his pursuers began banging at the door again with redoubled fervor. Clenching his teeth against the pain, Hollis pulled his arm free from the branch. His breath caught in his throat as he seemed to leave a portion of himself behind. Ripping a silk scarf decoration from the shattered arbor, the thief quickly wrapped it around his injured forearm and pulled it tight with his teeth. Hollis's eyes swept across the courtyard.

Three exits presented themselves. One led into the Courtesan's main room; that was no doubt full of patrons, a few of them would likely be people who would benefit from his capture. The second led into the alley behind the establishment; it represented the quickest and most direct route away from those who gave chase. Too obvious. The last lead to the kitchen. A tunnel from it lead to a shared storeroom with the tavern across the street. It had once been used by nobles craving their anonymity in the days before Torae's ownership of the Silver Courtesan. From there, Hollis could emerge from a rarely used exit from the tavern and hopefully disappear into the night.

The thief was able to get his makeshift bandage secured with a hasty knot by the time he reached the door to the Courtesan's kitchen. Without the time for subtlety, Hollis kicked it open and dashed inside. Toni leaned casually against a butcher block counter, a confident smile painted across their lips.

*****

"Good Evening, Lord Marcae," Toni purred, "In search of a midnight snack, perhaps?"

Hollis cursed his luck. His former rival must have been in the crowd when he made his ill-advised entrance. They obviously had seen through Torae's ruse. Hollis's knife leapt into his hand as if it had a life of its own. "As much as I enjoy reunions, I simply do not have time for one."

"So, I have gathered." They nodded toward the courtyard. "I very much doubt that Felst will think to look here. His mind tends to only work on the most direct paths. Close the door behind you and I am sure we will have ample time to reacquaint ourselves." Lifting the thin Slazean stiletto held casually in their left hand, Toni gestured to the door, "I am afraid I must insist."

Despite their nonchalant posture, there was a hard edge to Toni's eyes. Getting by them would be a lot more complicated than evading Felst and his comrades. While Hollis had been trained by Silvermoon and had honed his swordsmanship over two decades, Toni had spent much of that time with a knife in their hand, eclipsing his own skill with the weapon. In the cluttered confines of the kitchen, his Wallin Fahr would become a disadvantage, which may well have been their intent.

Hollis reached for the calming sensation gifted him by the Well in an effort to smother the panic rising in his gut. It was only partially successful. Through the 'Understanding', he saw the way Toni split their weight evenly between their feet, even when seemingly at rest. Held loosely, the point of their knife remained level with his sternum well within what the guild trainers called the 'kill box'. Toni's free hand was laid gently against their stomach, prepared to shove, grab or strike as needed. Even with the advantage that the 'Understanding' gave Hollis, the discrepancy between Toni's skill and his own made the outcome of a fight on their chosen ground an uncertainty.

What the Well's gift revealed, however, wasn't all dire. Toni appeared to be holding a purely defensive stance, although their expression showed no sign of trepidation. Their eyes remained steady and hooded while their posture broadcast relaxation.

Reaching behind him and swinging the door shut, Hollis kept his knife between himself and Toni. "I will admit to being intrigued."

Toni purred, "Why, Hollis, you are going to cause me to blush." He simply raised an eyebrow, prompting them to continue. "I imagine you have some questions."

"A few. For example, I was surprised when I found you had deserted your patron's door."

"Dhole may be the master of my guild, but he ceased being my patron long ago."

Hollis shook his head slowly. "Be that as it may, that action will no doubt bring with it substantial consequences."

Toni shrugged. "It was a calculated risk. If you had come for Dhole, there was not very much that Felst and I could have done to stop you from reaching him." Hollis couldn't suppress a smirk, a touch of pride coloring his heart. "Were I alone? Perhaps. But in his zealousness, the boy would have certainly gotten in my way." The feeling and its accompanying smirk faded as quickly as it rose.

"So, it was self-preservation?"

They shrugged. "Maybe. If your intent was other than murder, nothing would be lost besides a bit of his faith in me, which has unerringly dwindled in recent years. On the other hand, if you killed him, I would be free of his machinations without having to get my hands dirty. It was a win-win in my eyes."

Hollis scowled at them,. "Why does everyone seem to think me a murderer?"

Toni rolled their eyes. "Because we know you."

Exasperated, Hollis snapped, "Folk are capable of change." He felt a touch of shame rise in him, shame that hadn't been present before the events within the Well.

They held up their hand. "If you are going to profess that you have never killed any who did not deserve it, you can save your breath. Perhaps, as much as we struggle against it, we are both products of our patrons."

Desperate for someone to believe him, or perhaps to convince himself, Hollis growled, "I am no longer that person, Toni."

"Suit yourself. Your path of self-discovery was not the reason I sought this audience." they gestured around themselves. "Such that it is."

"I continue to be intrigued, even if my patience does begin to grow thin."

"Olm forbid." Toni's voice held the sharpness of sarcasm. Their eyes studied the door for a moment before they continued, "Why were you in the Great Library that night?"

"There was a disagreement as to ownership of a tome. I simply was clarifying the confusion."

"A book? You killed the curate over a book?"

Hollis held up a finger on his free hand, "First of all, I did not kill the curate. He was breathing when I made my exit." Lifting a second one, he chuckled and said, "Second, it was a fairly important book."

"So, if the choice was put to you: curate or book …"

He shrugged but remained silent.

"Changed man, my ass," they murmured under their breath. "Did you leave with the book?"

"I fail to see why that is relevant. In the interest of brotherhood, however, no; I was not able to locate it." Toni studied him through hooded eyes. "The library is a big place; the curate and his cronies arrived at a very inopportune moment."

"You sure stirred up a hornet's nest with not much to show for it."

"No one is perfect."

"Are you sure that you left empty handed?"

A bad feeling caused the hair on the back of Hollis's neck to stand on end. "I'm certain of it. Why do you ask?"

"One of the only advantages of being such a source of disappointment to Dhole is that he rarely spares any concern for what I may or may not be doing … or where I am doing it."

Hollis's heart went out to Toni; once universally accepted as the guild's chosen one, they'd fallen quite a distance. He felt a temptation to inquire further but they had moved on quickly, not giving him the chance.

"A representative of the Hand paid Dhole a visit the morning after the curate's body was found. He was intent on securing the guild's aid in finding you."

"Dhole insinuated as much."

Toni nodded. "But did he tell you that his desire for your capture was eclipsed by his insistence that anything found on you be brought immediately to the Ivory Cathedral?"

Hollis focused on keeping his face blank as he asked, "Is that so?"

"Any idea what the church may be missing?"

"None." His response was too quick. Hollis cursed himself for the mistake.

"Indeed."

"Are you going to ask me to turn out my pouches?"

Toni shook their head. "No need. We both know that, should you be in possession of such a valuable object, you would not carry it with you." They squinted at him. "You are not carrying it with you, are you?"

Smoothly, Hollis responded, "Carrying what?"

Their eyes darted again towards the door as raised voices filtered through it from the courtyard. Only with great restraint, Hollis resisted turning to look as well. "I am not sure that our audience will remain private forever." Toni's frustration was palpable.

"All good things must come to an end." Hollis let his eyes drift past them, his mind furiously searching for the most likely path through Toni should the door open.

"Then I will attempt to conclude our business with all possible brevity."

"I appreciate it, although I am not sure your comrades will feel the same."

Toni breathed a contempt filled chuckle, "At this moment, I am not particularly concerned with the feelings of my 'comrades'." The emphasis on the final word might as well have been made of sandpaper. "As strange as it may sound, given our tumultuous history, you always treated me fairly."

Hollis cocked his head to one side. "I am certain that at one point both of us considered rash solutions to the existence of the other."

"Before you were a changed man?" He frowned at them but nodded. "I will not deny it all the same. However, throughout our competitive years, you always dealt with me as an equal."

Hollis smiled broadly. "Equal is a little bit of an overstatement."

Rolling their eyes towards the door, Toni said through clenched teeth, "May I get through this or would you rather perform for a larger crowd?"

Dipping his head, Hollis gestured toward them with his free hand "Point taken. Carry on."

"All I ever wanted was to be the best thief in any room I walked into. I bought into the whole Brotherhood of the Night lecture. The guild judges you only on what you do, not who you are … or what. You never treated me as a freak —"

Hollis tilted his head. "Were you?" His question was asked as genuinely as his thoughts on the matter.

"I never thought so until …"

162

The door and what lay beyond it forgotten for the moment, Hollis stepped forward. "Is that what mired your advancement?"

Toni danced back a few paces, stiletto still held before them. "None of the masters said as much but people speaking behind your back do not always concern themselves with who hears their words."

"I will admit to being curious but the only thing that mattered to me during those nights of apprenticeship was keeping a step ahead of you. I am not too proud to admit that there were a few times where I feared you may get the better of me."

"A few?"

He let his shoulders slump a bit. "More than a few. You were one of the guild's best and brightest … you know, after me —"

"— besides you," they interrupted.

"Besides me," Hollis amended, "I find it hard to believe that anyone would overlook that in the name of …" He searched for the word in Trade Tongue but could only come up with the English word 'prejudice'. He settled for, "Personal taste."

Toni mirrored his smirk, "But do you truly find it so hard to believe, given the current leadership?"

"Dhole is arrogant, sure. He has a massively inflated sense of his own self-worth, absolutely. But tying one hand behind his back to spite the other, I never figured him for that big of a fool."

"And yet here we are."

"Here we are," Hollis agreed. A tense silence lingered between them for a long moment, the voices in the courtyard growing louder. "Where does that leave us?"

"That depends on your answer to my next question," Toni responded, nervously eying the door.

"I would suggest making it a quick one. I suspect that we are about to have company that will care about neither question nor answer."

"Did you kill the curate? Did you bring doom upon the guild for nothing more than your own selfish desires?"

"That is two questions, but the answer is the same. No, when I fled the library, Curate Rethmus still drew breath. If he died, it was not by my hand."

Toni's head snapped up as the door to the courtyard slammed open, revealing a half dozen men silhouetted in the setting sun. Hollis surged forward past his distracted rival and deeper into the dim room. He risked a quick peek over his shoulder and swore that he saw a toothy grin on Toni's face as they called out, "This way! He's escaping through the cellar!"

Thanks a lot, he thought, wondering to himself if, in the end, his answer had been satisfactory.

Chapter Twenty-Four
Into the Heart of the Beast

The Ivory Cathedral stood in the center of its own district, a brilliant testament to the glory of Olm in marble and gold. Unwilling to share space with the Great Library and the Academy Athenaeum, the greatest of the Lord of Dawn's churches was truly without peer. Professed to be open to all, in reality the cathedral was strictly the purview of the rich and influential. None would be turned away from its towering, gilded doors but access to the Cathedral District itself could only be attained after passing through no less than three city gates and the entirety of the High District. Those who safeguarded the 'quality of life' of those who dwelt there denied entry to those who threatened their carefully cultivated aesthetics.

There was a common wall between the Cathedral District and the Common Quarter but that was as close as most citizens would ever get to the church that controlled most of their lives. The words spoken by the Hand of Light, Olm's chosen vessel on Taerh, dictated more of their existence than the laws of the city, but virtually none of the common people would ever hear those words for themselves. Lower ranking priests would minister to the poor but those chosen messengers often spent every waking moment seeking a way to move beyond that distasteful task. The Hand would often claim that the church was built on the bedrock of its believers, but the truth was that they were given no more notice than the dirt beneath his feet.

As she gazed at the gilded adornments dripping from the cathedral's interior walls, Asaege found herself thankful that the people of the Ash would likely never see it with their own eyes. While each of them struggled day to day in order to feed their families, Olm's clergy lived in an enclave of privilege and excess. *One of these candelabras alone could feed a family of five for a year*, she thought. The circular main chapel measured nearly a hundred yards across and was lit by hundreds of them. The light shed was caught and fractured by jewel encrusted icons that crowded the flawless marble alter like so many trinkets in a tinker's wagon.

An artifact of her time spent within the Great Library, Asaege had kept the deep green, crushed velvet dress safe and unmarred in a locked trunk when she was cast out from the institution. With it, she was fortunate enough to be able to blend in with those passing through the Royal Gate into the High District that morning. Despite the confidence that should have provided, Asaege kept her hands hidden within the folds of her sleeves, conscious of the dirt that had been ground into her fingertips during the intervening years.

The multitude of voices around her blended into one steady buzz as she examined the mass of humanity gathered for Olm's Day services. Situated near the back of the Grand Chapel alongside 'the help', Asaege stood beside butlers, nannies and their charges. The wailing children and sour faced employees were necessary accessories to those seated further forward, even if they clashed with their current attire. Even here in the house of the Father of Justice, the city's stratification could be seen; the closer one's seat to the alter, the higher one's status was seen among Oizan's elite. The Lord-Mayor, his family and their guests occupied the entire front row.

A single clarion blast cut through the cacophony of voices; a second was enough to force them into silence. The third trumpet call announced the clerical procession's arrival. All eyes turned to a pair of ivory plated doors at the rear of the chapel. Slowly they opened, revealing a dozen silk and gold clad priests. Each carried an incense spewing censer on a six-foot pole of dark cherry. Behind the vanguard, walked another score of higher placed clergy decked out in cassocks decorated with beads of pearl, platinum and ebony. Next came a collection of bishops, their ceremonial garb even more ornate than those before them.

As the last of the bishops passed Asaege, the ethereal sound of a collection of harps arose from somewhere above her head. The trumpets called again in clear, pure notes.

With each blast, more harps joined the chorus until a tapestry

166

of melody filled the chapel. From within the darkness of the chamber beyond the vestibule emerged a stooped and frail figure dressed in a purple silk robe. Gold dripped from his neck and wrists like honey from a broken hive, giving the impression that he would be pulled to the ground by their weight. In contrast to his decrepit appearance, the Hand of Light carried with him an aura of power that seemed to take the air out of the chamber.

Behind and to the left of the Hand walked what Asaege assumed to be his newly chosen curate. While compared to the epicene countenance of the man before him the curate looked positively robust, the man was slim to the point of frailty but moved with the smooth gait of a jungle cat. In contrast to those that preceded him, the curate wore a robe of simple black fabric. His hands disappeared into voluminous sleeves held before him. What drew Asaege's attention, however, was the contoured leather mask that covered his face. Free of any adornment beyond the smoky lenses that served it as eyes, the mask was shaped to resemble an unremarkable human face. The lack of any contrast in color or texture caused a good deal of the detail to be lost except in the most direct light. It gave the illusion that his face constantly slipped in and out of shadow.

While the other clergy didn't spare as much as a sidelong glance for any member of the congregation until they reached the dozen rows nearest the alter, the curate seemed to study each face from behind his expressionless mask as he passed. When his dead, glass eyes settled on Asaege, she felt him linger there for a moment as if he searched for something. Just as a chill began to rise along her shoulder blades, the curate casually turned his gaze from her. She felt as if a great weight, unnoticed until it was gone, had been lifted.

She stared at the back of the curate's pitch-black cassock until he and the Hand reached the alter. With a smooth motion, the curate touched the Hand at wrist and elbow, aiding the man in ascending the marble stairs to where the alter stood. The Hand turned and raised both of his hands to shoulder level, his palms pointed out towards the crowd.

"May the Light of the Father be upon you." His voice carried easily to the last pew as if the words were shouted rather than whispered.

As one the congregation responded. "May your path always be lit by his mercy."

"You may be seated," the Hand muttered absently, gesturing to the gathered with a flick of his fingers. As priest and worshiper alike settled into their seats, the curate simply stepped back from the altar. He leaned against the wall, his black clad form settling between two massive tapestries that adorned it. The way they were hung, the area between them cast a shadow into which he seemed to disappear. Before Asaege could turn her attention to the phenomenon, the Hand began speaking.

"It is with a sad heart that I come before you this morning, brothers and sisters. Since last we met in the shade of Olm's embrace, a crime of tragic proportions has been committed in the shadow of this very cathedral. My dearest friend and most trusted curate, Rethmus has been taken from us … struck down as he walked the halls of knowledge in service to each and every one of you."

Asaege had to stifle a chuckle, letting her mouth drop into her upraised sleeve to hide the accompanying smirk. Rethmus's words as well as his deeds served only himself.

"While I am eternally grateful to the Lord of the Dawn for delivering to us Curate Reisling …" He gestured to where the masked man leaned casually against the marble behind him. "With that same breath, I curse the Bringer of Shadows for taking his predecessor from all of us."

She looked up slowly, all sense of mirth gone. *The man has no shame. Is it not enough to play politics with people's faith? Now he is making his own martyrs?*

"The Master of Beasts has taken many forms," he continued, "Some of these like the scorpion and the serpent are well known. These are shapes that we associate with cunning and treachery. The serpent bites the hand of those who reach beyond their place and the scorpion stings the ankle of those who tread outside the path of the righteous. These things we know." He paused, sweeping his gaze over those gathered. Even in the back of the chapel, Asaege felt his eyes bore into hers. "But tell me, brothers and sisters, how does someone know what their place is and what lies beyond it? How does one tell the path of the righteous from that built by the Father of Lies?"

The sound of a single coin dropping could have been heard in the silence that greeted his question. Asaege nearly jumped out of her skin when the Hand drove his fist into the pulpit before him and shouted, "Olm's words!" Instantly, his voice dropped to a softer tone, forcing all present to strain to hear him. "The words coming from the lips of the Father himself. They fall upon the ears of those who carry his light in their hearts … those chosen by him to guide his people into that light. All Olm wants is for all of us to step from the shadows and into his radiance. This is what I want for each and every one of you gathered here." The Hand gestured to the massive doors at the rear of the chapel, "This is what I want for every brother and sister beyond these walls."

"Unlike yourselves, however, they are not here to receive the words of Olm. They cannot find the time to gather here in order to hear them or … choose not to." He hit the last three words hard, emphasizing each one.

Asaege began to feel a fluttering in the pit of her stomach. *Is it me or is the Hand of Light insinuating that because these people can attend services, that makes them better than ... well everyone else?*

The Hand let his statement sit for a moment before continuing, "So we go out into the world as Olm bids us, bringing his words ... his will to those who need to hear them. It is a small charity but one that the Lord of the Dawn asks of those close to his heart."

Charity? He serves the Father of Justice ... where is the justice in the hoarding of knowledge.

"But what happens when his message is perverted? What are we to do when the words of Olm are used for purposes other than his own?

What indeed?

"There is a man in the Ash, brothers and sisters. This man speaks to those who do not know better. He counsels that lives of service are unworthy. This man's words deny that every person's reward lies at Olm's side. His words tell of rewards found right here ... right now." A collective gasp of disbelief swept through the congregation. "Can you imagine? Each of you labor in this life, knowing you will find your payment for that service in the next." As one, the gathered crowd shouted their agreement.

Asaege looked around at the collection of opulence gathered before her and sneered. *If each ounce of service bought these people a pound of gold, all of them would be poorer than the lowliest beggar in the Ash.*

"Furthermore, this man ... this coward does not dare speak his lies aloud!" The Hand's raised voice caused the grumbling congregation to quiet. "In the dark of the night ... the time reserved for the Bringer of Shadows, he etches his falsehoods upon the alley walls that bear witness to the very sins that Olm has labeled as forbidden!"

Revelation dawned on Asaege, *He is speaking about me.* She could not decide if she was more insulted by his mischaracterization of her message or his assumption that the Prophet was a man.

"To the most vulnerable of us, this 'Prophet'," he stressed the term, his voice dripping with sarcasm, "brings the most egregious of lies. They are left with only the shield of their own ignorance for protection."

A soft shared chuckle drifted among those gathered. It was over-shadowed by the Hand's booming voice, "But he deprives them of even this gift!" The chapel fell into shocked silence. "There are those in the slums who teach our poor victimized brothers and sisters to read so they may better believe his heresy."

A clamor of voices rose from the congregation. The Hand tried to continue, "They must be—" The remainder of his words were lost among the flood of angry voices. He slammed his fist into the pulpit once again, repeating himself, "They must be protected from that which they do not understand!"

The chapel didn't return to silence, but it quieted enough for his voice to be heard clearly once more. "Imagine a city ... a world where service is only to oneself and not the greater good. Ponder for a moment a situation where each of you was made to see to your own base needs rather than the business of running the city. Oizan would fall into chaos. Taerh would fall into chaos. Tell me brothers and sisters, who is the sole beneficiary of chaos?"

As one voice, "Sharroth" filled the air.

"That is correct. Only the Father of Lies reaps an ample harvest when chaos is sown, and I will tell you that harvest will feed none but those who bow to his will." The Hand pointed to the front row where the Lord-Mayor sat. "Even the reach of Olm's chosen has its limits. The Father of Justice must rely on his faithful. He depends on those with the strength of purpose to keep the machinations of his sinister brother at bay." He opened his hand and swept it across the crowd. "Who among you will refuse his call?"

Asaege brought her fist to her lips. *Siblings protect us. What has he done?*

Chapter Twenty-Five
Shadows of Ill Omen

Hollis cursed silently as the door creaked open. Never a sound sleeper, the thief had intentionally left the stairs leading to Bearon's extra room in ill repair as a means of thwarting any surprise visitors. Still, someone had climbed the rickety staircase while he fitfully slumbered.

Cradling his injured left arm to his stomach, Hollis reached behind his head, closing his fist around the knife that lay sheathed between the wall and bed. "Bearon," he began, "I told you I am fine. I swear you will make someone a fine mother someday." The last words were forced between clenched teeth as the chills that had haunted him all night caused them to chatter.

A hooded figure slipped through the door; slim and wiry they were the opposite of the stout Bearon. Hollis put the knife between himself and the intruder as he fought the fatigue and dull, body-wide ache that had plagued him alongside the shivering. Using his left elbow to muscle himself into a sitting position, the thief tried unsuccessfully to keep the weapon trained on the cloaked form. They crossed the room quickly and batted the knife aside with velvet-gloved hands. He exhaled sharply, trying to find a calm place among the depths of his aching head. The figure spoke, her voice sweet as water of a clear stream. "Hollis, why must you always be so …" Torae searched for the word, settling for, "You?"

171

Hollis allowed his body to slump back onto the thin mattress. "Habit," he offered.

She sighed, pulling at the thin blanket that covered his fully dressed form. "To hear Bearon tell it, you are dying."

Clenching his teeth against another bout of shivering, Hollis growled, "Bearon talks too much."

Torae took Hollis's hand gently in hers and pulled his arm into the feeble light of the rooms low burning lantern. He didn't resist. "Did those guild thugs do this to you?" He opened his mouth to answer but she interrupted him before he could speak. "I am unsure why I should care. You come into my place, attack one of my best customers and once again, leave me to clean up the mess."

He squeezed her hand. "Tor —"

Speaking over him, she continued, "I swear, you do not have the sense that Olm gives little children."

"Torae —"

"I told you to stay in the room. I told you not to go anywhere. But none can possibly know what is best for Hollis the Slender besides the infamous rogue himself." Torae pulled her hand from his weak grasp and crossed the room in hurried steps.

"Torae," Hollis snapped with more force. Pulling the lantern from the wall, she spun on him but remained silent for the moment. "I am sorry. I let my pride overwhelm common sense —"

"Something that you have precious little of in the first place," she scolded, coaxing the lantern's flame brighter.

"Be that as it may," Hollis conceded, "I brought trouble to your doorstep and I hope you can accept my sincerest apologies." More than a raised tone, his words shocked Torae into extended silence. He took advantage of it. "Since we have been children, you have taken care of me as much I have returned the favor, if not more. I believe I have taken that for granted. I hope to not continue in that vein."

Torae sneered, "Why do you only apologize when you are drunk or injured?"

He seized her in his gaze, "My words have nothing to do with this," he said, lifting his loosely bandaged left arm.

Shrugging off his objections, she set the lantern on the bedside table and began unwrapping the blood-stained rags. "We shall see where these sentiments are when you are on your feet again."

"They will remain," he assured her through tight lips as the cloth tugged at the ragged edges of his wound.

If the sight of the pus-laden wound shocked Torae, the woman gave no indication. "This does not look like the work of a blade," she com-

172

mented, unwrapping a damp poultice she must have brought with her.

"One of your bushes broke my fall but the aid did not come without cost."

Her eyes shot up to meet his, concern coloring their hazel depths. "Those bushes are treated with a cocktail of fertilizer and bug repellent. It is the only way they can flourish in such a sheltered location." She laid a damp bundle over the wound and began wrapping it again. "They are toxic in the best of circumstances; introduced into the blood, I am sure they are no less deadly."

"Well, shit," Hollis muttered, "You certainly are full of good news."

"Ask me ten times and I would never anticipate anyone would be foolish enough to impale themselves on my topiaries."

"I pride myself on being unconventional."

Torae laid her hand on the side of his face, wrapping her fingers under his jaw. "This is serious, Hollis."

"I am aware." Despite the smile he forced to his face, his deadpan delivery betrayed the direness of the situation.

"If we act quickly, a priest may be able to —"

Hollis shook his head, interrupting her, "I am not exactly in Olm's good graces these days."

"You mean the Hand's good graces?"

"Most people do not see the difference."

"Then what?"

"I still have some moves left, friends in low places if you will."

She raised an eyebrow, "Like who?"

"It is better you do not involve yourself. Friends may be a bit of an overstatement."

"Hollis," Torae began, scolding evident in her tone.

Closing his eyes, Hollis allowed himself to settle back onto the mattress. "Did you have any luck tracking down Plague Man?"

"Yes. Another one of my regulars saw him disembarking from a sloop a couple of weeks ago. Captain Fairborn. He does not have anything good to say about you, in case you are curious."

"I do not imagine he does. He was sure that it was Plague Man?"

"He is fairly distinct with that mask and cloak. Few would choose them willingly."

"I was afraid of that." The thief pushed himself into a seated position. "I need you to do something for me."

"More important than your life?"

"It could be." Slowly, so as to not betray how badly his hand shook, Hollis reached into his satchel where it hung from the bedpost. "Do you still remember Phaerick the shipwright?"

She nodded.

He extended a sealed letter to her; the end of it quivered like the hand of an expectant child. "Give this to him and tell him that it needs to find its way south."

Torae shook the letter in his face,."This is more important than treating the poison that is not so slowly killing you?"

Hollis shook his head. "Neither more nor less important, just differently so." He took her wrist in his weak grip. "Either the poison kills me, or it does not. That letter cannot change that fact. If I do survive, however, its contents will become essential."

She thought about it for a moment and then slowly nodded. "Promise me you will get help."

Hollis lay back again with great care. "I promise. Please, send Mother Bearon up on your way out."

*****

"You always seem to find your way into such interesting straits, my boy.' Seran's face looked grim despite his chipper tone. The slight Slazean leaned, cross armed against the door frame. "The absurdity of the fence's story gave it an air of suspicion but alas here you are."

Hollis squinted towards the voice, raising a trembling hand to shade his face from the room's dim light. Even the feeble illumination shed from the nearby lamp stabbed into his brain like needles driven through his eyes. "Nice to see you as well, Seran," he wheezed.

Seran stepped fully into the room, closing the door softly behind him. "You took a massive risk sending Bearon to find me."

Hollis fought against the tremors that wracked his frame to push himself into a seated position. "How so?"

A smile, inappropriate for the situation bloomed on Seran's lips as a low, rasping laugh built in his throat. "There was a time, boy, when you would not have had to ask that question."

"People change," was all he could manage before a breathless cough stole his voice.

Seran stopped just beyond arms reach, watching his former apprentice with an appraising eye. "No, they do not," he said simply. As Hollis collapsed back against the pile of pillows stacked behind him, Seran added, "Most put on a convincing enough show, perhaps even enough to fool themselves but in my experience, true change is beyond humankind."

"Ever the optimist," Hollis whispered, his eyes closed against the light-headedness brought on by his coughing spell. He heard the soft sound of his mentor's footsteps as he approached the bedside.

"Optimism is for the innocent and the foolish. The only thing it buys you is a knife in the dark." Silence hung in the room like a death shroud, only broken by Hollis's shallow, wheezing breaths. "Or perhaps an even less fitting demise."

Gritting his teeth against the stabbing pain that opening his eyes would bring, Hollis met Seran's gaze. "Have you come all this way to simply proselytize or did you bring what I asked?"

A wide smile still hanging on his face, Seran replied, "Can I not do both? After all, I may never find you a more captive audience."

"You may not have that …" Hollis began. His words were cut short by another coughing fit. Seran waited for it to subside with what seemed to be infinite patience. "… that audience for long if you keep it up," he breathlessly finished.

"You very well may have a point, my boy." Seran reached into the pouch at his waist and pulled free a small corked bottle of smoked glass. "This cost me quite a bit, Hollis"

"I will reimburse you."

"You cannot," Seran snapped but he quickly controlled his voice. Slipping back into a conversational tone, he said, "It's price was not paid in coin alone."

"Consider me appreciative," Hollis whispered, his strength nearing its limit.

"Appreciation does not interest me. Were it anyone else who called, I would not have come."

Hollis nodded, unable to muster the breath to speak. His eyes slumped shut, pinpricks of light flashing across the backdrop of closed lids. He heard the soft pop of the cork as if from a great distance. Strong fingers pried his jaws apart and forced the smooth neck of the vial between his lips. The liquid was cool and subtly sweet as it rolled across his tongue and into the back of his throat. It was thick like honey, seeming to clog his airway. The thief fought to keep from inhaling the lifesaving antidote into his lungs but found himself slipping into the numbing arms of unconsciousness.

*****

The first thing Hollis noticed as his eyelids flickered open was the mid-afternoon sun streaming through the room's only window. Shutters thrown wide, both the sounds and scents of the Ash flooded the room alongside the sunlight. Despite the fetid quality of the air, he drew deep lungful's of it. The tightness of the night before was gone and along with it the stabbing pain that light inflicted upon his eyes. Hollis slowly brought his hand up before his face, it showed no sign of its previous tremors.

His head snapped around as across the room, someone cleared their throat.

"I thought I would be forced to watch you slumber for another evening," Seran chided. He pushed himself from the threadbare chair and stood, "This experience has certainly confirmed that my true calling does not lie as a governess."

Experimentally, Hollis slowly sat up, relieved as the action wasn't greeted with the throbbing pains that had plagued him since returning to the room above Bearon's shop. "That may be for the best," he quipped. "You do not quite have the temperament for the vocation."

"Nor the interest in aging widowers." Seran approached his bedside, watching his former apprentice with a touch of something in his eyes that Hollis wasn't accustomed to seeing: concern.

Hollis swung his legs from the bed and set his feet on the floor.

"Easy, boy, no need to run before we see if you are fit enough to crawl."

He flexed his arms and chest, testing for signs of pain or weakness. Other than a gentle tugging and distant throbbing from his seemingly sutured forearm, all repercussions of his escape from the Courtesan seemed to have faded. "I am right as rain," Hollis muttered as he levered himself to his feet. Besides a brief head rush, he felt very much himself.

"I would consider it a kindness if you took it a little slowly all the same." Seran reached out to grip him by shoulder and elbow. "It took the last of my Umma's Tears to drag you back from the brink and I would be most put out if you wasted it by splitting that hard head of yours open."

Hollis allowed his mentor to guide him back onto the bed. "Listen, Seran," he began.

Seran held up a hand and said, "I am interested in neither apologies nor appreciation. What is done is done."

Hollis slowly nodded. "What are you interested in, then?"

His mentor dragged a chair closer to the bed before answering. "I would like to hear the story of how Hollis the Slender came to be poisoned in the establishment of one of his dearest childhood friends. I would love to know why one of my more thoughtful and cunning pupils would taunt the very man who holds the key to his readmission to the Brotherhood of the Night in his hands. These things would interest me greatly."

Through teeth clenched in anger rather than pain, Hollis hissed, "That corpulent sack of shit does not keep that particular gate."

Seran raised an eyebrow, "You seem to have some strong feelings about this."

"Damned straight, I do. Dhole has perverted the guild into his personal dictatorship."

His mentor slowly shook his head. "As all leaders with any years behind them are wont to do." Seran settled into the chair, crossing his right ankle over his left. "It has always been such for as long as any can remember. The Brotherhood is a convenient bit of propaganda to keep the naive in line." He studied Hollis with hooded eyes.

"Are you calling me naive?"

"I simply share a bit of hard-won knowledge. Make of it what you will."

"The guild survives through the strength of its members."

The Slazean laughed out loud, unable to speak for a moment. As he wiped the moisture from the corner of his eye with a callused thumb, he said, "It survives through the willingness of the rank and file to sacrifice themselves for the good of those at the top. In that, it is no different than any other nation … or church for that matter."

"I refuse to believe that."

"That is the thing about facts; they are what they are, whether or not you choose to deny them."

"Do you know what is just as consistent as facts? Change."

Seran leaned forward, his smile disappearing like smoke in the wind. "Change? So, you are a revolutionary now, are you?"

Without thinking, Hollis retorted, "If I need to be."

Shaking his head sadly, his mentor sat back, "There is neither profit nor longevity in revolution, boy. It is a hard enough struggle when you fight for yourself; there is hardly surplus to do so for others."

"So, you have always told me, old man." He could tell that his last words struck a nerve in his mentor. "Where has it gotten you? You tarry under the same thumb as the greenest apprentice."

"You know nothing of my mind, Hollis," Seran growled, "and you know even less of what plans are in motion as we speak."

Hollis felt realization like a cold rain descend on him. "You have designs on Dhole's position."

The corner of the Slazean's mouth turned up in a wry smirk. "At the very least. I did not say that I disagreed with the target of your ire, but simply the method you employed. A back is much more vulnerable to the knife that comes from the dark."

Hollis's shock stunned him into silence.

"That being said, an additional knife would make things far easier. "

He frowned at his mentor. "Even one that is hunted by half the city?"

"That is a conservative estimate," Seran remarked dryly. "But that is neither here nor there. You were correct in your statement that Dhole is not the sole guardian of your path back into the good graces of the guild. Were he gone, his replacement may well be more amenable to your return

… or could be convinced to be so."

The casual way that he spoke about the murder of the guild master made the hair stand up along the back of Hollis's neck. Although Seran's hard eyes were hooded, Hollis could see the cold calculations that went on behind them. Even without the 'Gifts of the Well', he was certain that his mentor's plans went beyond a simple knife in the dark … and it boded ill for any in his way. Hollis closed his eyes for a moment and attempted to center himself, drawing on the reservoir of calmness that lay just beneath the surface of his mind. When they opened, he was wrapped again in its comforting depths.

"Tell me more." The words slithered from between Hollis's lips like the serpent of Eden. He watched as the concerned wrinkles across Seran's forehead smoothed.

"Before I do, I need to know that your attention is devoted to this endeavor. One misstep could bring years of planning crashing down around my ears, as well as your own." The corner of Seran's eye twitched almost imperceptibly, whether in fear or anticipation, Hollis couldn't tell.

"As indirectly, my own life hangs in the balance, I cannot think of anything that would press more keenly on my mind."

Although he remained reclined against the back of the chair, Seran shifted subtly forward as if he appeared relaxed by force of will alone. "Is that so?" Hollis slowly nodded, watching his mentor from within the serenity of the Understanding. "You have not found any extracurricular activities to take your mind off of your woes?"

"If you have something to ask, you should get to the point, Seran."

"Someone has been stirring up trouble in the Ash as of late. It seems to coincide with the nasty business in the library that led to your excommunication from the brotherhood. Do you find that convenient?"

"Perhaps," Hollis drawled, relying on the 'Gift of the Well' to keep his racing thoughts from his face.

"I thought so as well. This Prophet, as they are coming to be known, has taken it upon themselves to transcribe passages from religious texts on walls throughout the Ash. The church seems fairly put out by the contents of this vandalism, leading me to believe that it is not simply the ramblings of a lunatic."

"Stands to reason. I am coming to the realization that those in power are invested in keeping everyone else in the dark."

Seran winked, "Those were my thoughts exactly. Combined with the rumor that on the same night that you were seen in the library, something of great value was found to be missing."

"Rumors often find hold where the truth dares to tread."

"Normally, I would agree, but all of this seems too coincidental.

Supposedly something is missing from the Great Library. The Binders will not reveal what it is, yet they search as if for their own souls. The church calls for the man accused of murdering the curate but seem more interested in his capture than his death. A mystery man appears in the only place that would give that fugitive sanctuary, spreading knowledge like it was seed in a fertile field. It is a twisted route, but a clear path nonetheless."

Hollis studied Seran out of the corner of his eye. If the certain tone of his voice wasn't enough of a clue, the self-satisfied look that sat upon his mentor's face like a bloated spider made it clear that his words were more than wild suspicion. "Are you seriously accusing me of being the Prophet? How could that possibly benefit me?" He hoped to shake the Slazean's confidence.

"I have been ruminating about that very question since assembling the puzzle pieces." Hollis's hopes were in vain. "I thought you could help me to satisfy my curiosity."

Avoiding the inferred question, Hollis simply stated, "Gladly. There is no advantage in it for me."

"Cute."

Hollis smirked. "So, I have been told … in the right light."

Seran ignored his deflection and said, "Perhaps it benefits another?"

"Did you not just get through telling me that the only cause worth fighting for is yourself?"

"You have been known to ignore my advice before."

The thief chuckled softly, "And look where that has gotten me." His mind reeled as he and his mentor played verbal chess, furiously jockeying to maneuver the other into a trap of logic.

"That is my point, boy." Seran leaned forward and laid his hand on Hollis's shoulder. Changing tactics, he slipped into the role of concerned father figure, "I hate to see you forced into an untenable position by the needs of someone else. You still have friends among the ranks of the guild, me included."

He is getting desperate, Hollis thought. *The first thing you taught me, old man, was that allies could be a weapon while friends always prove to be nothing but a vulnerability.* "Indeed?"

"If, as you say, you are not responsible for the actions of this Prophet, I have no doubt that you know who is." Seran released his arm and rose to his feet, "Or at very least could make an informed guess."

"And if I do?"

"A lot of powerful people have an interest in putting an end to his propaganda."

It is interesting that everyone assumes that the Prophet is a man.

179

Hollis nodded, "When your house is built on a foundation of sand, it is natural to fear the flood."

Seran locked eyes with his former apprentice. "It may come down to your life or his. The boy that I know will make the right decision when the time comes."

Despite his instincts, Hollis didn't avert his eyes. He drew on every bit of the Well-gifted confidence to keep the emotions that pulsed through him from his face. "I am not the Prophet, Seran, and I do not know who is." The lie flowed from his lips, sweet and smooth. "I have enough trouble dealing with my own problems." The thief felt Seran's stare as he studied his face. Before him stood the man who'd taught him how to lie … and to detect it in others. Even within his cocoon of serenity, Hollis felt the intensity of his mentor's scrutiny.

Just as Hollis thought his endurance was at an end, Seran turned on his heel. "Fair enough." With those two words the Slazean considered the conversation at an end. "I am glad to see you back on your feet, Hollis," he purred over his shoulder, "When you are feeling completely yourself, come see me." He stopped at the door, turning briefly. "We have plans to discuss."

*****

Hollis didn't hear Seran descend the stairs; the next sound that reached his ears was that of Bearon's tentative steps on the creaking wood. Rising slowly from the bed, Hollis was pleased to find that his strength had for the most part returned. His wounded forearm still hurt although the bandages wrapped loosely around it were free of blood.

By the time knuckles wrapped softly on the door, Hollis was on his feet and pulling on his shirt. "You need not knock in your own home, Bearon."

The door opened slowly revealing the fence's bearded face, filled with concern. "I am not fond of your friend," he began.

"He is not my friend," Hollis retorted, his attention focused on the heap into which his possessions had been thrown the previous night. Frowning absently, he crouched and began sifting through them. "It is somehow less and more complicated than that."

Closing the door behind him, Bearon crossed the room and closed the shutters. "I see. I did not think he would come initially."

The thief pulled his pouch from the pile and flipped it open with a flick of his wrist. "I had no doubt that he would come. It was in his own best interest. What he would do once he arrived had me more concerned, but everything worked itself out."

He could feel Bearon's stare burning into his back. "You did not know that he would bring you the antidote?"

Hollis shook his head, "I hoped that he would but if it was more beneficial for him to let me die, that is precisely what he would have done." He slipped the pouch's strap over his head before reaching for the pair of knives that lay beneath it. "He is nothing if not dependable. It all worked out, however."

"What are your plans now?"

Sliding the knives into their scabbards, one at his thigh and the other in the small of his back, Hollis sighed. "Seran's involvement has not made my situation any less complicated, but sometimes in complication lies opportunity."

"Truth be told, I am not overly fond of complication, Hollis. Undue attention is a liability in my business."

The thief picked up his sheathed Wallin Fahr and stood slowly. "You have something on your mind, Bearon." It wasn't a question.

"You know that I have always appreciated your patronage over the years …" The fence paused, searching for words that wouldn't sound ungrateful.

Hollis saved him the trouble. "But it is becoming a liability."

"Yes, but —"

"And my presence doubly so." He turned, belting his sword about his hips. "Do not fret, my friend, I understand. There is a saying. It is from a place far removed from Oizan. No autopsy, no foul."

Bearon scowled at him. "I do not understand."

Hollis pushed past his annoyance to paste a smile on his face. "It means that I do not hold your concern for you own safety against you." He squeezed the fence's shoulder, "You have been a good partner and an even better friend." Nodding to the pile of bloody clothes, he said, "Go to the guild and tell them that I threatened you and left in a hurry once my wounds were bandaged. Pay whatever protection they demand and answer any questions they have." He seized Bearon's eyes with his own. "As long as those answers do not involve Seran. He would not look kindly upon that."

Bearon swallowed a few times before he could speak, "Are you sure?"

Hollis nodded. "I am. Perhaps once I have straightened this all out, we can resume our working relationship."

"Thank you."

It saves you the trouble of asking me to leave again, Hollis thought, *and me the heartbreak of hearing the words*. "Be well, Bearon." The fence didn't follow him down the stairs. By the time the man found the courage to descend into the shop, Hollis was gone.

181

Chapter Twenty-Six
Shadow's Façade

Hollis leaned against the alley wall, cradling his injured arm against his stomach. The moonless night combined with building's shadow hid him from the view of the few passers-by in the narrow street. At the far end of the alley, Asaege painted her latest quote, oblivious to his presence. Even in the dim light, the large black letters stood out against the dun-colored wall. *One will rise claiming to speak in my name, hiding his intentions behind thundering indignation and a traitor's smile. Beware those who seek to conceal my words from the eyes of the faithful.*

As she added the last period with a flourish of her wrist, Hollis took a slow step forward. He purposely allowed his sole to drag against the filth that covered the cobblestone surface of the alley. Asaege's head snapped around. The brush dropped from her hand as she reached for the borrowed sword at her waist. It wasn't the blade that concerned Hollis, however. He felt the words that fell from her lips deep within his chest as they shaped the words of a spell. It didn't bode well for him, no matter what shape it took.

Hollis extended a hand palm outward. At the same time, he reached for the 'Serenity of the Well'. Months ago, it'd held off the magic of a herald; he hoped that hadn't been a fluke. Before he could find his own voice, the alley fell into silence, although the echo of words his mind refused to comprehend rang in his chest. The nail of Asaege's outstretched finger seemed to catch the light of a lamp on the street behind her. Rather than fade, the tip of her finger began to glow with an illumination of its own, soon engulfing the digit to the first knuckle. Before his eyes, the glow detached itself from the woman's finger and flew lazily but unerringly towards him.

"Asaege! No!" Hollis cried, shrugging his shoulders as if he could physically pull the cloak of calm tighter around them.

Her eyes widened as she recognized her target. Asaege reached out as if she could catch the blazing firefly, but it was beyond her reach. "Hollis!" A look of helpless fear descended over her features, leading him to believe that the spell was most likely gleaned from the book he'd gifted her with rather than one of the less potent cantrips that she'd mastered before leaving the library.

The 'Serenity' wrapped itself around Hollis's heart, muting the fear and doubt radiating from it. Freed of them, he remembered seeing the spell before. It had been one of Marcus's favorites. The glowing insect could devour matter, organic and non-organic alike, but it vastly preferred the former. As it fed, it replicated itself with astounding alacrity; the more they ate, the faster they reproduced until all that remained were bones and teeth. Marcus was a far more accomplished thaumaturge so it stood to reason that Asaege's spell wouldn't carry the same virulence, but it may not have to.

Time seemed to slow as they both watched the buzzing projectile pick up speed as it shot towards Hollis's chest. His every instinct cried out for him to turn and run but he knew that survival didn't lie in escape; the spell was far swifter than he was. He simply closed his eyes and focused on the Well granted peace. He formed an image of it in his mind as physical thing, a swirling, prismatic fog between him and the approaching spell. A low drone filled his ears, accompanied by a soft intake of breath from across the alley.

And then … nothing. A deafening silence dominated the night for a split second before the sound of hurried footsteps broke it. Tentatively, Hollis opened one eye and then the other. Asaege ran towards him, her face a mask of worry. On the filthy cobblestones, flickering like a low burning match, lay the product of her spell. As its glow faded, the insect itself became insubstantial and then disappeared as if it had never been.

Asaege's body struck him hard and caused him to stumble backward. She wrapped her arms around him, allowing him to regain his balance. Hollis looped his right arm around the small of her back, but his left was caught between their bodies. A sharp knife of pain exploded in his recently stitched forearm.

Gritting his teeth against the pain, he found himself reluctant to release the pressure on his injured limb. Hollis could feel the heat of Asaege's body against his skin; the gooseflesh it raised there dulled the pain into a distant ache. The force of her breath against his neck made his voice catch in his throat.

Hollis felt her gasp as if she were preparing to speak, but nothing emerged. Never at a loss for words, he searched for them now. Hollis felt her fingers at his back and the butterfly-light touch of her cheek against his chest. As suddenly as it began, the moment ended. Asaege stepped back, her jaw set. "What is wrong with you, Hollis? I could have killed you."

Blinking quickly, he fought to regain his senses. When he didn't answer her first question, she fired another pair at him in quick succession.

"Why would you sneak up on me? Do I not have enough to worry about?"

Gently cradling his left arm in his right palm, Hollis replied slowly, "I will agree that it was ill advised. The fault was entirely mine."

"Damn right it was," Asaege agreed. Her self-satisfied smile evaporated when she saw the grimace of pain on his face. "You are hurt. I must not have botched the spell so badly after all." Her concerned expression contradicted her words.

"I have seen the spell cast before and I do not believe you botched anything. That being said, I brought this particular injury with me." He lifted his arm and allowed his sleeve to fall towards his elbow, revealing the silk bandage that encircled his forearm.

"What happened?"

Hollis dismissed her question with a slow shake of his head, "A bit of ill luck in the midst of an equally ill-advised action."

For a moment, he thought she would press the matter, but she let it drop. "When you did not appear last night, I decided to give you the day before venturing out myself."

"If tonight proved anything, it is that you certainly can take care of yourself. From what I gathered from Marcus, that spell is neither simple nor for beginners."

"I am still not sure I performed it correctly."

Hollis laughed. "Do I hear a touch of disappointment in your voice that your glowing beetles of death did not make a meal of me?"

Asaege averted her gaze. "Of course not," but it was obvious that she wasn't being completely honest.

He sighed loudly. "You cast the spell just fine. Magic just does not affect me the same way it does most folk …" Her eyes shot back to him, a question evident in her stare. He continued, "In that it does not ..."

"Does not what?"

185

"Affect me … in certain circumstances."

"What circumstances are those?"

"It is complicated," he muttered more to himself than her as he approached her newest graffiti.

Thankfully, she'd let the matter drop before stepping up beside him. "I am kind of proud of this one. It is inspired by the Hand's most recent sermon."

"It seems a bit ominous."

Asaege shifted her gaze to the wall, but her eyes remained unfocused, "I suppose." The specter of trepidation hung in the air as she appeared to examine the quote and Hollis in turn studied her. Softly, she began. "So, I had an idea."

Hollis grumbled, "Five more frightening words have never been spoken."

She rolled her eyes and snorted softly, "You have not even heard it yet."

"Feel free to share, but I have a sneaking suspicion that more detail is not going to change my opinion."

"More and more people are coming to me in the hopes of learning to read," Asaege began, "And I am not the only one. Anyone who knows their letters is drawing crowds that many merchants would envy."

"The difference is that merchants get paid." She turned a hard glare upon him. "But that is not important. Please continue."

"Almost to a person, they want to read the words of the Prophet for themselves."

"That is not a good thing, Magpie. The fact that they are giving a name to the author of these," Hollis gestured to the message before them, "puts everyone in danger, most of all you and me." He stepped between her and the wall, blocking her view of it. "The fact that they are calling you a prophet —"

"Us," she interrupted, "and they are not calling us a prophet, they are calling us the Prophet."

"That makes it worse. People do not stay in power by allowing challenges to that power. The only safety a revolutionary can find lies in anonymity. If we give them a target, they will certainly oblige us by attacking it."

"That is where my idea comes in."

Hollis raised an eyebrow. "Why do I think that this idea does not involve hiding?"

"Because it does no such thing. If they are going to come for the Prophet anyway, which if I understand your logic, there is no way to avoid now, why shouild the Prophet not strike at them first?"

186

"I suddenly understand how Silvermoon must have felt," Hollis grumbled. Again, Asaege narrowed her eyes at him. "Please go on," he prompted.

"Thus far, the only people to read the passages we have written are those here in the Ash. The Hand can spin them any way he likes to his congregation, as they have not seen the words for themselves."

"Our nocturnal vandalism sessions have been successful thus far due to the fact that most in the Ash look the other way, if they do not outright support our actions." He turned and squinted into the distance, where a pair of spires stood against the low hanging moon. "That would change once we paint our first letter outside the Common Quarter. We might as well break into the Ivory Cathedral itself and paint passages from the Dialogues there."

Asaege smirked slyly and slow blinked at him. "Now that you mention it …"

Hollis frowned hard, "You cannot be serious."

"The Hand could not deny our words then. They would be there for all to see and more importantly to read."

"Is that worth the risk you are proposing?"

"For too long, the truth has been filtered through his agenda as a prism bends the light of a candle, causing it to split and distort into shapes so unlike its original message."

"And you believe that by merely reading these passages, his hold over Olm's faithful will be broken?"

Asaege took a deep breath, letting it seep from her lips slowly, "All words carry the power of the knowledge they convey. I know it sounds insane, but I believe these words in particular have power in and of themselves. I have no other explanation for the swell of devotion that even the rumor of them has evoked in the people of the Ash. The passages we have chosen are inspiring but not so much that they should motivate literally hundreds of people to learn to read in the space of a week. It is as if the words themselves carry the weight of Olm's will itself."

"And the more folks that see them —"

"— the more people will be affected by them. In addition, I believe the closer they are to the center of Olm's power, the more potent they will become."

Hollis rubbed at his eyebrow with a stiffened finger, "And, of course, that just happens to be the center of power for the man who hunts for us most passionately."

"The universe does certainly seem to have a sense of humor."

"That it does."

Despite the grim prospect before them, Asaege smiled softly. "Can I

187

assume that you agree with my plan?"

"It is not much of a plan … more a desired end result." Hollis looked into the depths of her face, so hopeful … so steadfast. He wasn't completely sure if it was what he found there or the low burning anger at the prospect of being hunted, but he wanted to see this to the end. "I cannot believe I am saying this, but yes, I am on board."

Impulsively, Asaege reached out and grasped Hollis's hand, squeezing it tightly. "The hard part is behind us; all that remains is the doing."

Hollis glanced from their intertwined fingers and her beaming face, unsure which pleased his eye more. *Focus, Hollis*, he thought, *breaking into the library will be like ripping a newspaper compared to the phone book that is the Ivory Cathedral.* "Oh, is that all?"

"Did you not tell me once that if there is a way out of a place, there is a way in as well?"

"Those were not my exact words, but the theory remains sound. I was within the walls of the Cathedral years ago. It was brief but I paid attention." Hollis's last visit had served double duty. He was primarily there to secure aid for Haedren, but he had used the trip to case the building for a fellow guild mate. The man had paid handsomely for the information, although Hollis was unsure if the heist had been successful. "I may know a way, but I would love to have another look at the inside before we give it a try."

"Any danger you may face acting on your memory's counsel is far outweighed by that of walking into the Ivory Cathedral in broad daylight."

Hollis turned on his heel, not releasing Asaege's hand. She didn't resist. The two moved slowly towards the mouth of the alley, relishing the shadow filled calm before the storm of what lay ahead of them. As they stepped out of the darkness into the flickering light of the lamp lit street, a broad shape turned the corner and blocked their path.

*****

Backlit from the street, details of the big man's appearance were lost in the space between light and shadow. Hollis noted clearly, however, his steel breastplate and sheathed longsword. Resisting the urge to push Asaege behind him and rush the soldier before he could gather his wits, Hollis squeezed his companion's hand and consciously forced an easy tone to his voice. "Good evening, milord," he chirped cheerily. He watched the man's frame stiffen with surprise his hand twitching towards the hilt of his sword; Hollis resisted the instinct to reach for his own.

The soldier's panic passed quickly, "Good eve to you as well." As he stepped forward out of the glare from the street, details of the man became clearer. Sans helmet, his chin length black hair hung loose around his face, free of any tie or ribbon. In the dim night, his brown eyes appeared virtually black as the soldier squinted at the pair. Hollis judged his age within a few years of his own, although the fine wrinkles at the corners of his eyes and mouth gave his features a gentle cast that contradicted the message sent by armor and blade.

Hollis felt Asaege's hand tighten in his own as her other one clasped his shoulder. Turning his body to place it between her and the newcomer, he kept his voice even. "If you will excuse us, it is late, and we would like to start for home."

The soldier raised an eyebrow. "Home? Where would that be?" Hollis couldn't help but appreciate his approach. The words held an interrogatory nature that was absent in his almost conversational tone. Something itched at the back of the thief's mind, forced aside by the immediacy of the present situation.

"We rent a small apartment over a shop on Butcher's Way," he lied smoothly. Butcher's Way held the lion's share of the Ash's butchers, grocers and fishmongers. Providing it as a location was almost as nebulous as not telling him anything. More importantly, it was a fair distance from either Bearon's shop or Asaege's home.

Hollis didn't break stride as he approached the soldier, intent on closing into knife range as quickly as possible. *Soldier or not*, he thought, *none can connect us to the Prophet ... and the graffiti behind us will surely do just that.*

"Oh," the man said, surprise evident in his voice, "perhaps you can help me a moment, then?" He shifted his body slightly, trimming a few inches from the space between himself and the alley's wall.

Hollis released Asaege's hand and tried to slide free of her grasp, but she clung tightly to him. The fingers of her other hand dug fiercely into the joint of his shoulder.

A twinge of fear sparked in his belly. She held fast to his right hand and with a freshly stitched wound in his left forearm, he wouldn't be able to draw the knife at his waist and stab the soldier before he was able to draw his sword. Once the thick bladed longsword came out, this would turn into a fight. Fights invited attention; which was the last thing the pair needed. "I am sorry, friend," Hollis purred, "We are in a bit of a rush."

The soldier extended his arm and laid his hand on the wall, effectively barring their passage. "It will only take a moment." His voice was conversational, without a trace of menace.

The thief tried again to extricate his hand, leaning his head against Asaege's. "Set me loose, Magpie," he hissed softly.

She whispered what could well have been the last words Hollis wanted to hear in that moment. "I do not feel so well. I think she is coming."

Still too far to hear their hushed conversation, the soldier stepped forward, concern evident on his face. "Is your companion unwell?"

Hollis realized he could not engage the man and deal with Asaege's imminent reflection at the same time. He laid his lips against her soft tresses, whispering into their depths, "Be in the moment. There is naught by our hands … my voice." Instinctively, he pursed his lips and kissed her lightly on the head. "There is nothing but us." He felt her tuck more closely into him.

The man before them took another step. "Do you require aid?"

The thief shifted his eyes up to regard him. "Thank you for your kind offer but she has simply allowed her desire for celebration to overcome better judgment." He kept his tone calm and his cadence smooth for Asaege.

The soldier held up his hands. "Of course. Of course."

Hollis gripped his companion's hand gently and moved towards the street. His thoughts were a whirlwind of trepidation and possibilities. Could he get Asaege somewhere safe and return to kill this man before he disappeared into the Ash's maze of streets?

"Just one question," the man continued, "if you do not mind."

Hollis felt frustration rise in his throat like bile. "I would really like to get my companion home."

"I understand, but it will only take a moment." Again, the soldier extended his arm to block their passage.

Through the clouds of exasperation and anxiety, realization dawned. Hollis had heard that voice before. It was less than a week ago, in Bearon's shop. He hadn't seen the Binder's face but his voice stood out in Hollis's mind. The way he maintained a conversational tone while relentlessly digging was quite remarkable. The thief's stomach dropped.

Beside him, Asaege murmured, "Hollis?" Ignoring the pain, he reached up to cradle her head with his left hand.

Pulling her head close to his lips, Hollis whispered, "You need to be still, Jillian. Our fate walks on a razor's edge." Shifting his eyes back up to the soldier, he said, "As long as it is only a moment."

"I am looking for someone and I am hoping that you can help me."

Focusing on keeping the maelstrom of emotions that swirled through him from his face, Hollis shrugged. "There are a lot of people in Oizan. Unless their fortune skews towards the dire, the Ash is not the best place to begin your search."

"From what I have gathered, he may indeed find himself in such dire straits." The soldier ran his fingers through the thick beard at his chin, "My issue is that there seems to be an inherent distrust between the

190

local people and anyone with a hint of authority."

"Do you blame them?" Hollis's tone carried an unintended edge. The soldier cocked his head but didn't comment. "The Ash does not seem to garner anyone's attention except when something needs to be taken from it."

"The only thing I wish to take from the Ash this night is knowledge." The soldier took another step closer; Hollis gave ground, turning his body to shift himself between the woman in his arms and the oncoming man. He ceased his advance immediately, bringing his hands up, palms out, again. "You have nothing to fear from me, I assure you. We are just two folks chatting. My name is Rudelph and I represent neither the city guard nor the templars of Olm."

"Then tell me who it is that you do represent, Rudelph? And who is it that you seek?" Hollis already knew the answer to the second question but needed to hear it.

"I am a Binder, sworn to protect the knowledge held within the Great Library with my life ... and beyond it if required."

"Protect it from whom?" The question came from under Hollis's arm. Jillian and Asaege seemed to grow more similar by the night. Or perhaps they always were.

The question clearly took the Binder by surprise. He paused before responding, "That is an excellent question, milady, and one not easily answered." He turned his attention back to the thief, "As to who I search for, that is simpler. Have you heard of Hollis the Slender down on Butcher's Way?"

The question wasn't unexpected, and Hollis had an answer prepared, "I have heard the name." Asaege's body had relaxed against his side, although her arm now loosely encircled his waist. "He is neither merchant nor laborer; in the Ash, that indicates that it is best to not look into his affairs."

Rudelph nodded slowly. "So I have been told. I fear, however, that my duty demands that I do just that. Have you heard news of what happened in the Library a week ago?"

Hollis shrugged noncommittally. "Word spreads here the same as anywhere else. Some priest or another was killed."

"More than a simple priest, the curate to the Hand of Light was slain. There are many who put the knife that pierced his heart firmly in the hand of Hollis the Slender."

"You said yourself that you represent neither the church nor the city. What interest is that to a librarian?"

The soldier chuckled softly. "You do certainly have a gift for understatement, my friend. While I would cherish the opportunity to serve as a simple librarian, I have taken an oath as a Binder."

"As you say." Hollis felt panic begin to rise within him again. When faced with a devoted man and a greedy one, he preferred the latter every time.

"The difference lies in the fact that librarians seek knowledge; I am charged with the pursuit of truth. It is a subtle distinction, but I assure you an important one."

Hollis took a step forward, moving closer to the wall. "The truth is that I cannot help you find the man you seek, Binder."

Rudelph didn't move to block his passage but turned to keep the thief in sight. "Cannot or will not?"

Icy fingers of dread clawed at Hollis's spine as he passed close to the soldier, releasing their grasp as he put himself between Rudelph and the street. "Cannot."

The Binder spread his hands helplessly. "Fair enough. Have a pleasant evening, …" He seemed to search for a moment. "I do not believe I asked your name."

Hollis shook his head but didn't respond.

"I see," Rudelph said. "One more thing though."

Darting a glance over his shoulder towards the street and freedom, Hollis growled, "And what is that?"

"It is funny … well not exactly funny, let us call it peculiar. An interested party insists that a book has been stolen from the Great Library. This work is of great value to them, but they are unwilling to provide the title or subject of said work. Yet they are more than forthcoming regarding their certainty that Hollis the Slender is the thief."

Hollis guided Asaege's body into the flickering light of the street. "Seems shady to me."

Rudelph allowed the pair to depart. "Indeed." It wasn't clear to the thief if the words were meant for him or the Binder himself.

*****

Hollis attributed the silence between them as they rushed through the Ash streets to Jillian's disorientation but as soon as he closed the door to Asaege's tiny apartment, the questions began in rapid fire English. "Who was that guy? Is he hunting you? Us? Why'd he let us go?"

The thief held up his hand and responded in the same language, "One question at a time, please." He could see more stacking up in her eyes, but she kept them to herself for the time being. "That was Rudelph and he's a Binder. They're like library security guards if in lieu of charging overdue book fines, they could just kill you."

"He didn't seem to be in much of a murderous mood."

Hollis pondered her words for a second before answering, "No, he

192

didn't, did he? I'm not sure whether that should give me hope or not."

"I'd like to take it as a positive."

Hollis nodded absently, his thoughts hurried and scattered. If he left Asaege's body in Jillian's care, he may be able to reach the alley quickly enough to track the Binder down before he left the Ash. If he could catch him by surprise, his Dwarven steel dagger would do the rest; if it came to a fair fight, however, Hollis was less certain of the outcome. Against thugs and common sell-swords, his fair skill with a blade, combined with the gifts of the Well, gave him quite an advantage. When faced with a trained soldier, though, that was quite a different story.

She poked him hard. "Hollis!"

The thief looked up, a frown stamped on his face. "What?"

"Didn't you hear a word I just said?"

He rubbed at his eyes. "I feel that when folks ask that question, they're already pretty sure of the answer."

"I said I didn't get a sense that he was antagonistic as much as curious. If you approach everything as a nail, you'll only ever use a hammer in response."

Hollis opened his mouth, a witty retort on his tongue but allowed it to slack closed. She was right. In the rush of so many enemies coming at him from so many directions, he hadn't stopped to think that not every party that had their eyes set on him sought his demise. The thief saved a little of the blame for Seran's cynical world view, passed on in his younger years. "You're pretty smart, Jillian," he said, "have you ever thought about becoming a teacher or something?"

"I'll look into that," she laughed, "for now, what's our next move?"

He raised an eyebrow. "Our next move? What are we in, a bad mob movie?"

She rolled her eyes,. "Rudelph is a potential ally. He's looking for the book —"

"Which Asaege would never consider giving back."

She smiled. "Believe me, I know. I can feel her raging in the back of my mind for just thinking about it, but there has to be a way to make peace with this man. Do we have enough allies that we can afford to toss one away?"

"Again with the 'we'"

Hurt flashed in her eyes. "I'm part of this too. Ever since I first reflected, I've been involved."

Hollis softened his tone, "I know and believe me, I appreciate your investment. It may have become too dangerous for you to continue, however."

"I have one of the journals and a plan for getting the rest."

He shook his head, "Absolutely not. It's come to my attention that Plague Man is in the city; he has been for weeks." The thief saw her swallow hard, but she didn't reply. "That puts him close to Asaege and through her, you. He's had more than enough time to put a plan in motion if he has one. Putting them in the same place at the same time you and Hector are in close proximity is a risk that I am not prepared to take."

She clenched her teeth. "It's a good thing that no one is asking you to. It's my risk, my decision." Hollis opened his mouth, but she cut him off, "When she wakes up, feel free to ask Asaege, she'll say the same. We aren't some helpless damsel as much as you aren't a white knight atop a wild stallion. We're in this together … all three of us, and we can use all the help we can get."

"You're very frustrating, do you know that?"

"So I've been told. Do you want to know what I found in the journals or not?"

Chapter Twenty-Seven
Innovation's Legacy

Jillian rubbed at her eyes with a knuckle. Despite sleeping like the dead for eight solid hours, she felt as if a portion of her still slumbered. Stifling a yawn, the woman took a deep breath as if trying to smother the feeling of fatigue with the crisp morning air.

Hollis had listened raptly to Jillian's summation of what she found in the journals but didn't evidence surprise. He'd been in the Traeth town square, had lived through the hellish battle that followed Haedren's escape. A quick perusal of the journal in her possession revealed that Hollis had played a part in the events documented on the remainder of its pages.

Although equal parts fascinating and frightening, the journal she had would add to neither the thief's understanding of his friends' fate nor either of their knowledge of the relic that Plague Man most likely now possessed. Both of those things lay in the building before her.

The florist's simple sign, Florist and Holistic Medicine now held a feeling of dread for Jillian. The knowledge of who stood on the other side of the frosted glass storefront gave the shop itself an aura of menace. She'd considered calling Cyrill to ask him to go with her but Hollis's warning about Hector's use for fellow reflections filled her with worry for her friend. If she was going to face him alone, at least she was able to enter the lion's den with open eyes. Jillian felt her confidence, rallied in the safety of her bedroom, begin to wane. She closed her car door and hurried across the parking lot before it could flee completely.

The small chime above the door rang like a church bell as Jillian stepped into the close, warm air of the shop. The cloying air drew a stark contrast to the cool autumn morning she left behind. The front room was identical to her last visit, but it now held a malevolent cast previously unnoticed. Among the close packed greenery stood vases filled with flowers well beyond their prime. Suspended between life and death, the bouquets hung flaccid in their dusty vases. Petals were curled in upon themselves; their edges rimmed in black, they clung stubbornly to their stems as if they too feared what lay on the floor below them. Rather than the comforting gauze of a greenhouse, the air reminded Jillian of the stale death shroud air of a tomb.

As her eyes swept the room, the only area that seemed alive was the table that held adder root. The table that held it was free of debris and dust. Unlike the funeral procession that was the rest of the shop, the adder root was vibrant and well-tended. The way the deep purple veins stood out against dark green leaves reminded Jillian of an old man's hand, parchment thin skin barely containing the blood vessels beneath. Her imagination bent the broken shadows that lay across the table into a rhythmic pulse; although it turned her stomach, she found it oddly hypnotic.

Before she found herself completely absorbed, the curtain at the rear of the room was pulled aside and Hector stepped out of the back room. A crooked smile split his face, although it reminded Jillian more of a sadistic boy burning ants with a magnifying glass than actual joy. "Jillian, right?"

Her response caught in her throat, so she settled for a quick nod.

"I never forget a face," he purred proudly. "What brings you back so soon? Cyrill isn't much for sharing?" His gaze dropped and lingered as he waited for her response.

Jillian felt a spike of anger and found her voice, "Something like that." When he didn't raise his eyes, she cleared her throat.

Hector met her glare and shrugged helplessly. "Where is ol' Cyrill this morning?"

"Like you said, if he doesn't have the sense to not argue with his dealer, I thought I might be better off flying solo."

He raised an eyebrow, "Is that so?" When Jillian didn't reply, Hector laughed sharply; it emerged as more snort than mirth. "Suit yourself." He turned his back on her, placing the counter between them. Over his shoulder, "What have you come in looking for?"

The tiny hairs on the back of Jillian's neck stood on end. *He knows,* her thoughts were a maelstrom, *I shouldn't have come alone. I should have at least told Marisol where I was going*. Her eyes darted across the counter's surface in search of something, anything she could use as a weapon. A large pair of scissors lay half open beside a messy stack of brown paper sheets. She flinched as Hector reached for them.

The corner of his mouth twisted upward as he snapped them closed and dropped them into a faded coffee can among the eclectic selection of pens. "No matter how careful I am, I always seem to leave something or another laying around." His eyes became hard. "But somehow, I never seem to really misplace anything."

Jillian swallowed hard but was able to choke out, "Dreamtime."

Hector clasped his hands before him, rubbing palm on palm. "Same as last time? A half?"

She nodded, finding her equilibrium once more. "It depends, same one seventy as last time?"

He tilted up his chin and regarded her for a moment. "I like you, Jillie. I think we're more alike than either of us would like to admit."

He knows.

"Let's call it one twenty … friends and family discount." Hector's voice dropped to a low growl as he said, "You want to be my friend, don't you, Jillie?"

Jillian heard her heart pounding in her ears, but she managed to keep her tone even. "Sure, Torie, I can always use more friends."

His grin disappeared like smoke on a windy day.

"I mean as long as we're friends, there is no harm in getting familiar, hmm?"

"Touché, Jillian. Give me a few to get it together." He emphasized her full name like he was driving a knife into the dirt.

"Thank you, Hector." She returned the favor. "Would you mind if I had a look around?"

Hector pushed his way through the curtain, offering, "Knock yourself out," over his shoulder as he disappeared into the back room.

Jillian wandered among the neglected flowers aimlessly, her attention on the narrow space between curtain and door frame. She watched as he pulled open the large walk-in refrigerator in the back corner and disappeared inside. As soon as she lost sight of him, Jillian dove through the curtain, her sights set on the small stack of leather-bound journals still piled beside the pair of antique chairs. Snatching the topmost book, she flipped it open to the first page and scanned it quickly. It was dated May 8th, almost a month after the last entry in the journal she already possessed.

The sound of Hector's thick soled footsteps announced his return. Jillian tucked the journal into her waistband and pulled her shirt down

197

over top to cover it. Impulsively, she grabbed the next book from the pile and fled through the curtain. By the time he emerged a moment later, she'd gotten her breathing under control. Jillian couldn't be sure if the ache she felt in her stomach was from the butterflies that fluttered there or the way the edge of the journals stabbed her viciously in the gut.

He extended the small sandwich bag towards her. "Here you go, I hope it's everything you were looking for."

Consciously trying to not contort her body, Jillian took the bag from him and tucked it into her back pocket. "Thanks, Hector."

He regarded her again with his piercing eyes. "You've got everything you came in for, then?"

She nodded. "I think so."

"I guess I'll see you again soon."

"See you soon," she muttered, turning for the door.

As it closed behind her, Jillian thought she heard him say, "You can count on it."

*****

May 8, 2010

We are still on his trail, although despite traveling deep into the night and forgoing sleep for the advantage, we remain three days behind him. Marcus believes he is using the ring properly; but the Walker was so rushed in her explanation, we can't be sure. Mika continues to harp on the fact that while we chase the words of the Herald, our quarry may be getting further away. Besides splitting up, I can think of no other options, however. Should Haedren command a fraction of the power that Theamon was capable of, I am not sure that any one of us could best him. Although I would never tell the others, I am unsure that even the three of us will be able to slay him and take the relic. If we had Ret's axe, I would feel more confident.

I only wish I could have made Roger believe our wild tale or had been able to convince the others to allow me to tell Stephen. He is young; but what Stephen lacks in worldliness is offset ten times by Hollis's guile. I was tempted to approach Hollis himself on this side; but I could not in good conscience pull him into a potentially deadly situation without knowing what effect it may have on Stephen on the other. I am sure that if he knew what was at stake, he would agree without a second thought and jump in with both feet. Perhaps that is why it is wise to exclude him; he has too much life left to live. If this all falls apart and goes wrong, at least I can live with the thought that he will have the bright future I know he is capable and deserving of.

The adder root began to fade that night. Although I yearned to see

198

Alice and Alan again, I dreaded what we would come back to after half a day. I could only hope that we are still in pursuit of Haedren and that my fear that we do not have the ability to defeat him does not come to fruition while I pass the day on this side. I worry what will become of us if while on this side, our personas on that were to die.

May 9. 2010

When I woke in Taerh, the sun was just peeking through the patch-work of trees surrounding our camp. Mika sat beside the low burning fire, putting whetstone to steel. The slow, rhythmic scraping grated on my nerves as much as the stone did on her sword's edge. As much skepticism as Roger had offered when I tried to convince him of my double life, Beatrice had shown acceptance. At first, she'd wanted to believe in the existence of Taerh more strongly than even my brother. Once George first reflected, that changed instantly. He has tried to explain to me the sensation of wielding the arts of a Thaumaturge but always follows any description with the statement, "But you can never really understand until you've actually done it."

Unfortunately, that is not in my cards. Through Silvermoon's mem-ories, I can get a sense of Marcus's character and if you remove the fan-tastical aspects of their lives, our brothers are more alike than they are different. Bright and enthusiastic, they both share a thirst for knowledge that seems to bring them joy through its pursuit alone. Both share an in-ner light and sense of humor that make even the darkest of times seem a little less so. I have found that I have some difficulty discerning whether Marcus or George is in control at any given moment.

On the other hand, Mika and Beatrice couldn't be more dissimilar. Beatrice is kind and selfless to a fault. She will spend fifteen minutes capturing and relocating a bug to avoid killing it. While a loyal friend, Mika most certainly is her own first priority. She is brash and abrasive even to those she considers friends. Those who she sees as 'sheep' (her words) are treated with benign neglect at best. Mika kills with little regard for the lives she takes. Truth be told, I think she actually enjoys it. I never have trouble deciding who is present when it comes to Mika and Beatrice. This night, the warrior reigned.

She watched me through hooded eyes, studying me as a cartog-rapher does a map. After a moment that seemed to stretch for ten times that, Mika finally spoke. "You realize," she began, "that when we do catch up with Haedren ... Theamon ... whoever, we will need Silvermoon and Marcus rather than the two of you." Although her tone was flat, the disdain was clear.

"I do not have much control over when and where I reflect."

She made a non-committal but still displeased noise.

"Two of you?" Marcus pulled his attention from the book splayed open in his lap long enough to join the conversation. Hanging from a limb above him, a lantern swayed gently in the morning breeze. "I assure you, Mika, I am quite myself."

"Hard to tell," she muttered, not taking her eyes off of me. "Perhaps you should abstain from the practice for the time being. Once 'Moon returns to the farm, the two of you can play 'swap the body' all you like."

"Reflect," I corrected.

"Whatever. My point is that you not only put him at risk, but while you and your friends are playing dress up, this is deathly serious for us." She gestured to include me, Marcus and herself. "If your little milkmaid slips in at the wrong time, we will both end up on the wrong end of Olm's hall." I felt my face tighten into a grimace but didn't trust myself to speak. "I can feel her, even now. It is like she scratches at the backs of my eyes but as in everything else, she finds herself without claws."

Taking a deep breath, I felt my anger smothered by the cloak of calm that I had come to know well. Despite the fact that I was in control, I could feel Silvermoon's presence in the back of my mind. It was a comfort that, even now, is hard to describe. "I understand your concern, Mika."

"I did not request your understanding. I asked you to leave our business to us."

"You realize that Silvermoon and I are of the same mind on this matter, correct?"

"He has mentioned it." She stood smoothly, like a snake uncoiling itself in preparation to strike.

A flash of panic eroded the edges of my fortress of tranquility but faded just as quickly. I pushed myself to my feet, standing to meet her advance.

"Hey!" It was Marcus's voice, sharp and insistent. Both of us turned to regard him. "If you two are through butting heads, I think that I may have found something that can actually be of use to us."

Mika squinted at him but ceased her approach.

"It was designed for something completely different, but there is a workable framework here," he closed the book on his lap and lifted it for us to see, "to sever the connection between the brooch and our comrade. There is no telling how much damage Theamon has done to his psyche but we could most likely deprive him of the power he now wields."

*****

On the facing page, written in another hand, was a block of text.

Barely a quarter of it was legible to Jillian; the parts she could read made very little sense to her. They seemed to describe varying tones of voice and differing emphasis on words that swam before her eyes as if the ink danced on the page. In the back of her mind, a sensation akin to a barely forgotten memory formed like an itch. Contrary to common sense, Jillian felt she should understand what lay before her.

Chapter Twenty-Eight
Shadow Play

People who feel secure in their sense of their own superiority rarely turn their myopic eyes downward. Hollis was glad that this theory held true within the gilded halls of the Ivory Cathedral. As the center of Olm's church in Granatyr, a virtually uncountable mass of humanity passed through its doors on a daily basis. None of them, be they petitioner or parishioner, could be allowed to see that the chosen of the Dawn Lord were fallible, breathing beings.

As such, the nuts and bolts of the great machine that was the Ivory Cathedral were expertly hidden behind curtain and mirror. Hundreds of laborers, pages and merchants came and went via a hidden highway of passages and tunnels.

Deliveries and disposals came and went without a whisper of notice among those under the vaulted arches of the church. During the day, these entry points were nominally monitored by low-ranking acolytes; in the depths of the night, those assigned to police the diminished but still substantial traffic were less than diligent. A pair of tattered cloaks and three silver nobles worth of fresh mutton were all that had been required to shuffle by a pair of only marginally awake sentinels. Once into the maze of catacombs that spider-webbed the building, it'd taken only moments for he and Asaege to find their way to the Grand Chapel.

In the thin hours after midnight, the cavernous chamber stood empty. Only a few scattered lanterns burned low to keep the night at bay, but the light was sufficient for the pair's work. Owing to the dangers inherent to their new surroundings, he and Asaege eschewed their normal pattern of her writing and him standing guard. In the name of haste, they were both forced to set brush to wall. To Hollis's frustration, Asaege was by far the quicker.

He was just completing his work on the first quote Asaege had written a week ago; she'd already finished copying her most recent one beside the altar and was beginning a new passage, chosen for this occasion. It read: *There shall be one among you to sound the call. When it is heard, my children, rise up, cast aside your chains and walk in the light once more.* She was just beginning the last sentence, her brush strokes both effortless and precise in equal measure. A sharp cramp in his right hand drew his attention to the fact that it hung suspended a few inches from the wall while he stared at Asaege's back like a schoolboy. Chuckling to himself, Hollis turned back to his work, finishing the last letters with a few wide flicks of his wrist. Rubbing absently at the back of his hand, he stepped back to admire his labor.

Each of my children are warmed by a measure of the flame used to mold Taerh itself. The rich and poor are as one in the eyes of the creator. Unsure if the words truly possessed the power that Asaege suspected they did, Hollis found himself swept up in the process all the same. When he'd been two distinct beings, separated by worlds and circumstances, Stephen had found satisfaction in lending a hand to those around him that lacked his advantages. It was that very same lesson that Silvermoon had attempted to pass down to him before his friend's death. Hollis couldn't help but smile at how, through a series of unexpected events, he seemed to be right where the forester had intended for him to be.

So lost in thought was Hollis that he almost overlooked the subtle flickering that danced out of the corner of his eye. Snapping his head around, he searched the deep shadows that cloaked the choir loft. At first, he was tempted to attribute it to his imagination but again in his peripheral vision something moved within the darkness. Hollis clicked his teeth together and made a sharp hissing sound to draw Asaege's attention. To her credit, she turned immediately.

Angling his body so that his back was to the loft, Hollis pressed his fist and one outstretched finger to his chest. He gestured to the darkness behind him with his eyes. Asaege was nearly through writing the newest message.

Despite the danger, she looked back helplessly at the incomplete passage. He sighed softly and pointed directly to himself and then over his shoulder. He then pointed towards her and mimed writing in the air

204

close to his chest.

A look of concern stamped on her face, she turned and quickly began painting again.

*****

Hollis had been blessed with remarkable night-vision; it was the only good thing left to him by his biological father. It certainly was nothing of a supernatural nature but had served him well throughout the two plus decades that followed their parting.

Once he began to climb the deep crimson carpeted stairs to the choir loft, he left the feeble lantern light of the main chapel. This was where he felt truly at home; there was something inexplicably comforting about the way shadow and stillness folded itself around him.

His footsteps barely raised a whisper as Hollis crested the stairs and moved into the claustrophobic clutter of the loft itself. Slowly lowering himself to one knee, the thief scanned the dim expanse before him. Disordered lines of benches and carelessly discarded choir robes in the darkness were spun into ominous shapes by his imagination. Pulling the cloak of serenity about his shoulder, Hollis squinted into the darkness, his body as still as the objects around him.

At the far end of the loft, a high arched door stood open. Beyond it a silhouette shifted, a deeper patch of shadow. Although his every instinct cried out for him to arm himself, Hollis remained motionless. His eyes remained single-mindedly fixed upon the yawning opening. Again, the shadow flitted from door frame to door frame. In the back of his mind, an itch formed; something about it seemed off.

As soon as the space beyond the door was again still, Hollis shifted forward on knee and toe. When the shape again dashed past the open portal, the thief froze in place. Almost instantly, his awkward pose caused tremors of pain to radiate through the small of his back and into his thighs. Despite the discomfort, he resisted the urge to shift position to relieve it. He waited the count of four slow breaths after the shadow disappeared from sight to allow his knee to settle again to the floor.

The thief focused his attention on the doorway as he forced his muscles to relax, letting the tension drain from them in a slow, steady flow. Again, the shape darted from one side of the arch to the other. The itch exploded into a haunting suspicion. Its actions were too predictable, its movements a little too smooth. With a practiced motion, Hollis pulled the thin stiletto from its sheath on his thigh and cocked his wrist in preparation for the shadow's next appearance.

When it appeared at the door frame, he threw the blade sidearm. It flew true, unerringly striking the shape center mass … and passed through as if it were nothing but air. Before the sound of his knife

205

skidding to a stop in the room beyond reached his ears, Hollis was at the choir rail. Below him in the chapel, Asaege stood with a leather clad arm looped under her right arm and around her throat. A matching leather gloved hand covered her mouth. The woman's cheek was pressed against a nearly featureless black mask. It had been described to him by Asaege in passing, one of a rush of details about the Hand's sermon the day prior. He'd been called Curate Reisling but Hollis had no doubt of the true identity of the man who wore it. On the Plague Man's lapel, the silver accents of the brooch caught the room's meager light.

Hollis's eyes searched frantically for something … anything to break his fall were he to leap from the loft; naught but hard wooden pews lay before him. "This is between us," he called, his mind racing but no plan answered his call, "you have no need of the girl!"

The expressionless mask cocked to the side, a muffled voice emerged, dripping with contempt. "You have no idea what I do or do not need, Slender One. You never have."

The thief began moving towards the stairs, hoping to keep the assassin occupied until he reached them. "Let her go and we can finish this."

A choking laugh echoed through the marble chamber. "My dear Hollis, I have no intention of finishing anything." Plague Man rotated his body to keep Asaege between himself and the thief. "As a matter of fact, I am just getting started." His words reverberated off the room's walls; they almost covered the creaking sound of footsteps on the stairs. "This is not about you. I imagine that it is quite a blow to your ego, but it never has been."

Hollis drew his sword quickly and took a careful step back to keep the archway beyond which those stairs lain in sight. "If you harm one hair on that woman's head, I swear —"

"— that I will not live to regret it?" Plague Man interrupted, his voice taking on an almost bored tone. "I have heard similar words from you before. If I recall, they were simply that: words. The half-breed … the priest … the dwarf. I have left behind me a trail of your former friends, but you continue to ignore the obvious."

Two broad shapes filled the doorway. Unlike the shadows that had lured him into the loft, these didn't lack substance. The thief took another step back, squaring himself with the more imminent threat. "Oh, really? What is that?"

Plague Man's next words were spoken in English, "I'm simply out of your league. As much as you want to be Val in Tombstone, you're more like Paxton in … well, anything. Definitely entertaining, but supporting cast nonetheless."

Any retort died on Hollis's tongue as two armed men came through the door. He lifted his foot, catching a stool under the sole of his boot. A swift kick sent it tumbling end over end towards the opponent closest to him. The man paid dearly for his enthusiasm; the lip of the stool caught him under the knee and caused him to tumble forward. He was left sprawled senselessly before the thief for a moment. That time was all Hollis needed to drive the blade of his sword between throat and shoulder; the man didn't rise.

"Unless my ears deceive me, Hollis," Plague Man called in a saccharine voice, "you have visitors. I'll leave you to it, the lady and I have business to attend to."

The thief spared a fleeting glance into the main chapel as the remaining swordsman cautiously closed the distance. Asaege struggled against the assassin but with her arm pinned above her head, he had an untenable advantage. As Plague Man dragged her backward, the patches of shadow that surrounded the altar seemed to flow like early morning fog about their ankles. Like an ice bath, the cold dread of helplessness seized Hollis's heart. "I am coming for you, Magpie!" The words felt hollow even as they emerged from his lips. "There is nowhere that you may hide from me!" Shouted through a clenched jaw, he wasn't sure if the statement was meant for his comrade or the Plague Man.

"We both know that to be untrue, Hollis. Your thin threats, as profound as they may sound, are becoming a touch pathetic." A rasping laugh echoed through the empty chamber. "Perhaps you should focus on the issue directly before you. I believe you are about to have your hands full."

Hollis took another step back, his gaze flashing to his opponent and then back to where the two had stood. All that remained was darkness and incense. Below him, Hollis heard the pounding of boots on marble. The man closing on him wore unadorned leather breastplate and breeches. *No doubt mercenaries hired by Plague Man for this very task*, he reasoned, *I assume that will not be the case with the approaching soldiers.* For reasons of his own, the assassin had wanted their interaction to go unnoticed; now that he'd made his escape, that secrecy was no longer required. Without a doubt, the approaching footsteps belonged to templars, men sworn to the cause of the Father of Justice … true believers all.

Hollis launched a back-handed swing, angling the hilt of his Wallin Fahr higher than its blade. It made contact with that of his opponent as the man parried. With a quick rotation, the thief reversed the momentum of his sword and let it slide along the mercenary's. Hollis's blade entered the soldier's thigh just below the hip, scraping bone before emerging from the far side. He went down in a heap, a blood curdling scream echoing through the chapel.

The thief lifted his sword, preparing to deal the coup de grace but found his hand hovering in midair. The man at his feet had his eyes closed tight against the inevitability of the blow, but it didn't fall. "I am no murderer," Hollis growled through gritted teeth, more to himself than his fallen foe.

The loft stairs squealed under the feet of mailed soldiers, cutting off his only path back into the main chamber. Behind him lay the 'servant's maze' and a potential escape. That escape, however, meant leaving Asaege to the tender mercies of the Plague Man.

The faces of the people he'd failed flashed in his mind, a highlight reel of guilt. Jeff. Beatrice. Renthroas. Mike. Jhorwynn. Each and every one of them had needed Hollis in their most desperate moments. Each and every one of them had died due to his absence or inability to save them. Plague Man had been responsible for the three most recent and seemed to revel in the fact. Like the perpetually feuding archaeologists in Stephen's favorite movie, there wasn't anything close to his heart that Plague Man could not take from him.

What if I cannot stop him again this time, he thought, *what if Asaege's name has to be added to the list burned into my heart?* A darkness that had nothing to do with the shadows that surrounded him settled on his mind. Although they'd known each other for only a short time, the thief felt a connection to the woman that both scared and exhilarated him. The feeling devolved into a hollow terror when he thought of her in the hands of that monster. Like the shock of cold water in his face, a thought sprang to mind. *Asaege is far from lost. Plague Man does not need to beat you as long as you give up and do his job for him.*

The Asaege he'd come to know would be fighting with all her might, how could he do any less?

But to continue this battle, Hollis would need to escape the ambush in which he currently found himself. *Hold on a little longer, Magpie*, he thought, *I will not give up on you, please do not give up on me.*

When the wounded man opened his eyes, Hollis was gone.

Part Two:

The End of Heart and Shadow

"Our lives begin to end the day we become silent about things that matter."

-Martin Luther King, Jr.

Chapter Twenty-Nine
Shadows of Defeat

Hollis crouched unseen, a deeper patch of darkness in the shadow between two buildings. Across a cobblestone plaza, stood the Ivory Cathedral in all its towering glory. The small outbuildings that flanked the courtyard served as storage and other day-to-day needs that the clergy sought to distance from themselves.

While their marble faces gave the impression of opulence, the illusion grew threadbare in the narrow passages between them. The pinky-width marble facades had chipped and fallen away in places, revealing the worn stone and daub surface underneath. He did his best to ignore the obvious metaphor.

His eyes scanned the night, alert for any hint of activity around the massive church before him. Immediately after his escape, templars had poured forth from a handful of doors like drones from a kicked anthill in pursuit of him. After a brief search of the plaza and an even more abbreviated one of the surrounding buildings, the soldiers dispersed. Two small knots of men rushed towards the Royal and Library Gates, the two points of egress into the Oizan proper. The remainder dispersed quickly, leaving the courtyard empty once more. *If Plague Man is going to move Asaege*, Hollis thought, *this would be the time to do it*. Yet, the plaza remained deserted.

A dull burning stung the back of Hollis's throat, a physical manifestation of the guilt he felt for abandoning his companion to the not so tender mercies of Plague Man. His mind was a violent storm of thoughts, all focused on what he could have done differently … how he could have reached Asaege before his enemy had called upon the dark magic held within the brooch. He cursed himself for a fool; he should never have fallen for the shadow play in the choir loft. That had been the domino that started the entire situation.

No, he thought, *it began when you did not retrieve that damned brooch from where the Walker had thrown it.* He replayed again and again in his mind the events at the Well. *Was it there when Walker fled? Was Plague Man gone by then?* He couldn't seem to bring the scene into clarity, even with the aid of the gifts given him by the Well itself. Frustration warred with anger and guilt in his heart, their conflict lodging itself like a lump in his chest.

Closing his eyes and rubbing at them with thumb and forefinger, Hollis tried to assuage his guilt by focusing on the path forward. He knew nothing of the brooch's powers besides what he had seen himself. If it was able to conceal its master in shadow, it was a real possibility that the cursed item could also use them to spirit Plague Man and Asaege away from the cathedral without ever having to enter the courtyard.

Frowning, the thief shook his head slowly. From the admittedly small amount he knew of thaumaturgy, actual teleportation was extraordinarily difficult. If the brooch's former owner, the Walker, had been able to command that particular ability, Hollis and his companions would never have been able to beat her to the Well of Worlds, no matter how fast they traveled. Yet when the Herald had arrived, he, Aristoi and Jhorwynn had been waiting for her.

At the thought of the dwarf's name, he felt the ball of rage buried in his gut flare again. Plague Man had been correct about one thing. He'd taken so much from Hollis and the thief had been unable to stop him. *What makes me think that I will have any more luck now?* Anger turned to despair. Like the unrelenting caress of the tide against the sand, his hopelessness eroded the cloak of calm confidence that the Well had placed around his shoulders. A frozen spear of panic transfixed his heart, dispersing his sense of tranquility like smoke before a sharp breath.

Hollis used the fingers at his eyes, to pinch the bridge of his nose and exhaled sharply. *Fear kills more men than the object of that fear ever could*, he thought, paraphrasing a line from his favorite book as a young man, *If it can be weathered as a ship does a storm, on the other side, only calm water and the ship remain.* The thief took a slow, deep breath and tried to remain in the moment before him. What had occurred before was the past; no matter how hard one tried to change it, the past remained forever etched in stone. What lay beyond his next breath was lost in the mists of the future, beyond his reach and, as such, unknowable. He could only affect the moment now.

He could feel the crisp air against the walls of his sinuses and taste the faint vestiges of incense on the back of his tongue.

By focusing on the inches of the now rather than the miles of the future, Hollis was able to smother the blaze of panic and despondency. Unable to extinguish it entirely, he was content that in lieu of a raging conflagration it simply smoldered. Slowly, the thief opened his eyes and allowed his perception to expand beyond his next breath. *It stands to reason that if they have not emerged by now, Plague Man has another escape plan in mind.* If that plan involved magic, there was little that Hollis could do about it, so he thought about outcomes that he could affect.

Asaege's paraphrasing of his own words came to mind: if there is a way out of a place, there is a way in as well. Sweeping his eyes across the plaza one final time to verify that no one remained, Hollis stood slowly and began circumnavigating the open area.

Dodging from shadow to shadow, he made his way to the church's 'service entrance'. To the thief's surprise, the outbuilding's gold painted doors were closed tight. Oddly fit to the frame that held them, flickering lantern light could be seen through the gaps. Something blocked the escaping illumination at waist height, indicating that the doors had been barred from the inside.

In their enthusiasm to catch him, the templars had also cut off Hollis's enemy's only subtle means of escape. For better or worse, whatever his plans for Asaege may have been, Plague Man was for the time being caught inside with his prisoner.

*****

A handful of copper commons bought Hollis three extra pairs of eyes to watch the most likely exits from the Ivory Cathedral as well as the silence of their owners … or so he hoped. The guards manning the Royal Gate quickly lost interest in the events within the chapel; with it fled any heightened vigilance that they may have mustered earlier in the evening. They were night watch after all. Overnight gate security didn't draw the best and brightest of Oizan's finest. The thief was able to join a cluster of students bound for a night on the town and slip through the gate without so much as a second glance.

Once into the High District, he was able to separate himself from the group and make his way to the Merchant's Quarter through an unlocked storm culvert. This unguarded thieves guild egress allowed him to bypass both the Garden and Market gates completely. Confident enough that his passage had gone unnoticed, Hollis felt comfortable rushing to

215

his intended destination: The Silver Courtesan. There was a possibility that he'd temporally exhausted any good will that Torae held for him, but his list of friends was becoming shorter by the minute.

After the uproar he'd caused with his last visit, the thief had thought better of walking through the front door. The shared storeroom served him as well as an entrance as it had an exit on his hurried escape nights before. Dim lighting and a low pulled hood had been all he required to slip through the courtyard (and past the damnable bush that had almost killed him) and into the brothel proper. This time, however, he avoided the business facing areas of the building, instead making his way to the small section that served as a dormitory for any employees who required as much.

Despite his repeated suggestions, the lock on the door to Torae's personal chambers matched the simple decor that pervaded the remainder of the hallway. Picking it took Hollis less time than if he'd possessed the key. In the interest of remaining in her good graces, he relocked it once he entered. Torae didn't seem as appreciative as he'd hoped when she stepped into the room to find him reclined on her bed.

"Sweet Umma," she cursed, bringing her hand to her mouth as she recoiled. Her shock turned quickly to anger. "Hollis," she hissed, "What are you doing here?"

Sitting up slowly, the thief chuckled. "If I did not know better, I would think you were not happy to see me."

"If you knew better, you would not be here." The daggers in her eyes softened. "Of course, I am glad to see you in better shape than I left you, but I am still trying to convince a plethora of interested parties that your presence here a few nights back was nothing but coincidence." Torae squinted at him, "Your repeated visits make that considerably more difficult."

"I could see that, Tor," Hollis muttered, "But I find myself in a bit of a bind."

"When are you not?" She paused as if waiting for an answer. She repeated, "When are you not?"

The thief climbed to his feet, "I will admit that my life has been … let us call it complicated as of late but as hard as it will be to believe, this time it is not my fault. Well, not completely anyway."

Torae regarded him with doubt hanging in her eyes. "It never is."

He tried to look incredulous but found himself without the energy to do so. "I understand why you may feel that way, Tor, but this time is different."

"How different?" The continued softening of her features indicated that perhaps she sensed the sincerity of his words.

"I cannot go into it at the moment." Torae's mouth began to tighten. "Believe me, it is better that way. I am involved in some seriously heavy things."

She raised an eyebrow. "Heavier than the death of the curate? Heavier than being hunted by half the city?"

"As hard as it may be to believe but yes. It is something that you do not want to know about."

"And why is that?"

Without hesitation, Hollis responded, "Because you would want to help. I have already lost one person that I …" The word on his lips was 'love' but he'd only known Asaege for a couple of weeks, give or take a day or so. He barely knew her much less loved her, but he couldn't deny the connection he felt.

"That you …" Torae prompted.

The thief shook his head, exiling the thoughts and their associated feelings to the back of his mind. "… that I feel responsible for. I will not … I cannot risk anyone else, especially not you."

"I am not a wilting rose. You, of all people, should be aware of that."

He reached out to lightly lay his fingertips on her forearm, "I am, Torae, but this is trouble you do not want … that you cannot afford."

"Then why come at all, Hollis?" The anger was back in her eyes, but it wasn't the hard steel of earlier. Her forehead wrinkled in frustration. "I cannot help you with something you refuse to share."

Hollis nodded. "I know. I need a place to think, somewhere free of all the noise to figure a way out of the storm that I find myself in."

Torae studied him for a moment before responding. "You always have a port here; we have seen too many of the same roads for me to turn you away."

"Thank you, To—"

Her voice cracked like a whip as she cut him off, "But we cannot … we will not have a repeat of the Dhole situation. Am I clear?"

"Thank you."

"Am I clear?"

The thief exhaled slowly, trying to allow the stress that ran though him like a live wire go with it. He was only partially successful. "I understand."

He saw her relax as well. "Sit down, then. For now, you are safe. I am not sure that I will be able to say that tomorrow but with the night winding down, you should have little to fear at the moment."

Hollis did as he was bid, allowing his body to settle once more onto the downy surface of her bed. It felt so soft beneath him, its depths singing a siren song to his weary body. It took an effort of will to shake off the tempting call.

"If you will not accept my help, there must be someone that you care for not quite as dearly that you may call upon."

A name sprang to mind immediately but given that Hollis had lied to his face during their last conversation, Seran may be less disposed to help him rescue Asaege. The prophet represented a thorn in his paw and her being removed from the picture could only benefit his mentor's plans. "There is someone …" Trepidation crept into his voice without intention.

Familiarity is not always a good thing. "Is there no one else?" Torae said, "There has always been something off about him."

"Off is one the nicer things that can be said about him but in my current straits, Seran may well be my only choice."

"What about the letter I delivered?"

Hollis nodded, a spark of hope flashing in his heart when he thought about the letter's intended recipient. Reality stamped it out before it had the chance to flare into flame. "There is no telling where its recipient is. The letter could take months to find her." He felt his shoulders slump. "No, Seran represents my last hope." A feeling of dread sliced into his gut like a knife. "If I had any other choice, I would take it."

Torae hooked her finger beneath his chin, forcing him to meet her gaze. Whatever she saw in his eyes caused any argument to die on her lips. "I can get word to him through a …" she searched for the most polite term, "mutual acquaintance." Seran didn't frequent upscale establishments like the Silver Courtesan; he preferred his companions with less shine on them. She let her hand fall to Hollis's chest and pushed him back against the piled pillows. "It will take some time … time enough for you to get some sleep. Whatever you have planned, I imagine it will not be aided by exhaustion."

Hollis fought neither her shove nor the gauzy curtain of weariness that settled upon him as soon as his head sank into the downy depths. The insistent heaviness of slumber, however, was unable to ease the crushing guilt that pressed down upon him in equal measures.

Chapter Thirty
Shadows of a Hope

A few hours of sleep did wonders for Hollis's physical wellbeing, the ever-tightening band of exhaustion behind his eyes had almost disappeared. His mental state, on the other hand, was a different matter. The hollow ache in the thief's heart had intensified into a throbbing pain during his nap.

Before he fought his way through the cottony depths of slumber, his mind was already a barrage of thoughts. How could he have slept while Asaege remained in the hands of that monster? While he lay wrapped in downy comfort, in what desperate straits did she find herself? Wouldn't that time have been better spent doing … well anything?

He pushed himself roughly to his feet, taking three steps before he felt the icy fingers of the stone floor clawing at his soles. Although Hollis's sword and daggers were arranged neatly on the chamber's modest table, his boots were nowhere to be found. He vaguely remembered Torae re-entering the room and pulling a thin blanket over him. At some point, she must have also taken his boots. Sinking to one knee, he peered beneath the bed.

"You will not find them there, Hollis," a voice behind him remarked. "As a matter of fact, if you were able to find them at all, it would defeat the purpose of me taking them in the first place."

The thief turned to see Torae framed in the doorway. He bit his lip lightly. "No boots on the bed?"

A sly smile graced his oldest friend's face, "There is that … but I have chosen to overlook it for the time being."

"So, you took my boots because …" He allowed his voice to trail off, waiting for her to fill in the blank.

"I will not fool myself into thinking that cold feet would stop you from making mischief, but I figured it would at least give you pause."

"I cannot stay here any longer. With or without Seran, I have to do something."

A second voice emerged from the dim hallway. "Then it is indeed fortunate that I was not otherwise occupied, boy." Seran stepped past Torae and into the room. His crimson hair was pulled back with a black ribbon that matched his silk shirt, worn over gray calfskin breeches. Whatever he'd been pulled from, there was little doubt that he had indeed been otherwise occupied.

"I hope that I did not pull you away from anything important," Hollis began.

His mentor studied him with a sidelong glance. "There is no need to be polite, Hollis. You hope no such thing." Without turning, he spoke to Torae. "Thank you for the escort, sweetheart, but we have important business to discuss."

Over Seran's shoulder, Hollis saw Torae's lips tighten into a scowl. She mouthed, 'You owe me,' before taking a step back. "I have business to attend to anyway." As she closed the door, she chided, "You boys behave," but her eyes never left Hollis's.

The thief walked to the table and wrapped his sword belt around his waist, acutely aware of the fact that Torae hadn't returned his boots. "Torae is a friend, Seran. There is no need to treat her —"

"— like a whore?" his mentor interjected. "I know that you and she grew up together, but your paths diverged long ago."

"Not so much," Hollis muttered, "we both get paid to take advantage of people and I would say that her way of going about it is more honest and a great deal more pleasant."

Seran dismissed his words with a sour look and wave of his hand as he continued to circle the room as if he were in a merchant's stall. "Is this why you dragged me away from my evening? I had hoped it would be something more …," he pulled open a drawer and peered inside, "… pressing."

Forcing the annoyance from his voice, Hollis said, "I need your help."

His mentor opened the double doors of the room's wardrobe and answered, "That much I have gathered. My inferred question would be

220

'with what?'"

Hollis buckled his stiletto against his leg and reached for the thick, dwarven steel dagger that had been Jhorwynn's final gift to him. "An associate of mine is in a bad way."

Seran turned, not bothering to close the wardrobe behind him. "An associate?" He nodded towards the door. "Or another friend?"

"It is complicated," was Hollis's reply. With the dagger sheathed at his back, he turned his full attention to his mentor.

"It always is. This bad way ... Would it have something to do with whatever has the templars all riled up, would it?"

The thief debated lying to him, but the truth would come out soon enough if Seran were to aid him. "It does."

"Damn it, boy. I thought I warned you to steer clear of the church. Zealots do not have the same concept of winning and losing as you and I. It makes them frustratingly difficult to deal with."

"Can we possibly skip the lecture? Time is truly of the essence."

"The lecture? Of course."

Hollis felt the temptation to relax but knew better.

Seran smiled; it was a predator's grin. "I do have some questions, however."

The thief remained silent and gestured for him to continue.

"This complicated associate, were they with you in the library?"

"She was."

Seran raised an eyebrow. "She, hmm? What are the chances that this mystery woman took something that did not belong to her while there?"

Through gritted teeth, Hollis replied, "Pretty good."

His mentor nodded slowly. "So, during our conversation following your recovery and —"

The thief didn't let him finish. "I never denied knowing that something had been taken from the library."

Seran scratched absently at his chin. "That much is true." A look that bordered on pride crossed his face. "Although you did claim ignorance as to the identity of the Prophet."

"So, I did. I still hold to the fact that I am not him." Hollis was careful with his pronoun.

His mentor didn't take the bait. A broad, toothy smile swept across his face, like a shark on a blood trail. "But you know who is, and you want my help to rescue her." He stressed the last word, his amusement clear.

"How long have you known?"

Seran snorted. "Are we telling the truth now?"

Hollis averted his gaze. "I did not want to get you involved." It wasn't a lie, just nebulously phrased.

"Until you needed my help." Like wine from a glass, the emotion drained from his face, leaving a blank slate. "Had you come to me earlier or at least been honest when I asked, perhaps we could have prevented things from getting to this point."

The thief felt his jaw tightening. *Or perhaps you would have used the information for your own agenda.* He resisted giving voice to his thoughts. "We are where we find ourselves."

"So, we are." Seran paused for a moment, considering. "Tell me, boy," he began, "what is in this for me?"

In a moment of true honestly, Hollis blurted out, "I need your help, Seran. I cannot do it alone." He was a boy again, with neither friend nor family.

His adopted father figure reached out, seizing his shoulder. "I want what is best for you, Hollis, I always have."

A spark of hope blossomed in the thief's heart. "Thank you —"

"— there is a price, however. Despite what the church tells you, charity is good for neither the soul nor the coin purse." Seran held up a finger. "First, if I aid you in this,, you will help me put Dhole in his proper place."

Hollis raised an eyebrow, "That being an unmarked grave?"

"Where else?"

"I do not see a problem with that."

Seran clicked his tongue against his teeth and held up a second finger. "Second, you need to find the boy I raised." He poked the thief roughly in the chest. "Whatever happened to bring about your recent change of heart, find your way past it." Through clenched teeth, he hissed, "What needs to be done requires the killer that you are, not whatever guise you have been pretending is truth since you returned."

The sudden venom in his mentor's voice took Hollis aback. "It is no guise, old man. Do not fool yourself, however. Even though I no longer snap at every breeze that tousles my fur, my teeth are no less sharp."

"We shall see, Hollis ... we shall see. First thing first —" Seran's next words were interrupted by the sound of hurried steps in the hallway. Both men turned, their attention fixed upon the door as it burst open.

*****

Torae stood in the open doorway, the thief's worn boots clutched in her white knuckled grip. "The city guard is here. Despite my insistence to the contrary, they have it in their heads that Hollis the Slender, murderer and heretic, is hiding somewhere in the Courtesan." She tossed them at his bare feet, "I do not get the impression that they are going to cease their search until they find him, or they strip the building for tinder. At

222

this very moment, they are knocking holes in my walls and interrogating the occupants of every room."

Hollis snatched up his boots and leaned against the table to pull them on. "How long do we have?"

She scowled at him, "Until they find you or until they drive away every patron I have spent a decade cultivating?"

He glanced at Seran and then back to her, "We will be gone in a matter of moments."

Torae's scowl remained. "That does me no good, Hollis. If they do not find you, they will not cease looking to my detriment."

The thief nodded. "Then find me they shall."

Seran snarled, "Are you insane?"

"Opinions differ," Hollis countered. "But finding and catching are two distinct things. Torae, how quickly can you clear out the kitchen?"

"Five minutes, give or take one or two. Why?"

"It is a confined space with an abundance of obstacles. It is also hot as Sharroth's Cage, putting armored men at a disadvantage; we will take every one of those we can find. Most importantly, though, is that there are a handful of exits." He smirked towards Seran, who nodded in appreciation. "With such a rich choice of holes to scamper through, the mice are almost certain to elude the clumsy paws of the cat."

"Why do I get the impression that escape is not your only goal?" Seran's voice held the flat tone of resignation.

Hollis's tone became flat. "Torae and her people did not bring this upon their own heads. Any trouble that we brought with us —"

"— you," his mentor corrected.

"Any trouble that I brought with me," Hollis corrected, "I intend to take with me."

Torae exhaled sharply, half snort half chuckle. "I honestly cannot wait to hear how you plan to do that."

He shook his head. "Be assured that once you do, your enthusiasm will cool. Take Seran with you downstairs to clear out the kitchen. When everyone is gone, meet me back here." He turned to Seran. "Do you think you can make pursuit as unsavory as possible, old man?"

A lopsided smile coloring his lips, his mentor nodded. "I think I have a few tricks left in my bag, boy."

Hollis turned his back and began to scan the room. "Go quickly, time is not our friend." He glanced over his shoulder at Torae. "You do not mind if I borrow some of your spirits, do you?"

Throwing open the door, she led the way into the hall. Her muttered words elicited a chuckle from the thief. "I am sure I do not want to know."

To no one in particular, Hollis responded, "You most certainly do not."

*****

The two small bottles tucked inside Hollis's vest ground into his ribs as Torae struggled against his gentle grip as if it were made of iron. "You do not need to sell it so hard," he whispered in her ear. Her only response was a stiff elbow to his hip. Perched at the top of the grand staircase, Hollis took the brief moment before they were noticed to take in the scene below him.

Two pairs of guardsmen were working over the Silver Courtesan's common room, their minds seemingly more focused on destruction than actually looking for anything. Polished chain shirts flashed in the flickering candelabra light beneath the forest green cloaks of their office. They ground painted porcelain shards beneath their booted feet as they stepped past the splintered remnants of once delicate lacquered side tables. Stray feathers hung in the air around the men, no doubt having found their freedom through the wide gashes in overturned silk couches. The men were nothing if not thorough.

So engrossed were they in their vandalism, Hollis thought he might have to draw attention to himself. A thick, scarred guard saved him the trouble. As he cast a Teigroosian vase to the floor, the man spotted him out of the corner of his eye. With a dumbfounded look on his face, the scarred guard turned to face him. "There he is!" The man's tone was unsure, as if coming across something he had no intention of finding.

Hollis raised his voice, intending for it to carry. "I am not going to be here for long. Stand back and keep your hands where I can see them or the whore is going to have one more hole than Olm had intended." Torae drove another elbow into him, this time deep into his gut. "I am only playing a part, Tor, it has to look real," he whispered into her ear. She joined him in his ruse by letting out a high-pitched scream. His head was so close to hers that it caused his ears to ring.

Without thought, all four guards took a step back. Hollis seized the opportunity presented by their shock to descend the staircase two steps at a time, Torae clutched against him. For her part, she continued to scream. That part the thief could have done without. To their credit, the men gathered their wits quickly, but not swiftly enough for them to charge him on the stairs. He shoved Torae from him as his feet touched the marble floor, aiming for the last intact piece of furniture in sight. Hollis paused only long enough to see her slump dramatically onto its cushioned surface before turning to rush through the kitchen door.

All of the lamps in the room had been extinguished; the only light that remained came from the cooking stoves' flickering flames. Reaching

224

into his vest, Hollis pulled free the two fragile bottles of Angels' Voice, thanking his luck that they had both remained intact. Similar in color and taste to Absinthe, the bottles of pale green liquor felt warm in his hand. The thief squinted into the dim depths of the kitchen in search of his mentor. A soft rap of metal on metal reached his ears, followed by another two in rapid succession.

Crouched beside a rack of pots, Seran tapped his dagger against a cast iron frying pan. The flickering light glinted off of its bright steel surface. Resisting the temptation to take the most direct route, Hollis dodged to his left around a large, free standing set of shelves just as the door burst open.

"He cannot have gotten far," a rasping voice called. "He will not be able to hide for long."

One of his pursuers must have caught sight of Seran because he shouted, "There! Get him before he gets to the door!"

The staccato of boots told the thief that, unlike himself, they'd taken the obvious route from one side of the kitchen to the other. It didn't take long for their folly to become apparent. The sound of a body hitting the floor was immediately followed by the cascading of cookware. The liquid hiss of what Hollis assumed to be scalding cooking oil against flesh was overwhelmed by the agonizing screams of whichever of the men had been directly beneath Seran's makeshift trap. It pulled at Hollis's heart, but he forced his sympathy down. Should these men lay hands on him, he would be fortunate if they merely killed him on the spot.

The thief circumnavigated the no doubt hazard filled central aisle, making his way to where he'd seen his mentor. As he reached the back wall of the kitchen, he saw a crouched form that could only be Seran beside a hastily arranged stack of boxes, knife at the ready. He softly tapped one of the bottles against the iron leg of an unlit stove. Seran tilted his head just enough to bring him into his peripheral vision and almost imperceptibly nodded before turning his attention back to the kitchen and the unsubtle guards making their way through his minefield of terror.

Where four had pursued Hollis into the dim room, only two crossed between him and his mentor. Further into the kitchen, the thief could hear the moans of the pair's comrades. What concerned him more, however, was the raised voices a little further away as reinforcements entered from the common room. They couldn't waste time in dealing with the closest men or risk being overwhelmed.

Seran must have come to the same conclusion because he leapt to his feet, his lithe body uncoiling like a spring. His full weight crashed into the boxes, bringing the entire stack toppling down upon the nearest guard. The wooden avalanche drove the man from his feet. Like a dancer,

Seran skipped across the splintered mess of crate and struggling guardsman. His Slazean stiletto held before him, Seran's left hand was clenched in a fist at his side.

The guardsman took a half step back, putting his straight bladed Granatyrian longsword between himself and the charging cutthroat. Tucking his right shoulder, Seran dropped into a crouch as he allowed his momentum to carry his left hand forward, opening his fingers. A cloud of pepper and ground glass filled the air, catching the feeble light for a second before striking his opponent square in the face. As the guardsman brought his free hand up to his eyes, the point of his sword dropped. Before the man could react, Seran was upon him, driving his thin bladed dagger into his side repeatedly. So slender was the knife that even the closely woven chain mail offered feeble protection.

Hollis heard the heavy footsteps of the second wave and stepped past the dying guardsman. He squinted into the dark, just making out the approaching group. As they passed the closest lit stove, he tossed the bottles towards it in rapid succession. As the first bottle broke against the iron surface, the flames within ignited it instantly. A small gout of flame erupted beside the leading figure. As the second bottle struck, the flame reached out as if alive and engulfed the man.

"That is all I have, and it will not slow them for long," the thief shouted to his comrade as he turned toward the door. "Although it should properly motivate them to give chase." Seran snorted by way of an answer and followed right on his heels. The door opened onto a narrow, refuse-filled alley but garbage wasn't all that clogged it that night. A half dozen armored shapes stood between them and freedom.

"At least it should be a short chase," his mentor quipped, driving the blade of his dagger under the door and giving it a short kick. "That is a short-term solution, at best."

Hollis drew his Uteli sword and stepped forward. "Three to one odds are not terrible," he offered. His voice didn't hold the optimism of his words.

He heard Seran pull a pair of daggers behind him. "I live my life in a way so as to never find out. Thank you so much for broadening my horizons." His mentor's sarcasm was sharper than his blades. A heavy weight crashed against the door, but the makeshift doorstop held for the moment. "Seems to be only one way forward, boy. Feel free to carry on."

The guards surged forward. If they'd moved together, the pair would have been quickly overwhelmed but in their enthusiasm, two of the guardsmen outpaced the rest. Hollis took the nearer one's overhand swing against his Wallin Fahr, slipping to the right and allowing it to deflect harmlessly away from his body. He struck out with a booted foot, striking the guardsman just above the knee. He felt the joint give way beneath his kick. As his opponent's injured leg collapsed beneath him, the thief brought his sword around and struck him in the back of the neck, between his helmet and chain shirt. The dying man folded like a discarded toy as Hollis allowed his momentum to carry him through, drawing his weapon free as he passed.

Seran was engaged with the other overenthusiastic soldier as Hollis moved towards those that had lagged behind. His mentor lunged and feinted in an attempt to draw his opponent's weapon far enough away from his body to close the distance.

Out of the corner of his eye, the thief saw the guardsman swing a little too wide and Seran slip inside his reach. Hollis was certain that their fight had entered its endgame. Corps-a-corps, there was little the man could do against Seran's furious knife work. The thief turned his attention to the four men in front of him. The odds had fallen to two to one, but they still remained steep.

Pushing the nervous electricity that pulsed through him from his mind, Hollis allowed the reassuring blanket of serenity to settle about his shoulders and studied the group before him. Although they were shield-less, the four guardsmen occupied the width of the alley. They approached cautiously, swords in a low, angled guard. Their numbers, combined with a careful advance, made them an intimidating obstacle. They could, if they so chose, hold off the pair until their comrades on the other side of the door finally broke free. At that point, Seran and his situation would become untenable.

Seran stepped up to stand beside him, the dead man's short, broad-bladed sword clenched in his fist. Adjusting his grip on his own, longer weapon, Hollis shuffled forward, testing his footing on the grime covered cobblestones. The only sound in the alley was the shuffling of booted feet as both sides took stock of each other. The tension was so palpable that Hollis's cheek twitched as if caressed by an unseen hand. He shook his head sharply and narrowed his eyes, trying to remain within the depths of his 'Gift of the Well'.

Again, a cool touch moved across his skin. Despite the unlikelihood of it in the stale alley air, it felt like a gentle breeze. A deathly stillness hung in the night, only broken by tentative footsteps. No offer of quarter was voiced; none would be given. Beneath the nervous shuffling, however, Hollis's practiced ears picked up something else. It sounded like a wordless tune, low and plodding as the strides of hopeless men. A spark of hope leapt to life in the thief's heart. Although he knew not the song, the voice was unmistakable.

The song's volume rose quickly, smothering the sound of footsteps as a wet blanket does a smoldering flame. As the melody grew in power, the wind returned in force. One of the approaching soldiers turned, trying to locate the source of the sound. Back lit by lanterns that lined the street stood a lithe figure, shadowy hints of thick braids hanging about their shoulders. Clutched in their hands was thick bladed weapon, more glaive than spear.

As she stepped into the dimly lit alley, Aristoi's features became clear. Her voice rang clearly, although as the words reached Hollis's ears, they slipped from his mind into the ether. It was the mark of magic, only those practiced in its use could understand the syllables that made up its language, much less retain them. The wind matched the volume of the Songspear's voice, causing her braids to float upon the sharp currents that whipped around her body. Also held aloft by the building maelstrom was an assortment of refuse from the alley, jagged pieces of masonry among the cloud of grime and garbage.

"What the —?" The guard who'd turned to regard Aristoi's arrival gave voice to a question that echoed in the thief's own mind. His inquiry was cut short as the Songspear stepped forward, spear held at the ready. The weapon proved unnecessary as she forced him into the wall of her personal hurricane. The guardsman recoiled as the wind buffeted him with its invisible but unrelenting hands. A barrage of fist sized mortar chunks struck him across the shoulder and head. A few even found their way inside his steel helmet. He dropped to the street with the rapid-fire sound of stone on flesh. As Aristoi took another slow step forward, the soldier's unconscious body rolled lazily from her path, coming to rest against the wall.

The trio standing between the thief and his savior glanced nervously over their shoulders. No words were shared between Hollis and his mentor as they leapt forward as one; none were needed. Seran stabbed low, catching the nearest guardsman in the gut just above his hip. As the soldier recoiled, he exposed his neck. Seran didn't allow such an opportunity to pass. His stiletto, held in an icepick grip found a home just beneath his jaw. Before the guardsman could recover, the knife was withdrawn and driven home again. A fountain of crimson erupted into the night as Seran shoved the already insensible man into his comrade.

On the opposite side, Hollis had driven forward, knocking the soldier's sword aside with his own. He angled the point of his weapon down and lashed out with the pommel. With a wet crack, dwarven steel met flesh and cartilage. The guardsman stumbled back, his free hand clutching his broken nose. Blood streamed through clenched fingers and ran down his forearm. The thief gripped his sword at mid blade and viciously drove it downward into the inside of the man's thigh just below his chain shirt. The soldier sank to one knee, head held in his stained hand, a lamb waiting for slaughter.

Seran's words ran through the thief's head: *What needs to be done requires the killer that you are, not whatever guise you have been pretending is truth since you returned.* The man at his feet offered no defense. With one swing of the sword in his fist, both the soldier and the threat he represented would be at an end. A year ago, Hollis wouldn't have hesitated. He would have bought his life with that of the helpless person before him. That was before the Well ... before Stephen. He knew in his heart, he couldn't go back. Never again would death be the cost of expediency. Retreating a step, Hollis turned his attention to the last soldier.

The remaining guardsman stumbled back, his head swiveling between the two men before him and the Songspear at his back. He took another step and pressed his back against the stone and mortar wall. The man looked as if he wanted nothing more in life than to drop his weapon, but his darting eyes spoke of his fear of doing so. Seran stalked the soldier like feral dog, the tip of his stolen sword making lazy figure eights in the air. Aristoi's voice fell into silence, although it seemed for a moment that it was held aloft on the quickly dwindling wind. Hollis caught his friend's eye for a second and saw her brows drawn together in concern.

"He is no threat, Seran," Hollis began. His mentor tilted his head to study him out of the corner of his squinting eye.

"Whose voice do I hear?" Seran asked, "The hungry boy of old or the sated man who has forgotten where he came from?"

Aristoi muttered, "Hollis ..." adjusting her grip on the spear she held before her.

The thief growled. "You heard me. One cowering man is not worth the time we would spend dealing with him." Another hollow thump echoed through the alley as the trapped guards threw themselves against the door. "Although, I would dare say his friends are hoping that we spend that time."

With one final glower at the frightened soldier, Seran slowly turned. "Have it your way." As he walked past the pair, a smile spread across his face, "I seem to have built up quite the appetite, perhaps we should stop for a bite to eat before continuing our evening's activities." His tone was casual, as if he'd just finished a relaxing stroll, not a life and death conflict.

Aristoi leaned in to whisper sarcastically. "He is pleasant. Why have you not introduced us before now?"

"Desperate times," the thief replied.

She frowned at Seran, muttering, "You should have written sooner."

Interlude: Rudelph
Purity of Oath

⟋

Rudelph walked by the objecting acolyte and opened the door to the Master Librarian's chambers before the boy could rise from his small desk. "No need to bother yourself, I will only take a moment of Master Thume's time," the Binder offered over his shoulder as he strode into the dim confines of the meticulously ordered room.

Its sole occupant looked up from the massive tome set before him with an expression of barely restrained anger.

Bran Thume, Master Librarian of Oizan's Great Library, wore every year of his seven decades like a badge of honor. His slightly clouded blue eyes stared out from between the lenses that perched on the bridge of his nose. With the voice of a practiced tenor, he asked, "What is it that I may do for you at this late hour, Captain Rudelph?"

"I just have a few questions, Master Librarian."

As Thume gingerly straightened from where he'd been hunched above the yellowed pages, he grumbled, "And they could not wait until morning?"

Rudelph shook his head. "Some things have been bothering me." He sank into one of the two overstuffed chairs set before the imposing oak desk that dominated the chamber. "They are just spinning around and around in my head. I fear that if I do not get them answered … well, I simply will be unable to sleep soundly tonight."

"How unfortunate for you," the Master Librarian sarcastically remarked, "but I am unsure how that warrants barging into my chambers unannounced ... uninvited."

"Well, Master Thume, allow me to explain. I assure you that I will not take up more of your valuable time than is necessary."

Thume sighed loudly and studied the Binder over the top of his reading lenses.

"Of course, allow me to get to my point." Rudelph leaned forward, resting his arms on the small, organized piles of papers on the desk's top. "As you must be aware, I have been assigned the task of tracking down a certain lost book." He paused, waiting for the Master Librarian's ascent, which the man gave with a terse nod of his head before continuing. "Excellent. The issue is that we have been made aware of a few perfectly helpful pieces of information regarding said book: the fact that something has indeed been stolen, as well as the date of said theft. In addition, we have been provided with the name of the alleged thief. All of this is, as I said, perfectly helpful but certain key facts seem to have been over-looked."

Thume's face contracted, seeming to fold in on itself. "And those would be?"

The Binder's face brightened, seemingly in direct correlation to the darkening of the Master Librarian's. "Thank you so much for asking. We are having some difficulty locating a tome for which we have neither subject nor title. The reasoning behind such an oversight has just been picking away at the back of my mind like you would not believe."

"Captain Rudelph," Thume began. "The library has charged you and your ... kind," he spat the word out as one would a rotten grape, "with doing as they are told." The Master Librarian pushed his reading lenses further up the bridge of his nose and returned his attention to the manu-script in front of him. "I suggest that any questions you have are directed in the pursuit of that ... and outside these halls."

Rudelph nodded a few times, "Excellent suggestion, sir ... excellent indeed. If you would indulge me for one more moment, however. I do be-lieve my last question holds some significance and ... well ... it directly relates to yourself."

Thume looked up again, his patience clearly at its end. He didn't speak, instead simply stared at the Binder.

Taking his silence for permission, Rudelph continued. "If you would be so kind, Master Thume, could you enlighten me on why the curate was in the library the night that the book was stolen?"

The librarian clenched his teeth and growled, "You know very well that Curate Rethmus was here searching for a religious text at the behest of the Hand of Light himself. Olm's chosen has blessed us with the privilege of safeguarding works of his holy mission. It is not our place to question how or when he makes use of them." Despite their irritated tone, the words themselves struck Rudelph as rehearsed, their cadence a little too practiced to not be rote. "Besides, the murder of the curate is none of your concern. Your one and only priority is the recovery of the stolen book."

Again, Rudelph nodded slowly as he remarked, "One man is dead and another's life hangs in the balance, it would seem that someone ought to make it their concern to get to the root of the matter …" seemingly to no one in particular. His gaze focused again on Thume. "But that is not important right now. I do apologize, however, perhaps I misspoke." The Binder leaned back in his chair, making himself more comfortable. "Although he was not curate at the time, I was referring to Reisling not Rethmus. It seems that a pair of laborers saw a masked man enter the library through the lower gate early that morning. Now that gate is reserved for deliveries as well as the comings and goings of people that the library wishes to keep out of sight."

Thume's eyes widened but he kept his thoughts to himself.

The Binder held up his hands, "I mean, how would it look to have common people seen entering a place of knowledge when those that it was meant for pay good silver for that same right?"

"I am not sure I appreciate your tone, Captain."

Rudelph dipped his head in deference. "I am truly sorry. I, of course, meant no offense. If I may continue?"

"If you must."

"When challenged by one of my brethren, this man presented to him something that caused the binder to snap to attention and allow him entry."

"You take the word of a —"

The Binder held up a finger. "If you would allow me to finish, I am sure you will find what I have to say interesting." He hardened his eyes, driving them into the Master Librarian.

The sudden change in Rudelph's demeanor set Thume back on his heels, giving the binder a chance to continue.

"This naturally made me curious as to exactly what an, at the time, unknown visitor could carry that would allow instant access to our hallowed halls with nary a question asked."

"I will have it looked into —"

Again, the Binder interrupted the man, "— I simply had to find out." Rudelph smiled softly at Thume but his eyes remained hard as steel. "As you know, mysteries do so plague my sleep." He released the librarian's gaze, looking about the room wistfully, "I felt that I just had to speak to the Binder in question. As you well know, everything that happens between these walls is documented, so it should have been simplicity itself for me to turn to the logbooks for that night. Within their pages, the name I sought should have been neatly written."

Thume leaned forward. "And tell me, Captain, what did you find?" his voice dropped to a self-satisfied rumble.

"That is where my interest really became piqued. In the logbook, the name of the Binder in question was smeared. Is that not peculiar? The names above and below were crisp and legible, but the one I needed? Utterly unreadable."

"An unfortunate thing. Were I you, I would have a word with the record keeper. This sort of carelessness should not be tolerated. I would expect better from the Binders."

Again, Rudelph held up a finger. "Again, sir, those were my thoughts exactly. To eliminate the possibility of this being a case of poor fortune, myself and the record keeper reviewed a year's worth of logbooks. Do you know what we found?"

"I would have no idea," Thume said, his voice taking on the sharp tone of defensiveness.

"I found that there were three other such occurrences. Each time, there was one name smeared beyond recognition while the rest of the page was in perfect condition. While I was unsuccessful in discovering the name of the binder on duty the night of Rethmus's murder, I was more successful identifying the others."

The Master Librarian swallowed hard but remained silent.

"... or should I say, other. The Binder in question in each instance was the same. Do you know what he had to say when I spoke to him about the coincidence?"

"As fascinating as this conversation is, I am afraid that I have work to do, Captain." Rudelph couldn't help but notice that Thume's hand trembled as he pulled the lenses from his nose. "Why do we not continue our discussion tomorrow evening?" He glanced towards the door and then back to the binder, never quite meeting his eyes.

Rudelph reached out and laid his hand on the librarian's wrist. "I only require a few more moments of your time, sir, if you would ..." He tightened his grip before continuing, all deference gone from his voice, "Indulge me."

"Mae'l!" Thume raised his voice to call for his assistant. The door remained closed, and the librarian's summons received no response.

"When I located him, Urael had nothing to say, of course. I certainly did not hold it against him as many would find it difficult to speak after three days dead."

"Mae'l!"

"Unable to inquire with the Binder in question, I turned my attention to what it was that our mystery man presented to him that had such a profound effect. Would you know what that would be?" With his free hand, Rudelph laid an embossed leather token on the librarian's desk. Pressed into its surface was the symbol of the Great Library. Thume tried to pull his hand free, but the Binder's iron grip held it firm. "The Master Librarian's token denotes a messenger on business of penultimate importance. It is under no circumstances to be questioned."

"I can explain," the librarian whined.

"I only have two final questions for you, Master Thume. What was Reisling's business in the library and why was he carrying your token?"

Chapter Thirty-One

A Complicated Legacy

Jillian sat with her head cradled in the palms of her hands. Mid-morning, a stabbing pain had taken residence up behind her eyes and continued to cling there despite the two ibuprofen she took with her lunch. With her students at recess, she still had some time to herself, but the soft ticking of her classroom clock eroded that time like wind against the desert sand. Alone in the dim room, she struggled to relax.

Under the pounding headache swirled a whirlpool of anxiety that Jillian couldn't seem to explain. As far as days went, this one was going pretty well. It'd been a rare day free of bureaucracy and mindless paperwork, certainly not a source of stress. She'd always been diligent with her finances, so overdue bills were surely not the source of the nebulous tension. Jillian's mind went to Asaege and Taerh. When she last reflected, she and Hollis hadn't left things in a dire place. While many hands were turned against them, a potential ally in the form of the Binder, Rudelph, had presented itself.

Only a hand full of hours had passed since waking had separated her from the other world. Could something have occurred in that time? Could their fortunes have turned since then? She took a shallow breath, picturing it as a gentle wave lapping the shore that was her anxiety. As she exhaled, a measure of the uncertainly was swept out with it.

She focused on her breathing and tried to block out everything else around her. Jillian felt the sensation of air tingling on the back of her tongue; she savored the way it stirred the sensitive skin beneath her bottom lip. *There is nothing but my breath. There is no one but me.*

As she fell into the comforting rhythm, an image formed in her mind. She sat cross legged on Asaege's simple bed in her small room. Across from her sat a grinning Hollis. Although she was alone in her classroom, she could almost hear his voice. *Close your eyes. Both eyes please. There is nothing outside this room ... outside of the two of us.* The tension within her changed to something else. Longing? Jealousy? Jillian immediately felt ridiculous. At best, Hollis was a world away. At worst, he was a figment of her imagination.

She could feel a warmth in her cheeks, shame washing across her face. Just the thought of dismissing her experiences as mere flights of fantasy seemed disrespectful to both Hollis and her reflection. Asaege felt more real to her than many of the people she worked with every day; in some ways, she felt closer to her other self than members of her own family. If her reflection felt the same, could her unease indicate Asaege's own frame of mind?

"I missed you at lunch." The voice cut through Jillian's reverie, snapping her out of her thoughts. She lifted her head to see Marisol standing in the doorway. "Are you feeling alright?" It was a simple question that left many more unasked.

Slowly standing, Jillian tried to shake off the vestiges of embarrassment and envy. "I'm fine. I just feel a little headache-y. Is that even a word?"

The corners of her friend's mouth curled in amusement. "I don't think so, but I understand. Some days, it's a wonder that my brain doesn't leak out of my ears." She walked slowly toward the front of the room. "The littles have ten or so more minutes left for recess. Can I assume that you haven't eaten?"

Jillian nodded her head slowly, even the slight movement set the back of her eyes burning.

"While eating isn't a sure-fire cure for a headache, not doing so is a great way to increase its duration. The lunchroom is closed, but I'm sure Trish still has a few slices of pizza left."

She screwed her face up, "You know I love pizza —"

"— It's the perfect food," Marisol interrupted.

"It is but school pizza is ..." Jillian searched for the words.

"Not exactly pizza?"

"Not in the strictest sense, certainly." Despite the ache that still hung behind her eyes, having her friend there made Jillian feel a little better.

"Maybe they have some left over chicken nuggets from yesterday?" Jillian muttered, "I'll take my chances with the pizza."

Marisol slipped her arm around her waist and turned her towards the door with a slow spin, "So we're off to see the lunch ladies then." Both women shared a laugh as they entered the hall.

*****

Jillian half sat, half leaned against the low lunch table as she ate the lukewarm food that could only be called pizza in the loosest interpretation of the word. That is to say that it combined bread, cheese and a tomato-based sauce.

Even in New Jersey, anyone trying to pass it off as pizza outside of school grounds would be subject to the justice of a mob of those with anything approaching a discerning palette. As much as she hated to admit it, getting some food into her stomach did reduce the constricting pain in her head.

"What?" Jillian asked, her mouth half full. She realized Marisol was watching her through hooded eyes, as if she were trying to unravel a mystery.

Her friend took a deep breath, obviously considering her answer. "There is something going on with you, isn't there?" While the words indicated a question, her tone didn't. "For the last week or so, you've been … not quite yourself."

"You have no idea," Jillian said, chuckling beneath her breath. Marisol raised an eyebrow. "I haven't been feeling very much like myself lately."

Marisol laid her hand on Jillian's shoulder. "Does it have to do with Charles?" A dark look of concern came over her face, shouting *I'll kill him*.

"Yes and no," Jillian said, "But not in the way you think. Sure, he was …" She thought for a second, settling on, "unpleasant but certainly not the worst date I've been on."

Marisol remained quiet, allowing her friend to muddle through her thoughts.

"I guess I've just developed a higher expectation recently."

Raising an eyebrow, Marisol cooed, "Did you meet someone?"

"In a matter of speaking, I guess so."

She replied with a single word: "Spill."

Jillian shook her head, "It's not that simple."

Marisol lowered her voice to a tense whisper, "Is he taken?" She lowered it further, "Married?"

"I don't think so but to say he is unavailable would be an understatement."

239

"Why is this the first I'm hearing about him?"

"It's complicated." She felt her eyes rolling of their own volition. "Really complicated."

"Maybe I can help you uncomplicate it. Tell me about him. Where did you meet?"

Without thinking about it, Jillian said, "He's a friend of a friend but there's a distance that is hard to overcome." *To say the least.*

"Distance is rough but if you two click, it's a problem that can be solved. Tell me about him."

Her pizza forgotten, Jillian leaned forward. "He's not my normal guy, rough around the edges but —"

"— in all the right ways?" Marisol eased closer to her. "Is he cute?"

Jillian shrugged. "I suppose." *It's hard to tell beneath all the dirt*, she thought to herself but she couldn't tell her friend that. "He's a gentle soul but has a dangerousness …" She averted her gaze, murmuring, "That sounds so bad. He makes me feel seen … seen and safe."

Marisol recoiled in surprise. "Since when have you looked to a man to protect you?"

"Never. But that's the thing, it's not macho, alpha male bullshit. It's as much a part of him as breathing. It's in the way he looks at me, the things he does. It's just obvious that he cares more for my own wellbeing than he does his own … with no expectations whatsoever." She felt a heat rise in her cheeks. She hardly knew Hollis, but through Asaege's memories, she felt as if she did. As soon as she thought of her reflection, a feeling of guilt opened like a pit in her heart. If Hollis's heart belonged to anyone, it was Asaege and here Jillian was gushing over him like a schoolgirl.

Her internal conflict led to a protracted silence, one which Marisol seemed happy enough to break. "So, when do I get to meet this scoundrel?"

Jillian just shook her head, grief for what couldn't be warring with shame over coveting that which belonged to another. "He's too far away. It'll never work." She moved away from the table as if in doing so, she could escape her feelings. "I've got to focus on what's right in front of me, the things I can do something about."

Marisol turned to face her, a pensive look hanging in her eyes. "It sounds like you have something specific in mind," she observed.

Forcing a smile to her lips, Jillian offered her arm to her friend. "Not at all." The lie felt like it burned her tongue as it emerged from her mouth, but she swallowed the feeling. "The children should be finishing recess. It would be good if we were there to meet them when they return." Although her feelings were uncertain, her duty to unravel the

240

mysteries held in the journals was less so.

*****

When I awoke in Taerh, the cold that surrounded me seemed to have soaked into my very bones. It played in stark contrast to the warm spring nights that had blessed us in our own world. Although I, Marcus and Mika sat sheltered beneath the woven boughs of low hanging pine trees, a large stretch of snow-covered tundra spread out before us. Perhaps a hundred yards in the distance, a small hill rose from the barren landscape, into which a roughly hewn cave had been carved. A pair of torches, cold and dead as the surrounding tundra, driven into the thick snow beside the opening bore mute witness to the importance of what lie beyond.

This was the Cave of Visions. After nearly a month's travel, it failed to live up to the image he had built in his mind. Silvermoon's memories hung about me like the smoky scent of a campfire long gone dark. Within the unremarkable cave was a pool both clear and luminescent. The Walker had called it the Well of Worlds; it was Haedren's final destination, supposedly the source of incredible power. In the wrong hands ... in the hands of whatever had control of Silvermoon's friend, that power could be turned to unspeakable things.

As we drew closer to this place, my mind has unerringly returned to the question of 'Why?'. Why have I put myself at risk in an attempt to end to a danger that isn't even of my own world? Why have I involved those closest to me in it as well? Why did I continue to reflect, even against the request of those I sought to aid? Why did I think I could take this task onto my shoulders when I have so much to lose?

The best answer I have been able to come up with is that it needs to be done. I'm not sure what brought me to this place ... at this time, but something did. While I never put much stock in fate, I can't help but feel that without our intervention, a great evil will be set loose upon this world. I am certainly not so naive as to believe that I am some chosen one, but I can't shake the feeling that I ... that we have an important part to play.

As I looked around the low burning fire, the faces of my two comrades told me all I needed. George's broody thoughts were clearly evident behind Marcus's stormy gray eyes. Mika's eyebrows were furrowed, a tight band across her forehead. Unlike the others, she continued to fight against Beatrice's reflection. She had made her opinion of the phenomenon as clear as an ocean daybreak. In our own ways, both Silvermoon and I have tried to convince her of the advantages that coexistence brings with it, to no avail. Beatrice has a strength of will that not many give her credit for, but Mika put her reflection's resolve to shame.

241

"It shouldn't be long now," I said in English, trying to keep my tone light. She simply nodded, obviously more occupied by her inner dialogue than my own words.

"I'm not sure if I should be relieved or scared out of my wits," Marcus responded in the same language.

"I don't know if they should be mutually exclusive. We put all of our eggs in one basket rushing here ahead of Haedren." Not only did Silvermoon's memories wash over me when I was reflected; his emotions were also laid bare before me. It had been he who first suggested forgoing the potential of ambushing his former comrade along his route in favor of doing so at the Well itself, when Haedren would be at his most vulnerable.

"It was the only reasonable course of action." Mika added her voice to the conversation, although she chose to do so in Trade Tongue. The fact that she responded to my words indicated that she understood what we had said, so her choice was certainly made more out of spite than anything else.

"No one is debating that." In the interest of keeping tangentially in her good graces, I switched to Trade Tongue as well. "It simply puts our back against the wall. We either fail or succeed here; there is no fallback position."

"If the wallflower stays out of the way, we will not require one." Before I could reply, she cut off my objection, "— And I am not interested in hearing once again about the benefits I could reap from integration; I have no interest in that particular crop."

I held up my hands in surrender. "As you will, Mika."

She nodded slowly, her green eyes locked with mine as if she could bore through me with them. "Since you have obviously disregarded my request to leave this to us, let us review the plan one final time."

Trying to ignore the venom that dripped from each word that emerged from her lips, I forced a smile to my own. "When Haedren and whatever cohorts he has collected arrive, we let them enter the Cave of Visions unmolested." She beckoned with her fingertips, indicating that I should continue. "Once they are inside the chamber, we cross the distance," I gritted my teeth, speaking through them, "Dealing with anyone left outside to prevent interruptions." No matter how much of Silvermoon's personality mingled with mine, I can't seem to get used to the casualness with which violence is treated in Taerh. My reflection did not revel in it, but he also didn't shy away from it when it seemed necessary.

I'm not sure if she felt sympathy for my conflict or if she simply acted in the name of expediency but Mika picked up where I had left off. "We shall enter the cave and I will engage Haedren while you clean up

242

whatever soldiers remain. Be quick. Be efficient. Steel is no match for that Sharroth-damned brooch." She turned to my brother, "Have you mastered enough of Marcus's magic to perform the ritual?"

Before he could respond, I interjected, "He will not be reflected when we fight Haedren." I saw Marcus's face pale.

Mika raised an eyebrow. "Have you both finally come to your senses?"

I shook my head. "Not as such. Marcus and George each have a role; George's can only be done from our world."

Irritation crept into her face. "When was this decided?"

"Does it matter?" Marcus's voice was clipped and angry. "You said you wanted us to stay out of it. When it comes to me, at least, you get your way."

"I did not say that I was disappointed. I am simply processing a change of plans." She turned her gaze on my brother's reflection, "It is an improvement, but a change nonetheless."

In an attempt to circumvent any further conflict, I cleared my throat to get Mika's attention. "We all hate last minute alterations but this one is necessary. George will offer us an opportunity to prevent the use of the Well if the three of us are unable to overcome our comrade on this side."

Curiosity replaced anger in her face, "How so?"

I saw Marcus's eyes dart left as he averted his gaze, a function of George's influence. Before I could answer Mika, he whispered in English, "I'm going to kill his reflection in our world."

She nodded appreciatively, "I didn't think you had it in you," in the same language.

His eyes shot up to meet hers, the set of his jaw indicating that he didn't take it in the complimentary manner Mika had intended. "If it needs to be done, we aren't left with much of a choice."

"How will you know it needs to be done?"

I put my hand on my brother's shoulder, feeling him relax beneath my grasp. "Certain aspects of George's connection to Marcus are stronger than even mine with Silvermoon."

"If I concentrate, I can ..." he seemed to search for a word, his voice deadpan, "I can remember what Marcus experiences as it happens. Should things turn against us, I'll ... I'll do what's required."

*****

Jillian dropped the book to her lap, a sudden feeling of dread filling her gut. Until this point, this situation had seemed part dream, part game. It'd been so far away. The worst thing she'd done was steal a few books from an unlicensed drug dealer, but on the page in front of her, in black and white, was a conspiracy to commit murder.

Sure, Hollis had told her how he'd spiked the adder root supply of the Walker's reflection but the journal described a premeditated plot to kill another person in this world based on nothing more than a dream. *What have I gotten myself into?* she thought, throwing the book from her.

It arced across her small bedroom and impacted the wall with a dull slap. Even out of reach, its leather-bound cover stared accusingly at her with unseen eyes. Although it sat motionless on the carpet, Jillian was unable to force her gaze from the journal. A panicked internal monologue deafened her. *What if I'm crazy? Could Hector be spiking his stuff with mushrooms? I don't want to be on the news!* Images from the eighties made for TV movie, Mazes and Monsters flashed through her mind. It'd been so bad that it instantly raised itself to cult classic status. Featuring a young Tom Hanks, the movie had been a heavy-handed indictment of role-playing games. Although most of it was inadvertently funny, the surreal scene where Tom Hanks' character completely loses his grip on reality and spirals into a heart-breaking fugue of waking dreams kept replaying in her memory.

Fighting the panic that quickened her breath into a bellows, Jillian closed her eyes and tried to shut out the looping montage. Balling her hands into fists tightly enough to dig her fingernails into her palms, she forced the images from her mind. Like the prow of a tall ship, the sharp pain cut through the chaos of Jillian's thoughts.

Pursing her lips, she expelled the air from her lungs as if blowing out a candle. Resisting the temptation to fill them again for a long second, she allowed the minutiae of the moment to fill her perception. The burning sensation in her chest, the stinging itch where her nails had creased her palms replaced the fear that had run rampant through her thoughts.

Despite her body's desire to take a gulping breath, Jillian drew in air slowly, trying to remain in the moment. One steady breath led to another as she built a wall against the panic that had risen in her. She settled back against the tumble of pillows piled against her headboard, a sudden and inexplicable sense of weariness rolling over her. As she exhaled again, memories as unfamiliar as they were frightening flooded her head.

Although she could feel the down comforter beneath her, recollections of unforgiving stone pressed against her cheek were so vivid that she could almost feel the frigid touch of it on her skin. She recalled the dim confines of a barren cell, only lit by the flickering of torch light through a tiny, barred window set into the door. Jillian's breath caught in her chest as Asaege's memories from the Ivory Cathedral mingled with those of her school day, neither set seeming more real than the other. She could see Plague Man's flat black leather mask in her mind's eye ... feel his willow-thin fingers digging into her arm ... smell the morgue-like

244

frigid air of the shadows through which he dragged her.

She wanted with all her being to open her eyes and put an end to the collage of recollections, but fear kept them shut tight. She remembered hints of movement in the darkness, just out of sight. Although they made no sound, Jillian recalled feeling their hunger.

As they emerged from the shadows, the feeble torch light burned her eyes like the noonday sun. She remembered bringing her hand up to shield them and feeling the slickness of her own blood against her forehead. The skin of her forearm and hand were covered by a dozen clear, perfectly formed bite marks. Although she couldn't remember any pain, they bled freely. Then her mind returned to the memory of the cell, its dank walls pressing in on her like a fist.

Gingerly, she opened her eyes, half expecting to see the stone confines of a prison. Instead, the neutral mauve and gray tones of her bedroom greeted her. The journal remained where she'd cast it, although it no longer held the same accusatory appearance for her. Whether or not her dreams were rooted in reality or not, she had to follow them as far as they would take her.

With a trembling hand, Jillian reached over to her bedside table and pulled out the plastic bag containing what she hoped were answers.

Chapter Thirty-Two

Heart in Darkness

By the time the door opened again, Asaege had lost track of how long she'd sat upon the rough stone floor. The hollow ache in her belly reminded her that no one had brought her food but she'd certainly experienced greater hunger in her life.

Asaege had relieved herself in the opposite corner some time ago but was unsure if her empty bladder was more an indication of time or the fact that she had also not been provided water. At one point, she thought she might have dozed off, a pleasant dream of a soft bed nestled under mauve and gray striped wallpaper flickering at the edges of her consciousness, but it'd faded quickly.

As the hallway's flickering torchlight flooded into the cell, Asaege struggled to her feet. In her haste, the rough surface of the wall ripped a few fresh scabs from her right arm, causing the wounds to seep once more.

Pushing the pain from her mind, she focused on the words that had been struggling against the chains of her thoughts since before she and Hollis entered the cathedral. Almost as if they sensed the proximity of their freedom, the syllables doubled in intensity. Asaege could barely hear her own thoughts above the clamor of the alien words.

Within the gifted book, she'd found an incantation that seemed within her ability. The author had named it 'Paelman's Purloined Luminescence'. It was an extrapolation on a cantrip taught to every apprentice, one that dimmed the light in one area and added it to another. At its root, it was a cheap parlor trick at best. The owner of the book, however, had altered it in such a way as to weaponize the resulting illumination. Asaege didn't think she could use the spell to its full potential but felt that even in her hands it could maim if not kill.

A thin silhouette appeared in the doorway, its heavy cloak casting a shadow deep into the cell. Relaxing the control keeping the incantation contained to her thoughts, Asaege allowed the words to bubble from her mouth in a torrent. The confines of the room were plunged into darkness as the first part of the spell took effect. She redoubled her focus on the figure that had stood before her, now hidden from her sight, as the last syllables emerged from her throat in a guttural growl. Between Asaege and the door, a soft glow began to form. Nebulous, it began to build, casting its light outward like a lantern towards the portal and the shape that stood within it.

Its brilliance raced across the floor, steam rising from the stone in its wake. Asaege kept her attention focused on the silhouette, her hands held before her as if she could guide the light with them. In truth, any alterations to the beam's trajectory would be made by force of will but, as with most spells, the gesture aided less experienced thaumaturges with their focus. 'Paelman's Purloined Luminescence' was an advanced incantation and as such, the only one Asaege had memorized as she wanted to take no chances.

The beam illuminated the cloaked form of Plague Man, bringing each contour of his leather mask into stark contrast. The cloak that surrounded him began to smolder instantly, small fires leaping to life in places.

Asaege brought her hands together, touching palm to palm as she concentrated on focusing the beam. As if it were an extension of her own body, the luminescence consolidated into a brilliant pane of light, no wider than a knife's blade. Cloth ignited and fell to ash in an instant, filling the cell with the scent of scorched wool.

Asaege felt a burst of hope kick her in the stomach as Plague Man pulled his arm across his chest, as if to protect himself. His silken sleeve burst into flames as he laid a gloved hand over the brooch at his chest. The shadows cast by the orb of light between them slithered across the floor as if alive.

A tentacle-like collection of them engulfed him while the remainder converged on the source of the illumination. Asaege separated her hands in a panicked attempt to fend off the interlopers, but it was too late. The animated shadows smothered her spell like a blown-out birthday candle.

Plague Man's rusty-hinge voice cut through the darkness. "I thought we might have a chat."

*****

Although the door remained open, the smell of burnt fabric still hung in the air of the small cell. The ruined remains of Plague Man's cloak lay crumpled beside his crouched form. Asaege took some small satisfaction that despite the fact that he still wore the brooch, he remained in the doorway.

"If you want to talk, you are going to have to start," she growled through clenched teeth, "I honestly have nothing to say to you." With the last of her memorized spells spent, Asaege was alone in her thoughts.

Before it was cast, the held incantation fought against her as if it had a will of its own. It had been a constant struggle not unlike forcing an addictive tune from your mind, only taken to the extreme. Prior to reading Marcus's book, the spells that she had mastered pressed upon her mind as an unintended memory brought to the fore by an errant scent. The incantations found within its depths carried with them a potency greater by magnitudes; their insistence to be set free scaled accordingly. Asaege had thought that once the resistance was gone, she would feel relief but found that she missed it.

Plague Man watched her, allowing the silence to stretch between them. It took Asaege a moment to realize that he'd yet to speak. He seemed to recognize that her reverie had come to an end. An unseen smile could be heard in his voice as he rasped, "Ah, my dear Asaege ..." The masked man put his hand to his chest in an exaggerated, mocking gesture of politeness. "... or do you prefer Prophet?"

"Asaege is fine." Her still clenched teeth turned the words into a hiss.

"Very well, Asaege, I happen to believe we have a great deal to discuss." Plague Man ran his gloved finger along the filthy stone floor before him. "I do regret that we could not speak somewhere a little more appropriate, but you and the thief left me little choice."

Surprising herself, she blurted out, "If you have hurt him —"

Clicking his tongue against his teeth patronizingly, he interrupted, "— you would be unable to do anything about it ... at least for now. Let us agree that we should dispense with such unpleasantness for the time being." Plague Man seized her gaze with dead eyes of smoky glass, "Both of us are painfully aware of our respective positions. Empty threats do neither of us any good."

His calm, almost pleasant tone caused bile to burn the back of Asaege's throat. She practically quivered with rage. Beneath her fury, however, a hollow sense of dread smoldered. Her thoughts turned to

249

Hollis. When last she saw him, he faced nearly untenable odds, yet his thoughts remained on her welfare. What might have been his final words were to put her mind at ease. *I am coming for you, Magpie.* He sounded so sure, even in those dire straits.

Their friendship ... relationship had begun in pretty unfavorable circumstances but at some point, her annoyance at finding him sprawled on her bed or slouched in her room's lone chair had turned to relief. A passing fondness had deepened at some point. So subtle was the change that she couldn't quite mark the time when it occurred. She simply found her thoughts, in this moment of imminent danger, turning to him, just as his turned to her hours before.

Again, Asaege became aware of Plague Man's expressionless mask studying her in her contemplation. He snorted softly. "I sense that the Hollis issue will be an obstacle to a constructive conversation." Casually, he wiped his glove against his breeches and stood, "I cannot attest for what became of him afterward, but he still breathed when he escaped the Ivory Cathedral." She could hear the effect of pursed lips on his next words. "Much to my chagrin."

She remained suspicious but allowed her desperate desire for his words to be true to convince her of their veracity. The nagging worry that clung to her heart with bittersweet claws remained but lightened its grip enough for rage and fear to overtake it for the moment. "He is not easily dissuaded, if he said he would return for me —"

Again, he cut her off with a casual flick of his hand. "— he intends to be true to his word. Hollis and I are well acquainted, although our history is paved with his intentions. To this point, they have proven to be at odds with reality."

Asaege's cold stare was her only response. In the time she'd known the thief, she had only seen real fear in him once. It had been when Plague Man's name was mentioned. *Obviously, there is more to their past than meets the eye*, she thought. Her faith in the man remained steady, but the gnawing worry clung to her mind, nonetheless.

"To be honest, I am less interested in him than you at the moment."

Fear once again gripped her heart. "No matter what becomes of me, the words I have written have found their way into the hearts of the people. Even you cannot silence them now!" she snapped, the rushed cadence of her words betraying her anxiety.

The way Plague Man rolled his shoulders reminded her of a contented cat. "Oh, I want no such thing. The paranoid fool in the Ivory Seat fears all words that are not his own; I am not so short sighted."

Asaege's eyebrow shot up in surprise, "Are you not his curate?"

He nodded slowly, "I am indeed, but if I am serving an impostor, what does that make me?"

"The Hand? An impostor?"

"Did your graffiti not say as much? Perhaps you understood it to be metaphorical? I assure you that it is quite literal; he turned his face from the light of the Lord of the Dawn a long time ago."

Taken aback, her mind began to race. *If he could no longer hear his god, of course he would need the Dialogues to keep up the charade that he was still in Olm's favor.*

Plague Man seemed to recognize her realization. "There you go. Now you are putting it together. In the Prophet, the most revered Hierophant Graceous Trim saw his greatest fears made flesh. With the disappearance of the book, he lost his last tie to that which kept him in power. When you emerged, quoting words taken from it without his careful editing, he was quite beside himself." Sitting back on his heels, he chuckled. "He was so desperate to keep his sandcastle of control safe from the coming tide that he overlooked my inability to secure the book from Rethmus on the night of his death. As I knew he would."

"Rethmus? That night in the library … the shadows … that was you? You killed the curate!"

He bowed his head slightly, "That it was … and that I did. You see, the Hand had grown tired of Rethmus's hold upon him. Power does not have the same allure when it is only at the whim of another. The curate had been feeding him sections of the Dialogues a little at a time, while withholding the text itself to retain his control." A short snort of a chuckle emerged from behind the leather mask. "It was actually pretty clever. There is no telling how long Rethmus could have strung the old man along if I had not come into the picture. Unfortunately for him, I did."

Asaege found herself leaning forward, engrossed in the revelation. "How did you know that the Curate had the book?"

"Why, the Hand, of course. He paid me handsomely to collect it and then eliminate the unnecessary middleman. It is a choice he will come to regret." The words dripped from his tongue like poison from an adder's fang.

She sat back quickly. "I do not have the book with me," she snapped.

"I know."

"I do not know where it is."

Plague Man shrugged. "I am less certain of that, but I am willing to give you the benefit of the doubt. I am sure, however, that you could find it in short order given sufficient motivation."

She found her mouth suddenly dry. "I will not get it for you. I would rather die than have it in Trim's hands."

251

"I think you will find that we agree on that point, although I am not sure I would go as far as placing my life on the line."

In her shock, Asaege blurted out, "What?"

"If I had wanted the Hand to have the book, I would have taken it from you in the library. Trim has had his time. He has become far too irrational and frightened to be of any real use to me."

"You are going to plot against the Hand of Light?"

"Going to? My dear Asaege, this conversation has been my plan all along. The shadows see all. They saw you when you snuck into the Great Library. They saw where you went and what books you showed interest in."

"You knew —"

"Where the Dialogues of the Chalice was before that night? My dear, I have known its location since before the Hand sought me out." Plague Man's voice took on a sorrowful tone, as if he no longer spoke to only her, "His downfall has been in the works so long, it boggles the mind." He shook his head slightly before continuing, "Although he contracted me, it was I who first circulated the idea to do so."

"What is your endgame then?"

"Power, of course. In the end, everyone's endgame is power."

"How do you plan to gain power by unseating the Hand of Light?"

"Without the favor of his god, Trim's only power lies in the people who believe in him. When he falls, those people will cry out for another to give their lives meaning … to tell them what to do. Sheep cannot be long without their shepherd, lest they become lost in the woods."

Asaege's mind began to spin. "Why would they follow you?"

"I do not want them to follow me, my dear. They have already chosen their shepherd … or should I say their Prophet."

She felt her breath catch in her chest when his intentions became clear. "I will not help you."

"Why not? What danger do I pose that Trim does not? You know who and what I am. Not every one of Trim's congregation will flock to you; some prefer things the way they are now. They will need a leader or there is no telling what chaos they will sow. Every hero needs a villain and vice versa. Would it not be best for all involved if they were each of the same mind?"

Asaege braced her hand against the rough stone wall, suddenly lightheaded. Gritting her teeth, she fought the dizziness. "You are insane."

Plague Man shook his head. "A more sane man, you will not meet. There is little doubt in my mind that the vast majority of the people would gravitate to you. Your message is one of peace and equality. There

252

are some, however, whose only concern is for themselves and their best interest. Those selfish, blighted people would remain loyal to the memory of their beloved Hand ... and the curate that keeps it alive."

She closed her eyes, her heart threatening to beat its way from her chest. "What do you get out of it? I will not take advantage of people's faith nor allow you to do so. Those in power have ground the powerless under their heels for too long."

"That is the beauty of our arrangement. Take everything they have. The more they lose, the more secure my hold becomes. I am interested in my own power; I care nothing for theirs."

Asaege could feel the cold solidness of the wall under her fingertips but still felt as if she were falling. In the shock of Plague Man's revelation, she'd overlooked the signs of reflection until it was too late.

Chapter Thirty-Three
Legacy of Fear

Jillian could feel her heart pounding in her … in Asaege's chest as she came to her senses. She half sat, half leaned against the uneven stone wall of a small cell. In the open door, stood a masked man, his back lit silhouette casting bizarre shadows on its stone floor. She hoped it was only the flickering torch light that made it appear that they breathed of their own accord.

As with previous reflections, her initial confusion gave way to a slow filtering of memory. Asaege's recollections revealed the figure's identity, the realization chilled Jillian to the core. Even if Asaege's memories hadn't supplied it, there was no mistaking the voice that came from behind the mask.

"You see, the situation is mutually beneficial for both of us. You are able to accomplish whatever charitable agenda that suits your heart." He again made a dismissive backhanded gesture with the fingers of his left hand. "And I am assured a core of loyal followers for my own needs." He paused briefly, as if expecting an immediate follow up question. When Jillian didn't comply, he tilted his head slightly, as if studying her for a split second before answering it anyway. "Which are my own business and should not interfere with yours in any real way. While I certainly cannot promise that our interests will not intersect in the future, I am sure that such conflicts will be minor and easily rectified."

It was obvious that Plague Man expected her to be a more active participant in the discussion, but her mind was still reeling from the stress of reflection. All she could manage was, "Alright."

Apparently, being agreeable wasn't the key. He took a few slow steps forward, his expressionless leather mask regarding her placidly. "Fascinating," he murmured, mostly to himself. A little louder, he mused, "Not to mention fortuitous." Plague Man approached slowly, his hands held at chest height, palms out. She couldn't help but notice that they stayed within easy reach of the brooch. "Miss Allen, I presume." His voice held a lilt of amused satisfaction. "I do not believe we have been formally introduced."

"I know who you are, Hector," Jillian hissed in English, her eyes glued to the dark steel and silver adornment.

"Close, my dear. Hector is not available right now; you will have to settle for the Plague Man." Obviously understanding her words, he chose to continue speaking in Trade Tongue.

Despite her dire circumstances, Jillian had to bring her hand up to hide her smirk. Plague Man had just referred to himself in the third person like a bad comic book villain. The air of seriousness in his voice only made the statement all the worse. She was forced to hold her breath momentarily to prevent a very inappropriate giggle from emerging from behind her hand.

Plague Man clearly misinterpreted the gesture, as his shoulders tightened slightly, pushing his chest forward in a proud gesture. "No doubt you have heard of me … or via Asaege remember having done so." He ceased his advance, stopping just out of arms reach. "You have nothing to fear from me in this moment," he said. His voice dropped as he continued, holding a tone of menace, "So long as we can come to an agreement."

All humor drained from Jillian's mind as the ramifications of her situation crashed in on her again. She sat in a prison cell, a world away from anything she knew. A cold-blooded killer stood between her and escape. "Your business is with Asaege. What do I have to offer you?" Jillian tried to keep her voice from shaking.

"Sweet, sweet Miss Allen," his voice was a gentle coo. "You do not give yourself enough credit." Taking a small step forward, he seemed to relish in the recoil it prompted. "Yours, perhaps, is the most important part to play … at least in my mind."

She remained quiet, not trusting herself to speak. At her continued silence, his chin rose an inch or so and some of the tension dissolved from his body, seeming to engender in him a not quite unwarranted, sense of satisfaction.

"My own reflection seems incapable of even the most simple tasks, the least of which is maintaining possession of those damned journals, much less acquiring those Stephen held before the events at the Well." Plague Man's voice took on a dark tone, as if forced through clenched teeth.

And I thought I had a rough relationship with Asaege, Jillian thought. *Compared to them, we're BFF's.*

"I know you have a trio of journals, taken from Hector."

She took a breath intending to argue, but he cut her off.

His words were terse and sharp, like razorblades carried on the wind. "Do not!" Jillian saw him consciously relax himself before continuing in a gentler voice. "Do not deny it. It does both of us a disservice. They were taken from the flower shop while his back was turned."

"What do you want with them?" Jillian's mind immediately went to the unreadable words and arcane symbols that she believed held the key to severing the connection between the brooch and its host.

"That is my own concern. I will assure you that it will not affect you for good or ill."

Who is doing us both a disservice now? She bit her bottom lip. "That is easy to say but while it remains a mystery, I have little proof to that effect."

"You are afraid that I seek to use you or someone close to you to fuel a Well." He seemed so confident.

Jillian's stomach dropped. She was so focused on the immediate problem of the brooch, the very real risk of her soul's use in Plague Man's 'ascension' had slipped her mind. "And if I am?" Her voice held a quiver that she prayed he didn't hear.

"From what Hector has gleaned from them thus far, there is little within the journals to point to the location of another Well."

Feeling a little more confident, she purposely switched to English again, "That doesn't guarantee that there isn't still information to be found in the missing volumes."

Plague Man paused a second too long, as if he were struggling to keep up. "That is true." He continued to speak in Trade Tongue. "I doubt there is anything I could say to convince you of the truth of my vow, which leaves us at an impasse."

"I'm starting to believe that's the case. You've given me no reason to trust anything you've got to say." Jillian doubled down. Continuing to speak in her native language, she filled her statement with as many contractions as she could. She couldn't see his face behind the leather mask, but noticed that his body pulled back on itself in a wince. It was yet another indication that he and his reflection were far from in sync.

Confusion and anger gave Plague Man's next words a lightning quick cadence. "What if I could offer you something in exchange?" His tone was soft, almost pleading. However, he quickly regained his composure. "What if I told you that Stephen was not beyond your reach?"

Taken aback, it was Jillian's turn to be set on her heels. "What do you mean?" she asked without thought. Instantly, she realized her mistake and tried to re-mediate the damage, "Why would I care?"

"You care, although I cannot imagine why. As much as I despise him, Hollis is … and has always been far and away the better part of the pair. Hector has his failings, but he can be quite useful when properly motivated. I know quite a good deal about both you and the nearly departed Stephen."

"Nearly departed?"

Plague Man nodded his head, "Due to a timely intervention … whether fortunate or unfortunate depends on your point of view, he clings to life in one of your …" he searched for the appropriate word. "Hospitals," it slithered from his lips like toothpaste from the tube.

"You're lying!" she snapped.

"I assure you that I am not. I honestly should give Hector more credit." Plague Man clasped his hands before him, the soft sound of leather rubbing on leather made the back of her neck itch. "He told me that you and Asaege were more alike than different. He told me that the way to you would lead through the thief's lesser half. I did not believe him … until now."

Jillian felt the muscles of her jaw tightening. "I don't even know him. What makes you think I even care?" A warm glow began in her chest. Her infatuation for Hollis was always something beyond her reach, the fanciful delusions of a dream.

But what if it weren't, she thought, *What if they could be together in the waking world.* Wasn't he the very thing she'd searched for in the dead eyes of on-line profile pictures and earnest faces of blind dates? Brave. Loyal. Steadfast. *Not to mention that there is literally no one else on the face of the earth who could understand what they both had experienced in Taerh.*

"To quote something from your own world," he began before switching to halting English, "The lady doth protest too much, methinks."

A nagging pang of worry rose to blot out the yearning of what could be. "I don't believe you."

Plague Man ceased wringing his hands and held up a single finger. "That is the thing, Miss Allen. Of all we have discussed this evening, I believe that is the one thing of which you have no doubt. In a different place and time, I think I would find it rather charming."

The soft edges of her worry sharpened into irritation. "How little you must think of me, Plague Man," she mockingly drew out the syllables of his name, "That you believe I would go weak in the knees at the promise of romance."

He shrugged casually. "Please excuse the assumption, I meant no offense." Plague Man clasped his hands together once more. "In case you have a change of heart, Stephen's possessions were turned over to a woman named Veronica Moses after his accident."

Irritation bloomed into anger, but the feeling seemed out of scale with Plague Man's implications. Hollis had told Jillian very little of his reflection's life; she had no reason to hold another woman against him. It dawned on her that the anger wasn't hers, nor was it directed at Hollis.

"Give my offer some thought, Miss Allen. I believe you know where to find Hector when you have made up your mind."

Jillian closed her eyes, momentarily fighting Asaege's reassertion of control. The muscles in her neck and face tensed in physical reflection of the mental conflict that raged within her. Thoughts of Hollis flashed in her mind, beating a counterpoint to the creature that stood before her. It was very evident in the way he spoke about him that Plague Man was engaged in a constant struggle with Hector, while based on the thief's stories, he and Stephen had always seemed to meet on common ground. They trusted each other.

Can I trust Asaege? There's only one way to find out.

Slowly, she released the tension in her body and gave into her reflection's influence. For a second, she felt as if her entire world stood upon a stretch of shifting sand and then the hazy softness of dream enveloped her. She didn't wake but watched through Asaege's eyes as if she were merely a passenger in her own body.

Chapter Thirty-Four
Heart to Heart

As Asaege came back to her senses, the sharp edges of her anger were softened by Jillian's acquiescence. Having been a mute witness to her reflection's conversation with Plague Man, she was prepared to answer his unasked question. "I would not hold my breath, were I you." Her tone held the sureness of stone and the finality of a noose. She could almost feel his frown through the leather mask as he studied her out of the corner of a smoky glass eye.

"You do not ever seem to cease surprising me," he remarked. "Asaege has returned, I presume?"

She didn't answer his query, simply stating, "We had not finished our conversation."

"That we did not." Plague Man still stood out of arms reach, looking down at where Asaege sat against the wall. "Even if your reflection does not see the wisdom of allying herself with me, I am sure you are able to see things with a more reasonable perspective."

Pulling her feet under her, Asaege leaned against the rough stone to lever herself into a kneeling position. She couldn't help but smile when Plague Man took a half step backwards. "As much as I dislike repeating myself: I would not hold my breath, if I was you."

His fingers twitched against his leather clad thighs, betraying the seething anger that he barely contained. "And if I were you," he hissed, "I would be more concerned with my own breath, specifically how long you will continue drawing it."

Slowly standing, she clenched her fists at her sides. "I am under no illusions that you hold my life in your hands." The truth of her circumstances spoken, there was no barrier of denial strong enough to overcome it. A stomach-churning terror rose to wrap it's skeletal hands around her wind pipe, cutting off her words. When she tried to speak, she found her throat tight and her mouth dry. "If you did not nee—" Asaege was forced to swallow hard before continuing, "If you did not need me, I doubt we would be having this discussion." She thought that pointing that out would buoy her confidence. It didn't.

"Need is a strong word, my dear. Your cooperation would assuredly make things easier but do not believe that they cannot be done without you." His tone was confident to the point of haughtiness.

She looked around the dismal chamber, trying to fight her way through the quagmire of despondency that threatened to pull her under. *Perhaps I can agree to his terms, at least for the time being*, her inner voice whispered, *there will always be time to turn the tables on him once I am in control of —.* The question was, in control of what? Asaege could already sense that the path of concession was proving slippery. *I never sought to lead. I simply wanted people to be in a place to make their own choices about what they believed and in whom they placed their faith.* Yet in the name of circumventing Plague Man's will, she'd already began thinking of those very same people as resources.

Rotten-honey feelings of guilt overpowered Asaege's fear as the potential repercussions of those concessions dawned upon her. No matter how it was phrased, any association with Plague Man was no different than embracing the sickness from which he drew his name. His foul heart was infectious. Although she would enter the arrangement with pure intentions, fully resolved to turn the tables on her partner at the first opportunity, she realized that by the time that chance presented itself, she would be too deep to make use of it. *I will be more like him than myself. No less a prisoner than I am right now.*

Asaege's mind spun with the implications, fiercely searching for a course of action that wouldn't lead to her death or corruption. Her panicked thoughts couldn't find one. She felt her shoulders slump, as she worked up the resolve to make the choice that, in her heart, she knew was right. *It is better to die as myself than live as someone I despise.*

"Then I suppose," she began softly. Like an avalanche set free from a mountain peak, the words came faster, "I suppose you are going to have to find a way to do just that." Asaege forced her shoulders back and set her jaw, "Because there is nothing that you can do … not imprisonment

… not death … nothing that will convince me to become like you." Meeting his smoky glass gaze once more, she said, "You want the same thing all petty people do: power. Power comes to those who deserve it, they have no need to chase it."

"Now I am petty? Powerless? Do I need to remind you who is locked in a cage and who holds the key?"

Asaege allowed her chin to drop, the burst of defiance spent. It gave way to despair once more. "Do what you want. Another will rise in my place. You do not have the strength to see your scheme to fruition. Your fear will always be twice the enemy any adversary could be."

Plague Man drew his hand back, preparing to backhand her. He paused, his arm hanging in mid-swing. "If I walk out that door, I shall not make this offer again." Slowly he allowed it to relax and drop to his side.

She barely raised her eyes, studying him through her halo of hair. "Even now, fear stays your hand. Even though your plan can carry through without me, you are afraid of what that may look like." Hopelessness threatening to overcome her, Asaege settled to the floor to sit tailor fashion on the cold stone. "We will see each other again, Plague Man, but I can guarantee that you will not enjoy our reunion."

"We shall see, my dear. We shall see."

She didn't give him the satisfaction of looking up as the heavy wooden door slammed, draping the cell in darkness once more.

Chapter Thirty-Five
An Unseen Shadow

Hollis didn't need to turn around to feel Aristoi's stare. He studied the Ash skyline through the open window, its shutters long since stolen. He wasn't sure what the failing twilight should reveal, but if there was inspiration to be found, he was clearly missing it. "Do you have something on your mind, Southerner?"

"Where should I begin?" The Songspear's voice was soft, only carrying as far as the thief's ears. "Your message left no doubt of the dire circumstances in which you have found yourself, although I had no idea how dire."

Hollis continued to stare into the night, his unfocused eyes not truly seeing anything. "He is going to do it again."

The abandoned building's dry rotted floor groaned beneath the Kieli's weight; the sound was her only reply.

"How much can Plague Man take from me, Aristoi? I should have stopped her … should have gotten her free of his reach the minute I heard that he was in the city."

"You are afraid of him."

The thief spun quickly, the rage on his tongue struggling to hide the fear in his heart. "I just want to get my hands around his scrawny throat!" Aristoi winced but stood her ground, allowing his fury to wash over and past her. Self-consciously, he lowered his voice, although the intensity of it wasn't diminished. "If he would stand still long enough, I would end … whatever this is between us. I do not fear him, I hate him. There is a difference."

The Songspear nodded slightly. "The two are not mutually exclusive. Your loathing of him … your anger at yourself … at everything you have lost, these things prevent you from seeing things clearly."

"What is there to see?"

"Perhaps you do not fear the man, but rather what he represents. For someone whose life depends on staying one step ahead of everyone around him, Plague Man presents a unique challenge."

Hollis tapped a finger against his temple. "The Well gifted me with ability to see everything so clearly —"

"— and yet he remains in your blind spot," Aristoi interrupted.

"And yet he remains in my blind spot," the thief agreed.

"And that frightens you."

"Damn right it does," Hollis hissed through gritted teeth.

"A wise man once told me that a hero is not someone without fear, but rather someone who acts in spite of it."

He raised an eyebrow. "Did you just call me wise?"

Aristoi shrugged noncommittally. "You have your moments." A wry smirk appeared on her face. "The real question is: what are you going to do with this revelation?"

The question struck Hollis like a hammer. Since Stephen's first reflection, Plague Man has been at the center of every loss he suffered, in either world. After a tense moment, Hollis admitted, "I am not quite sure. My first instinct is to say track him down and kill him. Be done with it once and for all."

"But …" she prompted.

"But that is, no doubt, what he expects from me … what he hopes I will do. He wants me to come at him straight ahead with blinders firmly affixed, giving him a chance to take away another thing I love." Hollis marveled at how comfortable the word was on his tongue.

Aristoi cocked her head but didn't comment on the later. "How would you proceed if last night were your first meeting?"

Hollis took a deep breath, letting it rest in his lungs before exhaling slowly. "I would figure out why he took Asaege rather than simply killing her in the chapel." Realization dawned on him in a rush. "If all he sought to do was hurt me, watching helplessly while she died would be more effective than risking me coming for her. He told me this was not about me; I just refused to believe him."

"Sometimes, even from the lips of liars comes the truth."

"After that business with the Walker, perhaps Plague Man has

266

decided he does not like the view from second place." The thief's brows tightened. "By now, he has to have realized that Asaege does not have the book."

"Do you believe that she will reveal its location?"

Hollis shook his head. "No, but enough torture will loosen even the most stubborn tongues." He was forced to swallow hard to prevent his gorge from rising at the very thought. Gritting his teeth, he tried to force the image from his mind. "Regardless, if he pries the information free, it will no longer be there." *If I cannot stop him from hurting Asaege*, he thought, *At least I can make sure that her dream does not die with her.*

"Why not just kill him?" The two spun at the sound of the voice. Seran leaned unconcerned against the sagging door frame, his arms casually crossed. "The dead make less trouble."

How long has he been there? How much did he hear? "If the opportunity presents itself, I certainly will not let it pass."

"The boy I knew made his own opportunities."

Aristoi sneered. "Children grow up. Not every solution is found at the point of a sword."

"Which is why I carry a knife, Kieli." The last word was laced with venom. When his eyes shifted to the thief, Seran's face was placid once more. "I shall ignore the fact that you lied to me, Hollis. If we know where this book is —"

"—he," Aristoi corrected, "He knows where the book is."

Seran ignored her, "Now that we have what Plague Man wants, creating that opportunity is simplicity itself."

"This is not about the book," Hollis snapped. "Drawing him out does us no good."

"This is about the girl?" Seran walked slowly forward, his steps barely eliciting a creak from the ancient floor. "Ignoring for the moment what the Dialogues of the Chalice could do for us personally …" Hollis didn't remember mentioning any specifics about the book, let alone its title. "… Plague Man is a blight on not only your life but countless others. What is one woman's life compared to that?"

"The fact that I have to explain it to you, old man, tells me that my breath would be wasted." The thief focused on each interaction he'd had with his mentor. In none of them did Hollis bring up the book, although Seran had certainly evidenced interest. He'd mistaken it for concern, but in retrospect Seran's interest in his former student's welfare had always been secondary. "Your involvement was never about me, Seran, was it?" A look of confusion clouded Aristoi's face, but she lifted her spear from where it leaned, nonetheless. She stood next to Hollis, firm resolve held in her eyes. Her unquestioning trust in him drew a stark contrast to the man who stood opposite them.

His mentor held out his hands in a pacifying gesture. "That is a terrible thing to say, my boy." His face was unreadable, even through the 'Understanding'; Seran had been playing games of deception for far too long. "I always had your best interests at heart. That book represents a unique chance … one that comes along once in a lifetime, if at all. There are plenty of women out there but opportunities at true power must be seized or be lost forever."

The thief snorted, "Plenty of women —", his body tensing.

Aristoi stepped between them, her voice low and dangerous. "Our intention is to rescue the girl; anything else is insignificant at the moment."

"I do not recall asking your opinion, Kieli." Again, contempt dripped from his voice.

The Songspear's lip curled, revealing bared teeth. Hollis swore he heard a rumble deep in her chest as she growled, "That is the second time you have spoken to me with disrespect. There will not be a third."

The thief placed a gentle hand on Aristoi's shoulder. For a split second, he could swear he felt muscles ripple under his fingertips. In an instant it was gone, leaving him to wonder if it was simply his imagination. "If you wish to withdraw your offer of aid, that is your choice. The plan remains the same."

Seran spread his hands into an exaggerated shrug. "As you will, boy. I told you that I simply sought what was in your best interest. If your interest is focused on this Asaege, then you shall hear no further argument from me." His words were conciliatory, and his face remained placid, but his eyes never left Aristoi's.

"You will not feel offended if I keep the book with me, though."

Daggers passed between his mentor and the Songspear, even as Seran chirped, "Of course not," in a light tone.

*****

The book in question was safely secreted in Hollis's satchel, but his imagination gave it a weight that belayed its size. He would rather have left it in any number of hides scattered across the Ash, but Seran knew him well enough that any that his mentor didn't have direct knowledge of wouldn't remain secret for long. The thief had carefully wrapped it in oilcloth before securing it in the bag. With it, he'd wrapped his dwarven steel dagger. The weapon's keen edge would slice cloth and flesh with equal ease should any unwelcome hands attempt to liberate the package from its nest.

The trio stood in what could have once been a cellar of some sort, although stagnate water pooled on the uneven stone floor. The cham-

268

ber's only light came from a battered lantern that hung high on the wall beside its only door. Behind them lay a serpentine maze of sewer tunnels, unused storerooms and cleverly disguised pass throughs. Hollis could feel the sluggish flow of fetid air that pulsed through the open arch in waves as they waited in silence.

"This is charming." Aristoi's low voice still split the air like a church bell.

"Raethe does not appreciate unexpected visitors," her two companions said in unison.

"The mind boggles at why that is a concern," she retorted sarcastically.

Hollis looked around suspiciously before leaning closer to whisper to the Songspear. "Some call him the 'King of Underfoot', it applies to both a physical and social stratum. Those who fall so far that even the Ash offers them no comfort can only seek solace beneath the society that scorns them."

The Songspear recoiled, raising her voice in surprise. "People live down here?" Self-consciously, she returned to a softer tone. "It is not fit for … well … anyone."

The thief nodded. "No matter how low you think you can go, there is always further to fall."

She studied him out of the corner of her eye. "You truly are a ray of sunshine."

"I am not in much of a sunny mood."

Aristoi nodded and let the subject drop. "This 'Underfoot' runs under the entire city?"

"Most of it, anyway. I imagine that if there were enough of value down here, the powers that be would make more of an effort to police it but …" Hollis swept his hand before him, indicating the room in which they stood and the dilapidated corridor through which they had traveled. "… you saw for yourself what they feel would be gained."

"I suspect that you do not share their point of view."

The thief shook his head. "I do not. No matter how distasteful, it represents a method of travel throughout the city without the need to pass through gates and the eyes they bring. That alone is worth more gold than the three of us could carry."

"Why has no one taken advantage of it? I imagine that at least those whose business is best done out of sight would be interested."

Hollis chuckled. "Remember what we said about Raethe not liking visitors?"

She nodded.

"That goes double for members of the guild … something to do with a disagreement over beggar territory a long time ago. It was before my time."

"No one has tried to take it by force?"

The thief shook his head. "Underfoot is virtually unnavigable without a guide. In addition, its corridors are so riddled with bolt holes and secret passages that there is no telling where or when its residents will emerge to defend their home."

"Better people have put more at risk for something of strategic value."

Hollis watched the door suspiciously, continuing to whisper to Aristoi without facing her. "It is my impression that a few guild masters, both better and worse, made attempts but in their time, each came to the same realization. While it may be worth the blood to secure the 'underways', that cost approaches insurmountable when you factor in what would need to be paid to keep it. The residents of Underfoot may be the dregs of society, but when pressed by the desire to protect their home … literally the last place they have to go, they put their dull teeth and broken knives to good use."

"It is certainly not the first tale of a people, forced to the edge of a cliff, fighting their way from the precipice."

The thief nodded absently.

Aristoi touched him lightly on the forearm, waiting until he turned his attention to her. "That begs the asking of an obvious question."

"Given Raethe's historical distaste for thieves, why have we come?"

The Songspear nodded but before she could respond, Seran spoke up from across the chamber. He'd been watching the arch through which they had entered. Hollis hadn't realized his mentor had been listening, but he should have known better.

"My Kieli friend, did you not realize that we traveled with Underfoot royalty?"

Hollis snorted. "Hardly."

Aristoi narrowed her eyes, a question hanging in them.

Willfully oblivious to his intrusion, Seran continued, "The boy is the only brother in recent memory to find his way through the maze into Raethe's court and emerge intact." Beneath his gently mocking tone, a whiff of something danced. To the thief's surprise, he thought it might have been pride. "A number of fools have tried over the years. Those fortunate enough to be found were rarely in one piece."

The Songspear chuckled. "You have been here before, Hollis?"

Hollis shook his head. "Not here precisely. It was some time ago; the chamber that I discovered has no doubt fallen into disuse or been abandoned since then." He shifted his glance to Seran briefly. "Even if

270

Raethe believed my promises of silence, a secret is no longer such once shared." He remembered clearly the tools that his mentor plied in the vain attempt to shake loose the location from him. As talented as Seran was with a blade, the true tools of his trade were more subtle. The man wielded flattery and threat, guilt and promise with astonishing skill.

Seran murmured, "You cannot blame me for trying."

The thief's disbelieving frown spoke volumes. He turned his attention back to the door without addressing his mentor's statement. "I was young and, despite all evidence to the contrary, unreasonably confident in my own immortality." In the time that the trio had been distracted from it, the door had opened.

Back lit by a hodge podge of dented lanterns and broken, candle-filled sconces, stood a slim figure. In a low, rumbling voice that reminded Hollis of gravel shaken in a glass jar, they announced, "Raethe, King of the Underfoot has granted you audience. Enter and be welcome, 'Urchin who would be Saint'."

Chapter Thirty-Six
Shadows of a Starless Sky

Raethe's audience chamber was carpeted in mouldering rugs and a variety of other less recognizable textiles. The room itself was layered in light and shadow, the illumination cast from the motley collection of lamps and candles that hung randomly from the roughly carved walls. Only a half dozen figures stood in the spacious chamber. Clad in tattered and stained rags, most of them were unremarkable to the point of inconspicuousness. These were people that people would pass on the street and not spare a second glance, whether from disgust for the wretch's station or shame for their own.

One man, however, stood out. His clothes differed from the others only in the fact that they stretched tight across his broad form. His left sleeve hung empty as a discarded snake's skin. Its cuff brushed against the worn hilt of a thick bladed short sword. It was the only obvious weapon in the room besides those carried by the trio. The one-armed man watched them step past Raethe's herald with the dispassionate glare of a lifelong soldier. Hollis felt the eyes inspecting him more effectively than any pat down ever could.

Behind them, engulfed by an over-sized but threadbare wingback chair, sat Raethe, King of the Underfoot. A rail thin man of indeterminate but advanced age, Raethe's unkempt white hair mingled freely with the bursts of stuffing forcing themselves through rents in the chair's far from pristine velvet surface. It made him appear to have a halo of dirty, swollen clouds and lent him an almost ethereal air. Sunken into wrinkled sockets, a pair of clear hazel eyes lashed out at those gathered before him with an intellect that contradicted his aged form.

"Now what do we have here?" Raethe's voice was like a rusty hinge on a summer night. "We never thought to see the day when the 'Urchin who would be Saint' would return to demand his payment."

In unison, Seran and Aristoi dragged their eyes from the King of the Underfoot to stare at Hollis. The Songspear mouthed, "Payment?"

The thief took a step forward, drawing a mirrored gesture from the one-armed soldier. "Demand is a strong word."

Raethe tilted his head and squinted at Hollis, obviously expecting something further.

"Your Majesty," Hollis provided.

Placated, Raethe allowed a smile to paint his pale lips. "Of course, it is … of course, it is." Humor drained from his face like wine from a punctured skin. "How would you describe trespassing in our domain without so much as a 'by your leave', expecting an audience rather than a knife between your ribs?"

Hollis swallowed quickly, his mouth suddenly dry. "Your words to me all those years ago were, 'You have done us a great service this day. You have returned to us a life we had thought lost forever. The Underfoot and its king owe you payment in equal measure."

The aged king leaned forward, his thick eyebrows knitted in irritation. "Were those truly our words?"

The thief nodded. "They were, Your Majesty."

Raethe pursed his lips, causing his face to appear like it was folding in on itself. The room fell into a tense silence, the hands of its occupants not straying too far from sword or knife. Slowly, his countenance uncoiled, and a broad smile returned to his face. "I suppose that I would have a hard time arguing with myself." His voice was light, with a casual quality that it hadn't previously possessed. "You returned to me one of my lost sparrows. Ask what you will of me and if it is in my power to grant, it shall be yours."

Those gathered breathed a collective sigh of relief. Although the tension in the room eased as hands strayed from weapons, a sensation very much like an itch plagued Hollis's thoughts. He closed his eyes and took a slow breath, finding his center quickly. When he opened them again, he did so in the midst of the Understanding. Raethe's supporters had begun to cluster closer to him, their concern not lessened but rather directed at another source. The king himself grinned at the thief as though he hadn't a care in the world, but his eyes held a glassy quality, seeming to watch something in the distance … something that only he could see.

"Speak up, boy," Raethe prompted. "There must be something you desire. You have come so far and risked so much to return Reis's child to his home." His expression still retained a dream like quality, although a small tremor began to cause the left side of his mouth to twitch.

Reis. Where have I heard that name before?

"Your Majesty," Hollis began, setting aside the question as he tried to focus his thoughts on what he was seeing, "I have come to ask for what I hope is a minor favor of you."

Seemingly oblivious to his words, Raethe turned to the closest of his people. "What ever became of that poor boy? His mother was taken from him so young … so suddenly." A dark expression crossed the king's face as he murmured to himself. "She was warned not to travel beyond our borders. That there was nothing for her or her son in the city above."

The rag draped figure leaned close to whisper in his king's ear. Raethe turned to regard them with surprise plain on his face. Hollis watched raised eyebrows tighten and wide eyes narrow. Realization dawned on the King of the Underfoot as the sun races across a meadow on a summer's morning.

"We did our best to protect them both." Raethe focused beyond his assistant, speaking to himself. "We cannot be held responsible for what goes on above our heads … beyond our reach." His voice began to increase in volume and tempo. "She took both of their fates into her hands when she fled from us. There was nothing we could do. The Upsiders have always feared us. That is why they drove us down here to live off of their refuse ."

The hair began to rise on the back of Hollis's neck as he came to the realization that Raethe spoke to himself alone, quickly working into a frenzy. That manic state wouldn't bode well for him and his friends. Focusing on keeping his tone calm and measured, the thief asked, "What became of the boy that I returned to you that day, Your Majesty?"

Raethe tore his gaze from whatever memory had held his attention and turned it on Hollis. The king's lips pulled back over his teeth as he snarled, "He accused us! He blamed us for the death of his mother!" Levering himself out of the voluminous depths of his makeshift throne, he struggled to his feet. "We cannot be held responsible for what goes on above our heads," he repeated, this time in a voice stained with equal parts rage and desperation.

The thief bowed his head slowly, but never took his eyes off of the frantic man. "Of course, you cannot."

One of Raethe's assistants reached for his arm but was batted away. "We protect our people!" The thin figure attempted again to steady the king; this time Raethe didn't resist. He simply turned and repeated, "We protect our people," in a quieter voice, somehow less certain. The rag covered head bobbed in agreement and guided his king into the chair.

"Of that, there is no doubt." Hollis's mind raced, searching for a way to return his audience to some semblance of order. As it turned out, Raethe took care of that himself. The King of the Underfoot tilted his head, his eyes hard and expectant. The thief added, "Your Majesty."

Raethe's expression brightened as he said, "Excellent. What may we do for you, Urchin who would be Saint?"

Fearful of another outburst, Hollis spoke plainly. "I desire free passage through your domain and a guide to lead me to my destination."

The king settled back against the uneven padding of his throne, his shoulders relaxing beneath the tattered robes that served as his vestments of state. "You intend no harm to any under my protection?" Hollis saw the old man's fists clench and the tension travel up his arms. Raethe's back arched as he sat forward once more.

The thief cut off the relapse by responding quickly, "Neither through my direct actions nor the effects of the same will I bring peril to you or yours. My business is with the Upsiders alone."

"Will your business lead to their diminishment?"

"If I am successful, yes."

Raethe folded his bony hands across his midsection. "Good. Where is it that you wish to go?"

Hollis weighed his words carefully, watching the king's expression. "The Ivory Cathedral." He held firmly to a hope that Raethe wasn't a religious man.

Again, a rag hooded head dipped in to mutter in his ear. The thief braced himself but this time, Raethe's reaction was one of amusement. "How appropriate," he said, his voice marred by a dry laughter. "Your request is granted, and our debt discharged."

That was too easy, the thief thought, wishing the assistant's face hadn't remained covered. At least that would have given him a chance to read their lips. He didn't need the Understanding to tell him that whatever passed between the two was related to his request.

The king continued, "As such, your presence in my domain will not be pardoned again."

As Hollis opened his mouth to agree, Seran stepped up beside him. "If I may have one moment of your time, Your Majesty." The thief seized his mentor's wrist in a vise like grip.

Raethe's jovial demeanor dropped from him like a shed cloak. "We are aware of you, Seran of Uldred … Knife in the Dark. Your reputation proceeds you."

276

Seran shook himself free of Hollis's hand, favoring him with a gloating smirk before returning his attention to the king.

"As for our time, every moment you spend within the Underfoot is one more than you draw breath. Neither you nor your brotherhood are welcome here."

"I have an arrangement that will prove beneficial to both of us. If you only —"

Raethe gestured to the one-armed man, "Vaunt, if he speaks again, it would please us to see you cut out his tongue … at the shoulders."

The soldier nodded, drawing his sword with the slow rasping sound of steel on leather.

"Your intrusion has been tolerated due to the debt owed to the Urchin. That debt has been paid and offers you no further protection."

Hollis watched his mentor out of the corner of his eye. He tensed as he saw Seran's jaw tighten, his eyes not focused on the King of the Underfoot, but instead his designated executioner. "Drop it," the thief hissed, elbowing him hard in the ribs.

Seran shifted his eyes to catch Hollis's. The twinkle found there contained no lack of confidence. As he looked past the thief, his brows furrowed when he saw that Aristoi had turned her back on Raethe. Instead, she focused on the room beyond the arch behind them. Hollis didn't have to turn to know that the previously empty chamber would be filled with those willing to give their lives to enforce their king's will.

"We would suggest you listen to your comrades, Knife in the Dark. Leave the Underfoot now or lose the chance to do so." Raethe leaned forward, his sharp elbows propped on his thighs. He appeared, for all intents and purposes, as if he sat in a theater awaiting the curtain to open.

Seran took a step back, his head bowed slightly. With a smooth motion, he spun on his heel and walked casually towards the arch. Aristoi followed closely behind, her head tilted to keep both the thief and his mentor in her peripheral vision. Hollis bowed again, this time more deeply. "My thanks, Raethe, King of the Underfoot."

His dark mood seemingly having passed, the king smiled broadly. "It is us who are grateful, Urchin who would be Saint. Your aid in dealing with the problem of the Reisling pleases us greatly. My Angel in Gray will be waiting to guide you to the Ivory Cathedral. Go with our best wishes."

Hollis froze in mid turn. *Child of Reis. Reisling? Curate Reisling? You have got to be kidding me.*

Raethe cleared his throat. "Urchin, you may take your leave." There was a trace of amusement nested within the irritation of his voice.

As if moving in a dream, the thief bowed once more and followed his companions.

Plague Man ... Reisling has been in my blind spot for longer than I could have ever imagined. I have written the tale of my pain in the pen of my own charity.

*****

Hollis's attention was pulled from his own thoughts by the rapping of Aristoi's spear against the splintering doorframe. His friend stood in the empty doorway, one arm wrapped casually around the weapon's shaft. Shifting his eyes back to the window, he was surprised to see the first fingers of the dawn pushing back the night. "I feel that we have been in this same position before," he joked.

"Indeed, and not that long ago. Burdens carried in silence are burdens carried alone, Northerner."

"That is profound, Aristoi, did you come up with it yourself?"

She shook her head. "I am afraid not. It was an adage of which my mother was fond. She would trot it out whenever she felt I was hiding something from her."

"How ..." Hollis searched for an appropriate word.

Smoothly, Aristoi provided it: "Infuriating?"

"Close enough. It is kind of you to pass along that particular gift."

The Songspear smiled softly. "I felt it was the least I could do." Her eyes watched him with patient intensity, as if by the mere weight of her stare, she could tease out of him the source of his concern. When that tactic proved insufficient, she pressed, "Are your thoughts still upon Plague Man?"

Hollis began to shake his head but stopped. "Yes and no. I cannot help but feel I am the cause of my own tragedy."

"The child? The one Raethe called Reisling?"

He nodded. "Not much more than a child myself, I happened upon a group of men gathered around what at first seemed like a pile of rags. That illusion was shattered when the whimpers reached my ears. In their circle was a child crying for its mother. Far from touching the hearts of the men, the mewling simply prompted a new chorus of laughter."

Aristoi didn't speak, she simply took a few slow steps into the room, leaning her spear against the wall beside the thief.

"They were in my child's eye hulking brutes, and I had just passed my twelfth summer. They were many and I was one, but their backs were turned and I had my knife." Hollis's eyes lost focus, seeing a place that only existed in his memory.

The Ash was as the Ash had always been: brutal and dirty ... a place where hope didn't merely go to die, it never was born at all. In its cluttered alleys, out of sight of prying eyes, unspeakable deeds were carried

278

out. That night was no different.

"The first of them fell before they were aware of my presence, my blade in his liver. I left him moaning on the ground and lashed out at the nearest of his companions before any of the rest could see me for what I was; Seran had taught me well. By the time they gathered their wits, half of their number were bleeding into the filth covered street. Two still remained, however; two full grown men faced a frightened boy whose luck and advantage of surprise had both expired."

The thief rested his hand on a small, fist sized pouch that hung from his belt. "Another lesson I learned early on was that any fight you escaped with your life was a battle won. The bloody pile of rags that once were the child's mother lay unmoving despite their pleas." He frowned. "It did not bother me at the time, although my relief in the moment has haunted me from time to time in the years since." He answered Aristoi's unasked question, "It made my choice easier. There would have been no way to escape that alley with two in tow. I would have had to decide between fleeing and thus leaving them both to their fate or defending their lives at the likely price of my own."

"What did you do?" Aristoi had crouched down beside her friend, a mixture of compassion and curiosity painted on her face.

Again, Hollis held the pouch in the palm of his hand, "Over the decades, I have traded it out for ground glass, but at the time, I always carried the finest sand I could find with me. A handful cast into the eyes will not kill a man … hell sometimes, it will only slow them momentarily. A moment was all I wanted that night." He made a snatching motion in the air. "While the men were clawing at their eyes, I grabbed the child and ran for all I was worth. That night, I guess that value was equal to the task."

"The body was Reis? That would make the child —"

"— Reisling, if I understood Raethe's implication. Curate Reisling …" The thief paused, waiting for recognition before supplying, "Known better to you and me as Plague Man."

"Son of a …"

He nodded. "My feelings exactly. In saving that frightened boy, I set loose on the world a cancer … a disease that killed at least three of my friends and now has the woman …" Hollis let his voice fade into silence.

Aristoi placed her hand on his shoulder. "This woman, Asaege, is more than a partner of convenience, is she not?"

Again, he nodded, "I cannot speak for her but yes, in my eyes she is different. In a short time, she has burrowed into my mind … my heart like …" His eyes drifted to the window once more, allowing his words to hang on the still night air.

279

"Do you love her?"

Hollis averted his eyes. "Love is a loaded word. It brings with it a great deal of complications. We have known each other for just under two weeks, neither of us could claim to love the other in that short time. Let us just say that I dearly want to find out if what is between us is more than infatuation; I have not been able to say that for a long time." He felt like his soul was laid open before his friend, naked before her gaze. It wasn't a sensation he enjoyed. "All of this becomes irrelevant, however, if I cannot —"

"—We," the Songspear corrected, her voice soft but firm.

"If we cannot pull her from Plague Man's clutches."

"We have defied worse challenges. At his root, he is only a man … a vicious, tricky one but a man nonetheless."

Hollis winced as he whispered, "He has the brooch." He'd dreaded delivering that particular piece of bad news to Aristoi but felt he could not delay it any longer.

She snorted roughly, as if she were trying to clear a foul odor from her nostrils. "You are full of good news."

"You can still walk away," the thief offered, "You have repaid any debt you owed me long ago."

Aristoi squinted at him. "I shall choose to forget that you said that."

"It would be a shame if I dragged you all the way here only to have to go up against the brooch a second time."

"You did not drag me anywhere. I was already in the city when your letter found me."

"That certainly is a convenient coincidence."

The Songspear shrugged, "Not particularly. I came here in search of you." Hollis's expression must have betrayed his momentary confusion. "You cannot be so naive as to believe that you are the only one with problems."

"I suppose not. My apologies for giving you that impression. Of course, I will be happy to help with whatever you need …" He paused searching for a delicate way to finish his statement.

As it turned out, true friends often don't need well-chosen words. "After your current issues are resolved." He opened his mouth to apologize but she waved away his objection. "I would have it no other way."

Hollis's head snapped around as a soft shuffling sound reached his ears from further inside the darkened building. He noticed out of the corner of his eye that Aristoi also searched the darkness for its source. His hand instinctively went to where his thick bladed, Dwarven steel dagger normally hung, only to curse himself for a forgetful fool. It still lay swaddled in his satchel beside the Dialogues of the Chalice.

A soft melody caressed his ears like the sound of a babbling brook as he instead pulled the thin stiletto strapped to his thigh and carefully stepped to the other side of the open door. The tune came from the throat of the Songspear, its words so quiet that he could barely make them out. Even so, his mind allowed them to fade into the fog of forgetfulness as soon as they touched it. The song's effects were as subtle as its notes. The very air of the room began to take on a soft glow akin to that of the blessed few moments of predawn just before the sun extended its reach beyond the horizon. Far from blinding, it gave them just enough light to discern shadow from solid.

Following the thief's lead, Aristoi moved to the opposite side of the doorway on cat's feet. He could see the almost imperceptible movement of her lips, as if she were whispering to herself. *The months have certainly done right by you, my friend*, he thought. When last they parted, she'd been bound for her home in Kiel. Her Long Walk at an end, a piece of lost lore recovered for her people. She'd shared with him a hope that the secret of the Well would be enough to buy her full membership into the ranks of the Songspear. Based on the power she had shown here as well as in the alley outside the Silver Courtesan, Hollis had no doubt that her wish had been fulfilled.

Despite their dire circumstances, a small smile came to the thief's lips. It was good to have Aristoi back at his side. In her, he'd found something rare in his life. Silvermoon, Mika and the other members of the Band of Six were as close to him as family, but in their eyes, as well as his own, he was always a younger brother. Hollis stood beside them but always a step behind. Similarly, he'd found a new family in Renthroas, Rhyzzo and Ulrich but with the three of them, it was he who felt protective. The thief saw each of them as siblings to be looked after, even as they grew into men in their own rights. In the Songspear, he'd found an equal; he trusted her as he did his own mind.

As such, when she stepped back and gestured to the door and then to the center of the room, he nodded and sank into a crouch. She meant to lure whoever approached into the room, where the length of her spear could be brought to bear. Hollis would deal with anyone who followed behind. Softly sliding his right foot back, he perched on the balls of his feet, preparing to leap forward before his presence was detected.

For a tense moment when Seran stepped through the door, Hollis feared that she wouldn't stay her hand. The tension between the two of them hadn't improved since the incident in the alley. His trust in Aristoi was validated; she angled her spear towards the ceiling and allowed her song to drift into silence. Behind his mentor came a thin boy, still not in his teens, dressed in mottled gray breeches and over-sized tunic.

Unaware of his barely escaped peril, or at least expertly hiding his knowledge of it, Seran smiled a toothy grin. "My good and dear friends, this is the Gray Angel sent by the King of the Underfoot." The boy lowered his head in a shallow bow, keeping his hands tucked into the long sleeves of his tunic. "With our fellowship complete, do either of you see any advantage in further delay?"

Hollis's frown was lost in the darkness of the room. Seran seemed almost too eager ... too enthusiastic. *This is the man who drilled caution and planning into me from the day I came under his mentorship. More times than I can count, I heard: 'Plan twice, execute once, else the execution become yours'. Why is he so keen on moving quickly?* Other than his heightened paranoia, the thief could come up with no reason to waste any further time. "I can think of none."

Seran rubbed his hands together. "Wonderful." Gesturing to the boy, he said, "After you, Gray." Without a word, their guide turned and stalked from the room. As his mentor followed, Hollis caught Aristoi's attention. He pointed to his eyes and then to Seran's retreating back. He received a knowing nod in return. Catch-22 wasn't one of Stephen's favorite books; he'd only read it once in high school. He couldn't bring the exact wording to mind, but the gist of the quote resonated with him in that moment. *Just because I'm paranoid, doesn't mean I'm wrong.*

Chapter Thirty-Seven

A Tragic Legacy

Jillian awoke, an overwhelming sense of despondency hanging around her like a foul stench. Her bedroom, still blanketed in the predawn dimness, inexplicably brought to mind the dismal stone cell in which Asaege languished. The clock that sat on her bedside table confirmed it was a little before six am. When she tried to close her eyes again, memories of the prison returned full force.

Her heart pounded in her chest as the stone walls, only figments of her memories, closed in around her. Fumbling for the small lamp beside her bed, she tried to come to grips with not getting back to sleep.

Jillian rubbed at her eyes, still stinging from fatigue, as she pushed herself up into a sitting position. Laying innocently in the pool of light shed by the tiny bulb were the pair of journals she'd taken from Hector's shop. Her hand hovered over them for a moment before she snatched them both and dumped them into her lap. For a moment, she simply stared at the books as they lay in their down and cloth nest. *Such innocuous things*, she thought, *who would think that within their pages was ... what? Another world? In a manner of speaking. The hopes of a good man, doomed to tragedy, etched by his own hand? Certainly.* As sad as Jeff's story was, at least for him, it was over.

His legacy, however, was left in Jillian's hands alone. Gone were any of those involved in the events documented, but in those entries was the key to solving their murders. *Oh, and the key to neutralizing the brooch and depriving Plague Man of his power before he carries through on his threat to kill Asaege ... and through her me.* The weight of the responsibility laid upon her shoulders suddenly felt insurmountable. The desire to simply slump back against her pillows, closing her eyes against all of it was strong, but she knew what waited for her behind her eyelids.

Jillian took a slow breath and gritted her teeth against the temptation. She couldn't cover her eyes and hope someone else would take the burden from her. It was hers alone, whether or not she had chosen it for herself. Asaege depended on her, and through her reflection, her own life hung in the balance. *Hollis will come for her,* she thought hopefully. While the thought lifted her spirits slightly, she couldn't bear to put her fate in the hands of another; it was something that she and Asaege agreed on.

She couldn't help feeling a tinge of jealousy, despite herself. While neither she nor her reflection could rely on a white knight to save them, there was no doubt in Jillian's mind that the thief would move heaven and everything beneath it to try. *Hollis has proven in a few weeks to be more loyal and caring than most of the men I have known combined.* A strong sense of foolishness drowned the envy as she remembered her responsibilities. To take her mind off of it, she picked up the newest journal and began scanning it for anything that could help with them.

*****

Haedren had been waiting for us. When I came to myself in Silvermoon's consciousness, his memories barraged my awareness. It was overwhelming to process them in the midst of the vicious melee. Out of the corner of my eye, I saw Marcus slumped against the roughhewn wall of the cave. A shadow without apparent source engulfed his body in its depths. Although neither chain nor bond held him in place, Marcus struggled as if manacles secured him at wrist and ankle. Worse, however, was the almost liquid sound of choking emerging from his mouth. His head thrashed side to side as if trying to force something out of his throat.

I found myself standing opposite Mika, our former companion between us. ~~My~~ Silvermoon's meticulously crafted ash bow lay broken near the chamber's entrance. His sword felt familiar in my hands, although I could count on one hand how many times I had held a weapon outside of reflection and have a few fingers to spare. My momentary distraction had provided a few seconds respite from the two-front war Haedren had been fighting. He didn't waste the advantage.

The priest stepped back, free of the sword held impotent in my fist. Mika followed him, her sword held low at a forty-five-degree angle. Even in my confusion, she was breathtaking to watch. Her steps were smooth

284

and controlled; she covered an amazing distance almost effortlessly. Although she kept her gaze focused on her opponent, her lips pursed into a scowl. Beatrice had reflected with us, but I could see no sign of my friend in the expression of her reflection. Between clenched teeth, she hissed, "I warned you to leave this to us."

Haedren ceased his retreat, lunging forward swiftly. His mace lashed out in an attempt to bat aside Mika's straight blade. Rather than meeting it head on or pulling back, she stepped into the blow, shifting to her right at the last moment. Her sword connected with the thick wooden haft of the mace, redirecting it away from her. Mika continued her motion, allowing her wrists to break, rotating the sword in a tight circle to strike at Haedren's head. He reflexively lifted the butt of his weapon and interposed it between his skull and Mika's weapon. The force of the blow drove him back another step.

Able to shake loose of my initial disorientation, I rushed to her side. As I had done in the past, I allowed Silvermoon's reflexes to act without the chains of my conscious thought. The Uteli blade lashed out, catching him in the side just under his left armpit. The chain shirt he wore beneath his midnight black tabard kept the edge from his flesh, but my drawing cut sliced a wide gash in the leather garment. Neither tabard nor chain shirt could cushion much of the impact itself, however. I felt something snap under the force of the swing. Haedren grunted softly and favored his side as he took another step back.

Sensing an opening, Mika leapt forward in an elegant thrust. Haedren tried to bring his mace around to parry but it only served to drive the point of her sword deeper into his gut. His legs collapsed beneath him like a suddenly string-less puppet. She drew her blade back, preparing to drive it home again but from her perspective she could not see the small iron and silver brooch that was pinned on Haedren's chest like a frog upon a log. Before my eyes, its silver accents ceased reflecting the chamber's torchlight and fell into inexplicable shadow. His hand snaked out to grip Mika at the calf, leaving a dark stain upon her leg.

"Mika, stop —" was all I could manage before the tip of her sword vanished into the quickly growing pool of darkness. The leading quarter of the blade disappeared into the shadow, only to reappear instantly from Mika's calf in an eruption of blood and steel. The unexpected pain forced a cry from the lips of the warrior as her leg threatened to give out beneath her. Mika stumbled back in a hitching limp. I watched as the shadows collected above Haedren's heart raced towards the wicked wound in his midsection as if they had a mind of their own. When they receded, the only evidence of the wound was a ragged, blood-stained gash in Haedren's tabard and chain shirt. The flesh beneath was smooth and unmarred.

Deep in the back of my mind, I felt an insistence pushing me to cease being a witness to what went on before my eyes and continue to act. I recognized it as the sure confidence of Silvermoon. My grip tightened around the hilt of the sword and swung down at Haedren with all my might. Our former comrade tried to roll out of the way, contracting his body to take the blow against his shoulder rather than head or neck. Again, as if it sensed the danger to its host, the spreading pool of shadow oozed across his chest and engulfed his upper arm.

Able to pull back some of the force of the blow, I saved Mika from a more grievous wound, but the enchanted shadows conveyed what momentum remained to their twin perched like a leech upon her calf. Her leg finally gave out beneath her, although she had the presence of mind to scramble backward out of Haedren's reach. Consciously tearing my gaze from Mika's predicament, I saw Haedren slowly climbing to his feet, a mocking smile pasted on his face. The large patch of shadow, having separated into a half dozen splotches, swept across his body in a series of hypnotically random patterns.

"You cannot defeat me, Forester," he said, "No matter how many of you are in that brain of yours."

Words appeared in my mouth unbidden, doubtlessly provided by my reflection. "We have chased you far, Haedren. This ends here … this ends now."

Holding his mace casually in his right hand, the priest regarded his left hand as tendrils of darkness flitted between his fingers. "My dear Silvermoon, you are so very close to the truth. What lies between us will indeed end tonight, but while it is true that you followed me here, you did not chase me. I led you to this place by the nose as a bull to the slaughter." With a sweeping gesture of his shadow covered hand, Haedren pointed behind him. As if a curtain had been drawn, shadows receded to reveal a subtly glowing pool. "They call it the Well of Worlds. Its origins are shrouded in myth and legend, but its purpose could not be clearer. For the price of blood, it offers the power to change the world. Your blood will pay for my power."

The Well itself seemed innocuous, perhaps even inviting. The warm glow that emulated from its still waters called to the heart as much as the body. Surrounded on three sides by elegantly carved torches, a crude stone altar crouched before the pool. Offerings of gold and bone trinkets dotted the top of the dais. The flickering torchlight revealed a pile of bodies stacked in a tangle of limbs between the altar and the Well.

"I wish I could say I was sorry, but I would not do you the disservice of lying to you in your final moments."

286

I gestured to the corpses. "Has there not been enough death to-day?"

Haedren frowned. "Oh ... them? They simply stood between me and our reunion. They could offer me no more than resistance. It is you and your friends that hold the only key that I am interested in. Those who would be Children of the Well are a specialized breed. They must span two worlds, be of both and yet neither. The promise of the Well has been denied me too many times. I had thought the false hand finally offered me the opportunity to seize what was mine."

"False Hand? Theamon?"

Haedren nodded. "The same. But you know how that ended. Denied the magic commanded by Theamon, his reflection had grown old while he retained his youth. The fool's reflection was beginning to have a change of heart as he approached the winter of his life. Sadly, in his conflicted state, he was no match for you when your final confrontation came. Fortunately for me, the broken priest presented himself so readily."

My mind reeled, both Silvermoon and I believed it had been Theamon's spirit that had possessed Haedren but apparently, something far older had gotten a hold of both of them. "What are you?"

"I have been accused of being many things. The only one that should matter to you is executioner ... your executioner."

Out of the corner of my eye, a flash of movement was the only warning of Mika's approach. In a stumbling run, she rushed Haedren, her shield held before her. Haedren turned to meet her rush, the shadows that covered his body coalescing on his chest and arms. She struck him hard, tendrils of darkness crashing over the edges of the shield like waves on the beach. When they receded, the wood looked as if it had been gnawed on by dozens of mouths.

As he was driven back by Mika's charge, I stepped into him, gripping my sword halfway up the blade as I did so. Using not only my momentum but hers as well, I drove the point of my sword into Haedren's back. It separated leather jerkin and chain rings with equal ease. The motion also caused the blade to slice through my own heavy leather gloves and lay my palm bare as well, but it had been worth the injury. Haedren's shadows, occupied as they were with Mika's attack, could not prevent me from impaling their master.

The priest let out a scream, equal parts pain and rage. As his cry fell to silence, I could hear the ragged intake of breath that suggested a punctured lung. Mika raised a mailed fist and struck over her shield at Haedren's head. The sound of metal on flesh and bone was sickening, although instinct allowed me to withdraw my sword and stab him again.

287

The crimson agony in my left palm almost caused me to drop the weapon, only through adrenalin and hatred was I able to maintain my grip. I felt as if victory were within our reach.

Much like my own lacerated grip, that reach proved more slippery than I imagined. Mika pulled her fist back to strike again but with it she drew a clot of shadows. By the time her arm pistoned forward, they had covered most of her arm. Mika's punch never landed. A high-pitched, keening scream emerged from her, and she used her shield to push the priest away. From within the darkness that wreathed her arm, a soft rain of blood pattered on the cave floor.

My left hand a mass of pain, I was forced to release the blade and rely on the strength of my right to drive the sword further into Haedren's body. As Mika fell back, his shadows were able to realign their attentions on me. The majority of them clustered around the sword wound but a section concentrated on the offending object. I twisted my weapon one final time before releasing it. It was not a second too early; the polished steel of my Wallin Fahr disappeared into the darkness to the sound of teeth on metal.

Haedren's body spasmed with a liquid cough as he turned on me. Dark, half congealed blood dripped down his chin as he seized me with his maddened gaze. Slowly reaching back, he pulled the sword from his body and dropped it to the ground. The blade was pitted as if it had been left to the elements for years and there were actual bite marks in the leather wrapped hilt. His shadows swarmed around him like a hive of angry bees. "All you have done is delay the inevitable," he said in a hoarse murmur that grew stronger as he spoke. "The power of the Well is mine, stolen from me by inches until all that was left was shadow and whisper."

My blood felt as if it chilled in my veins. I had become clear to me in this, our last meeting, that whatever had driven Haedren, and Theamon before him, to the depths of depravity was much older and more dangerous than any of us could have expected. If, as the Walker had explained, the Well of Worlds played a part in bringing order and light into Taerh, the being contained within the brooch must represent the opposite: chaos and darkness. I'm not sure what would happen if something like that was able to roll the clock back on progress, but I was not prepared to find out.

"And Shadow and whisper is what you shall remain," I hissed. When faced with Theamon's magic, Silvermoon's and my connection had been able to bolster us against its influence. I had no reason to expect that it would not do so again. I could not have been more wrong. I surged forward, snatching my pockmarked sword from the ground with my uninjured hand. Haedren gripped his mace in both hands, raising it to meet my advance, its head wreathed in undulating shadows.

288

Gritting my teeth against the pain, I grabbed the mace's shaft with my injured hand. There was little strength in my grip, certainly not enough to prevent him from pulling it free. Fortunately, maintaining control of his weapon was not my primary goal. With both of his hands occupied, nothing remained between my blade and his thigh, exposed beneath the protection of his chain shirt. Although scarred, the steel of my sword still maintained enough of an edge to slice through his thin leather breeches and into the flesh beneath. Combined with the overextension caused by jerking his weapon from my grasp, the leg wound caused him to collapse to the stone floor once more.

Bolstered by our shared certainty that whatever dwelt inside the former priest, Silvermoon and I were of one mind, one soul. I felt the warm, comforting cloak of our connection settling across my shoulders as everything seemed to slow around me. As if suspended between two ticks of a clock, I saw Mika struggling to her feet. Her arm was ravaged by jagged cuts and vicious bite marks; in places the wet crimson-ivory surface of bone could be seen. Her face was set in an expression of resolve: hard glare and clenched jaw.

Haedren's eyes held something quite different. Fear hung in the depths of them in equal measure with doubt. In the moment, as I continue to do in this one, I wondered if they were a gateway into the mind of the man I had known or whatever controlled him. That moment was short lived. In his fall, the mace was torn from his hands. The shadows that had surrounded its head did not dissipate, however, nor did they return to their master. Instead, they raced towards me with a single minded, almost malevolent intelligence.

Foolish in the confidence of our connection, I stood my ground. The shadows struck me with the force of a gentle spring breeze, their lack of strength catching me off guard. In my surprise, I glanced down to find them flowing up my legs like a geyser. Where my body fell into darkness, pain followed. I felt the delicate agony of steel splitting flesh mingled with the bone crushing torment of razor-sharp teeth sinking into my body. What was worse, the shadows brought with it a frigidness that I can't describe. More than freezing my body, it wrapped its icy fingers around my very soul. The warm serenity of my connection with Silvermoon evaporated like oil on a quenched sword, leaving behind only fear and confusion.

My numb legs gave out beneath me, and I collapsed to the floor. Haedren flashed a smug smile before turning from my prone form to engage Mika. She swung her shield as if it were an extension of her arm, aiming for his chin. The priest raised his arm, interposing it between her attack and his face. Wood and limb met in the thunder of breaking bone.

Haedren let out a sound that was half grunt and half scream, but the smile still remained plastered on his face. He took a step back, allowing his shattered arm to dangle at his side.

"Where are your clever words now?" Mika taunted as he continued to retreat. She pursued, putting her body between the altar and her opponent. "Why do you run from me? Did you not want to use me to fuel the Well? Here I am, come and get me."

"Ah, but my dear, I have no need to pursue you." Haedren's voice betrayed none of the pain that his broken arm must have been causing him. "You are delivering yourself into my hands just fine on your own." He glanced down at Mika's long shadow cast by the flickering torches behind her. Shifting his eyes to meet hers, Haedren slowly lifted his boot and placed it across the neck of the shadow beside him. The effect was immediate; Mika lifted her hands to claw ineffectually at her throat. "With your final thoughts, please know how grateful I am for your sacrifice."

The sight of Beatrice's reflection, and through her Beatrice herself, in dire straits, shocked me into action. Although the living shadows continued to flow over my body, leaving pain and terror in their wake, I forced my way through the fugue that surrounded me. I put one foot in front of the other, moving towards Haedren on trembling, aching legs. My mind searched franticly for Silvermoon's presence, but it seemed obfuscated at every turn by a heavy fog of agony and fear.

Haedren pivoted to face me, his foot still firmly planted on the neck of Mika's shadow. The woman herself continued to fight against the unseen force that had seized her throat, unable to even make a sound. "I only require one of you, Silvermoon. Either Mika or Marcus will more than suffice. Do not fear, though, Those Who Dwell in Shadow have need of you ... they are eternally hungry."

As the darkness reached my chest, I could feel taloned fingers clawing at me as if in an attempt to bore themselves into my flesh. My steps slowed as the pain grew almost unbearable. Through willpower alone, I was able to continue my forward momentum, but I was quickly losing the battle against terror and blood loss. In the back of my mind, I could feel Silvermoon's consciousness struggling against the power of the shadows. Each time that I felt our mental hands clasped together, they were torn apart by another, fresh agony.

Within arm's reach of Haedren, I lashed out at him with desperate fingers only to have my hands batted away as one would rebuff a child. The clumsy attack exhausted the last of both my vigor and hope; I tumbled to the ground in a heap of misery. Before my quickly dimming vision, I saw Haedren staring down at me, his expression a mixture of pity and disgust. *"This outcome was always a certainty, but I find myself disappointed that you did not offer more of a challenge."* He shook his head slowly. *"After Theam —"* A wracking cough convulsed Haedren's body, spraying me with thick, bloody mucus. *"After Theamon, I thought —"* Haedren tried to continue but was once again interrupted by a spasm deep within his chest.

He clutched franticly at his heart, *"What have you done?"* His voice was at the same time accusatory and pleading. The shadows that surrounded me fell from my body and raced across the short distance that separated us. His chest was swarmed by a cloud of ever-shifting shadows, their frantic movements betraying their panic. Despite their presence, Haedren continued to gasp for breath, his lips flecked with blood and spittle.

My eyes went to where my brother's reflection laid entrapped by another of Haedren's shadows. Although darkness engulfed his body, his eyes seemed to shine forth with a defiance that could only come from his own connection to George. As if from miles away, Marcus spoke three words: *"It is done."*

"No," Haedren whispered between ragged breaths. *"No!"* With his final breath, he was able to force enough air from his lungs to vent his anger before collapsing lifeless to the stone floor.

Upon his death, all evidence of Haedren's power evaporated. Mika dropped to her knees, furiously gulping deep lungful's of air. Marcus struggled to his feet, no longer constrained by the mystic shadows. With the darkness that had enveloped me gone, I was able to see the effects of it. I almost wish I hadn't. My leather breeches had been torn to reveal the skin beneath. Deep slashes and ragged bite marks covered my legs and abdomen; in areas, whole chunks of flesh were missing.

Haedren's words echoed in my mind: *"They are eternally hungry."* I swallowed roughly in an attempt to contain my gorge.

We had won, but at what cost? On the three hour —

*****

Jillian had been so enraptured by the story unfolding within the pages of the journal that she almost hadn't heard the insistent barking from the apartment below her.

Stupid dog, she thought, *what's it barking at now?* She never heard the dog bark at anything but her coming or going from her apartment and certainly never once she'd moved into her bedroom. *What does that dog have against me?* A frigid shock of fear ran down her spine. *It's not just me, he barks whenever anyone enters the apartment.*

Chapter Thirty-Eight
Plague's Legacy

Jillian strained to hear anything below the high-pitched yapping. Did she hear a soft squeak of a rubber sole on the cheap linoleum that covered the floor of the entryway? Was that the groan of a loose hardwood slat in the living room that maintenance had refused to fix?

Her eyes swept her bedroom, searching for anything she could use to defend herself. On her dresser, a small paring knife lay beside an empty Amazon box. She'd meant to break down the box and recycle it days ago but with current events, it'd slipped her mind. She was suddenly grateful for that lapse in memory.

Picking up the knife, Jillian was surprised by how comfortable it felt in her hand. Unbidden, Asaege's memories flooded her mind. Living in the Ash, even the most amicable carried a knife and knew how to use it. Softly padding across the cheap low pile carpet, she held the knife stiffly at her side. As Jillian eased the door open, she heard the soft bump-rustle of someone rummaging through her school bag. A furtive glance back to the bed caused a sick feeling to rise in her stomach. *Were they looking for the journals?* Impulsively, she reached down and snatched a pair of jeans from the floor and tossed them over the leather-bound books.

The rustling stopped suddenly; Jillian froze in place, afraid she'd made enough noise to be heard in the next room. Taking a furtive step back from the door, she strained her ears but could only hear the beating of her own heart. *What if it's not the journals they're after? What if this is just a break-in?* Her eyes darted to the knife in her hand and then to the cell phone sitting on her bedside table. She cursed herself for not calling 911.

The soft whoosh-whoosh of slow footsteps began down the short hallway. Looking between the half open door and the phone, she made a quick lunge for the phone. As she snatched it from the table and ran her thumb along the screen to wake it up, the door slowly creaked open. Jillian turned, the phone cradled to her chest and knife held out before her.

A half-smoked cigarette hanging from his lips, Hector stood in the doorway. "Obviously, I've not woken you," he offered.

"Get the fuck out!" Her voice sounded more desperate than she would have liked, but no less so than she felt.

He held his hands up, palms out, "Believe me, nothing would give me more pleasure but I'm afraid you have a couple of things that belong to me."

"I have no idea what you're talking about, Hector," she lied. Her phone held at her side, Jillian pressed the power and volume buttons with her middle and pointer fingers to bring up the emergency interface. Without looking, she thumbed the screen in the center. Depending on her memory of her phone's layout, it would either power off or dial 911. She prayed for the later as she pressed and held the volume down button. There was no telling what Hector was capable of; it was better to keep him talking until the police arrived.

"I think you do, Miss Allen. Normally, I couldn't have cared less about a few books more or less, but our shared acquaintance insists. We both know what he's capable of if he doesn't get his way."

"So, you decided to break into my apartment and threaten me?" She made sure to enunciate each word.

"I'm not sure I would call picking that Mickey Mouse lock breaking and entering. You should really invest in a real dead bolt."

"I was sleeping and woke up to you riffling through my apartment." Jillian extended the knife another few inches towards him in an attempt to draw his attention from the phone at her side.

"Would you rather I called?"

"Yes," she snapped. "Yes, I would've." She paused a second for emphasis before blurting out, "Are you high?"

Hector shrugged, not denying it. "Says the kettle to her drug dealer."

Jillian pulled her hand behind her thigh and ended the call before letting the phone drop onto the bed. *If I didn't turn the blasted thing off, the operator should have enough to send the cops. If not, there isn't*

294

anything I can do about it now. "Do you wonder why Plague Man is so interested in those two particular journals?"

"So now you suddenly know what I'm talking about?"

"Did you believe me when I said I didn't?"

"No."

"Well, there you go." She shrugged. "Why does he want them?"

"Who knows with him." A look of weariness crossed Hector's face as he confessed, "He's a nut job."

Despite herself, Jillian smiled. "That's an understatement. So why work with him at all?"

He scowled. "If you read the journals, you must have come across the stuff about the Well. Who wouldn't want that kind of power?"

"Is it worth it, though, if you have to tie your fate to that man?"

Hector studied her as if she were speaking a different language. "Of course, it is. Power shared is still power."

"Have you read them?"

"The journals? A little bit here and there."

"That's a lot more than Plague Man has. Any knowledge he has of them comes from you." Realization dawned in Hector's eyes. "Have you read anything in them worth risking getting stabbed for?"

His face contracted as he thought about it, before slowly shaking his head. "Not that I can remember."

"And you don't find that peculiar? Plague Man needs these books so bad but has no way of knowing what is in them?"

Hector set his jaw and frowned at her. "It doesn't matter. Just give me the books and neither of us needs to get hurt."

She ignored him. "But what if he does have a way to know what's in the books?" She tapped her temple with a forefinger. "What if you and he are not alone in there?"

"What do you mean?" His voice raised in pitch, panic coloring its tones.

"You've been reflecting since before the Well, correct? Before he took the brooch?"

He nodded, squinting as if he were working something out.

"Have you noticed a difference in him since then? Has he been the same?"

Hector shook his head, "Now that you mention it …" He allowed his words to trail off as his forehead wrinkled in concentration, as if he contemplated answers to questions only he could hear.

"There is something in the brooch … something far older than the object itself, perhaps even older than the Wells themselves. You may be willing to share power, but I don't imagine it feels the same."

"He has been more demanding recently, somehow more single minded yet less focused. It almost seems as if he is —"

"Someone else," she finished for him, "or something else?"

Hector's face tightened as realization clearly dawned on him. He parroted her original question back to her. "Why does he want them?"

"Well, that's the sixty-four-thousand-dollar question, isn't it?" Jillian spoke her next words carefully, unsure of how he'd react. In their quest for power, would Hector and his reflection make an accord with whatever devil clung to the brooch? "Unlike you, I have read more than a little of the journals. While I'm not sure what they hold that it wants, they are quite clear that Plague Man wasn't the brooch's first owner, nor was the Walker before him. Perhaps within those pages lies the secret to thwarting whatever it had planned for those that held it previously … what it intends for you and your reflection."

Hector frowned, his thick brows tightening as his brow furrowed. For a moment, Jillian felt a sharp pang of doubt. *Did I misread his intent? Are he and Plague Man already lost to the 'shadows' or worse willingly working with them?*

He slowly lifted a hand to scratch at the week's growth of beard on his cheek. "How do I know you're not lying to me? I'm getting the impression that you would say anything to stop me from taking the books."

"Just because I don't want you to have them, doesn't mean I'm lying to you." Even though Jillian's body quivered in fear, she took a step forward. "The only way you could know for sure is to read them." Her lip pulled back in what she hoped was an intimidating sneer. "And that simply isn't happening."

"You're playing a dangerous game, lady. If what you're saying is true, anything I learn would be passed to whatever is inside the brooch. That would damn me to a non-speaking role in whatever Off-Broadway production that the thing has in mind." She felt herself relax for a second, until his next words. "But if you're lying to me, it ends up being the same script, just another playwright."

Out of the corner of her eye, Jillian saw the strobe of alternating red and blue lights against her bedroom blinds. "Well, Hector, you should make your choice quickly," she jerked her head towards the window, "before the police make it for you."

His eyebrows shot up in surprise, looking between the window and Jillian. "You called the cops?"

She picked up her phone from where it lay on the bed, turning it so he could see her call history. Her most recent call was to 911. "As you were coming down the hallway." Uncertainty hung in his eyes. Seizing on the advantage, Jillian pounced, "If you decide to believe me and leave without the books, you may be able to flee the building before they get out of the car. If you try to take them, I can't say I can stop you but I'm pretty sure that I can delay you long enough for the police to do so."

"It's not much of a choice."

"It wasn't meant to be."

*****

It didn't take the police long to take her statement. With Hector having picked the lock rather than forcing it and not actually taking anything, they lacked any real enthusiasm for even doing that. Jillian stopped counting how many times she was asked if his presence was of a more personal nature than a larcenous one. She was so keen to have them leave that she let their stern warning about the consequences of filing a false police report go without comment.

A quick search on You-Tube yielded a very informative video on turning a dinner fork into a makeshift door lock. Within an hour, Jillian was back in bed, her mind slightly more at ease. Beside her, the journals still lay beneath the hastily tossed jeans. With no trace of the trepidation that had plagued her earlier in the evening, she snatched the topmost book and searched for where she'd left off.

*****

We had won, but at what cost? On the three hour journey to the closest settlement less than a dozen words were shared between the three of us. Mika rode ahead of Marcus and I, vacillating between spurring her horse forward in an attempt to coax greater speed from us and slowing to allow us to catch up. Of the group, she was most eager to reach civilization, such that it was in Rangor.

We had agreed that Haedren's body, along with the brooch should be left behind until we could put together a plan to safely transport it. None of us wished to become the slave of whatever entity resided within the object. The ritual that Marcus had discovered could sever the connection between the brooch and its host but wasn't sure he could destroy it outright. The thought of such a powerful and dangerous relic left behind made us all nervous but Mika most of all.

Marcus rode beside me, lost in his own thoughts. Although he would answer direct questions, usually with a simple nod or shaking of his head, he seemed to be keeping his own counsel. From the little that I understand about the completeness of Marcus and George's connection, it went both ways. As my brother struggled with what he had done on Earth, his guilt filtered back to his reflection. If I had not been so preoccupied with my own concerns, I would have put it together. I should have put it together.

Instead of thinking about my companions, my mind wrestled with

297

the revelations I had made within the cave. For so long, we had chased Haedren in the hopes of prying him away from the influence of Theamon's spirit, only to find out that the former Hand of Lies was, in his own way, a victim of whatever force dwelt within the brooch. I analyzed and reexamined the events of the past months, searching for any clue that we had missed ... some way we could have prevented the situation entirely. By the time we reached the small seasonal village of Agmar's Watch, I was no closer to an answer.

Despite the fact that none of us had eaten since dawn, Marcus indicated his lack of interest in sharing dinner with a simple six-word announcement: "I am going to lie down." Without waiting for a response, he walked into the darkness of the ramshackle building that served us as borrowed lodgings. Mika and I sat before the small cooking fire outside the hut. At first the silence that hung between us was only broken by the soft snapping of the fire and distant sounds of the night.

"Your grand plan almost got all of us killed." I was so surprised by her voice that I didn't immediately respond. I suppose she took that as agreement and continued. "It worked out for the best, but it could have easily gone the other way."

"No plan survives contact with the enemy," I offered, "Mine was no different." I tried to keep my voice confident, but I knew she was right. I had not allowed for the potency of the brooch and how completely it had possessed Haedren. Immediately, I felt guilty for my projected arrogance. "I am sorry, Mika. I know my ... our presence here is not what you would have wanted."

"I have never made a secret of that, but," she paused, a rare, gentle smile coming to her lips, "you made a decent enough accounting of yourself."

"Kind words from the Queen of Snow? Be still my thrilled heart." In a gently teasing tone, I continued, "Did they hurt? Do you perhaps need to lie down?"

"Do not make me take them back." Gone from her voice was the razor edge that it normally held for myself or any of my reflecting friends. "Queen of Snow, hmm? I would have thought you would have gone with the Ice Queen."

I shook my head. "Ice is too obvious. When you hear it, you are automatically put on your guard. Snow begins soft, setting your mind at ease. You only become aware of the danger as it swallows you in its frigid embrace." I matched her smile, "It seems more fitting somehow."

Mika sat back, taking a deep swallow of the honey mead before her, contemplating my words for a moment. As she placed her mug back on the rough tabletop before her, she nodded appreciatively. "In a strange

298

turn of events, I find myself unable … or at least unwilling to argue with you."

"Sun's got to shine on even a dog's ass some days," I muttered in English.

She laughed in a series of short exhalations. "As much as your language sticks in the throat, it truly shines at colloquialism."

I spread my hands, bowing slightly as I agreed, "It certainly has its moments."

We sat in silence for several minutes, me savoring the elk stew before me and she nursing her drink. Mika broke the stillness with a statement that was also equal parts question. "There is more to that cave than we were told."

I nodded slowly. "Our time there, short though it was, left me feeling …" I searched for the word.

We both found it at the same time. "Unsettled."

"Having never been cursed with an abundance of curiosity, I find it strange that my mind tenaciously returns to that place … to the Well." Mika seemed almost angry with her revelation.

It was a welcome confession, as I will admit to feeling a low-key obsession with the cave. Up until that point, I had not placed a name on it but the Well had not been far from my thoughts since we had departed.

Mika gazed through the gaps in the ill fitted shutters, through which the tundra moon glimmered. "I feel as if we would do ourselves a disservice if we did not satisfy our shared questions before heading south again. Haedren's body and the brooch will not remain undiscovered forever, unless we wish to leave them both where they lay, we will need to return anyway … sooner rather than later preferably."

"I am assuming that your idea of soon would be this evening?"

"Am I correct that you are as unwilling as I to leave the brooch where it may corrupt someone else?"

"You are. The brooch presents a threat to anyone who possesses it, but that threat increases a hundred-fold when you factor in the power of the Well —"

"— which we still do not understand," she interrupted. She held up a finger. "Theamon." She added a second and third to it as she continued, "Haedren and even the Walker are fascinated by it. We cannot afford to be the only ones in the dark about its significance."

"Walker is our friend," I snapped, a little too quickly than I would have liked. Looking back on it, I think that I was trying to convince myself as much as Mika. The Walker's reflection, Samantha, is both friend and mentor; I cannot accept that she served some sort of ulterior agenda.

"The Walker is a Herald," she corrected, "Heralds do not have friends, only pieces in whatever game they play among themselves."

As much as I wanted to argue with Mika, my interactions with the Walker had convinced me that she and Samantha were very different people. "I suppose it would not do any harm to have another look after we have collected the brooch and removed Haedren's body from the cave."

As we were saddling our horses, I felt the adder root fading. As always, my reflection began to feather around the edges, becoming more dream and less reality. As my grasp on Taerh began to slip, I felt Silvermoon's consciousness move forward until I watched the body that had been in my control a moment ago pull itself into the saddle. I woke safe in my own bed a second later, my beautiful wife at my side.

Slipping from our bedroom without waking her, walked the two blocks to George's house. I wasn't surprised that my brother stood on his porch waiting for me, a cigarette held between pursed lips. Although I had believed that he had given up the habit years ago, it apparently still had its claws in him. We sat side by side on the stairs until the sun came up, although I don't believe he looked at me once. All of us did things while reflected that we regret but somehow taking place a world away, in the depths of a dream, they seemed less dire.

To save our lives and those of our reflections, George was forced to take matters into his own hands, here on earth and completely awake. I can see how his actions weigh upon him … in every distracted word, every nervous gesture. For the good of us all, my brother sacrificed a part of himself. Whether you call it his soul, his conscience or his heart, he feels the loss acutely. Although he dismissed the offer out of hand, once I am finish documenting my thoughts, I'm going to call a college friend of mine. I think George needs both a therapist and a priest, Bryan is both. No matter if George chooses to talk to him or not, I have decided that last night was his final trip to Taerh. His psyche has been wounded in the defense of Beatrice and I; he needs time to heal and that can't happen in the other world.

As for myself, the hours between now and when I can reflect again will no doubt drag. I find myself as interested in the secrets of the Well as Silvermoon and Mika. I just hope that together we can pry loose whatever significance it has before it can be used against us.

*****

The pages following the entry were blank. Jillian flipped back to the last lines. She felt gooseflesh rise on her arms as the realization dawned on her that they represented the author's final thoughts.

300

Chapter Thirty-Nine
Heart of the Matter

Asaege sat with her back against the cold stone wall, her arms wrapped around her knees. The only light that filtered into her cell came from the small, barred window in the thick wooden door.

For a while, she'd replayed her conversation with the Plague Man, searching her memories for something that she may have missed. She hadn't had another visitor since he'd taken his leave; she was left to her own thoughts with neither food nor water. *He no doubt hopes that after some time, fear and misery will soften my resolve.* What truly frightened Asaege was that she wasn't sure that he was wrong.

Closing her eyes, she tried to focus on something beyond her growling stomach and sandpaper throat. Without meaning to, her thoughts went to Hollis. The empty cramps in her gut turned to serrated claws of worry as she thought of his last words to her. Deep in her heart, she feared that the Plague Man sought to use her captivity as a method to put an end to whatever issues remained between them. *And all I can do is sit here, an unwitting bait*, she thought bitterly. *If only I had Marcus's book, I know that I could find something to put a fly in that arrogant bastard's oil.*

She sought to seize on anything to force her thoughts from what had become the two most important men in her life: one she hated and the other she felt herself growing to love. As clearly as recollections of her own life, Jillian's memories filtered into her mind. They were spotty in places, as if they were of a night too full of wine, but she could extrapolate enough to understand the context of them. She saw words written in a bold hand across the page of a leather-bound journal. Among them was what she thought could be an incantation that she couldn't seem to bring into clarity. She saw in her mind's eye a man she didn't recognize, dressed in strange clothes and standing in front of the same mauve and gray striped wallpaper from her earlier dream.

With the images came a deluge of emotions: fear, anger and concern. She could feel that her reflection was wracked with worry for Hollis as well. A tinge of jealousy hung among the other sentiments like smoke on an evening breeze. Asaege couldn't be sure if it belonged to herself or Jillian. As a feeling of resentment built in her heart, Jillian's memories began to fade from her mind. She shook her head vigorously, as if through the motion, she could shake loose the bitterness as well.

Taking a deep breath, Asaege let her head settle back against the wall and released her unintentional vise grip on her knees. She let her legs stretch out before her as she exhaled smoothly. With her breath, she tried to expel from her heart her jealousy and irritation for her reflection. While not able to completely purge her bad feelings, she felt herself reaching an accord with the foreign memories in her mind. Jillian's revelations about the brooch hit her like a frigid winter wind, chilling her to the core.

If the brooch was more than a simple trinket of power, instead some sort of prison for a malevolence as old as the Well itself, it put her conversation with the Plague Man into perspective. Of course, he wouldn't care about the welfare of those who would turn from Olm's true word; it would be in his best interests to encourage strife and dissatisfaction. In the hearts of the fallen, the seeds of temptation could grow deep roots. Never again would the force within the brooch need to wait for souls to corrupt, they would be as wheat before the scythe.

Asaege furrowed her brows, trying to bring the incantation upon the journal page into clarity through force of will. The harder she tried to remember it, the less substantial it became in her mind. She felt as if the memory itself fought against her. Before she realized it, her steady breathing had become ragged and labored. *Fighting against Jillian is essentially fighting against myself. That is a battle that neither of us can win*, she thought.

Reluctantly, she let the image of the journal page fade from her mind. Instead, she focused on memories that came more easily.

She saw a woman in her mind's eye that she didn't recognize yet looked strangely familiar. Her wide smile and deep brown eyes evoked a light, warm sensation within Asaege's chest. Although she'd gotten to know many fellow students in her time within the Great Library, none had cared enough for her to reach out after her fall from grace. *Here is the face of someone whose friendship is as unwavering as her smile*, she thought as the memory faded into another.

A sea of young faces watched her with rapt attention, their eyes sparkling with excitement. Her own voice rang in her ears, speaking about the history of a world that wasn't hers. Beyond the words, however, the passion that filled Asaege's heart made her feel as if she were flying. Reflected in those children, she saw genuine enthusiasm and affection. Beneath it, the barest whisper of frustration echoed, but in the summer sun of the moment, that irritation was as the faded memory of winter's chill. Jillian's fond memories of her classroom mirrored Asaege's own recollections of teaching her neighbors to read. As this reminiscence too began to dissipate, she felt an overpowering temptation to seize it … to hold onto the unbridled joy that teaching brought to them both. Grudgingly, Asaege let it wane, another rising to take its place.

She saw her own hands reach forward, clutching Marcus's book to her chest. As if from a distance, she heard her own words: "I never said that!" Hollis stood an arm's reach away, a smile painted on his lips that in retrospect was less arrogance and more affection. *One of Jillian's favorite memories is of me.* Asaege felt her breath catch in the back of her throat. *Out of all her own experiences, she finds joy in one of mine.* Even in her gloomy surroundings, her heart was lifted by the thought that she could share that moment with someone who appreciated it as much as she did.

Within Jillian's memory, Asaege could feel the weight of the book in her arms, smell its aroma of aged leather and parchment. She could even make out the dust motes held suspended in the afternoon sun. Asaege marveled at how they danced in the stray beams that filtered through the ill fitted shutters of her room. It was a detail that she'd missed in the excitement of the moment, but here in the reminiscence of her reflection, it lived forever.

Her eyes shot open as an idea ran through her like a bolt of lightning. *What else dwelt in Jillian's reflected recollections? What other shards of my life, lost to my memory are forever memorialized in hers?* Asaege could feel her excitement building as she closed her eyes again and slowed her breathing in an attempt to return to the place of serenity in which she and her reflection melded. To her surprise, it came easier this time.

A wash of memories caressed her consciousness like a warm spring breeze. With a gentle act of will, Asaege guided the flow towards a specific memory. At first, the recollection of the first time she examined Marcus's tome was pale and feather-edged, more fog and insinuation than clear image. Resisting the temptation to try to force it into clarity, Asaege let the memory carry her along, focusing on the details that were lucid. She allowed herself to feel the rough texture of the parchment between her fingers and smell the almost sweet scent of the melting candle beside her.

Slowly other details around her became sharper until the memory was as complete as if she stood within it. Before her on the page the words of the softening spell stood out in crystal clarity. With no more effort than she would need to delay blinking, the recollection froze before her mind's eye. Asaege's heart began to race; with her excitement, the image began to blur. Fearful of losing her only opportunity of escape, she focused on her breathing again. As she felt herself relax, the book became sharp once more.

With a gentle mental nudge, the memory proceeded once more. Her hand slowly turned the page as her eyes devoured the formulae on the revealed page. After an agonizing moment, Asaege watched herself grasp another page between shaking fingers and turn it. Before her was the spell that she sought. Again, she willed the memory to pause so she could more completely study the words before her.

In its most basic form, Levae's Charm of Changing allowed the thaumaturge to change the size of inanimate objects. The accompanying notes detailed slight changes to emphasis and pronunciation to affect animals and even people, but Asaege doubted if her understanding of thaumaturgy in general and this spell in particular were up to the task. In the end, its most basic application was more than enough for her needs. *Let us just hope it works*, she thought as she took a deep breath and began reading the words before her closed eyes.

At first, Asaege felt as if she forced them from between swollen lips. She'd always cast from carefully cultivated memorization, imprinting them on her brain using mnemonic devices taught to her during her brief apprenticeship. Reading them aloud without the benefit of that practice felt awkward. Twice she felt the energy gathered by the spell begin to turn on her due to a mispronounced syllable. She quickly stopped and allowed it to dissipate before beginning again.

On her third attempt, something felt different. The words flowed from her mouth as if each was carried along by the one before it. As each touched her mind's eye, it rolled forth along her tongue and into the air. The energy collected by the spell caused the fine hairs on her forearms to rise. *Now for the difficult part.* Asaege continued to read the words in her memory, but also formed an image of the thick wooden door of her cell. She felt the tightening grip of anxiety around her chest as she tried to maintain focus on two disparate images simultaneously.

As the last syllable fell from her lips, it seemed to reverberate in the air, repeating itself over and over. The casting of the spell seemed to have lasted forever but in reality, it had been less than a dozen heartbeats. Asaege slowly opened her eyes to see the door undulating with the echo, almost as if it were breathing. With each perceived intake of breath, the wooden portal shrunk in on itself. In a few seconds, the door became too small to be contained in its frame. With the sound of splintering wood, it pulled free from its hinges and fell outward.

Asaege crept to the now open doorway and peeked around the corner. The area outside her cell was empty, a short expanse of hallway flanked by a half dozen closed doors on either side. It ended in a blank wall to her right. No voices were raised from behind any of them, nor did the sound of alarm reach her ears in response to the sound of the door falling to the stone.

Staying low, she slowly made her way to the right and towards what she hoped was freedom.

Chapter Forty
Chilling Shadows

Hollis looked around appreciatively as Gray led the way through the tunnels. They were larger than he'd expected, high enough to stand completely and wide enough for three of them to walk abreast if they didn't mind getting cozy.

A small, rust colored stream wound its way down the center from somewhere out of sight. The thief breathed shallowly, as the combination of stale air and the cloying scent of unchecked mold gave the air a decidedly unpleasant odor. Beside him, Aristoi had wrapped a length of cloth around her face in an attempt to keep it at bay. From the way her brows were furrowed, it wasn't as effective as she would have liked.

Seran trailed behind the group, but Hollis could feel his eyes on his back even if he couldn't see the man himself. Many years had passed since the thief had come to the realization that his mentor could only be trusted to be loyal to his own best interests. Through some blessing of fate, those interests had never conflicted with Hollis's own. *But somehow, I feel that something is different this time*, he thought. Instantly, he felt a blush of shame. Had Seran not come to him in his hour of need? Had he not brought him, at great cost to himself, the Tears of Umma?

A thought like an itch at the back of his neck whispered to him that the elder thief never did anything without reason. *The question remains, what am I missing? He has not hidden his desire for the Dialogues, at least in any meaningful way. Perhaps he delved into his personal store of trinkets in a bid to keep me alive long enough to wheedle its location from me, but he is very aware that I now carry it on my person. If he wanted it that badly, he would have tried to take it already.* Again, a wave of guilt washed over him. Seran had taken Hollis in when no other would; he was just as responsible for making him the man he was as Silvermoon could have claimed. Perhaps beneath his cold exterior, Seran held in his heart a soft place for him.

Then what is he hiding? Hollis's mind kept coming back to that thought. He was certain that even without the Well-gifted 'Understanding' he would have picked up on the oddities of Seran's behavior over the last few nights. Added to the look of genuine shock in the eyes of the guild members he killed in Bearon's shop, it was clear that the man was hiding something. *All I can hope is that whatever he is planning has the courtesy to wait until we have rescued Asaege.*

The mere act of mentioning her name, even in his own thoughts, conjured her image in his mind. Her sly smile and soft eyes flashed at him from the depths of his imagination. With the image, came a flood of emotion that caused his heart to flutter. The thief clenched his jaw as if through that physical act, he could bite back the feelings welling in his chest.

For as much as Seran judged the man that Hollis had become based on the boy that he'd known, his mentor was correct in one regard. If the four of them were going to infiltrate the Ivory Cathedral, find and rescue Asaege, he was going to have to rediscover the heartless killer he once was. While he rejoiced at his rediscovery of the heart he once thought lost, those same emotions would serve him poorly in these circumstances. Reluctantly, he forced her image from his thoughts, instead drawing the comforting embrace of the 'Understanding' around him in an attempt to lose himself in the details that it revealed.

He watched Gray as the boy walked in front of them. His steps were sure, almost as if he knew these tunnels as intimately as Hollis knew the streets that had reared him. There was more to his stride, however. The way he held his shoulders back and his chin high demonstrated pride in equal measure to his confidence. Even factoring in the spotty nutrition available to the citizens of Underfoot, Gray couldn't have been older than twelve. Hollis was the same age when he was permitted to work the streets by himself as an apprentice thief. He knew well the satisfaction that came with the trust of those whose opinion you valued.

From the darkness behind them came a burst of soft scratching. It was so brief as to have been lost in the sound of their own footsteps had Hollis not had the benefit of the Well's gifts. He shifted his head towards

Aristoi, keeping both the ways ahead and behind in his peripheral vision. The Songspear seemed unaware of the sound. Although Hollis had no lack of confidence in his friend, she definitely seemed preoccupied.

Even with her face covered, he could see her nose wrinkled against the tunnel's stink. Although it was malodorous, the odor was far from the worst that he'd experienced. In the time that he'd known Aristoi, she'd never demonstrated a sensitive nose or weak stomach. Her reaction to her surroundings were evident in her bearing. She seemed to be curled in on herself, as if under a great weight. *Perhaps I just have never noticed before*, he thought. Although he tried to dismiss it, something continued to nag at him. Like Seran's recent behavior, he couldn't quite put his finger on what bothered him.

Again, the sound of scraping reached his ears. This time it was clearer, evident to him the brushing of leather against stone. They were being followed. He softly snapped his fingers twice to get Gray's attention before lightly laying his hand on Aristoi's shoulder. The woman's head snapped around, her eyes wild for a moment. As quickly as the feral gleam appeared, it dissipated but Hollis couldn't dismiss it as his imagination. *Another time*, he promised himself. He tilted his head to indicate the tunnel behind them before touching his forefinger to his right ear. With no further prompting, the Songspear turned on silent feet and scanned the darkness, her weapon at the ready.

Gray crept up beside them, also squinting past the limit of their low burning lantern. A few breaths later, Seran crossed the barrier between shadows and light, his face contorted in question. In the depths of the 'Understanding', Hollis noticed immediately that the inquiry wasn't mirrored in his eyes. Their calculating depths were empty of uncertainty.

The thief hissed one word, meant for the two figures nearest him. He was no longer concerned if the warning reached his former mentor. "Ambush."

*****

A half dozen figures stepped from the darkness to stand beside Seran; behind them Hollis could see the hint of at least another dozen silhouettes. He slowly drew his sword, not wasting his breath to ask his mentor for an explanation. Their guide took a cautious step back, drawing a knife from within his flowing tunic. Beside him, Hollis could hear a hum beginning to build in Aristoi's throat.

Dropping his eyes to the side, he asked wearily, "Are you ready to show me some of your new tricks?" The Songspear took a slow breath and then nodded her head. He wrapped his left hand around the hilt of his Wallin Fahr, below his right. "I knew I could count on you," he rumbled as he raised his eyes, a smirk painting his lips despite their disadvantage. Hollis hadn't realized how much he'd missed the Kieli until that moment. Since Asaege was taken, the thief had been seized by the profound feeling of solitude, despite the aid he'd received from Seran and Torae. With Aristoi at his side, he felt as if he no longer walked alone.

"Alright, who is going to be first? There is an excellent chance that the three of us do not leave this tunnel alive, but I guarantee that we are not going to be the only ones."

Just when he thought that Aristoi couldn't contain the building sound any longer, she opened her mouth. Her lips shaped it into words that broke against his ears like the ocean against a pier. Their force was undeniable but the words themselves slid from his mind like water through his fingers. Beneath his feet, the dirt and stone of the tunnel floor pulsed in time with her song.

She would not bring the tunnel down around our ears? he thought, *would she?* For an agonizing second, Hollis felt his confidence in his comrade wavering. That doubt faded with the shaking under his boots. Across the ten feet that separated the trio from their gathering opponents, however, the building earthquake only intensified. The six zealous figures seemed to lose their enthusiasm as they quickly began to back pedal. The thief figured all they needed was a slight nudge to push them into retreat. He was glad to provide it. "Or we could just bury all of you and continue about our business. I am not sure about you folks, but I am becoming more confident in our chances by the moment."

The figures turned and fled into the darkness, leaving Seran standing alone amid the intensifying vibrations. Unlike his companions, he seemed unfazed by the effects of Aristoi's song. He casually reached into the folds of his vest and pulled forth a gold and ivory object that reminded Hollis of a cigarette case from Stephen's world. It was another of Seran's trinkets. A quick flick of his thumb caused the case to snap open, revealing a flat black interior. Its effect was immediate and absolute. Between breaths, the feeble light of the lantern was extinguished, and the tunnel dropped into silence. In the darkness, Hollis pictured the Songspear clawing at her throat in a panic, although he could neither see nor hear the gesture.

The silence was broken by a sharp click as Seran closed the lid. As if a hood was removed from his head, the ambient sounds of the tunnel returned. Behind his mentor, two figures put flint to a pair of lanterns, stabbing Hollis's eyes with their sudden light. As he'd imagined, Aristoi clutched her throat, straining to force a sound from her lips. Seran held the trinket up. "I hope you do not find my little toy inconvenient; I do so hate to find myself unprepared."

Hollis snapped, "You had best make sure I am dead, Seran," surprised to find his own voice intact. "Because you can be assured that I will not rest until you are so." His narrowed eyes bore into the man he once called a friend. His intense focus caused him to momentarily overlook other familiar faces revealed by the lantern light.

"I am sure that will not become an issue." Guild Master Dhole definitely looked more intimidating than the last time they'd met, but that wasn't difficult as the last time Hollis had seen him, the man had been half naked and tied to a bed. Beside him stood his protege, Toni.

Hollis clenched his jaw in rage, hissing between his teeth, "Dhole, I thought I recognized your stench."

"Guild-Master Dhole, if you please. As in 'Guild- Master Dhole, please just let me die'."

Hoping that his face didn't betray the very real dread that pulled at his heart, Hollis snapped, "There is as much chance of that happening, as of you spending time with someone that you do not need to pay."

"How dare you!" The guild-master boomed.

The thief tried to keep his voice even as he responded, "Daring has nothing to do with it. Remember our last conversation took place with you in the midst of just such a transaction." He forced a chuckle. "I do hope you asked for a discount as I am sure it was not what you had intended."

Even in the dim light, Hollis could see the color rise in Dhole's face. An unhealthy shade of crimson flowed upward from beneath his collar, settling just under his receding hairline. "You have brought embarrassment to the guild ... cost us more than even your own overestimation of your worth."

"I would not be so sure; I have been told that I am pretty arrogant."

"Do you ever shut up?" Dhole growled. "Of the many things I will be glad to be rid of with your passing, I think I will celebrate the sound of your voice the most." Toni stood beside the guild-master, watching him with a look of apathy that was so perfect it almost had to be practiced. "The guild has decided your fate, Hollis, there is no avoiding it now. Before you stand odds that even your inflated ego could not believe you could overcome."

Beside Hollis, Aristoi's hand dropped to grasp her spear again. The only sign of the fear that must be pounding through her veins like her blood was the tip of her tongue flicking out to wet her lips. Even with the combination of the gifts of the Well and the Songspear at his side, the thief couldn't find it within himself to disagree with Dhole's words. "I would rather die with a pair of loyal companions by my side than live a century with the knowledge that I betrayed the trust of my brothers and sisters." His eyes bored into Seran, who studied his fingernails casually in the dimness of the tunnel.

Looking up at Hollis's words, his mentor simply favored him with a quick wink before returning his attention to his hand.

The guild-master laughed. "Then it will be my pleasure to grant your wish." He took a few steps forward to stand beside Seran with his protege matching his pace. Within the confines of the 'Understanding', Hollis noticed that Toni seemed to be more focused on Dhole than himself. "Let us test the commitment of those in which you have placed such faith, shall we?" Dhole forced a smile to his lips. "Boy. Woman. If you turn your back and walk away now, I guarantee that none of mine will pursue. In Hollis, you have tied your fate to a stone. Take the chance to discard him before he drags you to your deaths."

The thief heard the sound of dirt crunching under boots around him. The first was Aristoi settling her feet more firmly on the tunnel floor in preparation for the battle ahead. Unfortunately, the second was Gray backpedaling into the darkness. *I cannot blame him*, Hollis thought, *It is not his fight.*

"That leaves only two," Dhole mocked, "Your odds are worsening by the moment. In recognition of your past contributions to the guild, I am willing to make one final offer of mercy. Give me the book and I will agree to make both of your deaths quick."

Hollis glanced over to Aristoi, who simply shook her head. "What makes me think that is a lie?" Hollis drawled. "It must be the fact that your lips are moving."

The guild-master's hand went to the short, chopping sword at his waist. Seran's fingers fastened about his wrist. "Lord Dhole, do not allow Hollis to get the better of you." He locked eyes with the thief before continuing, "Despite his bravado, he should understand the situation he finds himself in." When Dhole tried to pull his wrist free, Seran seemed reluctant to release it, leaving his arm awkwardly draped across his body.

Toni laid their hand on his extended shoulder. "Guild-Master, Seran is correct. His confidence is unwarranted. What has he done to deserve it? Nothing." Their words were tinged with contempt. "Your actions, on the other hand, speak for themselves."

Dhole once again tried to free his arm but between Seran and Toni, he seemed immobile for the moment. Hollis saw the beginnings of fear touch his muddy brown eyes. "You delivered the guild from more than a century mired in tradition and brotherhood, into a new era of barely veiled indentured servitude." Realization warred with terror in the guild-master's face as Toni slowly drew their dagger. "In the name of your own aspirations, you placed chains around the throats of each and every one of the Brotherhood of the Night."

312

"Toni," Dhole snapped, "release me this instant!" Unable to muster conviction, he opted to replace it with volume. Behind the trio, the remainder of the guild forces erupted into a chorus of confused murmurs. "I knew the moment I saw you, that I should have left you for the mongrels." The guild-master turned to Seran, his eyes pleading. "If you would rectify my mistake, I will make it worth your while."

Seran tightened his grip on Dhole's wrist and slowly shook his head. "My dear Guild-master Dhole, bribery is the last frantic gasp of the truly desperate." He slowly tucked the gold and ivory trinket back into his vest and drew his own dagger. "My neck was among those you sought to bind." Seran leaned close to the guild-master's face and harshly whispered, "Nothing you have is worth my freedom."

As one, Toni and Seran drove their blades into Dhole's body. The man slumped to his knees after the first stabs, but the pair continued their assault. Behind them, as if Dhole's murder had been a signal, a number of the thieves in the shadows fell upon their companions. Hollis and Aristoi remained frozen in stunned silence, watching the carnage before them helplessly. In what seemed like seconds, it was over. A dozen young thieves stood behind Seran and Toni, the bloody body of former guild-master Dhole at their feet.

Hollis shook loose from his shock. "Was this your plan all along?"

His mentor reached into the folds of his vest and pulled free the trinket once more. "Of course, my boy. Your ignorance was a necessary conspirator, however." He thumbed open the case and Gray's forgotten lamp flared to life once more.

"Son of a bitch!" Aristoi roared, her voice restored.

"I will admit that certain portions of my ruse were less regrettable than others."

The thief placed a restraining hand on the Songspear's arm. "Now is not the moment," he mouthed to her before turning his attention to his mentor. "This is what you have been hiding all this time." It should have been a question, but it wasn't.

Seran shrugged, "I was honestly concerned you would figure it out sooner. Did you truly believe I would choose that corpulent sack of mediocrity over my own apprentice?"

"The thought crossed my mind."

"Shame on you, boy. Shame on you."

"Not to cut short this, oh so compelling back and forth," Toni said, "but are there not better things that we can be doing?"

Hollis looked over his shoulder to see Gray abashedly stooping to pick up his discarded lantern. "Now that you mention it ..."

Seran laughed, throwing his arm around the thief's shoulders, "I would say our odds have just improved dramatically."

He shrugged off his mentor's embrace. "Only as long as there are no further surprises. Your hostile takeover could have put everything at risk."

"Noted," Seran agreed.

"Would someone like to fill me in?" Toni's voice was a mixture of interest and annoyance.

"In a moment," Hollis held up a finger to them before turning to Aristoi. "Are you alright?"

She nodded once, her eyes filled with fire, all of it directed at Seran. "I am having a few trust issues is all."

"You and me both. Do you think you can work around them for the time being?"

Again, she nodded. "I know what is at stake."

Hollis squeezed her shoulder. "Aristoi —"

"— I know," she interrupted. "I have not asked you my favor yet. Perhaps you will regret requesting my aid."

"Never." Hollis then crossed the distance between the group and where Gray stood, lantern held in both hands. The boy wouldn't meet his eyes.

"I—"

The thief shook his head. "You owe me nothing beyond showing the way. Is that going to be a problem?"

"No."

"Good." Without turning around, Hollis announced over his shoulder, "We will be moving on to the catacombs below the Ivory Chapel. Anyone who wishes to leave now is free to do so." None of the gathered thieves took him up on his offer. "Then let us be on our way."

Out of the corner of his eye, he saw motion in the darkness. His sword already drawn, Hollis pushed Gray behind him and brought it up to a guard position.

As the figure emerged from the shadows, the blade fell from his fingers. Hollis rushed forward and wrapped his arms around Asaege's waist and crushed her to him, those assembled forgotten for the moment.

314

Chapter Forty-One
Heartfelt Reunion

Asaege's trepidation of the group gathered in the tunnel evaporated when she heard the bass tones of Hollis's voice. With great effort, she restrained herself from running to him. As she entered the circle of light, the reactions of those gathered were instantaneous. Hollis stepped protectively in front of a small rag draped boy while the Kieli warrior woman at his side lowered the broad bladed spear in her hands. Behind them, more than a dozen figures reached for weapons.

Asaege almost had time to regret her bold approach before Hollis had cast his sword aside and enveloped her in his arms. The suddenness of the gesture caused her to tense for a second, before melting into his embrace. She was so lost in the moment that she was barely aware of his companion's richly toned voice as she allowed the tip of her spear to angle towards the ceiling. "Asaege, I assume."

Hollis didn't react to the Kieli at all.

For the first time since meeting him, Asaege found the man without words. His face buried in her neck; she felt his quickened breath stirring her unkempt hair. With her arms looped around his neck, the days' growth of stubble on his head prickled at her skin but Asaege didn't feel the least temptation to pull away. In the midst of the terrors of her time below the cathedral and in the presence of the Plague Man, this moment seemed to blessedly go on forever. In Hollis's arms, those things melted away like ice in the afternoon sun. A voice at the back of her mind whispered that there were more pressing things to be attended to. Asaege simply declined to listen for the time being.

Without planning to, she pressed her lips against his neck between his ear and shoulder. The intimate touch of skin on skin caused electricity to pulse through her veins. Asaege pulled him closer, riding the sensation like the fast-running waters of a wild river. She felt his fingers grip her light shift dress, as if he never intended to let her go.

In a husky whisper, he spoke into her hair, "I … I told you I would come, Magpie." His hands still intertwined in the fabric of her dress, Hollis lightened his grasp in an attempt to look at her. Asaege only reluctantly allowed him to put space between their bodies. "I told you I would come."

In breathy tones, Asaege replied, "I know. I just thought I would meet you halfway." She couldn't contain her smile as her eyes devoured his face, thrown into rugged contrast by the flickering lantern light. "I —"

He cut her words off by pressing his lips hard against hers. The current caused by her brief kiss against his neck exploded into the rush of lightning. Lost in the moment, Asaege pulled Hollis close, crushing her body against his. Around them, all else ceased to be. She only knew of him … the strength of his arms, the heat of him against her body, the insistent demand of his lips on hers. For one glorious moment, the universe began and ended in that embrace.

*****

Asaege sat on a pile of rubble across from Hollis, their fingers intertwined in the intervening space. Around them stood the mismatched trio of his comrades. To his left stood the warrior woman, her spear tucked nonchalantly against her shoulder. There was a comfortable familiarity between them, but there was no indication that it was more than their experiences with the Well. The other two were members of the thieves guild; of them Asaege was far more partial to Toni. Although Toni's cool, professional demeanor was off-putting at first, Asaege preferred it to Seran's often dramatic and insincere platitudes.

"With Lady Asaege free from the foul clutches of the Plague Man, the matter should be concluded." Seran's voice dripped with honey but beneath it hung sour notes of contempt.

"It may not be that simple," Hollis responded. "If the book or Asaege plays a part in this grand plan of his, he is not likely to give up so easily. Doubly so if he has the power of the brooch at his disposal."

"We allowed it to slip through our fingers once," Aristoi added. "I am not prepared to do so a second time."

"That makes two of us," Hollis agreed, "It is too dangerous to be

316

left in his hands. Walker was able to shake off its influence; I am not sure the same can be said for Plague Man."

"Either way," Toni spoke up, "we can ill afford to allow him to add to his power, whether mystical or political."

Asaege frowned at them, "What is the thieves guild's interest in all this?"

Toni's face tightened. "Dhole made arrangements with the city leaders in an attempt to secure for himself a seat on the council. I recently discovered that part of that agreement was to have the guild act as the council's secret police. We could move freely where the city guard could not. Many apprentices, too afraid to ask questions, did not challenge the fact that they were stealing from those whose worth was far below the cost of the job."

"I had no idea," Hollis said.

Toni shrugged "Neither did I … or at least not clear enough of one. I knew that he was lining his pockets at the expense of the Brotherhood but I only came to understand the entirety of his machinations two nights ago."

"He is dead now," Asaege said. "I repeat my question. What is the guild's interest in Plague Man?"

"If you will excuse my turn of phrase, the unholy alliance between church and council would have us turn against our own," Toni said. "It is rare that those who grew up with full bellies turn to our profession, even rarer that they join the guild. We are often the last rung before someone descends into hopelessness. Those 'polite society' treads beneath their heels are our pack, not our prey."

"Are you saying—," Hollis began.

Toni finished for him, "If things are going to change, the guild will, for once, be on the right side of it."

"I will admit to being surprised by that," Asaege said, "Do you speak for the entire guild."

"Any that held allegiance with Dhole have been dealt with," Seran added, "Toni and I agreed that it made sense from both the standpoints of business and morality." His face twisted as he uttered the last word, as if choking on the taste of it. "If the rich hold all the money, it is counter intuitive to stand on the same side of the table as them."

"How pragmatic," Hollis muttered.

"I thought so." Seran's toothy smile reminded the thief of an alligator deciding whether to eat you now or save you for later.

Changing the subject, Asaege offered, "I am not sure that a few quotes constitute a movement."

"There is power in words." It was the first thing Aristoi offered in the discussion. "They cut deeper than steel and fortify a heart more completely than armor does the flesh that it surrounds."

"I have seen with my own eyes the effects of those few quotes, Prophet." Toni watched Asaege inquisitively. "I have heard them spawn words of their own, words of defiance and insurgence. The flame has already been lit. It will not take much to fan it into an inferno."

"I never meant to …" Asaege allowed her words to trail off. She had meant to say that she didn't want to start a revolution, but didn't she? People … her people were suffering in poverty and ignorance, kept there by powers that benefited from keeping everyone around them small.

"It does not matter what you meant," Hollis's gentle voice rose, "you have given voices to those who have been too long mute. You have shined a light on a lie that has for too long been spoken as holy truth. The misery with which the common folk have been saddled is not divinely decreed. It comes from the greed of those whose lives depend on keeping them face down in the mud. I am not sure you can undo that, even if you wanted to."

"While not easy," Aristoi said, "it is a noble cause … one that is too important to be co-opted by either Plague Man or whatever lies within the brooch."

Hollis added, "You were right to doubt the sincerity of his offer to settle for the dregs. I know not the motivations of the brooch, but I am all too familiar with those of the Plague Man." A specter of sadness fell over his deep brown eyes for a second, as he seemed to settle into his own thoughts. Before the silence became awkward, the thief filled it. "If we can get the brooch from him, we can at least minimize its role in his plan."

Asaege squeezed Hollis's fingers lightly, drawing his attention. "What if we did not need to take it from him? What if we could remove the threat of it once and for all?"

A smirk came to the thief's lips. "Well … that would definitely be better. I sense that you have a plan."

She nodded. "There is a ritual that should be able to sever the link between the brooch and whatever lies within it. If I could perform it, the brooch will become nothing more than a gaudy bauble."

"I am hearing a lot of should's and could's." Seran's voice held apprehension.

"Nothing is without risk," Aristoi snapped, her eyes hard as they stared at Seran.

"Do you have this ritual?" Hollis asked.

"Sort of."

The thief tilted his head. "Sort of?"

318

"Jillian has it … in the journals." Asaege could feel Hollis deflate some. She quickly added, "She and I have had some real breakthroughs recently. I think we can do it."

"Who is Jillian?" Toni asked.

Hollis dismissed their question with a wave of his hand, his attention focused on Asaege. "Alright. If anyone can do this, it would be the two of you." His words sounded confident and sincere.

A spark of pride bloomed in her chest. It was followed by a twinge of terror. *What have I done?*, she asked herself, *We were able to cast one spell against an unmoving door. I have now committed to perform a lost ritual that I have never seen against the single most dangerous man I have ever met.*

Hollis brought her hand to his lips and lightly kissed her fingertips. The faith in his eyes almost made her believe anything was possible. Almost.

"Perhaps we should find our way out and come up with an actual plan to put into motion," Toni announced, "We are certainly not going to find Plague Man in the middle of this tunnel."

"I would not be so sure about that." A leather masked figure stepped out of a collection of shadows Asaege hadn't seen coalesce.

*****

Those gathered stared in shock as Plague Man stood in their midst. From the swirling shadows behind him emerged a group of templars, swords drawn, and shields raised. Hollis jumped to his feet, his Wallin Fahr halfway out of its scabbard before he reached them. Aristoi's spear leapt into her hands as if it had a will of its own and the pair moved forward as if they shared a mind. On their heels, Seran moved in a half crouch, a thin dagger in his fist.

"Ambush!" Toni called to the thieves that were scattered around the chamber. To their credit, most of them were already moving towards the interlopers. Toni drew their broad bladed Mantrian short sword and moved to their left, their intent to prevent the templars from flanking their position was obvious. A few steps behind, Toni's guild forces mirrored their movements. In the dim light, it seemed that the templars were outnumbered but not outmatched. While the thieves were dressed in soft leather and homespun, the soldiers wore chain mail shirts and each carried a stout wooden shield.

Fear that had nothing to do with her own safety burned the back of Asaege's throat. Plague Man's thin Slazean sword lashed out, missing Hollis's exposed cheek by inches. The assassin was only denied a follow up cut because he had to leap backwards out of the path of the thief's own sword. The undulating shadows behind him reached for Hollis with

319

hungry fingers. He danced back out of range of their greedy grasp, but Plague Man followed him, closing the distance. He brought the shadows with him. To Hollis's right and left, Aristoi and Seran kept the soldiers flanking Plague Man at bay, although their techniques couldn't have been more different.

Aristoi relied on the length of her weapon, thrusting it deftly where the templar's shield was not. Unable to get within range to strike at her, the soldier was forced to block furiously. Each time he attempted to bat aside the spear, Aristoi simply withdrew it, causing her opponent's weapon to be out of line for a parry. Before the templar could recover, she would thrust again. Often, it would meet the sturdy wood of his shield but occasionally, the point of the broad bladed weapon would sink into a shoulder or thigh, splitting chain links to draw blood. All of these wounds were trivial, but Asaege assumed they would factor into a battle of attrition.

Seran, on the other hand, fought as closely as he could to his opponent. He seemed to be in constant motion, circling the soldier to grab and pull at the edge of his shield. At such close range, the templar was forced to grip his sword halfway up the blade and use the hilt as a club, but even then, his weapon was no match for the speed of Seran's knife work. Where an opportunity presented itself, Seran would drive his stiletto into the soldier, its thin blade slipping between links and through the padding below.

Forcing her eyes from the battle, Asaege turned her thoughts inward. Although the timing wasn't as they had intended, the plan remained the same. If any of them were going to escape with their lives, the brooch had to be rendered inert. Asaege tried to slow her breathing, but the sounds of combat prevented her from finding a peaceful state of mind. She saw Toni grab one of the thieves by the collar and gesture back at her. Although their words were lost in the cacophony, their intent was clear. Two guild members broke off from the soldiers and took up positions between Asaege and the melee.

"Do not worry, Prophet," one of them shouted, "they will need to kill me before I will allow them to lay so much as a hand on you." His companion nodded his agreement. Each of their faces was set in an almost fanatical grimace.

Asaege smiled in thanks but suddenly felt uncomfortable. *These boys are not much older than my former students, yet they are willing to lay down their lives ... for me?* She closed her eyes in an attempt to block out the images around her, most of all the look of zeal stamped on the faces of the two boys before her. She focused on her breathing, trying to find that place within herself where doubt became confidence. Each time she felt the cottony fingers of connection brush her heart, a clash of metal or cry of anguish would intrude on her thoughts, and it would be lost. Gritting her teeth, she held in her mind the mauve and gray confines of Jillian's bedroom.

She could feel the soft bed beneath her and smell the sweet, earthy scent that pervaded the air. Once again, the soft embrace of her reflection settled on her shoulders but still the image of the room remained static and distant, like a painting before her eyes. Asaege was jolted from her attempt as a grunt of pain erupted so close, she felt that she could touch it. Before her, a templar towered over the two boys meant to protect her. The quiet one gripped his belly, as if by the act alone he could contain the innards that threatened to spill forth. His partner didn't appear as confident as he had a moment before.

He looked back at Asaege, terror as plain on his young face as if it were stamped there. Tears burned the back of Asaege's eyes and blurred her vision. She drew a borrowed dagger and moved forward. "No," the boy snapped before turning his attention back to the soldier bearing down on him. His short, chopping sword hacked at the templar's unprotected leg. The man, having overlooked the boy, didn't bother to block. The blade sank into the soldier's knee with a sound like butchered meat, causing him to crumble to the ground.

Asaege's protector fell upon the downed man like a rabid animal, swinging his sword wildly. When he turned from his savaged foe, blood covered his face and chest in broad, crimson stripes.

Between ragged breaths, the boy repeated, "So much ... as a ... hand."

Chapter Forty-Two
A Shadow Most Perfect

Hollis backpedaled just inches ahead of the probing tentacle of shadow that reached over Plague Man's shoulder. Although the move kept the malevolent darkness out of range, it also separated him from his comrades.

To his right and left, Aristoi and Seran held his opponent's guards at bay. Each time he dodged out of the shadow's reach, Plague Man's long strides devoured the space he left behind. He couldn't help but notice, however, that the closer he drew towards the lantern's light the less substantial and slower to respond the shadows became.

A quick glance over his shoulder revealed that Gray's lantern lay abandoned on the tunnel floor; the boy was nowhere to be seen. *I should have seen that coming*, Hollis thought, but was having trouble holding it against him. *At least he left the lamp*. Before the thief had time to ruminate further on Gray's departure, Plague Man pressed in on him, his thin Slazean sword leading the way. Hollis wasn't surprised to see its length slick with some sort of viscous substance.

The thief extended his sword, meeting Plague Man's and allowing the later to slide along its blade. He stepped towards his opponent before the assassin could withdraw his weapon, keeping the Wallin Fahr in contact with the Slazean steel. Plague Man's left hand snaked out, a stiletto held in his fist. Hollis removed his left hand from the hilt of his sword, using it to bat aside his opponent's wrist. A second too late, the thief thought to trap Plague Man's knife arm. He withdrew it before Hollis could close his fingers around his wrist.

Plague Man wasted no time in thrusting forward again with the knife. His own hand out of position, Hollis opted to lash out with a booted foot, low and hard against the assassin's knee. Although the thief's kick made contact, his opponent shifted his leg backward and robbed the blow of most of its momentum. In doing so, he also stole most of the force from his own stab; the slim blade did no more than carve a shallow furrow into Hollis's leather vest just under his ribs.

As their master fell back, his diminished shadows surged forward to keep the thief from pressing his advantage. Unable to halt his forward motion, Hollis's empty hand dipped into their dim depths. Instantly, pain exploded in his gloved hand, as if he'd plunged it into a snowbank. Before he could withdraw it, the thief felt bone crushing pressure in his fingers as unseen mouths tried to bite through the leather of his glove.

He drove his Dwarven steel blade into the mass of shadows, its gleaming surface catching the lamp light behind him. As it passed into the darkness, Hollis felt the slightest lessening of the pressure in his hand, giving him the chance to pull it free. The glove was riddled with deep punctures and ragged tears.

Before the thief could recover, Plague Man surged forward once more and forced him back a few steps. Behind the assassin, the shadows ebbed and flowed, as if they were testing the flickering lamp light. Hollis pivoted on his back foot and launched a halfhearted lunge, stopping his opponent's charge. Even in the embrace of the Well's gift, the thief was having issues tipping the fight in his favor. The 'Understanding' allowed him to anticipate Plague Man's actions to some degree and stay a trembling step ahead of him but when it was turned on the shadows he commanded, he saw nothing but a void.

As twisted as it seems, he thought, *Walker was far less dangerous. At least if you took away her magic and the brooch, she was just an old woman*. Plague Man, on the other hand, was a skilled fighter in his own right; the brooch raised him to another level. Deep in his embrace of calm, Hollis felt a twinge of fear.

Why had his gift not stopped the shadows as it had with Walker's magic? Why could the 'Understanding' not pierce their murky depths? He had no further time to explore these mysteries as Plague Man lunged forward again, his body blade-like and low to the ground. Shadows clung to his skin like honey, seemingly strengthened by the proximity to the brooch.

Hollis sidestepped swiftly, taking his body out of line with the assassin's weapon. As he did so, he brought his sword down in an over-hand swing. Plague Man raised a shadow draped forearm, interposing it between the thief's blade and his body. Hollis felt his sword strike something, although it felt less like bone and sinew than raw meat. When he withdrew the Wallin Fahr, shadows not blood dripped from its edge.

Out of the corner of his eye, Hollis saw a guild thief go down with a templar's sword in his chest. With the rest of the thieves engaged, the soldier broke off towards where the Songspear fought one of his comrades. Although her words were swallowed by distance and surrounding noise, but her mouth moved rhythmically.

The effects were apparent to all. Although she stood deeply entrenched in the flickering shadows, the grasping dimness seemed hesitant to approach her flame wreathed spear. They receded, forming a path to allow the templar to approach from outside Aristoi's peripheral vision.

"Left," Hollis shouted, praying that his voice could rise above the clamor that rang through the chamber. Without diverting her attention from her opponent, the Songspear swung her weapon wide, causing him to retreat. Mid swing, Aristoi turned her wrist over and dropped the spear's point to the floor. Where its tip scored the stone, a conflagration rose to shoulder height in an instant, forming a wall of flame between the Songspear and her unseen attacker. With a short series of sinuous steps, she pivoted to bring her spear to bear on both foes.

Turning back to his own opponent, it became immediately evident that Hollis's distraction had cost him. Plague Man had recovered and was mid thrust before the thief could bring his sword to bear. The point of the assassin's blade entered under his right arm. Only Hollis's reflexive rotation of his body prevented Plague Man from impaling his lungs and heart. Instead, it scraped along his ribcage and exited cleanly just under his shoulder blade. Hollis fervently hoped that enough of whatever noxious substance had coated the weapon had been lost so as not kill him outright.

The thief brought his elbow down on Plague Man's collarbone with as much force as the awkward angle afforded him. He felt the assassin crumple slightly under the blow.

Gripping his opponent's head with his free hand, Hollis pushed him away, dragging himself off Plague Man's sword at the same time. No trace of poison remained on the steel blade. *All I can hope is that the majority of it is not in me now.* Bringing his sword into guard position once more caused Hollis to wince, but the pain was manageable for the moment.

Unable to afford another lapse in concentration, the thief narrowed his focus on the assassin. He became lost in the ebb and flow of their deadly dance. Seconds melded into moments as one became indistinguishable from the other. Each time Hollis began to turn the tide, to find his way through the steel tapestry woven by Plague Man, brooch-born shadows would press in and drive him back. Each time, he was able to work his way around the undulating dimness, the assassin's sword and dagger were there to greet him.

Crouching down, the thief scooped up the lantern in his left hand from where Gray had abandoned it. As he gathered himself for another press through the shadows, a glint caught Hollis's attention. Beyond the wall of pulsating darkness, a brilliant point of light hung. Holding the lamp before him, the thief danced through the press of shadows between himself and Plague Man. As they pulled back from the flickering illumination, the assassin came into clear view. Behind him, Hollis could see Seran creeping forward, his dagger glowing of its own accord. Where the weapon passed, the darkness that hung around it evaporated like rain on hot cobblestone.

Shadows have been known to hide the sins of men, but obviously they also whisper their secrets as well. As stealthy as Seran thought himself, he couldn't sneak up on the brooch pinned to Plague Man's chest. The assassin gestured towards Hollis, causing the darkness to thicken about him before turning to deal with his mentor. Like a pack of ebony lemmings, the shadows charged into the circle of lantern light. The first wave crashed against the pool of luminescence and faded to nothingness but like a swarm of bees, soon overwhelmed the lamp's illumination.

As Hollis was draped in a frigid cloak of darkness, the last thing he saw was Seran's raised dagger shining like the noonday sun. That image imprinted on his eyes, the thief's vision failing him. In the cold, pitch black, he heard slithering things surrounding him, their rasping movements creating a symphony of dread. Suddenly, their activity ceased, draping the thief in a stifling shroud of silence. Lasting barely the span of a breath, the stillness was broken as in unison the unseen creatures pounced on him. Grasping talon and fang filled maws tore at him from every direction. Hollis brought up his Dwarven steel blade, swinging it wildly. In its path, his attackers abandoned their assault and fell back, only to descend on him again once it had passed.

A sudden cry of pain and surprise echoed through the darkness, taken up by the creatures that surrounded the thief. Suddenly, the shadows around him receded, revealing Seran standing above the kneeling form of Plague Man. The shining blade of his stiletto was half buried in the assassin's back.

Inky shapes writhed on Plague Man's skin, unable to come within six inches of the wound or the weapon that caused it. Seran was all toothy grin. "Essence of Daybreak," he proclaimed before a tidal wave of shadows crashed upon him from every direction, sweeping him away.

Hollis heard rather than saw the meaty impact of Seran's body against the tunnel wall. The only part of him visible was his right hand, still clutching his luminescent knife. Muffled screams could be heard from within the darkness as his fingers slowly opened, allowing the weapon to clatter to the stone floor. Seran's hand twitched spasmodically as the shadows rose to claim that as well.

A quick glance around revealed that with the exception of a hand full of small pools, the entirety of the brooch-born shadows were concentrated on Seran. Hollis leapt forward, bringing his sword down on the injured Plague Man. The assassin dove to the side but wasn't quick enough to avoid a deep slash across his thigh. When he attempted to roll to his feet, his leg wouldn't support him, and he collapsed to the ground once more.

Unwilling to sacrifice his advantage, the thief pressed forward, swinging his sword in short, chopping motions. It was all that Plague Man could do to scramble out of the way on hands and heels. Thick patches of shadow swarmed over his body, blotting his thigh wound from sight. They couldn't approach the Essence-smeared wound on his back, however. Hollis quickened his pace, scoring two deep gashes on his opponent's chest and arm. In a panic, the assassin rolled over and crawled on hands and knees towards one of the few remaining patches of shadow. The thief was able to spear him through the back before he reached it and disappeared from sight.

His own breath echoing in his ears, Hollis frantically scanned the chamber for any sign of his opponent. Half of the guild forces lay bleeding (or worse) on the stone floor, but they were giving as good as they'd gotten, having whittled the templars' numbers down to less than a half dozen.

While the thief had fought Plague Man, Aristoi had evened the odds arrayed against her; a single desperate templar hid behind his shield in a vain attempt to weather the Songspear's assault of cold iron and flame.

Hollis pivoted, preparing to aid his mentor when a hint of movement in the shadows behind Aristoi caught his attention. Before he could shout a warning, Plague Man emerged. There was no sign of the injuries inflicted by either himself or Seran's glowing knife.

To her credit, the Songspear sensed his presence at the last moment. She spun to face him, bringing the butt of her spear around at chest height. Like water of stone, the assassin ducked below the swing and drove his sword into her gut.

Aristoi's leather-clad back bulged for a second before the point of Plague Man's blade emerged in a bloody explosion. She collapsed to the ground like a broken doll.

*****

Hollis shouted in wordless anguish as he charged Plague Man. The wounded templar tried to interpose himself between the thief and his master. Hollis dropped down into a baseball slide, drawing his blade across the soldier's legs as he did so. Dwarven steel met flesh and bone. It wasn't close to an even contest. The templar fell to the stone floor, only two thirds of the man he was previously.

Digging the heel of his boot into the broken ground, the thief popped up and took a pair of stumbling steps before falling back into an even gait. The shadows behind Plague Man pressed forward like a wall of shifting mist but Hollis didn't slow his rush. The frigid confines of the darkness rolled over him like a spring sun shower as he passed through. Plague Man was so taken by surprise that he couldn't raise his weapons in time before the thief reached him. Hollis dropped his shoulder at the last second, rising up as he made contact with the assassin, driving him into the air and away from Aristoi's prone form.

Plague Man landed hard on the ground but was immediately surrounded by shadows. Bolstered by them, he rose quickly, showing no ill effects from his fall. Hollis stood over his fallen friend's body, his face twisted into a hateful scowl. "You have failed another one, Hollis," the assassin cackled. "When are you going to realize that while it is my blade that ends their lives, you are the one responsible for each and every one of their deaths?"

Hollis glanced to where Asaege stood surrounded by a trio of thieves, safe for the moment. Nodding to himself, he shifted his eyes back to Plague Man. "It may be convenient for you to believe the filth that falls from your lips, but that does not make it true. You think that the brooch gives you power but in reality, it only perpetuates the story of your life. You will always serve the will of another."

"Is that so?"

The thief nodded, "Indeed. As much as you rail against it, you are … you will always be that scared, wailing child I rescued all those years ago. Unable to muster your own purpose, you serve others and claim theirs for your own."

Plague Man's lips pulled back into a snarl, "Those words will make a fitting memorial for you, Slender One."

Settling deeper into the calming cloak of the Well, Hollis shrugged. "I can think of worse things to put on my gravestone." Still unable to pierce the brooch's shadows with the 'Understanding', Hollis focused on their current master. "My death will not change the truth of my words, though. As much as I hate to admit it, you did not exaggerate your skills.

328

You are an extraordinary weapon; it is a shame that you will forever be wielded by another."

The assassin's growled response was lost in the clamor of battle hanging in the chamber, but its intent was clear as he leapt forward. His eyes were narrowed in pure hatred. Alongside him, the patch of shadows surged forward. Plague Man was past the cat and mouse game of attrition; he sought Hollis's death in as immediate and overwhelming way as possible. The thief's reflexes demanded he fall back before the assault, to engage the unholy alliance on his own terms. He stubbornly stood his ground over Aristoi's body. *I will not abandon you to shadow*, he promised, unsure if blood still pumped through the Songspear's veins.

The flickering fingers of darkness struck him first, freezing the flesh beneath his leather vest and stealing the breath from his lungs. In his mind's eye, he conjured an image of the Well's gift as a physical garment, draped around his shoulders. It didn't completely drive away the icy embrace of the shadows, but it dulled it considerably. When the maws of whatever dwelt within the darkness sought to sink their fangs into him, it cushioned their bites as well.

Plague Man burst through the shifting dimness a second later, his thin, Slazean sword probing the air like a serpent's tongue. Hollis's Uteli blade met each thrust, turning it aside. He kept his left hand free and open at his side, prepared for the inevitable low dagger thrust from the assassin. When it came, masked by the murky shadows as it was, the thief almost missed it. He barely slapped it aside before it was driven home in his gut.

The assassin's knife attack had brought the pair into close quarters, where both of their long weapons would be of no use. Plague Man's dagger, on the other hand, was perfectly suited for such tight spaces. Before his foe could recover, Hollis brought his free hand up to grip his sword by the blade and swung his elbow into Plague Man's face. He felt bone crack under the blow. His opponent stumbled backward, the shadows still clinging to his body already racing for his broken jaw.

Having forced the assassin beyond knife distance, Hollis released his half-blade grip and swung his sword in a sweeping uppercut. Plague Man's own weapon met and redirected the strike. When he retreated a step, the shadows he controlled remained where they were, enveloping Hollis in their deadly embrace. The longer Hollis remained there, the less of a barrier his manifested protection offered. Already, he could feel sharpened teeth tearing at leather and silk in search of the flesh and blood beneath. Like a moor spawned fog, the shadows began to steadily rise, threatening to plunge him into darkness once more.

Sweeping his Wallin Fahr before him, Hollis tried to keep both the shadows and Plague Man at bay. As panic began to filter through his Well-born serenity, the darkness intensified around him.

The assassin surged forward in a sudden lunge just as the last vestiges of his protections faded.

Parrying by instinct, Hollis managed to deflect the blow before he was plunged into black. He wouldn't see the follow up strike. More than likely, that would be the one that ended his life.

Chapter Forty-Three
Stalwart Heart

Asaege watched helplessly as Hollis was swallowed by the shifting darkness. Instinctively, she charged to his aid. Her mad dash was prematurely ended by the three thieves arrayed between her and the few remaining templars. Violently shaking off their grasping hands, she snarled, "He is in trouble."

The boy who'd saved her life earlier placed his body in front of her. "You are too valuable, Prophet. Hollis was aware of the possible results of his actions."

"I cannot just watch him die," she retorted, her voice almost pleading.

"Would he have you follow him into that death?"

The answer was, of course, no but it didn't cool Asaege's desire to rush to the thief's side.

"We need to flee, Prophet," another of the thieves said. "When he is through with Hollis, Plague Man will turn his attention to us."

In Asaege's chest, terror warred with the whispers of her heart. The logic of her protectors resonated with her but the thought of Hollis being taken from her so soon tore at her soul. *I certainly do not want his sacrifice to be in vain. He risked everything to come for me when he had nothing to gain but my safety. I cannot ... I will not abandon him now.* Unbidden, a thought intruded on her internal monologue. *You know there is one way to put an end to the threat to both Hollis and yourself.*

She took a step back, her hands held before her. "I need another moment."

"If we wait much longer, none of us may escape with our lives." The boy's jaw was set but his eyes betrayed the fear he must have been struggling to contain.

"Go," Asaege blurted, "Save yourselves. I will be right behind you." She added, "I promise," in an attempt to sweeten the offer.

All three thieves shook their heads. The boy spoke again, "If the Prophet falls, so too does what she represents. If you remain, so do I." His voice quivered but his tense posture revealed his resolve. The other two agreed, although somewhat less enthusiastically.

Disappointed, she murmured, "You all have to make your own choice." Sinking to the floor, Asaege crossed her legs tailor style before closing her eyes. She focused first on blocking out the sounds around her, although when Hollis's muffled cries reached her ears, her heart felt like it would burst within her chest. Asaege felt the trail of a single tear as it rolled down her cheek, but kept her eyes shut tight against the horrors that occurred yards from where she sat.

Asaege withdrew into herself, letting the cacophony of pain and death around her merge into a persistent but indistinct hum. *Jillian, where are you?*, she pleaded. She conjured the picture of her reflection's bedroom again. It came easily but was once more devoid of life. In a panic, Asaege reached out for the feelings that she and Jillian shared: the joy of teaching, the warmth of true friendship, the desire to do something more with their lives. In turn, each came easily enough but none held any real substance; they were whispered echoes in the night rather than the roaring orchestra she sought.

At the edge of her perception, Asaege sensed movement around her but stubbornly pushed it to the back of her mind. She plunged back into her memories of reflection, searching for the key to throwing open the doors to her connection with Jillian. It came suddenly and from an unexpected emotion. In her desperation, Asaege's mind kept coming back to what brought her to this place.

It would have been easy to dismiss it as a series of unfortunate consequences arising from her impulsive decision to steal a book that had significance to her. There had been so much more to it. At any point, she could have returned the Dialogues; as a matter of fact, Hollis had brought up the option on more than one occasion. Each time, she'd adamantly refused, and that refusal led Asaege and everyone around her here. What had been the point?

An alien thought touched the back of her awareness. *The same rea-*

son Jillian stood up for the young boy in her class. To do nothing in the face of injustice is its own crime. Asaege had seen the suffering around her, just as her reflection had felt Timothy's pain in that moment. If either of them had remained silent, their lives would have been spent suffering for a sin that could never be atoned for. Each of them sought to leave behind a legacy worthy of pride, a legacy that would live in the hearts of those whose worlds were made better by their sacrifice. Like the sun emerging from behind a storm cloud, Asaege's consciousness was bathed in the comforting warmth of communion.

Although no words were exchanged between the reflections, each knew the other as intimately as they did themselves. When Asaege brought to mind Jillian's room this time, it was filled with the thick, woody scent of her burned herb and the warm comfort of her most cherished possessions.

Resting on Jillian's crossed calves was a leather-bound journal. On the open page before her were the delicate letters and carefully drawn diagrams that Asaege couldn't mistake. Clear as an autumn morning, the ritual of severing was within her reach.

Her eyes still clamped tight, Asaege extended a finger and traced in the dirt the intricate patterns she saw in Jillian's memories. Resisting the temptation to open her eyes to review her work, she drew in fits and starts afraid of making an error. In answer to her rising panic, the quiet confidence of her reflection enveloped her like a velvet blanket. Safe in its confines, Asaege's finger moved like a shark's fin through the thick layer of soil before her.

As the last stroke was complete, Asaege's hand hovered above the diagram that she hoped matched the one in her mind. Beside it in the journal were the words that would bring it to life. For such a significant spell, the formula was brief to the point of being terse. Four lines were all that separated success from failure. For a moment, Asaege's voice caught in her throat. As a theory, the ritual seemed a miracle beyond her hope. The reality of what could follow chilled her to her core, even though the cloak of serenity remained wrapped around her shoulders.

What if it doesn't work? What if I mispronounce a word ... if the diagram is incomplete? A wave of doubt crashed upon Asaege, threatening to crush her beneath its weight. She felt Jillian in the back of her mind, struggling to drag her from the quagmire she was creating for herself. Mentally reaching out for her reflection's hand, Asaege pushed aside the insecurities that assaulted her from every direction.

Asaege began speaking haltingly, but as her confidence returned, the words came more quickly. The syllables themselves carried a power that she was unprepared for. At the midpoint of the spell, the energy that she bent to her will threatened to take her breath from her. Gritting her teeth, she pushed through; unlike the spell she cast within the prison, Asaege couldn't afford to restart the spell. She would have but one chance to complete it and save Hollis.

Carried along by the words of the ritual, Asaege was taken by surprise when they came to an end. The sound of her voice hung unnaturally in the air as she opened her eyes. In the dirt before her was a perfect copy of the diagram from the journal page. Standing over her seated form were all three of the thieves that had pledged to protect her. Just beyond them, a second templar's corpse had been added to the first. Across the chamber, Hollis's form was lost within the clot of shadows that surrounded him. They couldn't confine his pained cries.

Plague Man had turned his attention from the trapped thief and fixed his gaze on Asaege. If the man didn't know the significance of the power that hung in the air, whatever was contained in the brooch surely did. His lips pulled back in an angry sneer as he started towards her. In front of Asaege, the three figures turned as one, their faces set in expressions of grim determination.

The echoing sound of her own voice called to Asaege as she averted her eyes from the rushing assassin. Focusing her attention on the figure once more, she gathered her wits before drawing the energy of the spell into herself. As soon as she accepted it, a burning sensation rippled across her skin as the captive power demanded its freedom. Opening her hand, she slammed it palm first into the center of the diagram. The effect was instantaneous.

The darkness that had engulfed the thief ceased to be from one second to the next. He slumped to the ground beside Aristoi's motionless form. Dozens of ragged wounds covered his face and neck, their edges already black with gangrene. His leather vest and breeches were shredded, revealing more injuries beneath them. To Asaege's surprise, Hollis tried to drag himself to his feet, despite the agony that was evident on his face.

Plague Man fell to the floor mid stride as if he were clubbed to the ground. His arms shaking as he pushed himself to his hands and knees, he pulled the leather mask from his face and gasped for breath. His puss slicked skin was midsummer moon pale as he glared at Asaege with a shocked expression. Hollis's account of the man's face was insufficient to describe its sore marked surface.

The silver and iron brooch lay upon the ground between them. Its once pristine surface was pitted and scorched as it smoldered in the dirt.

Templars and thieves alike ceased their hostilities as a buzzing grew to eclipse the sound of steel on steel. It quickly built into a roar, filling the chamber with its furious tones. Asaege thought that within the clamor,

334

she could make out an inhuman voice shouting its rage to the heavens. As suddenly as it began, the sound disappeared, leaving the tunnel blanketed in such absolute silence that it impacted those gathered like an explosion.

The first to regain his wits was Plague Man. He climbed shakily to his feet and fled past the templars and into the darkness of the tunnel, leaving his loyal soldiers to their fate.

Hollis had crawled to where Aristoi's motionless form lay before Asaege had shaken loose her shock. Pushing past the three thieves, she rushed to him. Falling to her knees, she wrapped her arms around his ravaged body. He tried to protest when she tore a strip from the hem of her dress and vainly tried to clean the blood from his face.

"I'm alright," he rumbled, in his confusion slipping into English.

"No, you're not," Asaege retorted in the same language.

"I'm al ..." He paused to catch his breath, "I'm alright."

Asaege called over her shoulder, "We need help over here!"

"I trained under a stitch," Asaege's devoted young protector shouted, rushing to her side. In the Ash, where none could afford the cost of Olm's blessings, street doctors were the best one could hope for. Within the ranks of the thieves guild, they had adopted the title of stitch, as most of their tasks involved some matter of sewing flesh.

Asaege turned to see that Hollis had rolled Aristoi on to her back. Her lips and chin were drenched in blood but miraculously, the Songspear's mouth moved slowly, as if trying to speak.

Hollis lowered his head in an effort to make out her words. A laugh erupted from the thief, which in turn caused him to cough uncontrollably for a moment. He looked up at Asaege. "She asked me what I am waiting for? Plague Man is getting away."

Chapter Forty-Four
Chasing Shadows

Hollis glowered down at Aristoi. "You nearly scared the life out of me." When she tried to speak, he slid a hand beneath her neck and supported her head. "For once, remain silent. Help is on the way."

Beside him, the thief could feel Asaege's body lightly pressing against his own. Shifting his gaze to her for a moment, he saw worry and relief etched on her face in equal measures. Forcing a smile to his lips, he winked at her with a half-swollen eye before turning back to the Song-spear.

One of the guild members, an apprentice known as Alister the Lesser, knelt beside Aristoi and carefully unbuckled her leather vest. The boy worked deftly, despite missing the ring finger and pinky on his left hand. "They call you Eight Fingered Alice," Hollis said, giving him an appreciative nod.

"That is correct, Lord Hollis."

"Hollis is fine," the thief countered, "I hope you are a better stitch than you are a piano player."

His attention focused on the Songspear's wound, Alice missed his attempt at humor and simply nodded absently. Hollis didn't need to ask the severity of her injury; the boy's face answered that question better than words ever could. A dark shadow crossed Alice's features before he met Hollis's eyes. "There is nothing I can do. Plague Man's sword impaled kidney and bowel. Perhaps if we could reach a priest …" The boy let his voice fade into silence, the remainder evident in his tone. Aristoi wouldn't survive the trip, even if it could be made in time.

"He is still in your blind spot." The Songspear's voice was weak, barely heard over the voices that echoed in the stone chamber.

Hollis looked down at her. "Plague Man is the last thing on my mind at the moment."

She coughed lightly, speckling her lips with fresh blood. "That is … that is precisely his plan. While you are blind—" Another more vigorous cough wracked Aristoi's frame. "… blinded," she tenaciously continued, "he once more escapes his sins."

"Do not concern yourself with that. Once you are back on your feet, we will hunt him down together."

"That may well be …" The Songspear paused to catch her breath before continuing, "Too late." Lifting her hand slowly, Aristoi gestured to the clumps of bodies that littered the tunnel. "He carries upon his soul the weight of every life lost this night … on both sides." She gripped Hollis's face weakly, forcing him to look her in the eye. "Would you allow him to shake them loose as he did those of Mike? Jhorwynn?"

The thief felt Asaege's hand on his bicep, her silent support acting as an anchor amid the maelstrom of emotions that battered his heart. "I will not leave you."

Aristoi laughed, although it quickly morphed into a choking cough. After she'd composed herself, she whispered, "What if I promised to be here when you return, Northerner?"

"I would not believe you."

Aristoi nodded gravely. "Perhaps you are correct." She pointed across the room with a trembling finger. "I am considering moving over there once I … catch my breath. I am hoping the air is a touch fresher."

"I think you should save your strength."

With the same hand, the Songspear gripped the front of Hollis's leather vest. "Do not be foolish. The more you argue, the …" She closed her eyes and took a few shallow breaths before continuing. "… the larger his lead becomes." Aristoi weakly tried to pull the thief closer; he relented without a struggle. In a rasping whisper, she said, "We both know that eventually you will heed my advice. Save us both an argument for which I am unprepared and go after him now."

"I —," Hollis began.

The Songspear cut him off, "All of this is for naught if he is allowed to escape."

The thief nodded solemnly and plucked Aristoi's hand from his vest and laid it gently on her chest. As he slowly rose to his feet, he felt Asaege's shoulder under his arm. "I will stay with her," she whispered. She laid her head against his chest, seeming unwilling to release her from the embrace. "Come back to me, Scoundrel."

Looking down at her with soft eyes, Hollis smiled. "There is nothing on the face of this world or any other that could stop me, Magpie."

*****

Between the state in which Plague Man left the tunnel and the 'Understanding', Hollis had little trouble picking up his trail. His own injuries, however, made following it with any speed a difficult proposition. Each of his wounds were of little consequence, but those consequences seemed to add up very quickly. As he moved through the labyrinth of unused tunnels, the small streams running through them combined, gaining width and volume until its rushing waters dominated the center of every branch he came upon.

Fortunately, this made tracking Plague Man easier as his paths of egress became fewer and fewer as unflooded tunnels became the exception. Hollis was so focused on ensuring that his quarry didn't escape by way of an unnoticed side passage that he almost failed to notice that the one he followed abruptly ended, forming a steep waterfall into the chamber below. Pulling up short, the thief barely avoided haplessly tumbling over the precipice.

The sudden shift of his weight required to halt his momentum dropped him to his back. From that reclined position, Hollis was able to see beneath the broken floor of the tunnel and into the area beyond. There, not two hundred yards distant, he saw Plague Man navigating the rubble strewn chamber. Not bothering to stand, the thief slid forward the last few feet and dangled his legs over the edge. He released his torch and let it fall to the floor below before rolling onto his belly. Adrenaline temporarily overcoming the pain of his injuries, he was able to scramble down the rough stone and mortar cliff, dropping the last dozen feet to the ground.

As he tucked his shoulder and rolled in an effort to absorb some of the impact, Hollis felt the patchwork of wounds on his back tear open again. He tried to put the pain from his mind as he pursued Plague Man in an awkward, loping jog. The assassin looked over his shoulder and did a double take before quickening his pace. Hollis couldn't help but smile to himself. *I would say it is like the geriatric Olympics*, he thought, *but that would be a terribly unfair slight to the aged.*

In the end, their race was less a matter of speed or endurance and more a case of kismet. The tunnel through which they moved ended just as the one above them had, except in a gap too wide to be jumped. Rather than opening to the chamber below, the ledge overlooked a thirty-yard drop into a natural cavern. Plague Man's look of consternation told the thief that the wall didn't have the convenient hand holds of the one behind them.

Hollis slowed his pace as he drew his sword. "It looks like our chase has come to an end."

Taking one final look over the edge, Plague Man turned to face him. Unused to seeing him unmasked, his disease ravaged face took Hollis by surprise. "So it appears." Wearily, he pulled his Slazean sword from its scabbard. "It seems that our chaotic relationship also has reached its conclusion as well."

The thief gritted his teeth and hissed, "Chaotic? You murdered my friends. You framed me for the death of the curate, so you might take his place. You kidnapped the woman I —"

"Love?" Plague Man suggested.

"It is complicated," he growled. "On top of all that, you seem to have single-handedly launched a holy crusade against me and mine."

"The last part was more of the Hand's idea … but your point is valid nonetheless." With his free hand, Plague Man drew his stiletto and carefully advanced on Hollis.

The thief didn't draw his own dagger, preferring to keep his left hand empty for the moment. He opened his mouth, but any words that may have followed were stolen by the assassin's sudden lunge. Put back onto his heels, Hollis deftly deflected the first thrust but nearly missed the dagger strike that followed. He slapped it aside, taking a sliding step backward, out of the range of his opponent's shorter blade.

Plague Man gathered himself for a second thrust but seemed to think better of it as Hollis extended his Wallin Fahr before him in a defensive guard. "Let us suppose you are finally able to follow through with the threats you have been making each time our paths have crossed. I believe it unlikely but for the sake of argument, in your compromised state, you are able to find yet another miracle. What then?" The tip of his sword shot forward in a feinting strike, pulling back before Hollis's blade could make contact with his own.

The thief shuffled forward, dipping the point of his own weapon into a short thrust. Plague Man beat the half-hearted attack aside, but Hollis had retreated before he could take advantage of it. "I guess I celebrate the fact that neither I nor anyone else needs to look over their shoulder for you."

"But at what cost? I have taken so much from you but, in the end, you can only kill me the once." The assassin moved to the side, his feather-light steps seeming to seek a flanking position from which to launch his next strike.

Hollis remained where he stood, simply pivoting to keep Uteli steel between himself and his opponent. "In this circumstance, I think that would be enough." The predicted attack didn't come. Instead Plague Man shifted his weight to his lead foot, a clear indication that rather than lunging forward, he perhaps considered fleeing. Two quick steps brought the thief even with him, a third put the assassin's back to the sheer drop one more. "As long as you are in a talkative mood, I do have a question."

Plague Man's lips pursed in frustration. "Do tell," he grumbled.

"I saved your life on that Ash street, years ago. Why make it your purpose to haunt mine?"

The assassin stifled a laugh. "Once again, Slender One, you fail to see what lies right in front of you. It is not about you ... it never was."

"You keep saying—"

Plague Man cut him off, "—that is not to say that I did not derive satisfaction from your suffering." With two gliding steps, he lunged forward, his sword flashing back and forth in a side-to-side pair of slashes.

Hollis rocked back on his heel, allowing the first swing to pass within inches of his savaged leather vest. Before the assassin could launch his return strike, he brought his sword down in an overhead cut. The blow drove Plague Man's blade towards the ground. Lashing out with his lead foot, the thief aimed a kick at his foe's gut.

Plague Man collapsed backwards into an awkward roll, coming back to his feet as lightly as a cat. Hollis turned the failed kick into a short charge, denying the assassin a moments respite. As the thief neared his opponent, he launched a clumsy thrust his foe easily turned aside, skipping backwards out of range of any blows that would follow. Hollis allowed him his retreat, as it brought him closer to the precipice.

Desperately, the assassin hissed, "Do you know why that is?"

He sees his predicament, Hollis thought, *he will try to worm his way out any way he can. Do not allow yourself to be distracted by his words.* Slowing his steps, Hollis focused on remaining in a position to prevent Plague Man from dashing by him as the noose tightened. "I will admit to some curiosity in that matter."

Plague Man's eyes darted from side to side, searching for a path past the thief. "I lost everything that night. My mother. My hope of a better life. Most importantly, I lost my freedom."

Despite his own words of warning, Hollis was taken aback by the assassin's confession. "Your freedom? I returned you to Underfoot ... to people who would shelter and care for you."

Plague Man leapt forward, trying to take advantage of the thief's momentary lapse in attention. Hollis's blade was there to meet him.

Falling back, he growled, "Did you ever contemplate why a mother and child from Underfoot would be unaccompanied on the streets of the Ash … at night?"

Realization dawned on Hollis. "You were seeking escape."

"We were seeking escape," the assassin agreed, "and that was something that Raethe took very personally, especially when it came to me."

The thief fought to maintain his concentration amid his curiosity. "You were his—"

"— he never said as much. What he did lay claim to was my mother and through her, me as well."

"You would have died in that alley; whether quick or not would have depended on your luck but the outcome was never in doubt."

"I would have preferred death to another moment under Raethe's thumb. It took me five years to finally escape him again and leave the Underfoot behind. He made every moment of it as miserable as possible, and I have you to thank for each one."

"I had no idea." Despite the thief's hatred for the Plague Man, his words were heartfelt.

"Of course, you did not but that did not make me despise you any less. It was fortune's poor humor that brought us together again. I did not seek you out, but I will admit to finding satisfaction in taking everything from you, as you once did from me. My only regret is that you never sought the solace of death, as I had many a night."

So enraptured was Hollis in his newfound insight into the life of his enemy, that he was a beat too late in reacting to the assassin's frenzied attack. The thin, Slazean sword speared his thigh, sending bolts of pain throughout his leg. Only by sheer will power did the thief remain standing. Stumbling backward, Hollis deflected blow after blow as one ran into the other. Unable to find an opening to turn the tide, he remained on the defensive.

Plague Man continued to press his attack, making use of his lighter weapon and momentum to keep the thief on his back foot. With each flurry, he attempted to duck around his foe, but each time Hollis shifted to block his escape. The assassin feinted towards the thief's wounded leg, bringing his dagger up at the same time. Hollis saw through the ruse at the last moment, but Plague Man's weapon still drew a burning line along his ribs.

As Hollis recoiled from the weapon's stinging bite, the assassin tried to rush past him. Out of instinct, the thief extended an arm and caught Plague Man across the throat. They both went down in a heap, their weapons clattering to the stone floor. The assassin snarled as he clawed at Hollis's eyes. Fending off the attack with his left hand, the thief drew his broad bladed Dwarven steel dagger from its silken prison in his satchel. It had been a gift from Jhorwynn, another in the tragic list of Plague Man's victims.

An expression of triumph pasted on his face, the assassin grabbed Hollis's free hand in the bony fingers of his right hand. As he pulled back his left fist, preparing to drive it into the thief's unprotected face, that look changed to one of shock as Hollis stabbed the dwarf's gift into Plague Man's side. Rolling his wrist, Hollis reversed the assassin's grip on his arm and drew him close. Throwing his hip out to the side, the thief rolled on top of Plague Man and pinned him under his superior bulk.

Before Hollis could stab him again, the assassin drove his knee into his injured thigh. Agony forced the thief's fingers open, and the dagger fell from his grip. His black silk shirt darkened further by the blood that poured from his chest wound, Plague Man stumbled to his feet, the thief's own dagger held before him. Hollis rolled onto his back, both his and his opponent's weapons out of reach.

"And now we each see our way ..." Plague Man paused to find the breath that he couldn't seem to catch, "... our way to the end of our road together."

Beneath him, the thief felt a fist sized object digging uncomfortably into his kidney. He tried to put it from his mind as he desperately searched for something to use against the assassin standing above him. Any way he shifted, the lump seemed to tenaciously remain in place. Plague Man approached slowly, seeming to savor the moment.

"If you can take any small consol—" The assassin was forced to take a deep, rattling breath before continuing, "... consolation from your end, it could be that you ..." Another breath. "... you no longer have to watch me kill your friends." Towering over Hollis, a crimson toothed smile spread across Plague Man's face. "I am going to take great pleasure in doing so, but at least you do not have to watch."

Hollis dropped one of his hands to pull the object out from under him, to find that it was a time worn pouch. The pouch he'd carried for years ... the very pouch whose contents had, in a manner of speaking, put him into his current predicament. Roughly tearing it open, the thief dug his hand in and pulled out a fist full of what was held within. As Plague Man dropped to one knee, the thief's own dagger clutched in his fist, Hollis threw a hand full of powdered glass in his face.

The assassin stumbled backward, clawing at his eyes. The broad-bladed dagger fell forgotten to the ground. Hollis tried to rise but his wounded leg wouldn't support his weight. He was only able to scramble forward on hands and knees towards the discarded weapon. Snatching it from where it lay, the thief looked up to see Plague Man with the precipice at his back. He alternated between pawing at his bleeding eyes and swinging his fists wildly in an attempt to ward off imagined blows.

As Plague Man took another half step backward, his heel hung over empty air. In a second that seemed to be frozen in time, the assassin threw his arms out to the side in a vain attempt to regain his quickly deteriorating balance. Blood from his lacerated eyes formed crimson tears on his cheeks as he met Hollis's gaze. In their crimson stained depths, all the thief could read was hatred. As quickly as it'd been suspended, the timeless instant came to an end. Plague Man disappeared over the cliff, leaving only a shrill scream hanging in the air.

With as much speed as he could muster, Hollis limped to the edge. In the still pool below him, a quickly spreading cloud of blood hung in the water around the still body of the assassin. At a loss for what to do next, the thief searched for a way down that he knew he wouldn't take. Feeling more empty than he'd thought he would in this moment, Hollis turned and slowly retraced his steps.

Chapter Forty-Five
Shadows Fade

Hollis's thigh had moved beyond throbbing by the time he found his way back to his comrades. All he felt below his hip was an unrelenting cloud of formless pain. Plague Man's sword had missed any major blood vessels but each step he took added another note to the symphony of agony in his thigh. The thief gratefully accepted the crescendo as he stepped from the side tunnel.

Two guild members took a handful of menacing strides towards him before they recognized his battered form. Scanning the chamber, Hollis saw that, true to her word, Aristoi had relocated to a more favorable corner. Although she leaned heavily on her spear, she stood on her own as she spoke quietly to Asaege. Clearing his throat, Hollis shouted, "Do not believe a word she says, Magpie, she is quite an accomplished liar."

Both women turned their attention to the limping thief. "If any would know a liar, Northerner," Aristoi called back, "it would be you." Beneath her cynical tone, Hollis heard a note of relief.

He didn't have to interpret Asaege's feelings of his return. She rushed across the room and into his arms. Wincing as he accepted her weight as well as his own onto his injured leg, the thief didn't protest. Pushing the pain from his voice, he purred, "Well, good evening to you as well, Milady."

Asaege playfully slapped at his chest, "Aristoi and I were just debating going in search of you." She nestled her head against his shoulder, her breath hot on his throat.

"Is that so?" Hollis asked. "When I left, my dear friend was only in search of her last breath."

"I feel much better," Aristoi retorted, giving the pair their space.

"So it seems," the thief called. Dropping his voice to a whisper, he remarked, "Suspiciously so."

Asaege looked up at him, wordlessly mirroring his concerns with a furrowed brow. "That is a discussion for another time," she muttered. "For now, let us be grateful for your friend's good fortune." With her aid, Hollis slowly crossed the chamber to where the Songspear stood.

"Well, the two of us certainly cut an impressive pair of figures, do we not?" Aristoi extended her right arm, palm pointed toward the ceiling. The thief laid his own on hers, each grasping the other's wrist. "It does my heart good to see you again, Hollis."

"I could say the same …" Hollis paused, debating his next words. True to his nature, he blurted out, "I have questions."

The Songspear let out a hoarse laugh. "Another time, Northerner. Another time."

Asaege pinched him sharply under the bicep and remarked, "I may have heard that advice somewhere before."

The thief joined in Aristoi's mirthful chuckle. "So you have." He released her arm and gestured at those gathered around them. "Obviously we triumphed."

"When Plague Man fled, he took the remaining templars' will to fight with him." Asaege nodded towards a group of guild members speaking quietly with Toni and Seran. "Calmer heads decided to allow them to retreat rather than press our luck."

Aristoi frowned. "I have a feeling that despite the wisdom of that choice in the moment, it may come back to bite us … sooner rather than later."

"I would love to argue with you," Hollis said, "but your logic is solid."

"It is a gift," the Songspear chided.

The thief opened his mouth to respond but decided to let her words pass as the two new guild masters approached the trio.

"It appears you have a little fight left in you after all," Seran remarked. "I trust that we will not need to concern ourselves with the curate any longer?"

Hollis shook his head. "I certainly hope not."

His mentor's face lit up. "Most excellent. All in all, I would call this a successful endeavor."

346

"I am sure that our dead brothers and sisters would argue the point," Toni inserted.

Seran dismissed their objection with a casual backhanded flick of his fingers. "We had no way of knowing that the templars would get involved. Given the unexpected complication, I believe we adjusted better than I could have anticipated."

Toni's face darkened, their brows tightening above squinted eyes. "There were always going to be losses, but that does not give us leave to not mourn them."

"Why do I feel like I am half a day's march behind what is going on here?" Hollis asked, staring intently at his mentor.

Toni answered instead, "Your situation represented a perfect storm that served to hide our intentions until it was too late for Dhole to do anything about them." They softly snickered, "He really hated you."

The thief growled, "The feeling was mutual." Tightening his grip on Asaege, his voice lowered to a rumble, "I do not find fault with the end result of your coup, simply your use of the lives of me and mine to accomplish it."

"We put our own lives at risk as well," Seran interjected.

"That does not help as much as you want it to, old man."

His mentor simply shrugged casually. "What is done is done."

Toni stepped between the two men. "I understand your complicated feeling, Hollis."

Through gritted teeth, the thief said, "Complicated does not begin to cover it."

"But," they continued, "Dhole and his use of the guild as his personal key to the halls of power put all of you in this position to begin with. It is true that none of you were foremost in our minds, but you benefit from our actions nonetheless."

Hollis took a breath to reply, but Asaege placed a restraining palm on his chest. "What do you plan to do with those keys now?" she asked.

Toni glanced over to Seran who nodded slowly. "Our feelings on the matter have not changed. If the Prophet seeks to set the common folk free, the guild stands beside her."

The thief frowned hard. *Alliances of convenience are often cast aside when they cease to be so,* he thought but remained silent. He respected Asaege's judgment; it was her choice.

"It will not be an easy path to walk," Asaege said. "For now, our adversaries hold most of the cards."

Toni chuckled. "Then it is indeed fortunate that we have some experience in larcenous pursuits." Their smile dimmed, as their expression became serious. "We know we have a fight before us, but if the Brotherhood of the Night ever meant something ... is going to continue to hold any meaning, it is a fight that we must be a part of."

A tense silence hung in the air for a moment, those gathered unsure of what was left to say. Asaege settled for, "Thank you."

"We are the ones who owe you gratitude, Prophet."

Hollis felt a mix of pride and weariness. In a matter of hours, their conspiracy had found staunch allies, but the struggle was far from over. He began to limp forward, forcing Asaege to rush to keep up with him. When she met his eyes, his only explanation was, "If we are about done with the mutual gratitude society, we should probably find our way to the surface. The fight is certainly not going to come to us."

Chapter Forty-Six
Revolutionary's Heart

Asaege hadn't known how much the subterranean tunnels had begun to close around her until she emerged from them into the night air of the University District. Her back ached from helping Hollis keep his weight off of his injured leg and without realizing it, she'd been breathing in shallow bursts to keep the dank, heavy air from sitting in her lungs like mud. Asaege closed her eyes and allowed the evening breeze to play across her face.

"I never thought I would be so glad to smell Oizan air," Hollis said as he lifted his arm from across her shoulders and limped gingerly forward. "Toni," he called, "do we still have that pass through into the Maple District?"

They shook their head. "It was closed down by the librarian's cronies a month or two ago."

"Well, that is an unfortunate bit of timing. There is no way that we," he indicated their ragged looking group, "are going to pass through either the Library or Cathedral Gate unmolested."

"I hope you are up for a climb," Seran said as he turned to face the imposing wall that separated the University District from Common Quarter beyond.

"There has to be another way," Asaege inserted, eyeing the thief with concern.

In a calm tone that didn't match her words, Aristoi said, "We may have more pressing matters to attend to. Our presence has not gone unnoticed."

Asaege followed the Songspear's line of sight to see a group of armed men approaching through the Library Gate from the direction of the Ivory Cathedral. Hollis shuffled back a few steps, trying to reorient himself towards the new threat.

Without a word, a quartet of guild members stepped in front of the group, their daggers held low; Alice was among them. "Make a break for the wall, Prophet. I think ..." he paused as if he were bolstering his will, "We can hold them off long enough for the rest of you to escape."

Ashamed that she was contemplating it, Asaege looked to Hollis. His right leg was slightly bent, his toe barely touching the ground as he kept as much of his weight from it as possible. If given ten-fold the time that Alice and his companions were able to buy them, the thief wouldn't make it to the wall, much less scramble up its stone surface.

As if he heard her thoughts, Hollis shook his head. "Fly, Magpie." He limped forward to join the small group of thieves. "I was prepared to risk everything to wrest you from Plague Man's hands, I certainly cannot allow you to fall into those of these men now."

"No," she cried. "I will not leave you!"

"I know." The thief looked back at her with sad eyes. "There was always the chance of a situation like this coming up." Asaege felt Aristoi's fingers close around her forearm. "I have made arrangements for it." Focusing a hard glare on the Songspear, Asaege fought against the stronger woman's grip. "I am sorry, Asaege." Hollis allowed his eyes to linger on her for a moment before turning away and drawing his sword.

"I do not relish this task," Aristoi said by way of an explanation, "but I am sworn to it." Asaege felt hot tears sting her eyes; those tears glistened too in those of the Songspear. "I beg you to not make this any more difficult than it needs to be." Asaege could feel Aristoi's resolve balanced on the edge of a razor.

Asaege resisted for the first few steps, but as a mixture of anger and grief threatened to swallow her, she relented to the Songspear's insistent pressure. *We have come too far*, she thought, *and been through too much to have it end like this*. Desperately she reached out for her connection to Jillian but through the storm of her emotions, she couldn't locate her reflection. So deep within her own thoughts was Asaege, that it took her a moment to realize they had stopped. In a fugue, she turned her eyes to the wall ahead of them.

Backlit by the gibbous moon, a scattering of figures moved along its top. *Archers? Templars?*, Asaege thought. In the end, it wouldn't matter.

350

Whoever they were, they stood between the group and escape.

She and Hollis would be together this night, just not in the way either of them had imagined.

*****

Behind her, Asaege heard the first sounds of steel on steel as Hollis and his young thieves engaged the templars. She tore her eyes away from the silhouettes on the wall and glance over her shoulder. In the flickering torchlight, she could just make out his shape amid those of the bulky soldiers, the burnished surface of his dwarven steel blade a lustrous beacon in the night. Moving with a nimbleness that should not have been possible with his injuries, the thief wove his way through the templar ranks, seemingly one step ahead of their swords.

Hope rose in her heart until he stumbled, his leg seeming to give out beneath him. Falling to one knee, an armored shape towered over him, his weapon raised above his head. One of the smaller shapes darted in, striking at the soldier's broad chest under his upraised arm. The sound of steel piercing flesh reached her ears a split second before the templar's scream of pain. Hollis lurched to his feet and brought his Wallin Fahr around in a tight arc. Blade met throat and the injured soldier slumped to the cobblestones. The templars' press denied the thief the opportunity to celebrate as he was forced to push his savior behind him and meet their next assault. From the shadow of the Ivory Cathedral, a large group of reinforcements surged through the gate. Hollis's holding action wouldn't survive their addition.

Turning her attention back to the wall, Asaege saw that more shapes had gathered along its summit. From them arose a cry, almost a rhythmic chant. Over the distance and veiled by the life and death sounds of combat behind her, she could not make out the words.

"Stay out of bow range," prompted Aristoi.

Seran squinted into the night. "I do not think they have bows," he observed, his voice as calm and even as ever. "As a matter of fact, none of them seem to be brandishing anything larger than a chair leg."

A few of them were highlighted against the night sky before their forms were lost against the backdrop of the wall. Whoever they were, they were beginning to climb down. Those that remained, continued the chant. Although the words brushed her ears, Asaege still couldn't make them out. For a gut wrenching second, she thought they may be thaumaturgical in nature. Closing her eyes, she let her senses expand but found no indication of power hanging on the wind.

Bodies brushing against her own prompted her to open her eyes and look around. The guild members were slowly withdrawing towards the still active melee behind her. At some point, Aristoi had released her arm

351

although Asaege couldn't pinpoint exactly when. Both of the Songspear's hands were wrapped around the shaft of her spear. Asaege didn't need to reach out to feel the energy that collected around Aristoi as she began to sing beside her.

Asaege stood her ground as the people around her pushed past. She squinted into the shadow cast by the wall, willing the shapes that moved within them to come into focus. Although her eyes couldn't pierce the darkness, as the figures came closer, their chant became more comprehensible.

Arcane syllables fell from Aristoi's mouth as the air around them both hummed with barely restrained power. Trying to block them out, Asaege strained to make out the words that the approaching figures were reciting. When they finally became clear, she impetuously gripped the Songspear's shoulder and shook her vigorously. Her concentration broken, Aristoi's song fell into silence. She turned on Asaege, the anger plain in her eyes.

"Listen," was Asaege's only response.

Still nebulous, the chant increased in both clarity and volume with the passage of every second. "—nd the ca—" Asaege prayed she was correct, that her guess was justified and in interrupting the Songspear's spell, she hadn't doomed them both. "—ound the call! Sound the call!"

The chant was part of a larger passage that was imprinted on Asaege's recollections as if carved in stone. *There shall be one among you to sound the call. When it is heard, my children, rise up, cast aside your chains and walk in the light once more.* She'd written it herself upon the walls of the Ivory Cathedral itself two nights ago. She would have expected it to have been scrubbed from their surface before she found herself thrown into her tiny prison cell, but words, especially words of power always sought freedom.

As the first figure stepped into the moonlight, Asaege was unsurprised to find it was Trelis the tinkerer rather than a soldier intent on her demise. Behind him, came Prent, the bootblack's son, and his brother Mehr. Each of them carried the chant upon their lips. She turned to Aristoi with a relieved smile pasted on her face. "We have nothing to fear." Behind the three commoners, twice their number emerged, adding their voices to the mantra. "They are here to walk beside us."

Aristoi did a quick double take and then shouted above the din. "If we are going to walk out of here, they need to be legion."

Closing her eyes, Asaege reached out for Jillian's consciousness. She found it easily and without delay. Drawing on her reflection's memory of Marcus's book, Asaege quickly found the spell she sought. Her eyes flickered open slowly, the formulae thrashing amid her thoughts, demand-

352

ing to be set free. "I think I can arrange that."

Turning back to the monumental structure of the wall before her, Asaege let the words of Trologue's Transmutation pour forth. Instantly, the top of the wall began to sway as it struggled under its own weight. The figures silhouetted against the moon flattened themselves against the ridge as a ten-yard section drooped like wet parchment. In the midst of the spell, Asaege could feel the power coursing through her as the words drew it in, focused it and expelled it at the wall.

More than anything she'd tried before, the incantation swept her along with them. More and more of the wall fell under its influence, causing its surface to cascade in on itself like a waterfall. Although her eyes remained open and locked on the scene before her, Asaege didn't see the small shapes running for their lives along the ledge; she only saw her will made reality. She only felt the indescribable rapture of bending the universe to her whim. Deep inside her consciousness, Asaege fought against her primordial nature but like a leaf caught in a flood, she couldn't find her bearings enough to mount an effective resistance.

Aristoi's sharp elbow in her side gave her enough of a distraction to bring her baser instincts to heel, although it felt like damning a river while still caught in its flow. Steadily, she was able to slow the current of power pumping through her mind until it was only a trickle and then cut it off completely. Before her, a fifty-yard wide fissure scarred the surface of the stone wall separating the Common Quarter from the University District.

Through the hole, swarmed a horde of commoners, their voices thunderously raised on a single chant: "Sound the call!"

At their head was a small figure dressed in an over-sized gray tunic.

*****

When the mob crashed against the tight formation of templars between them and Hollis, Asaege's hopes swelled. The soldier's line bent and threatened to break, but in that moment, the templars demonstrated the difference between passionate civilians and trained soldiers. They condensed their forces, forming themselves into a tight wedge and allowed the sea of humanity to break over them. Bodies fell on both sides, but as precious seconds passed, less and less soldiers fell to the ground. Homespun offered little protection against steel.

Asaege drew her own borrowed dagger and followed behind Aristoi's flashing spear towards where Hollis held a small island of empty cobblestone amid the soldier's ranks. His half dozen guild mates had dwindled to only two: himself and Eight Fingered Alice. Still, the pair stood back-to-back giving as good as they got. The thief's thigh wound bled freely, coating his leather breeches in a thin layer of blood. He had abandoned his two-handed grip on his Wallin Fahr in favor of wielding his thick bladed dagger in his left fist.

As Aristoi's spear darted past a templar shield to impale its owner between his shoulder and collarbone, Asaege saw Hollis dip low and drive his right shoulder into one of the soldiers surrounding him. Letting out a pained shout, the thief rose suddenly and set his opponent off balance. As the man stumbled, Hollis drove his dagger into his gut three times in rapid succession. The templar crumpled to the ground, his life spilling on to the cobblestones. When the soldier's comrade surged forward to take advantage of the thief's unprotected back, he met Alice's short, chopping sword. The boy stepped into the gap, allowing Hollis to rise and press his back against Alice's shoulders; the dance began anew.

Asaege lashed out with her dagger as a templar attempted to flank the Songspear. The point of the weapon failed to penetrate the soldier's chain mail covered ribs but it deterred his continued advance. Only ten yards separated the pair of women from where the two thieves fought but it seemed an insurmountable distance. Asaege briefly considered casting again from the book in Jillian's memory but discarded the option immediately. Between the cacophony of battle around her and the very real concern of one of the templars around her taking the opportunity to kill her, she didn't think she could find a calm place from which to commune with her reflection.

With a sudden lunge, the Songspear forced herself between a pair of soldiers. Pivoting, she brought the butt of her spear down against the extended knee of the closest. With the sound of a turkey wing being wrenched from its carcass, the joint separated and the man dropped writhing to the ground. Aristoi swung her weapon in a short arc, discouraging the second soldier from pressing towards her. As the fallen templar dodged backwards out of range of the thick blade, the Songspear brought its butt down again. This time, it struck the downed soldier in the temple. He didn't stir again.

Only a pair of templars stood between the two of them and the circle of steel that surrounded Hollis. Asaege felt the power of Aristoi's song before its notes reached her ears. It was a slow, mournful dirge that seemed to build in volume as her spear wove a hypnotic pattern in the air. Each sweep of Aristoi's weapon turned aside a frantic blow from the soldiers that pressed her. With each blow so deflected, the next one seemed to have less force behind it. In contrast, as her opponents weakened, the Songspear's motions only seemed to grow swifter and more powerful. As she brought the shaft of her spear down against the flat of a shield, the sound of shattering bone echoed even among the clamor of steel around them.

354

The last templar stumbled backwards, tripping over his own feet as if he hadn't the strength to lift them from the ground. Asaege knew she should have finished him off, allowing Aristoi to continue forward but the look of terror in his eyes stayed her hand. Without so much as a glance back, the Songspear stabbed down into the downed man's side. Asaege heard the point strike the stone beneath the soldier's body.

The circle before them opened as the templars at its edge turned to confront the spear wielding warrior. Behind them, Asaege saw Hollis lunge forward. The tip of his Dwarven steel blade entered the surprised soldier's back just above his hip and emerged through his chest in an explosion of blood and severed chain links. Alice dodged backwards with a two hopping steps, pressing his back once more against the thief's. The ring of soldiers expanded to engulf Aristoi and Asaege, closing more tightly around them as the four comrades stood united. *At least we are together*, Asaege thought, although it brought her less comfort than she would have liked.

*****

The mob harried the edges of the templar forces, but their clubs were proving no match for sword and shield. Aristoi, Hollis and Alice had formed a triangle around Asaege as she tried to put their dire circumstances from her mind in order to commune with her reflection. Each time she tried, however, she felt Jillian's panic compounding her own. Neither of them could seem to find a place from which to pull upon the tome locked in their memories.

"They are moving to block our escape," Aristoi noted. Although her voice remained calm amid the chaos blooming around them, Asaege could hear a quiver begin to build.

"I see that," Hollis added. His voice was a mixture of anger and frustration. "If we could break free, we could make for the gate."

"Not all of us will make it through," Alice said.

"I know." Sadness colored the thief's tone. "If the mob presses the guards, in the confusion a few of us may be able to slip through."

Asaege snapped her eyes open, "We cannot leave these people to die."

He looked over his shoulder, his furrowed brow and tight lips indicated the conflict in his heart. "It is that or we can all die here together."

She scanned the melee. In the dim light, she recognized dozens of faces. These were people she spoke to every day; she'd read for them … taught them to read for themselves. They were her people, her friends. There had to be another way.

Hollis leapt forward, his sword flashing like silvered lightning. His first blow bounced off his opponent's shield, leaving a sizable notch in its

355

wake. The follow up swing caught the templar in the arm between gauntlet and armor, severing it just above the wrist. Before his comrades could react, the thief danced awkwardly back into their tight formation.

"Whatever we decide, it is going to have to be soon." Asaege could see the way he favored his right leg as the adrenaline pumping through him began to reach its limit.

"We could make for the library," Asaege suggested. "There is a series of tunnels beneath the building that lead into the Common Quarter … for deliveries and such. If we move quickly enough, we could barricade the entrance behind us and buy everyone some time."

The Songspear looked at Hollis, who nodded quickly. "It could work but we would need to clear a large enough swath that we can move as a group. I do not think they will be gentle with stragglers." A small smile blossomed on his lips. "Do you think you can supply that, Southerner?"

Aristoi's answer was a soft rumble in her chest. Rather than mirroring the sly smirk of her comrade, the Songspear's face betrayed a fear that Asaege hadn't seen in the woman before. Sounding more like a deep growl than any sort of song, the sound built until those around her could feel it in their bones.

Aristoi's nostrils flared, and her lips pulled back from her lips in a bestial snarl. The tempo of her breathing increased as if she were mustering her resolve before an act that frightened her more than the melee around her.

Throwing her head back, Aristoi let loose a primal howl that cut through the night. It's haunting notes rolled forth from her lips like black blood from a gut-wound. Its effect was immediate. Asaege felt as if her heart was wrapped in frigid razor wire. Sweat formed on her brow and ran into her eyes as they frantically searched for an escape from whatever unnamed fear had taken up residence in her chest. Around her, Asaege could see that she wasn't alone. She was surrounded by the white faces and wide eyes of sheep in the presence of a wolf.

In the midst of the maelstrom of terror, stood the Songspear and the thief. Hollis slowly inhaled through his nose, releasing a measured breath through his mouth, clearly in the throes of the serenity of the Well. Aristoi, on the other hand, shifted restlessly from foot to foot. Her entire body was a bowstring, a taut, barely restrained instrument of violence. Like ripples on a pond, the effects of her song rolled forth across the battlefield.

When the Songspear tilted her head back down, there was a cold glimmer in her eyes.

In the midst of the magic born terror, Asaege swore that the moon was reflected in their depths, like some sort of animal. Aristoi fell silent for a split second as she focused on the press of templars between them and freedom. She took a deep breath and narrowed her eyes, as if she fought against something just under the surface.

When she resumed her undulating song, it seemed concentrated on the men before her. A few templars turned to flee, but most simply dropped their weapons and fell to the ground.

Although some of the manufactured fear fell from around Asaege's heart, not all of it fled. Sweat burned her eyes as she strained to hear anything past the insistent pounding of her heart in her ears. Around her, she could see that the people not directly in front of Aristoi were regaining their senses. Hollis didn't wait for them to do so, he interlaced his fingers with Asaege's and limped forward with as much speed as he could muster. Alice darted after them, but Aristoi was slower to follow. A hungry glint hung in her eyes as she slowly began to smile. It wasn't a comforting gesture.

The boy pivoted as only young muscles can and made his way back to the Songspear. When he laid his hand on her arm, she snapped her head around, the round shape of her mouth bending into a U of tense lips and bared teeth. "We have to go," Alice prompted, pulling on her contrary to every indication to do otherwise. Aristoi's dangerous aspect passed like clouds across the summer moon. Her face regained its calm bearing as she sprinted forward, pulling Alice behind her.

In pairs and trios, the members of the mob broke from the paused melee to follow the group. By the time the group reached the Great Library's capacious courtyard, a seemingly unbounded tide of humanity trailed behind them. "There is a tunnel entry just ahead," Asaege called, supporting Hollis's weight as his strength began to falter. Just as they reached the palatial steps leading to the library's entrance, the massive oak doors slammed open. Backlit in the warm glow of a huge accumulation of lanterns, stood more than a dozen Binders, arrayed in full armor.

Asaege's heart sank. The library guardians stood between them and their last hope of escape. Behind the fleeing mob, the templar force had regained their senses and moved to cut off a retreat in that direction. She felt the thief slump beside her as his reserves of fortitude faded. "I'm sorry," he whispered in English, "I —"

She placed her fingers against his lips, "Don't. If it wasn't for me, you would never have gotten involved in any of this. I should have left well enough alone."

Hollis laughed. "Magpie, I wouldn't trade away a minute of my time with you for a lifetime of peaceful moments." He looked down at his blood covered thigh before amending, "Perhaps I'd let a few minutes go." He wrapped his hand gently around her wrist and softly kissed her fingertips. "You reminded me of the man I want to be rather than the man the world has made me."

Asaege's breath caught in her throat as for a second, the world faded around the two of them. "I love you," she admitted quickly. "I know it's insane, but —"

"My heart is yours, Asaege." The thief pulled her fingers from his lips and laid them gently against his chest. "It has been since the moment we met, I'm sorry it took me so long to realize it."

A sharp elbow to Hollis's ribs brought the tender moment to an end. "If you both do not mind," Aristoi chided, "there are some immediate matters that need tending to."

The Binders moved forward slowly. As they descended the stairs, Asaege saw that among those that remained on the landing, a hand full of silk clad librarians stood, their hands bound before them. Most prominent was Bran Thume, the Master Librarian. Even in the dim light, Asaege could make out his indignant scowl. When the helmed Binder leader reached the bottom of the steps, he showed no sign of slowing his stride. The mob curiously cleared his path and let him pass between them.

Hollis took Asaege's hand in his and began limping after the group. In answer to her questioning glare, he shrugged, "Obviously they are not here for us." Cautiously, she followed the thief. The Binders ignored the gathering commoners and marched towards the templars. The people at the edge of the mob started moving towards the wall. All of them stopped when the Prophet passed by.

A collective cry of joy arose among the gathered soldiers as the gathering of commoners split to reveal the Binder commander and his forces. A templar in gold and ivory embossed armor stepped forward to meet him, his brows tight in confusion. "We do not require your aid, Binder. Within this rabble are the individuals responsible for the death of both Curate Rethmus and the Hand of Light himself."

"Thanks, Plague Man," Asaege heard Hollis mutter.

"If you would be so kind as to turn them over to us along with the stolen property in their possession, these people can return to their holes and you can be about your business."

The Binder commander reached up to pull off his helm, tucking it beneath his arm before speaking. "I believe there has been some sort of mistake." Asaege's heart leapt as she recognized him. In the dark alley where they first met, Rudelph had been dressed more simply, but there was no mistaking the man's voice.

The templar took an impatient step forward. "I assure you there is no mistake. If you would —"

Rudelph cut him off, his voice sharp as a knife edge. "Lieutenant, if this man takes one more step towards me, see that he never walks again."

Two Binders drew their swords and flanked their commander. The nearest snapped, "Gladly, Sir." The templar froze in his tracks.

His voice returning to a conversational tone, Rudelph said, "I am sure you will find that we will pose more of a challenge than a group of unarmed civilians. Would you care to test that theory?"

The soldier shook his head. "We are not looking for any issues. Give us the criminals and the book." His voice was less sure.

"We often find things we do not seek. The Binders are sworn to the Great Library and the knowledge held within ..." he glanced back to where Thume stood bound, "... not to the librarians ...not to the city ... " He turned his eyes back to the templar before him, "... and most certainly not the church. The book you seek belongs to us. You have no more claim to it or anything else behind these walls than these people do."

"But —" the soldier interjected.

Rudelph cut him off again without his voice losing its patient tone. "As to the alleged crimes that occurred on library grounds, there have been some complications that have yet to be sorted. Without a crime, there can hardly be criminals." He studied the templar before him, allowing the silence between them to grow awkward before adding, "Is there anything else I may do for you this evening?"

"We cannot allow the false prophet to continue spewing their heretical ramblings. She does not fall under your purview. You will deliver her at very least." Conviction filled the templar's voice, but he came short of taking that prohibited step.

Nodding his head, Rudelph smiled. "Ah ... I see your confusion. Whether, in your opinion, she is false or not, the Prophet brings understanding to the people, as demonstrated by the gathering before you."

"This is a riot. It is no more of a gathering than occurs when you kick an ant hill. Drones are easily agitated but will eventually settle back into their place." A wordless murmur began within the common people.

Rudelph spoke over it. "Opinions differ but as long as she serves the cause of knowledge, the Binders stand with her." A cheer arose behind him, but the Binder continued as if he hadn't heard it, "You could, of course, attempt to take her by force ..." In unison, the assembled Binders struck their swords against their shields in a deafening crash. "... although at this juncture, I would recommend against it."

The templar leader took a few steps backwards before turning to face his men. "We will return to the Ivory Cathedral ... for now."

"Excellent choice. In an effort to prevent any future misunderstandings, I think it best for the University District to be free of templar presence for the moment." Rudelph's words were met with a scowl, but he continued unperturbed, "Any entry by force will be met in kind."

Turning from the retreating backs of the templars, Rudelph chuckled lightly. "Lieutenant, would you be so kind as to make sure our guests get home safely?" He locked eyes with Asaege. "Lady Prophet, if you could ask a few of your followers to accompany my men, I believe it would be best to present a united front."

She could feel a relieved smile spread across her face. "Gladly, Rudelph ... Captain?"

"There is no need for formality, my dear. After all, unless I miss my guess, our fates have just become inextricably bound." Rudelph took a deep lungful of night air, "The wind always tastes sweetest when it carries the scent of change, do you not agree?"

"I am not sure I would go that far," Asaege responded, "but I appreciate the allegory."

Rudelph handed his helm to the closest Binder and extended his hand. As Asaege grasped his arm by the wrist, he said, "We have much to discuss; when the sun reveals our deeds, we would do well to greet it with a unified purpose."

She released Hollis's hand reluctantly and raised an eyebrow.

The thief's only response was, "How does it feel to be a revolutionary?"

Part Three:

The Epilogues

"You're off to great places! Today is your day! Your mountain is waiting, So get on your way!"

- Dr. Seuss

Epilogue One
Shadowtorn Heart

Hollis tried to rise, but Asaege's firm hand pressed against his chest and forced him into the bed again. "Brother Traemont wanted you to rest for a full week. Remind me how far into your recovery we are?"

"Two days," the thief grumbled. The street preacher had been among the mob on the night that people had termed 'The Call'. His intercessions to his god accelerated Hollis's healing, turning a crippling wound into what the thief considered a minor annoyance. His opinion wasn't shared among his friends. Switching to English, he said, "I'm feeling much better; no harm can come from a short walk."

She looked down at him, responding in kind, "If by no harm, you mean tearing up the inside of your thigh like shredded chicken, I agree."

"If your intent in speaking your otherworldly tongue is to hide your intentions from me, Northerner, I am afraid you waste your time. Your stubbornness knows no language."

Switching back to Trade Tongue, the thief complained, "Do not tell me you are taking her side."

"It is not about sides, Hollis. You owe me a favor and I need you in good health if you are going to be any good to me."

He settled back against the pile of pillows with an exasperated sigh. Secretly, Hollis was glad for the respite. With Plague Man dead and more people flocking to the banner of the Prophet by the day, there had been little need of him. Between the Binders and the reinvigorated Brotherhood of the Night, Asaege's rebellion was holding its own against both the city and the church.

The Common Quarter and University Districts both remained firmly in rebel hands. As word spread, pockets of resistance were springing up across Oizan. A bloody dock worker strike had closed the port, tightening the noose around the council's throat. The revolution was far from over but if things continued in this direction, it had a real shot.

"We wanted to wait until you were feeling better to tell you ..." Asaege began.

"We?"

The Songspear nodded. "My road takes us north —"

Hollis pushed himself upright into a sitting position, "I cannot possibly leave now."

Asaege laid her hand on his shoulder. "You can and you should. While we were fighting for our lives, Jillian finished reading the journals. Your three friends were able to slay Haedren and prevent him from using the Well."

"And yet the Well was dead when I reached it this past summer," Aristoi inserted.

"Your friend's final journal entry mentions Silvermoon and Mika's plan to travel to the site ... alone. The entry was dated the day of his death."

The Songspear half sat on the edge of Hollis's bedside table. "When last I traveled the Rangor Wastes, a formidable warrior sought to unite the tribes against their southern neighbors. She was dark of hair and darker of eye, an outsider whose skill with a blade was beyond anything seen for generations."

"A dark eyed swordswoman? That could be anyone." Although the words were for his friends, Hollis truly tried to convince himself.

"I am told she wields an Uteli long blade bound in sharkskin." Aristoi paused to let her words sink in. "Does that sound familiar?"

The thief slumped back. "Even if it is Mika, I have responsibilities here."

Asaege smiled sadly at him, "The true killer of your friends is in reach, Hollis. Although you believe your responsibilities are here, if you do not finish what you have started, you never will be."

He reached up to squeeze her hand. "You are my future, Magpie."

Caressing his face with the back of her fingers, Asaege said, "There can be no future for either of us until you put to rest the ghosts of your past."

Epilogue Two
Soul's Poison

The bruised and battered man collapsed to the muddy shore, his reserves of strength having been depleted hours ago. After the last of his fortitude abandoned him, he'd persevered on hatred alone. From his position on the riverbank, he could see the outline of Oizan against the setting sun. The city had brought him nothing but frustration and pain since he stepped onto its accursed docks again.

Once his home, Oizan had been no more than an open sore in his memory for more years than he'd spent within its walls. He had always believed that when he returned to the city, it would be to place it under his thumb like an insect that had stung once too often. In reality, it had escaped his grasp to sting him once again.

Too arrogant to turn his eye inward in search of blame, he replayed the events of the last few weeks in his head trying to pinpoint where his plan had gone awry. Each time he thought about his downfall, one person kept slithering his way into his brain. The man's stomach tightened with rage each time his smirking visage appeared. This time Hollis had truly been at his mercy. It had cost him a measure of his freedom, but it was a price he was willing to pay.

In the end, it was an Ash-born nothing that had snatched from him the justice that he so richly deserved. In doing so, she'd also pulled his carefully laid plans down around his ears. In the span of a few days, he'd gone from having true power within his reach to grasping nothing but mud. Like her lover, Asaege wanted to involve herself in matters beyond her station. She who fashioned herself a teacher would instead learn the error of her ways.

The Plague Man would instruct her in this.

Once her education was complete, her death would serve as a lesson of its own to the meddling thief.

About the Author

A child of the 80's, SL Harby grew up playing Dungeons & Dragons and classic video games. An only child, he was bitten early by the reading bug, cutting his teeth on the masters of modern fantasy. His days were spent inside the worlds created by Howard and Lieber, Moorcock and Tolkien.

A perpetual Jersey boy, SL Harby now lives in South Carolina with his wife and muse, Jessica, and their bad ass rescue dog, Tallulah.

Shadows of the Heart is his second novel, the second in the planned Well of Shadows series.

Other Works by SL Harby

Well of Shadows Series

Shadows of a Dream (Available Now)
Shadows of the Heart (Available Now)
Shadows of Betrayal (Available Winter 2023)

Well of Shadows Short Fiction

What Lies Beneath: Chronicles of the Thief - Prequel One
One Man's Bastard: Chronicles of the Thief - Prequel Two
Song of Darkest Sin: Songs of the Spear - Prequel One
Song of Desert Wind: Songs of the Spear - Prequel Two

Made in the USA
Middletown, DE
26 August 2024